About the

Carole Mortimer was born in England, the youngest of
three children. She began writing in 1978 and has now
written over one hundred and seventy books for
Mills & Boon. Carole has six sons, Matthew, Joshua,
Timothy, Michael, David, and Peter. She says, 'I'm happily
married to Peter senior; we're best friends as well as
lovers, which is probably the best recipe for a successful
relationship. We live in a lovely part of England.'

Regency Rebels

Regency Rebels:

The Dukes' Return

CAROLE MORTIMER

MILLS & BOON

First Published in Great Britain 2023
By Mills & Boon, an imprint of HarperCollins*Publishers* Ltd,
1 London Bridge Street, London, SE1 9GF

www.harpercollins.co.uk

HarperCollins*Publishers*
Macken House, 39/40 Mayor Street Upper,
Dublin 1, D01 C9W8, Ireland

ISBN: 978-0-263-31955-2

MIX
Paper | Supporting
responsible forestry
FSC™ C007454

This book is produced from independently certified FSC™ paper
to ensure responsible forest management.

For more information visit: www.harpercollins.co.uk/green

Printed and Bound in the UK using 100% Renewable Electricity
at CPI Group (UK) Ltd, Croydon, CR0 4YY

ZACHARY BLACK: DUKE OF DEBAUCHERY

To all of you, thank you for reading my books.

Chapter One

Late February, 1815, outside White's Club, London.

'What the—?' Zachary Black, the Duke of Hawksmere, came to an abrupt halt as he climbed into his carriage and noticed the shadowy figure already seated on the far side. The lantern inside was turned down low, preventing him from seeing if it was a man or woman who sat back in the shadows. 'Lamb?' He turned to look accusingly at his groom, silver eyes glittering in the soft glow of the flickering lamp.

The middle-aged man straightened to attention. 'She said as 'ow you was expecting 'er, your Grace,' he offered questioningly.

His intruder was a woman then, Zachary processed grimly. But certainly not one he had been expecting.

Unless…

He had just spent the evening and part of the night at his club with his four closest friends celebrating the forthcoming nuptials of one of them, Marcus Wilding, the Duke of Worthing, and his ladylove, Lady Julianna Armitage. Their wedding was due to take place later on today.

Zachary had briefly toyed with the idea of marriage himself the previous year, a decision forced upon him by the circumstances of his father's will. But his attempt to secure a wife had gone so disastrously wrong he was reluctant to repeat the experience. However, his cynicism did not prevent him from wishing Worthing well in the venture. Indeed, he had done so until almost dawn.

Which now caused Zachary to wonder if perhaps the woman in his carriage was a part of those wedding celebrations? Possibly a gift from Worthing? And perhaps each of Zachary's other three close friends would all find a similar present awaiting them in their own carriages?

Maybe so, but Zachary intended to remain cautious until convinced otherwise. The war with Napoleon might be over, and the Corsican currently incarcerated on Elba, but these were still dangerous times, and finding an unknown woman waiting for him in his carriage was certainly reason enough for him to stay on his guard.

'Hawksmere House, Lamb,' he instructed tersely as he climbed fully into the carriage and the door closed behind him. He took a seat across from the mysterious woman, placing his hat on the seat beside him as the carriage moved forward.

Zachary's sight had now adjusted enough to the gloom for him to note that the woman wore a black veil, one that covered her from her bonneted head to her booted toe. Such an effective covering prevented Zachary from being able to tell if she was old or young, fat or thin.

Deliberately so?

No doubt.

Zachary maintained his silence. This woman had sought him out, and therefore it was incumbent upon her to state her reasons for having done so.

To state whether she was friend or foe.

Georgianna's heart was beating wildly in her chest as she looked across the carriage at the silently watchful Zachary Black, the Duke of Hawksmere. A man, should he discover her identity, who had every reason to dislike her intensely. And rumour had it that the hard and cynical Zachary Black was a dangerous man when he disliked, intensely or otherwise.

Georgianna repressed a shiver as she straightened her spine before greeting him huskily, 'Your Grace.'

'Madam.' He gave a terse inclination of his head, his fashionably overlong hair appearing the blue-black of a raven's wing in the dimmed lighting. His silver eyes were narrowed in his aquiline face; his brows were dark over those pale and shimmering eyes. He had sharp blades for cheekbones above an uncompromising and sculptured mouth and stern jaw.

Georgianna's gaze was drawn down inexorably to the spot just beneath that arrogant jaw, to the livid scar visible above the white of his shirt collar. A wound so long and straight that it almost looked as if someone had attempted to cut his throat. Which had no doubt been the intention of the Frenchman wielding the sabre which had been responsible for the injury.

She repressed another shiver as she hastily returned her gaze to the dark and saturnine face above it. 'I realise my presence in your coach might be considered as an…an unorthodox way of approaching you.'

'That would surely depend upon your reason for being here,' he drawled softly.

Georgianna's gloved hands were clenched tightly together beneath the concealing shroud of her black veil. 'There is… I have important news I need to… to impart to someone I believe is an acquaintance of yours.'

The man seated opposite her in the carriage did not appear to move, his expression remaining as mockingly indifferent as ever, yet Georgianna nevertheless sensed a sudden, watchful tension beneath that indifference.

'Indeed?' he murmured dismissively.

'Yes.'

He raised those dark brows. 'Then I may assume you did not intrude upon my carriage with the intention of sharing my bed for what is left of the night?'

'Certainly not!' Georgianna pressed back in shock against the comfortably upholstered seat.

He continued to look at her with those narrowed and merciless silver eyes for several long seconds. 'Pity,' he finally drawled. 'A satisfying tumble would have been a fitting end to what has already been a most enjoyable evening. Pray tell, then, what is this important news you so urgently need me to impart to an acquaintance of mine? So important, it would seem, that you wilfully used subterfuge and lies with which to enter my carriage, rather than call upon my home during the daylight hours?' he prompted mockingly.

Now that she was face-to-face with Zachary Black, albeit with her own face obscured beneath the black veil, Georgianna was asking herself the same question.

At two and thirty, the arrogantly disdainful Duke of Hawksmere was a man she believed few would ever approach readily.

Admittedly, his prowess on the battlefield, with both sword and pistol, was legendary. His prowess in the bedchamber equally so. But he was also a gentleman rumoured to deal with both in the same cold and ruthless manner.

A coldness and ruthlessness, as Georgianna knew better than most, said to be frighteningly decisive.

So much so that she had no doubt that were he to identify her he would not hesitate to halt the carriage and toss her unceremoniously out into the street.

That he might still do so, of course.

She drew in a deep breath. 'It is rumoured, or more precisely I have reason to believe you have certain… connections? In government?'

Zachary remained lazily slouched on the plushly upholstered seat of his ducal carriage, his expression of mockery and boredom unchanging. But inwardly he was instantly on the alert, not caring for the way in which this woman had hesitated before questioning his connections.

It implied that she had some knowledge of his having worked as an agent for the Crown this past four years. Information which was certainly not public knowledge. Indeed, his endeavours in that area would be of little use if it were.

He gave a dismissive shrug. 'I have many acquaintances in the House, if that is what you are referring to.'

'We both know it is not.'

'Indeed?' Damn it, who was this woman?

A younger woman, from the light and breathless sound of her voice, and possibly unmarried if her shocked reaction to the suggestion she was here to share his bed was any indication. She also appeared educated from her accent and manner of speaking, although that veil still prevented him from knowing as to whether she was fair or dark, fat or thin.

Or what she knew of his connections in government.

'Yes,' she asserted firmly.

'I am afraid that you have me at something of a disadvantage, madam. While you claim to know a lot about me, I do not even know your identity,' Zachary dismissed coldly.

Georgianna doubted that the arrogantly assured Zachary Black had ever been at a disadvantage in his privileged life. Nor was he under one now, for this was his carriage, and their conversation one over which he ultimately held power. As he always held power over all who were allowed, or dared to, enter his privileged world.

A power, a proximity, that she frankly found overwhelming.

She had forgotten—chosen to forget?—that the duke was so immediate, and his personality so overwhelming, that he seemed to possess the very air about him. Air perfumed with the smell of good cigars and brandy, no doubt from the evening he had just spent at his club with his friends. There was an underlying hint of the sharp tang of lemons and an earthy, insidious aroma she could only assume to be that of the man himself.

Allowing her personal nervousness and dislike of the man to bedevil her now, after all she had gone through, was not going to help Georgianna's cause in the slightest.

'It is not necessary for you to know who I am for you to arrange for me to meet with one of those gentlemen,' she continued determinedly.

'That is for me to decide, surely?' The duke leisurely picked a speck of lint from the sleeve of his black evening jacket before he looked up and pinned her once again with those coldly glittering eyes. 'And why come to me on the matter? Why not simply make an appointment and impart this knowledge to one of those gentleman yourself?'

Georgianna's gaze lowered. 'Because I very much doubt any of them would agree to meet with a mere woman. Not without the recommendation of someone such as yourself.'

'You underestimate the influence of your own sex, madam,' Hawksmere drawled derisively.

'Do I?' Somehow Georgianna doubted that.

She had been barely nineteen ten months ago when her own father had accepted on her behalf the offer of marriage she had received from an influential and titled gentleman, all without giving any consideration as to whether or not Georgianna would be happy in such a marriage.

Her now-deceased father, she reminded herself dully, having learnt upon her return to England just yesterday that her father had died nine months ago, and in doing so making a nonsense of the anger she had felt towards him in regard to that betrothal.

'I believe so, yes,' Hawksmere dismissed harshly. 'Either way, I am not in the habit of listening to news imparted to me by unknown women—most especially one who feels it necessary to lie her way into my presence—let alone recommending that anyone else should do so.'

Georgianna had expected this distrust and cynicism from a man whom she knew allowed very few people into his inner circle of intimates—the four friends from his schooldays, also dukes, being the exception. Those same four friends with whom she knew he had just spent the evening and most of the night.

'Who I am does not have any bearing on the veracity of the information I wish to impart,' she maintained stubbornly.

'In your opinion.'

'In the opinion of any patriot.'

Zachary Black raised a mocking brow at her vehemence. 'A patriot of what, madam?'

'Of England, of course.' Georgianna glared beneath the veil.

'Ah, yes, England,' he drawled drily. 'I trust you will forgive my ignorance, but I had thought England to currently be at peace? That we had held celebrations in honour of that peace just this past summer?'

'That is the very reason—' Georgianna broke off her outburst in order to draw in a deep and controlling breath. Being anything less than in control in this particular gentleman's company was not wise when he was more like than not to take advantage of it. 'I can trust in your discretion, I hope?'

He raised those mocking brows. 'Should that not have been something you ascertained before you decided to invade the privacy of my carriage?'

Yes, it should, and Georgianna had believed that she had done so; she would not have approached the Duke of Hawksmere if she had not known he was exactly the gentleman she needed to speak with initially.

And yet, alone with him now in his carriage, and presented with the perfect, and wholly private, opportunity in which to convince him into speaking on her behalf, she found herself hesitating.

To the country at large the Duke of Hawksmere was nothing less than a war hero. He'd fought bravely and long in Wellington's army and had been severely wounded for his trouble. That he had also worked secretly for the Crown was not so widely known, but just as heroic. It was Georgianna's personal dislike of the man which now caused her hesitation.

Alone with Hawksmere in his carriage, so totally overwhelmed by the sheer presence of the man, Georgianna could not help but be aware that he was also a man known for his ruthlessness.

Once again she straightened her shoulders as if for battle. 'You may pretend and posture all you like, your Grace, but I have no doubt that, once we have spoken a little longer, you will choose to speak on my behalf.'

Zachary would admit to being somewhat intrigued and not just by the information this young woman so urgently wished to impart. It was the woman herself who also interested him. Her voice might be young and educated, but it had also sounded slightly naïve when she stated her impassioned loyalty to England. Her claimed loyalty to England?

And Zachary still wondered what she looked like beneath that concealing veil.

Was she fair or dark? Beautiful or plain? Slender or rounded?

Zachary now found himself curious to know the answer to all of those questions. To see this young woman, if only so that he could look upon her face and judge for himself as to whether she spoke truthfully or otherwise. These last four years of working secretly for the Crown had shown him only too well not to trust anyone but his closest friends. How easily this could be an elaborate trap, a way of piquing his interest, before this mystery woman proceeded to feed the English government false information.

And his interest was most assuredly piqued.

To the extent that he no longer felt the least effect from the wine and brandy he had enjoyed with his friends earlier on.

So much so that he had no intentions of allowing this young woman to leave his carriage without first ascertaining exactly who she was and how she came to know things about him she should not have known.

He glanced out of the window to see that dawn was just starting to break over London's rooftops.

'Then might I suggest…' he turned back to the young woman, just able to discern the pale oval of her face beneath that veil now '…as we will reach my home in just a few minutes, that now might be as good a time as any for you to confide at least a little of that information?'

Her hands twisted together beneath that veil. 'I— It concerns the movements of a…a notable personage, currently residing on an island in the Mediterranean.'

It took every ounce of Zachary's considerable self-control not to react to this statement. Not to show, by so much as the twitch of an eyelid, that her information might be of interest him.

Who in hell was this woman?

And what exactly did she know?

He turned once again to look out of the window, as if bored by the conversation. 'As far as I am aware I do not have any acquaintances currently residing on a Mediterranean island.'

'I did not say he was a personal acquaintance of yours—'

'Then I cannot see what possible interest any of this can be to me,' Zachary cut her off harshly; even mentioning that the noble personage in question was a he could be dangerous.

Having chosen his servants himself, Zachary trusted them implicitly. But that did not mean he wished to test that trust by allowing any of them to overhear the details of his conversation with this woman and her implication that he was an agent for the Crown.

A young woman whose eyes now glittered across the width of the carriage at him from beneath that veil. Dark eyes. Brown or possibly a deep blue, he could not tell.

'I assure you, it will be of great interest to…'

'You have run out of time, I am afraid.' Zachary returned her gaze coldly as the carriage came to a stop outside Hawksmere House. 'Perhaps you would care to come inside and finish the conversation there?'

Said the spider to the fly, Georgianna mentally added as she gave another shiver of apprehension. Being alone in this man's carriage with him had been more than a test for her nerves. Entering Zachary Black's home with him would push her well beyond her limits of daring.

Although many might think otherwise, she acknowledged heavily, knowing her reputation was beyond repair as far as society was concerned. And most assuredly so in Hawksmere's cold and condemning gaze.

What would he say or do if he were to learn exactly who she was? Would he shun her, as all of society now shunned her? Or would he exact the revenge she had long been waiting for? That Sword of Damocles which she had felt balanced above her head for so many months now.

Zachary Black, with his reputation as the coldly ruthless Duke of Hawksmere, was not an enemy any sane person would voluntarily wish upon themselves.

And yet Georgianna had done so.

And done so willingly at the time, in the belief that she had no other choice in the matter. It had only been in the months since that she'd had time to reflect, as well as deeply regret, her previous actions. To appreciate exactly what manner of man it was she had chosen to make her mortal enemy.

After just a few minutes spent in the company of Hawksmere, and being made totally aware of the dangerous edge beneath his smooth urbanity, was enough to confirm that he was the type of man who would never forget a slight or an insult.

And Georgianna had insulted him most grievously.

'I think not, thank you,' she now answered him coolly.

'I really wish you had answered differently.'

Georgianna was not fooled for a moment into thinking that Hawksmere's words of regret were because he was still under the misapprehension she was a lady of the night and he wished to bed her. His tone had been too unemotional, too calmly conversational, for that to be true.

She pressed back against the shadows of the carriage as the groom opened the door and the duke rose to his feet before stepping down on to the cobbled road, placing his hat upon his head before turning to hold out a hand to her.

'Our conversation is far from over,' he murmured pointedly as she made no attempt to take that hand.

'If you will just agree to speak to—speak on my behalf, your Grace,' she corrected as he frowned darkly, 'then I will return in a day or so for your answer. For now I choose to wait here a few minutes longer, before quietly leaving. I believe it preferable if we were not seen leaving the Hawksmere ducal carriage together.'

He raised one dark and mocking brow as he turned from dismissing the listening groom. 'Are you perhaps under the misapprehension that your preferences are of any interest to me?'

'On the contrary, I am sure they are not.' Georgianna continued to press back into the shadows. 'I was thinking of your own reputation rather than my own.'

Hawksmere gave a humourless smile. 'I am informed by my closest friends that my reputation is that of a gambler and an irredeemable rake.'

And Georgianna now believed that to be a reputation this man had deliberately fostered, as a way of diverting attention from the fact that he worked secretly as a spy for the Crown.

Oh, he was also undoubtedly both a gambler and a womaniser. He had more than enough funds to accommodate a liking for the former and both the arrogance and dangerous attraction to ensure he could satisfy the latter. He could surely have any woman who might come to the attention of those piercing silver eyes.

Well, almost any woman, Georgianna reminded herself, knowing that one woman, at least, had escaped the attentions of both that silver gaze and the man himself.

'No doubt you are,' she conceded softly. 'I would nevertheless still prefer to remain in the carriage until you are safely inside the house.'

Zachary was not a man known for his patience. Or his forbearance. Or, indeed, any of those admirable qualities that made certain gentlemen of the *ton* so acceptable to both the young débutantes and their marriage-minded mamas. The opposite, in fact; he and his four closest friends had earned the sobriquet The Dangerous Dukes amongst the *ton* this past ten years or more, and one of the reasons for that had been because they were none of them amiable or obliging. Or in the least interested in marrying any of those irritatingly twittering young women who appeared year after boring year on the marriage mart.

Zachary's brief flirtation with the idea of marriage had been out of necessity rather than inclination, his father's will demanding that he be married and have an heir by the time he reached the age of thirty-five, or forfeit the bulk of the Hawksmere fortune. The scandalous end to that betrothal meant that Zachary had delayed repeating the experience as yet. Although, now aged two and thirty, he appreciated that his time was assuredly running out, and he would soon be forced to once again take his pick of the Season's beauties.

Worthing was to marry later on today, of course, but as he was to marry the younger sister of another of The Dangerous Dukes, it did not signify; the beautiful Julianna Armitage was neither twittering nor irritating.

So far in their acquaintance, Zachary had not found the earnest young woman behind the black veil to be either of those things either, though.

'You consider I am in some danger, then?' he enquired mildly. 'From yourself, perhaps?'

'Certainly not,' she gasped. 'I assure you, I did not come here to cause you any more harm—' She broke off abruptly even as she seemed to cringe even further back against the carriage seat.

'More harm?' Zachary's eyes narrowed even as he leant forward until his shoulders filled the doorway of the carriage, his gaze searching on that veiled figure. 'Who are you?' he prompted harshly.

'I am no one, your Grace.'

'On the contrary, you are most certainly someone.' He reached into the ever-lightening gloom of the carriage to grasp one of her arms before pulling her along the seat towards him. A soft and slender arm that answered at least one of his earlier questions; the young woman beneath the veil was slender, very much so.

'Let me go.' She struggled against his hold, her gloved hand moving up in an effort to try to prise his fingers from about her arm. 'You must release me, your Grace.' There was now a distressed sob in her voice as her attempts failed to secure her release.

'I think not,' Zachary said slowly.

It had never been his intention to just allow this young woman to leave. Not since she had mentioned having information on Bonaparte, not by name but by implication.

Besides which, his curiosity to know more about this woman had only deepened with her comment about inflicting more harm.

The implication surely being that she had caused him some personal harm in the past?

If that was the case, then Zachary intended to know exactly who she was and in what way she might have caused him harm.

To that end he leant inside the carriage and pulled her easily towards him, until she fell forward across his shoulder despite her struggles.

'What are you doing?'

'I should have thought that was obvious.' Zachary backed out of the carriage before straightening to heft his feather-light burden more comfortably on to his shoulder, his arm tight about the backs of the young woman's thighs. He shot the curiously observing Lamb a grimly satisfied grin as he stood beside the horses' heads, holding the reins to keep them steady. 'The lady has expressed a fancy to pretend she is being kidnapped by a lusty pirate and carried off to his lair.'

Georgianna gave an indignant squeak at the deliberate and mortifying fabrication, before turning appealingly to the stoic-faced groom. 'Do not believe a word of it,' she pleaded desperately, the blood having rushed to her head and now causing her to feel slightly dizzy. 'I am certainly being kidnapped, but not by any lusty pirate.'

'Quiet, wench.' The Duke of Hawksmere gave her a hearty slap on her backside to accompany the piratical instruction. 'Wish me luck with my plundering, Lamb,' he added drily, 'for I am certain I shall need it.'

'Not you, your Grace.' The groom grinned his enjoyment of the entertainment. 'Women are much like feisty mares and I've never known of one of 'em as you couldn't tame to the bridle.'

Georgianna's cheeks were aflame with colour, her light-headedness giving the whole situation a dream-like quality. One in which she felt like the spectator at a theatre farce.

What other explanation could there possibly be for the way she now dangled over one of the wide and muscled shoulders of Zachary Black, the dangerous Duke of Hawksmere?

To now be jostled and bounced as he carried her up the steps of his town house, through the open doorway, before taking the three-pronged and lit candelabrum from the surprised and haughty-faced butler into his other hand?

The duke continued on through the entrance hall before taking the steps two at a time as he carried Georgianna easily up the wide staircase to the bed-chambers above.

Chapter Two

'Remove the veil.' Zachary looked down grimly at the young woman he had just seconds ago dropped unceremoniously on top of the covers on his four-poster bed. The lit candelabrum he had placed on the bedside table allowed him to see the way her petticoat and the skirt of her black gown rode up and revealed slender and shapely ankles. Catching him looking, she hastily pulled the garments down again. Unfortunately that concealing veil had remained irritatingly in place. 'Now,' he ordered uncompromisingly.

Georgianna looked up warily through her long lashes at her towering adversary as she scrabbled further up the bed, as far away from the ominously threatening Duke of Hawksmere as it was possible for her to be. 'I have no intentions of removing my veil.'

'Are you in mourning?'

Was she? Her father had certainly died in the past year, but even so that was not her reason for wearing the veil.

'If you have to think about it, then obviously not,' the duke dismissed coldly. 'Remove the veil. Now. Before I lose what little patience I have left,' he added warningly.

Georgianna's response to Hawksmere's dangerously soft voice was to sit up straighter in the lush pile of snowy white pillows at the head of the four-poster bed. 'You cannot treat me in this high-handed manner.'

'No?' His tone was low and menacing. 'I do not see anyone rushing to your rescue.'

Her cheeks flamed with heat as she continued to look at him from beneath lowered lashes. 'That is because you told your groom... Because your servants now think...'

'That I am continuing to play my part in your erotic fantasy and am now ravishing you?' Hawksmere completed derisively.

'Yes.'

The duke gave a grimly satisfied smile. 'And can you tell me truthfully that you have never had such a fantasy? That you have never dreamed,' he added, sensually soft, 'of a swashbuckling pirate carrying you off to his ship before having his wicked way with you?'

Of course Georgianna had once had such fantasies. What young and romantic girl had not dreamed of being carried off and ravished by a wicked pirate, or perhaps a dashing knight, who would then fall instantly in love with her and keep her for ever?

But she was now twenty years of age and felt much

older than that in her heart. Nor did she have any faith left in romance and love. She knew only too well that the reality did not match up to the fantasy, that the wicked pirate or the dashing knight invariably had feet of clay.

'Those are the daydreams of silly young girls who do not know any better,' she dismissed flatly.

'And you do?'

'Oh, yes,' she assured with feeling.

Hawksmere's lids lay heavy over his eyes as he smiled down at her mockingly. 'In that case, might I suggest you stop behaving like the ridiculous heroine in a lurid novel and remove your veil?'

Georgianna did not see that she had any choice in the matter when the duke was so much bigger than she was and could so obviously force her to his will if he so chose. And his mocking assertions earlier as to his reason for bringing her to his bedchamber meant she could not expect to receive any assistance from Hawksmere's servants, either.

She had, Georgianna now realised, placed herself completely at the duke's mercy.

And those cold silver eyes, and the uncompromising set of his arrogant jaw, confirmed that this man gave no quarter, to man or woman.

She slowly raised her shaking hands to where the pins held the veil in place. 'You will not like what you see,' she warned as she slowly began to remove those pins.

Hawksmere raised dark brows. 'Are you disfigured in some way? From the pox, perhaps?'

'No.' She sighed as she placed the pins on the night table beside the candelabrum of three flickering candles.

'Ugly, then?' he dismissed uninterestedly. 'Something my bedchamber has certainly not seen before.'

And such a richly ornate bedchamber it was, too, and entirely fitting for a duke as wealthy and powerful as Hawksmere. The curtains at the windows and about the four-poster bed were of a rich blue velvet and the furniture was heavy and dark and at the height of fashion. A thick, predominantly blue Aubusson carpet almost entirely covered the floor while a cheery fire burned in the large, ornate fireplace.

The room was almost as magnificent as the duke himself, attired as he was in tailored evening clothes of black jacket and breeches, and waistcoat of fine silver brocade, his linen snowy white, a diamond pin glinting in the neckcloth at his throat.

The same magnificent duke whose mistresses were rumoured to be some of the most beautiful women in the land.

'I am neither ugly nor beautiful, I am merely a woman.' Georgianna's hands trembled even more as she began to remove the concealing black veil.

'Then I fail to see what it is you believe I shall dis—' Zachary stopped talking as the veil came off completely and he was able to look at the woman's face for the first time.

She had lied to him because she was most certainly beautiful. Very much so. Her hair was raven-black beneath her bonnet, equally black and shapely above eyes hidden by the lowering of the longest, darkest lashes he had ever seen, her nose short and straight. Best of all was her magnificent mouth, the lips full and pouting, and surely meant for a man to kiss and devour? And other, much more carnal delights.

That was Zachary's first thought. His second was something else entirely as he eyed that pale face, that delicious mouth, in frowning concentration. 'Do I know you?'

Georgianna almost choked over the hysterical laughter that rose in her throat, at having Zachary Black, of all men, ask if he knew her.

If he knew her?

Not only was it highly insulting to have him look at her with such quizzical half recognition, but it also made a complete mockery of her having bothered to wear the black veil as a disguise in the first place; she had fully expected this man to take one look at her and remember exactly how, and why, he knew her.

'Perhaps if you were to cast your mind back to last April, your Grace, it might help to jolt your memory?' she prompted sarcastically.

'Last April?' Zachary's lids narrowed as he studied her more closely. 'Take off your bonnet,' he ordered harshly.

Her brows lowered as she looked up at him for the first time without that concealing veil and revealing deep blue eyes, the colour of violets in springtime.

Unforgettably beautiful eyes, even if the rest of this woman's appearance, apart from that tempting mouth, had changed beyond all recognition.

If this young woman was indeed whom Zachary suspected she might be, then the last time he had seen her she had been plump as a pigeon and stood only an inch or two over five feet in height. She'd rosy, rounded cheeks, ample breasts spilling over the top of her gown, and curvaceous hips a man would enjoy grasping on to as he parted those plump thighs and thrust deep inside her.

She now appeared so slender that a puff of wind might blow her away. Indeed, Zachary knew from carrying her up the stairs that she weighed no more than a child of ten. Her skin was very pale against the black gown buttoned up to her throat, her breasts small, waist and thighs slender, as were the shapely calves and ankles he had glimpsed earlier.

She sighed. 'I am growing a little tired of your instructions, Hawksmere.'

'And I am beyond tired of your delay,' he returned angrily.

'Perhaps if you were to consider using the word please occasionally, especially when addressing a woman, you might meet with more co-operation to your requests?' She reached up slender hands to untie the ribbon beneath her pointed chin.

Zachary's hands were now clenched so tightly into fists at his sides that he knew he was in danger of the short fingernails piercing the skin. 'I reserve such politeness for women who have not invaded my carriage by the use of falsehood and lies. Now, remove the damned bonnet.'

Georgianna knew from the violence in Hawksmere's tone that she had now pushed him to the limit of his patience. Perhaps beyond that limit, for those silver eyes glittered dangerously in that harshly handsome face, his hands clenching and unclenching at his sides as if he were resisting the urge to reach out and place them about her throat before squeezing tightly.

If he had finally recognised her, then she had no doubt that was exactly how he felt.

Georgianna glared up at him defiantly as she finally removed the offending bonnet, revealing thick, ebony curls secured at her crown, a shorter cluster of curls at her temple, and the slender nape of her neck.

'Well, well, well.' Hawksmere gave a predatory smile, that silver gaze remaining on Georgianna's face as he began to pace slowly at the foot of the bed. His sleek and muscled body seemed to flow with the dangerous grace of the predator he now resembled. 'If it is not Lady Georgianna Lancaster come to call. Or perhaps I should now be addressing you as Madame Rousseau?' he added scornfully.

Leaving Georgianna in no doubt that this man, Zachary Black, the arrogant Duke of Hawksmere, now knew exactly who she was.

She felt the colour leach from her cheeks, her heart once again beating erratically in her chest, as she saw how the duke's silver eyes glittered with a cold, remorseless, and utterly unforgiving anger.

An anger that turned to scathing satisfaction as he saw the answer to his question in her now-ravaged expression. 'So your gallant Frenchman did not marry you, after all, but merely settled for having you warm his bed,' he stated mockingly as he ceased his pacing and suddenly lowered his lean and muscled length into the chair beside the ornate fireplace, those devil's eyes never leaving Georgianna's deathly pale face for a moment.

An icy coldness settled in Georgianna's chest. Her limbs felt heavy with fatigue, her lips so numb she doubted she would be able to speak even if she tried.

But she did not try; she knew that she deserved whatever scorn Hawksmere now chose to shower upon her head.

However, being carried so unceremoniously up to the duke's bedchamber and forced to reveal her identity was not supposed to have happened.

She had intended to meet Hawksmere in the darkness of his carriage, under the guise of anonymity, making her request for him to arrange for her to speak to someone in government, before fading into shadowed obscurity as she awaited an answer to that request. Fully aware it was all she could expect from Hawksmere, following the events of ten months ago.

'And is your French gallant here in England with you?' Hawksmere now prompted softly.

Georgianna drew in a steadying breath. 'You must know that he is not.'

He raised dark brows. 'Must I?'

She blinked back the sting of tears in her eyes. 'Do not play cat-and-mouse games with me, your Grace, when I have no defences left with which to withstand your cruelty.'

Zachary felt cruel. More than cruel. Despite his

outward calm, he had an inner longing to punch something. Someone. To take out his anger, his frustration with this situation, on living, breathing flesh.

Oh, not Georgianna Lancaster's tender flesh, of course; he had never hit a woman in his life, and as deserved as the anger he felt towards her might be, he was not about to start now by so much as placing a finger upon that smooth alabaster skin.

For, unlikely as it might seem, it truly was her, Zachary acknowledged incredulously as he continued to study her through narrowed lids. And he could surely be forgiven for not having recognised her immediately, when she was so much paler and more slender than she had been a year ago. When those beautiful eyes no longer brimmed over with a love of life.

With love for her erstwhile French lover?

If that was true, then, she had got exactly what she deserved, Zachary dismissed coldly. Disillusionment. Betrayal.

Unless…

'When did it become obvious to you that your lover was not the French *émigré* he claimed to be when he came to take up residence in England, but was actually a spy sent here by Napoleon himself?' Zachary channelled his anger into biting words rather than physical retribution. 'That his name was not Duval at all, but Rousseau?'

She bowed her head. 'Not soon enough.' The tears spilt unchecked over those long dark lashes before falling down her pale and hollow cheeks.

Not soon enough.

Zachary knew exactly what that meant. 'Did he ever have any intention or marrying you, do you think?' he scorned. 'Or was it his plan all along to just use you to hide his true identity?'

'What a truly hateful man you are.' Georgianna buried her face in her hands as the hot tears fell in earnest, sobbing brokenly at the same time as she knew that she wholly deserved Hawksmere's anger and his scorn. His disgust.

For she truly was a disgrace. That romantic fool whom Hawksmere had described earlier.

A young and romantic fool who had believed André loved her, that they were running away together, eloping, in order to be married. That he'd acted as her saviour, rescuing her from the prospect of a loveless marriage. Only for her to discover, once they reached a chaotic Paris, the city still in turmoil following Napoleon's surrender, that her lover had never had any intentions of marrying her.

Something André had wasted no time in revealing once he was safely back in France. Their elopement, he had told her, had acted only as a foil; as a way of hiding his real reason for fleeing England so suddenly and returning to his native France.

Something she felt sure that Hawksmere, as a spy for the Crown, must surely now be aware of. Not because he had any interest in learning what had become of her, but because André and his fellow conspirators—Bonapartists—were men whom England needed to watch.

'How you personally feel towards me has no bearing on the importance of the information I have brought back with me from France,' she now assured the duke dully.

'France?'

'Yes.'

Hawksmere shrugged those wide shoulders, elbows on the arms of the chair in which he sat, his fingers steepled together in front of his devilishly handsome face.

'Information which must surely be tainted by the mere fact that your word is not to be trusted. That you might now be a spy yourself, come to give the English government false information on your lover's behalf.'

Geogianna's eyes widened at the accusation. 'I told you I am a loyal subject of England.'

'One who has willingly been living in France with her lover this past ten months.'

'I have not seen or spoken to André Rousseau for many of those months,' Georgianna denied heatedly.

At first she had been too ill to leave France; once recovered, there had been no money to enable her to leave, even if she had wanted to. Which in reality she had not, knowing herself to be unwelcome in England after disgracing her whole family, as well as herself, in the eyes of society.

A family she was sure must have disowned her completely following her elopement with André.

So, yes, she had remained in France, all the time keeping her ears and eyes open to the plots and plans that so abounded in the streets, the shops, and the taverns of the city. Plots to liberate Napoleon from the Mediterranean island of Elba, where he now reigned as emperor of just twelve thousand souls.

Which, she reminded herself determinedly, was the only reason why she would ever have deliberately sought the company of the Duke of Hawksmere.

'No?' The duke eyed her mockingly.

'I gave you my word.'

'And I, of all people, have good reason to doubt your every word, Georgianna.'

She sighed. 'Your distrust of me is understandable.'

'It is kind of you to say so,' Hawksmere drawled with obvious sarcasm.

A flush warmed her cheeks at the deserved rebuke. 'I am well aware that I wronged you.'

'You wronged and disgraced yourself, madam, not me.' Zachary stood up restlessly to stride over to the window and look out into the park below as he wondered if such a strange and ridiculous situation as this had ever existed before.

Here he was, the powerful Duke of Hawksmere, fêted and fawned upon by the elite of the *ton* and society as a whole, alone in his bedchamber with Lady Georgianna Lancaster, a woman who had behaved so disgracefully in the past that if it were publically known, he doubted society would ever open its doors to her again.

A young woman whom Zachary had good reason to believe would never enter his bedchamber, under any circumstances.

And she had not come willingly this time, either, he reminded himself, but she'd been carried up here, thrown over his shoulder with no more concern than if she had been a sack of coal, her indignant protests at his actions completely ignored.

Because Zachary had not known who she was at the time, could have no idea that it was Georgianna Lancaster hiding beneath that veil and bonnet.

And if he had?

Would he have behaved any differently if he had known of her identity?

That identity, her history and association with André Rousseau, would have made it impossible for Zachary to simply ignore her. Or the information she said she had come here to impart.

'I apologise for my past wrongs to you.'

'I have absolutely no interest in your apologies, Georgianna, in the past or now,' Zachary assured her scathingly as he turned back to face her, his cool expression masking the shock he once again felt at the changes these past ten months had wrought in her.

Georgianna Lancaster's face was now ghostly pale rather than rosy as a freshly picked apple. Her violet eyes now dark and haunted, her alabaster skin stretching tautly over the delicacy of the bones at her cheeks and throat and her figure wraith-thin.

Because, as she claimed, she had been seduced, before then being abandoned by her French lover?

Or because of the nervousness of possibly days or weeks spent considering the enormity of the deception she was about to practise on her lover's behalf?

Zachary was wary and cynical enough to know that the rift that apparently now existed between Georgianna Lancaster and André Rousseau could all just be a ruse. And that she might have only returned to England to carry out her lover's instructions of passing along false information to the English government.

Until Georgianna revealed the full details of that information, Zachary had no way of knowing what was true and what was not.

Georgianna raised her chin, determined that Zachary Black should hear her out. Whether he wished it or not. The cold mockery in those glittering silver eyes, which now looked down at her so disdainfully, conveyed that he did not.

Her own eyes lowered so that she no longer had to look at that disdain. 'I have information.'

'Well?' he prompted hardly as she hesitated.

'It is Bonaparte's intention to leave Elba shortly and return to France as emperor.'

He shrugged wide shoulders. 'There have been rumours of his escaping Elba since he was first exiled there.'

'Oh,' Georgianna murmured flatly before rallying. 'But this time it is true.'

'So you say.'

Her eyes widened in alarm at the boredom of his tone. 'You have to believe me.'

'My dear Lady Georgianna, I do not have to do anything where you are concerned,' the duke assured softly as he crossed the bedchamber on stealthy feet, until he once again stood beside the bed on which she still sat. 'What were your lover's instructions regarding what you should do next, I wonder?' he prompted conversationally as he sat down on the bed beside her. 'If met with resistance from me, were you to then attempt to seduce me in order to gain my trust?'

Georgianna could only stare at him with wide and apprehensive eyes as he now sat so dangerously close to her his muscled thighs were just inches from her own. Close enough she could feel the heat of his immense body, smell the clean scent of lemon and sandalwood and that hint of the brandy and cigars he had enjoyed during the hours spent at his club earlier tonight.

So close that she could now see the black circle that rimmed those silver irises looking down at her so disdainfully. She noted the tautness of the flesh across aristocratic cheekbones. The top one of those sculptured lips curled back with the haughty disgust he so obviously felt towards her. That livid scar upon his throat a warning to all of how dangerous this gentleman could be.

As if to confirm that danger he gave a slow and sensuous smile.

'Feel free to begin any time you wish, Georgianna.'

Her alarm deepened at the cold mockery she saw in those hard silver eyes looking at her so contemptuously. 'I have no intention of attempting to seduce you.'

'No?' he drawled. 'Pity. It might at least have

proved amusing to see just how much your French lover has taught you this past year.'

'I told you, I have not so much as spoken to André in months.'

'And I am expected to believe that claim?' the duke drawled. 'To accept your word?' His jaw tightened, a nerve pulsing beside that livid scar at his throat. 'I am to accept the word of a woman whom I am only too well aware does not know the meaning of the word honour, let alone trust?'

Georgianna flinched at the icy dismissal of his tone. 'I was very young and foolish when you knew me last.'

'It was only ten months ago,' he cut in harshly. 'Am I now to accept that you have changed so much in that short time? That your word can now be trusted? The word of a woman who did not hesitate to cause disgrace to her family and herself just months ago in her desperation to elope with her French lover?'

Each deserved and hurtful word was like a whip lashing across Georgianna's flesh. Her eyes flooded anew with stinging tears, her body quivering at the landing of each successive and precise blow to her sensitised flesh.

She gave a weary shake of her head, unheeding of the tears still falling hotly down her cheeks. 'I am asking you to accept that the information I bring is completely removed from my own behaviour. That it is most urgent, even imperative, that you believe me when I tell you it is Bonaparte's intention to leave Elba soon and take up arms once again.'

'When, precisely?'

Her gaze dropped from meeting his. 'If you could arrange for me to speak with someone...'

'You do not trust me with this information?' He raised incredulous brows.

'Forgive me, but I have learnt this past ten months not to trust anyone completely,' she answered dully.

Zachary studied her between narrowed lids, hardening his heart to the tears that still lay upon those pale and hollowed cheeks. He reminded himself that this was the woman who had thought nothing of deceiving her own father, and the man who was to have been her husband, in order to run away with the Frenchman who was her younger brother's tutor.

It might be true that she had not seen André Rousseau for some months. Just as it might also be true that Georgianna Lancaster's unmarried state meant that she had reason to regret ever having eloped with the Frenchman in the first place.

But it might be just as true that this was all just a ruse and that she had been sent here by that lover to deceive and mislead the English government.

If the first of those things was true, then it was of no personal concern to Zachary; the woman had made her choices and must now live with them. No, it was the little information Georgianna Lancaster had already imparted, in regard to Napoleon's intention to soon leave Elba, which interested him.

For no matter what he might have said to Georgianna Lancaster, no rumour of Napoleon leaving Elba was ever ignored.

His nostrils flared.

'And I have no intention of so much as telling anyone of your presence back in England until I am satisfied you have told me all that you know.'

'Please.'

'Poor, bewildered Georgianna,' Zachary mocked the pained expression on her beautiful face as he slowly lifted his hand to gather up one of her tears on to his fingertip, looking down curiously at that tear before allowing it to fall to the carpeted floor at his feet as his gaze returned to her face. 'Did you really imagine it would be so easy to convince me of your sincerity? That I would listen to your information, be so concerned by it that I would then immediately arrange for you to speak to someone in the government?'

She swallowed. 'You must.'

'I have already told you I must do nothing where you are concerned, Georgianna,' Zachary thundered before quickly regaining control of his temper. A control he lost rarely, if ever. Testament, no doubt, to the anger he still harboured towards this woman. 'What have you really been doing these past ten months, I wonder?' he mused grimly.

She blinked. 'I told you, after André— Once I learnt he had merely been using me, I had no choice but to leave him.'

Zachary was fully aware that her violet gaze could no longer meet his own. A sure sign that she was lying? 'And what did you do then?' he prompted. 'How did you continue to live in France, Georgianna, with no money and, as you claim, no lover's bed to warm you?'

'It is not just a claim.'

'I am afraid that it is.'

Georgianna looked up at the duke apprehensively, not fooled for a moment by the calm evenness of his tone. 'What do you mean?'

He returned her gaze contemptuously. 'I mean that you have made a mistake in claiming Rousseau would ever have allowed you to leave him.'

Georgianna ran the tip of her tongue across suddenly dry lips before speaking huskily. 'Why do you say that?'

He gave a derisive laugh. 'My dear Georgianna, if you really were just the foolish romantic you claim to be, then once your usefulness to Rousseau was at an end he would have had no choice but to kill you for what you already knew about him, rather than simply allowing you to leave.'

She drew her breath in sharply, the colour draining from her cheeks even as she felt the burning in her chest and temple, a painful reminder that André had attempted to do exactly that.

She still cringed at the numbing disillusionment, the cruel and frightening way in which she had discovered André had never cared for her, but had merely been using her. And the shock, the devastation of learning that André intended to rid himself of the nuisance of her by taking her out of the city before killing her.

That he had not succeeded in doing so had been more by chance than deliberate intent.

And Georgianna had the scars, physical as well as emotional, to prove it.

Zachary remained unmoved by the haunted expression on Georgianna Lancaster's suddenly deathly pale face. Her elopement with André Rousseau, the mystery of where she had been and what she had been doing this past ten months, were all more than enough reason for him to distrust every word that came out of her delectable mouth.

And he did still consider it a delectably sensual mouth, he conceded regretfully. The sort of mouth that he had once imagined doing wild and wonderful things to his body—

Zachary stood up abruptly. 'Fortunately, the decision as to the truth, or otherwise, of the information you wish to impart, does not rest with me.'

'Then with whom?'

Zachary looked down at her grimly. 'There are others—less gentle than myself—who will decide the matter.'

'I do not understand.'

'You will, Georgianna.' Zachary hardened his heart to the increased bewilderment in those violet-coloured eyes. 'Have no doubt, you most certainly will.'

She stared up at him with fearful eyes. 'You cannot mean to— You are saying I shall be tortured, in order to ascertain whether or not I am telling the truth?'

'The English government does not resort to torture, Georgianna.' Zachary bared his teeth in a hard and mocking smile. 'Not openly, at least,' he added softly.

'You are trying to frighten me,' she accused emotionally.

'Am I succeeding?' he taunted.

'You must know that you are.' Her slender fingers tightly gripped one of the downy pillows.

'Poor Georgianna,' Zachary drawled mockingly. 'Are you even aware of your father's death?' he prompted sharply.

'Yes. I learnt of it yesterday when I returned to England.' Her lashes lowered. 'I— Do you have any news of Jeffrey?'

'He is well, I believe. Inheriting the title put paid to Cambridge, of course,' he drawled dismissively. 'But he fares well with his new responsibilities as Earl of Malvern, with the aid of his guardian.'

'Who on earth…?'

'I am sure your belated concern for your brother is all well and good, Georgianna,' Zachary continued dismissively, 'but it will not succeed in deflecting me, and others, from the suspicion that you might also now be a spy for Napoleon.' He gave a mocking shake of his head. 'And to think, just ten months ago the situation was all so very different. That if you had not run away, then all of this might now be yours.'

All of this, Georgianna knew, being the Hawksmere houses and estates, the title of duchess, and the Duke of Hawksmere himself as her husband.

All of which would most assuredly have been hers,

if she had continued with the betrothal her father had accepted on her behalf and married Zachary Black, the aloof and enigmatic Duke of Hawksmere.

It was every young girl's dream, of course, to receive an offer of marriage from a duke, to become his duchess, revered and looked up to by society.

It might also have been Georgianna's dream, too, if her father had once consulted her and not instead roused her stubbornness by accepting Hawksmere's offer without so much as discussing it with her.

If she had truly believed she could bear to be married to such a cold and arrogant man as Hawksmere, a man she had no doubt did not love her.

If she, stupid romantic fool that she had been, had not already believed herself to be madly in love with another man, a penniless tutor, whose situation in life had appealed to her young and too-innocent heart. The man she had believed to be in love with her.

As opposed to this man, Zachary Black, the icily composed Duke of Hawksmere, whom she knew had not loved her, but had only offered for her because she was the eminently suitable, and malleable, nineteen-year-old daughter of the Earl of Malvern.

Chapter Three

Georgianna had been flattered but terrified when her father first came to her and proudly told her of the offer of marriage he had received, and already accepted, on her behalf, from the wealthy and powerful Duke of Hawksmere.

Until that moment Hawksmere had been a gentleman Georgianna had never so much as spoken to and seen only rarely, and then only from a distance, at several of the *ton*'s entertainments during the past two Seasons. The toplofty gentleman had much preferred his clubs, and the company of his close friends, to the bustle and formality of society's much tamer entertainments.

But even viewed from a distance, Hawksmere had seemed intimidating to her, and aged one and thirty years to her nineteen, their twelve years' difference was so obvious in experience as well as age.

His demeanour was always one of icy disdain as he habitually looked down his arrogant nose at the crush of guests assembled at those entertainments. And the terrible scar visible upon the duke's throat had caused Georgianna to tremble every time she so much as glanced at it, as she imagined the raw savagery that must have been behind such an injury.

The very idea of her ever becoming the wife of such a haughtily cold and frightening gentleman had filled her young and romantic heart with fear. Especially so when the two of them had not so much as spoken a word to each other. Indeed, the only possible reason Georgianna could think of for the proposal was that, as the only daughter of the Earl of Malvern, Hawksmere must consider her a suitable candidate to provide his future heirs.

The dukedom aside, even the thoughts of the intimacy necessary to provide those heirs with such a terrifying man as Hawksmere had been enough to cause Georgianna's heart to pound fearfully in her chest.

Besides which, she was already in love and had been so for several months. With André Duval, the handsome and charming blond-haired, blue-eyed French *émigré* her father had taken pity on and brought into their home, so that he might help to prepare her younger brothe,r Jeffrey, for his entry into Cambridge.

That same handsome and charming blond-haired, blue-eyed Frenchman who just weeks later had so unemotionally taken her out to a wood outside Paris with the intention of killing her.

Tears of humiliation now burned Georgianna's

eyes as she looked up at Hawksmere. 'As I said, I was very young and very foolish,' she said dully.

'And now you are so much older and wiser,' Hawksmere taunted.

'Yes.' Georgianna's eyes flashed darkly. This man could have no idea of how much older and wiser she was, how much even a loveless marriage to him would have been preferable to the fate that had befallen her.

He eyed her pityingly. 'I trust you will forgive me when I say I do not believe you?'

'I very much doubt that you have ever needed anyone's forgiveness, least of all mine, to do just as you please.' She sighed as she moved to the edge of the bed before standing up. 'Very well, Hawksmere. Arrange to take me to your torturers now and let us put an end to this.'

Looking at her from between narrowed lids, Zachary could not help but feel a certain grudging admiration for the calmness of Georgianna Lancaster's demeanour and the slender dignity of her stance. A dignity so at odds with the frivolously young and plumply desirable Georgianna Lancaster of just ten short months ago.

Zachary had not been consciously looking for his future wife the evening he attended the Duchess of St Albans' ball, only making that brief appearance because the duchess had been a friend of his deceased mother. He had thought only to while away an hour or so out of politeness to that lady before making his excuses and departing for somewhere he could enjoy some more sensual entertainments.

Indeed, he had been about to do exactly that when Georgianna Lancaster had chanced to dance by in the arms of some young rake. Even then it had been her eyes which first drew his attention.

Eyes whose colour Zachary had never seen before. Long-lashed and violet-coloured eyes, laughing up merrily into the face of the gentleman twirling her about the ballroom.

It had taken several more minutes for Zachary's hooded gaze to move lower, for his body to respond, to harden, at sight of those delectably pouting and sensual lips, the swell of full and creamy breasts above her gown and curvaceous, childbearing hips.

To say that his arousal at her abundance of femininity had come as something of a surprise to him was understating the matter.

Normally he did not so much as glance at any of the young débutantes paraded into society every Season, having long ago decided they were all prattling flirts who sought only a titled and wealthy husband, none of them having so much as a sensible thought in their giddy heads.

Georgianna Lancaster did not look any less giddy than her peers, but at least his manhood had sprung to attention at sight of her, a necessary function if one was in need of an heir, and, he had decided, the daughter of the Earl of Malvern would do as the mother of that heir as well as any.

He had even convinced himself that her youth was an asset rather than the burden an older, more demanding woman might become. He would be able to mould Georgianna to his ways; he could wed her and bed her, enjoy that lusciously ripe body to the full whilst he impregnated her, before then leaving her to enjoy her role as the Duchess of Hawksmere, and so allowing him to return to the more sophisticated entertainments he preferred.

Or so Zachary had decided as he had looked upon Georgianna Lancaster that evening ten months ago.

What he had not considered at the time, or for some days after the announcement of their betrothal appeared in the newspapers, was that Georgianna Lancaster had not been the one to accept his offer of marriage. That, young as she was, she had a mind of her own. She had no intention of becoming the wife of a man, even a duke, she neither knew nor loved.

Or so she'd stated in the letter she had left behind for her father to read after she had eloped with her French lover, and which Malvern had reluctantly shared with Zachary when he had demanded the older man do so.

Zachary's mouth thinned as he remembered the days following Georgianna's elopement with her French lover.

The formal withdrawal of the betrothal in the newspapers so soon after it had been announced.

The condolences he had received from his uncles and aunts.

Most humiliating of all, perhaps, had been the knowing looks of the *ton*, all of them aware that Zachary Black, the haughty Duke of Hawksmere, having finally chosen his future duchess, had then just days later been forced to retract the announcement when that future bride had withdrawn from the betrothal.

Or so the story had been related to society at large. Very few people were made privy to the knowledge of Georgianna's elopement with the young and handsome French tutor.

Certainly none knew that it had been discovered, after the elopement, that the French tutor was not who he'd claimed to be, but was in fact a spy.

As Georgianna Lancaster was herself now also a spy, at the behest of her French lover?

She certainly knew far too much of Zachary's private business, of his connections, to be the complete innocent she claimed to be.

'Your Grace?'

Zachary's eyes narrowed as he returned his attention to the here and now. 'If only it were as simple as that, Georgianna,' he bit out scathingly. 'Unfortunately, there are several aspects of your story which the two of us will need to discuss in more detail.'

'Such as?'

'Such as why you chose to come to me, of all people, with this fantastical tale.'

'It is not fantastical or a tale.'

'Why me, Georgianna?' he persisted.

Her lashes lowered over violet eyes. 'I—I can see no harm in my admitting that it was André who informed me that you had long been acting as a spy for the Crown.'

Zachary gave a humourless smile to cover the inner jolt her words had given him; if Rousseau knew of the work he carried out in secret for England, then surely it followed that others must also? 'Could you not have found more stimulating pillow talk?' he said scornfully.

Georgianna's cheeks coloured at the insult even as she straightened the narrowness of her shoulders determinedly. 'He taunted me with the knowledge when he…when he…'

'Yes?'

She raised her pointed little chin. 'When he admitted that he had never been in love with me.' Her lashes lowered, her voice husky. 'When he told me that he had deliberately seduced me, then used our elopement as a way of leaving England. That there were now some who suspected his real reason for being in England.'

Zachary nodded abruptly. 'He had only just been put under more intense investigation at the time of your elopement.' And if Rousseau now knew of Zachary's own secret work for the Crown, then his usefulness in that capacity had surely come to an end?

'How disappointing for you,' he drawled dismissively in order to cover his inner disquiet.

Violet eyes flashed rebelliously. 'Do not dare to mock me, your Grace.'

All humour faded as Zachary's mouth thinned in displeasure. 'Your behaviour these past ten months dictates that I shall now dare to treat you in whatever manner I please, madam.'

The fight went out of Georgianna as quickly as it had flared to life. She bowed her head, totally shamed at the truth of the duke's words. She had behaved like a fool ten months ago. A stupid and naïve fool who had fallen completely for André's charm.

A charm that had completely deserted him the night he had taunted her, mocked her, for having run away with him, a spy for Napoleon. When the man to whom she was betrothed, the man she had run away from, was in fact the honourable one and more of a hero to England than any but a select few knew.

'That still does not explain how you knew where I should be this evening.'

Georgianna raised her head wearily, too tired now to do any more than answer Zachary Black's questions. 'I returned to England by ship yesterday.'

'Does your brother know you are returned?' he prompted sharply.

'No one but you knows.' She gave a sad shake of her head. 'It would have been most unfair to burden Jeffrey with that knowledge.' Much as she might long to see her brother again, to know if he at least was able to forgive her for her past recklessness, he was still but nineteen years of age, and newly become the Earl of Malvern, with all of the responsibilities that title entailed. He did not need to be burdened with the knowledge of the return to England of his disgraced sister, too.

'Obviously you did not feel a need to treat me with the same consideration,' Hawksmere rasped disdainfully.

She winced. 'I have explained why you are different. Why I had no choice but to seek you out and speak with you.'

'But not how you knew where I should be this evening,' he reminded grimly.

'I made it my business to keep a watch of your comings and goings as soon as I arrived in London yesterday, in an effort to speak with you alone. This evening, spent at your club, to celebrate the nuptials of your friend, offered me the opportunity I needed.'

Hawksmere gave a dismissive shake of his head. 'I should have known if you had been following me.'

'Obviously you did not.'

Which was worrisome, Zachary acknowledged with a frown. It implied a complacency on his part now they were no longer at war, a laziness, if he had failed to realise he was being so closely watched.

He straightened. 'This has all been very interesting, I am sure, but I have several other things that require my attention this morning, not to forget a wedding to attend this afternoon. So I am afraid I cannot waste any more time on this particular conversation just now.'

She nodded. 'I am staying at lodgings in Duke Street—perhaps you can send word to me there once you are have decided what to do?'

'Oh, no, Georgianna, I am afraid that will not do at all,' Zachary drawled drily, grateful for the approximate knowledge of where she was staying in London. And that no one but he was aware of her presence back in England.

She stilled warily. 'What do you mean?'

'I mean that, for the moment, I cannot allow you to leave this bedchamber.'

She gasped. 'You cannot keep me a prisoner here.'

He eyed her mockingly. 'Can I not?'

'No.'

'And, pray tell, who is to stop me?'

Her hands clenched at her sides. 'You are attempting to frighten me again.'

'And succeeding?' Zachary prompted mildly.

'Not in the least.' Georgianna clamped her lips stubbornly together as she refused to show any fear at Hawksmere's threats.

As she refused to ever show fear again, of anything, or anyone, after the way she had suffered at Rousseau's hands.

Which did not mean that Georgianna was not inwardly quaking at the icy determination so clearly shown in Hawksmere's expression.

She repressed a shiver at how, just ten months ago, she had so narrowly escaped becoming the wife of this cold and ruthless gentleman. A man, Georgianna had no doubt, who would have settled her in one of his ducal homes following the wedding and then repeatedly bedded her, until she had filled his nursery with his heir and his spare. After which, like many of the gentlemen of the *ton*, he would no doubt have abandoned her to find her own entertainments, whilst he returned to the life he had enjoyed before their marriage.

Such, Georgianna knew, was the life of many wives in society. A loveless and boring existence.

A life she had hoped to escape when she had eloped with André.

Only to then find she had placed herself in an even more dire position than becoming Hawksmere's unloved duchess.

Did she regret her elopement of ten months ago?

Of course she did.

If she could live that time over again, she would have remained in England with her family.

And become the wife of Zachary Black, the Duke of Hawksmere instead?

Never!

Despite all that Georgianna had endured these past months, despite all that she might still have to endure, she did not have a single regret in regards to refusing to become the wife of the Duke of Hawksmere.

She would never marry at all now, of course. How could she, when her reputation was now such that no gentleman would ever consider making her his wife? And to lie about her past, to pose as a widow, perhaps, in order to marry a lower-born gentleman, was a deceit she refused to practise on any man, or any children born into that marriage.

No, Georgianna had accepted that she would spend the rest of her life alone. As she fully deserved to do, when her impetuous actions of ten months ago had resulted in such shame and scandal.

'Do not look so sad, Georgianna.' The duke deliberately chose to misunderstand the reason for that sadness as he crossed the bedchamber on predatory soft steps, until he now stood just inches away from her. 'I may be busy for the rest of the day, but I shall return later this evening. And when I do—' those glittering silver eyes held her mesmerised as he slowly raised a hand and allowed the hardness of his knuckles to graze softly over the warmth of her cheek '—I am sure we shall be able to think of several ways in which to keep you entertained, during your incarceration in my bedchamber.'

Georgianna gasped as she heard the intent beneath that softly sensuous voice. Just as she now flinched as the hardness of those knuckles travelled the length of her throat before moving lower, lingering to caress the swell of her breasts through the material of her gown.

Leaving her in absolutely no doubt as to what those entertainments might be.

Her cheeks burned with humiliated colour as she pulled back from those caressing knuckles. 'I may have fallen from decency in society's eyes, Hawksmere, but I assure you I have absolutely no intention of becoming your plaything.'

The duke eyed her derisively. 'The arousal of your breasts, from just the merest touch of my knuckles, tells a different story,' he drawled mockingly as he glanced pointedly downwards.

Georgianna's startled gaze followed the direction of his mocking gaze, her face paling as she saw what Hawksmere so obviously saw; those rosy berries that tipped her breasts were now swollen and full, and could clearly be seen outlined against the soft material of her gown buttoned up to her throat.

Because they were aroused?

By Hawksmere?

Impossible.

Oh, he was handsome enough to set any woman's heart beating faster. But it was a dangerous attraction, a challenge those silver eyes proclaimed no one woman would ever be able to satisfy.

Too much of a challenge, it was rumoured, for any woman, high- or low-born, married or unmarried, to resist sharing the duke's bed once he had expressed an interest.

But Georgianna was not one of those weak and susceptible women. How could she be, when she found Hawksmere no less intimidating now than she had ten months ago?

Except…

There was no denying the physical evidence of her breasts having become aroused by his lightest of touches.

Not with desire but fear, Georgianna instantly assured herself.

Because Hawksmere had just threatened to keep her here, a prisoner in his bedchamber, for as long as he chose to do so.

She straightened her spine. 'You cannot keep me here against my will,' she repeated firmly.

'I can do anything I wish with you, Georgianna,' Zachary murmured with satisfaction, mocking her response, her undeniable arousal at his caress.

An arousal which Zachary knew no woman could fabricate or control.

As he had been unable to control his own arousal

as he had lightly caressed the engorged tip of her breast.

Despite her having run away from marrying him ten months ago, Zachary could not deny that he still physically desired this woman. In his bed, beneath him, to be buried to the hilt between her thighs.

Try as he might, Zachary had found no explanation for that sudden clench of desire when he had looked at Georgianna Lancaster ten months ago, and he had none now, either. It was enough to know that it still existed.

A weakness, in the current circumstances, best kept to himself.

He stepped back abruptly. 'As I said, I have other things to occupy me this morning, but I will go downstairs now and arrange a breakfast for you, and then I advise that you get some sleep.'

'I am not hungry, nor shall I sleep.'

Zachary's eyes narrowed on her critically, noting the hollows in the paleness of her cheeks, her slenderness beneath the unbecoming black gown. 'You are grown too slender.'

'I said I am not hungry.' Those violet-coloured eyes flashed again in warning.

Another show of temper Zachary did not care for in the least, as he stepped deliberately closer to her, so close that he could see the way the pupils of her eyes expanded as she now looked up at him apprehensively.

'Nevertheless, you will eat all of the breakfast I have brought up to you.'

She maintained her ground even as a nerve pulsed rapidly at her throat, no doubt as evidence of her inner nervousness. 'And I have said I shall not.'

Once again Zachary felt that grudging admiration for her stubbornness; not too many people dared to stand against him, least of all women. She was a very young woman at that, and one who did not as yet appear to fully appreciate the danger she had placed herself in by choosing to step back into his life.

He gave a slow and deliberate smile. 'I advise you not to defy me, Georgianna.'

She eyed him rebelliously. 'Why should I not?'

He gave a nonchalant shrug as he murmured softly, 'Because I shall win and you will lose.'

Georgianna repressed another shiver of apprehension as she heard the arrogant certainty in his voice. As she acknowledged that, through her own stupidity this time, Hawksmere now had her completely at his mercy. She was his prisoner, to do with as he wished.

Hawksmere smiled confidently as he seemed to guess at least some of her thoughts. 'I shall be locking you in here in my absence, of course, and taking the key with me. And I advise that you not bother giving yourself a sore throat, or knuckles, by screaming or shouting, or banging on the door for my servants to release you whilst I am gone,' he added derisively. 'I shall make sure to inform them, before I depart, that it is all part of the erotic play between the two of us, and that the more you ask to be set free the more you desire to stay here and await my return.'

'You truly are a monster.' Georgianna's cheeks burned with humiliated colour.

He shrugged. 'I have never made any pretence of being anything else.'

The implication being, Georgianna knew, that she was the one who had practised deceit, when she'd lied to her family and her betrothed in order to run away with André.

And that Hawksmere believed she was lying to him even now.

Except she was not. And Hawksmere's decision to keep her locked up here, and his threats, did not change the fact that time was more the enemy than this arrogant duke. 'You will speak to someone this morning on my behalf?'

Hawksmere's mouth thinned into an uncompromising line. 'I have no plans to do so until the two of us have spoken again, no.'

'But you must,' Georgianna gasped desperately. 'Napoleon…'

'Enough, Georgianna,' Hawksmere rasped his impatience with her persistence as he grasped her arms, his silver eyes as cold as ice as he looked down the length of his arrogant nose at her. 'I have not had the opportunity to sleep, either, this past night, and my patience is now at an end.'

'But…'

'I said enough, Georgianna,' he thundered.

Tears blurred her vision. 'You have every right to be angry with me, to despise me for my having ended our betrothal in the way that I did.' She gave a weary shake of her head. 'Take your revenge upon me any way you please. I do not care what you do to me, as long as you take my warnings seriously.'

'And if it is my wish to claim your body, for your having run from me, from our betrothal, ten months ago?' he taunted softly.

She shook her head. 'As long as you also listen to me in regards to Napoleon.'

'One more mention of that man's name and more pressing responsibilities be damned, I shall be forced to begin that punishment now!' the duke warned darkly. 'Now that I think about it, it might be best if I were to request that you remove your gown,' he mused hardly. 'You will be less likely to attempt an escape if you are half-naked.'

'I will not take off my gown.' Georgianna pulled out of his grasp to move quickly away from him, her hands held up defensively in front of her rapidly rising and falling chest.

Zachary studied her through narrowed lids as he noted the wild panic in those beautiful violet-coloured eyes. Much like a deer the moment it realised it was caught in the sights of the hunter's gun.

All because he had asked her to remove her gown?

Surely a woman who had shared one man's bed for the past ten months would not be quite so averse to the idea of another man seeing her naked?

Unless…

'Did he hurt you?' Zachary scowled darkly.

That violet gaze sharpened. 'What?'

His mouth thinned. 'Did Rousseau hurt you?'

'Of course he hurt me! How could he not, when he used me to make good his escape?'

'That is not the type of hurt I am referring to, Georgianna.' Zachary took several steps towards her, coming to a halt as Georgianna shadowed those steps by moving back, until she was now pressed up against one of the velvet curtains hanging at the window. 'I have no intentions of harming you, Georgianna.'

She gave a choked and bitter laugh. 'You have just threatened to take away my gown.'

'And that is all I have threatened.'

She gave a shudder. 'It is enough!'

Zachary's eyes narrowed. 'Some men like to give pain to their bed partner during lovemaking, as a way of heightening their own arousal.'

She gasped. 'Do you?' Pale and slender fingers now tightly clasped at the throat of that unbecoming black gown as she stared at him with dark and shadowed eyes.

'No, I most certainly do not,' Zachary assured grimly. 'But I am beginning to suspect that Rousseau did. Do you perhaps share his perversion?'

'No!'

'I am glad to hear it.' Zachary's eyes narrowed. 'But has he left lasting marks upon your body you would not wish another man to see?' he added harshly, surprised at how violent it made him feel to think of there being so much as a single bruise administered to that alabaster skin, let alone any lasting reminder of the man Rousseau.

Georgianna breathed shallowly, not sure she understood all that Zachary Black was saying to her. Not sure she wanted to understand.

Surely lovemaking was exactly that? An expression of the love a couple felt for one another? Or if not love, then at least a tenderness, a caring, for the other's welfare?

What the duke was describing, the deliberate inflicting of pain, did not sound as if it could be any of those things.

And yet Georgianna did indeed bear scars, and ones inflicted upon her by André Rousseau. Not the visible scars to which Hawksmere seemed to refer, of course, but they were damning none the less. A testament to the scorn, the total uninterest in which André had held the impressionable young girl who had forsaken all for her love of him.

'I can see that he did.' Hawksmere obviously took her silence to be her answer, his expression grimmer than ever. 'And you still love such a man?' he added disgustedly.

'No.' Georgianna choked in protest; how could she possibly love a man who had treated her as André had?

To her everlasting shame, Georgianna was no longer sure she had ever really loved André, or whether she had not just been in love with love itself.

A year ago she had been so young and idealistic, had believed in love and romance. And the handsome and penniless Frenchman employed by her father had seemed so much more romantic, so much easier to love than the intimidating and distant Duke of Hawksmere. To the extent that Georgianna had woven all of her dreams about the golden-haired and romantic Frenchman in order to run away from marrying the dangerous duke.

Reality had proven to be so much less than those silly, romantic dreams.

Not that she believed Hawksmere to be any less dangerous now than she had previously. The opposite, after the things he had said and done to her today.

But she certainly had no romantic dreams left in regard to André Rousseau, either, or indeed any other man.

Hawksmere's top lip curled up in distaste, silver eyes a pale glitter between narrowed lids. 'Again, this is something we will have to discuss further upon my return. No doubt we shall have the opportunity to discuss many things during the hours we spend here in my bedchamber together,' he added pleasantly.

'How long do you intend to keep me here?' Georgianna stared at him disbelievingly.

'As long as it takes to get to the truth,' Zachary assured uninterestedly.

She gave a desperate shake of her head. 'Have you not listened to a word I have said? Do you not understand the urgency of the things I have told you?'

He eyed her mockingly. 'I have listened to the little you decided to share with me, yes.'

'What will it take to convince you of my sincerity?'

'More than you have already told me, obviously,' Zachary drawled drily, brows raised questioningly.

A frown creased Georgianna's forehead as she obviously fought an inner battle as to how much more she intended revealing to him.

Finally she gave a defeated sigh. 'Napoleon is to leave Elba before the end of this month.'

'And you come to me with this story now?' He raised sceptical brows. 'With the end of the month just days away?'

'I did not—' Georgianna gave an impatient shake of her head as she accepted that to Hawksmere this was still just a 'story'. 'I only learnt of the plan nine days ago and I could not immediately get passage from France. I...' Her gaze lowered. 'André has men placed at all of the ports, watching and waiting for anyone who might wish to betray Napoleon.'

'And yet here you are,' Hawksmere drawled disbelievingly.

She nodded. 'But I had to bide my time and make good my escape when the chance came for me to join a large family travelling together. I was all the time fearful that someone might recognise me. Am I boring you, your Grace?' she prompted sharply as the duke gave a yawn.

'As it happens, yes, you are.' He nodded unapologetically.

'But...'

'I really am uninterested in listening to any more buts or arguments just now, Georgianna,' he rasped harshly.

Georgianna looked up searchingly into his hard and implacable face. Noting the cold glitter of his silver eyes. The tautness of the skin across sculptured cheekbones. The sneering curl of his top lip.

The determined set of his arrogant and unyielding jaw.

She knew in that moment that all of her efforts of appeal for Zachary Black's help had been a waste of her time.

That this man despised her so utterly he would never believe a single word she said to him.

Chapter Four

Zachary was irritable and tired by the time he returned home several hours later, his morning having proved to be a frustrating one.

Not least because the man he had wished to speak with, the man to whom he had reported this past four years, was unavailable, and likely to be so for the next few days, as his deputy had informed Zachary. It happened, of course, but it was frustrating, nevertheless.

He had duly passed along the relevant information to the deputy, of course, but even so he still felt a sense of dissatisfaction.

It was true that there had been dozens of rumours of plots and plans to liberate the Corsican from Elba these past months and each and every one of them had necessarily to be investigated.

What if Georgianna were telling the truth and Napoleon really did mean to leave Elba before the month's end and return to the shores of France? Possibly as emperor? That would not suit Louis or England.

Zachary had also requested to look at the file they had accumulated on André Rousseau these past months, hoping it might shed some light upon Georgianna Lancaster's own movement. There had been no sightings of her in Rousseau's company for some months. No sightings of her at all, it seemed, since a week or so after she and Rousseau had arrived in Paris together.

A curiosity in itself.

Where had Georgianna been all this time? And what had she been doing? For that matter, if she had not been with Rousseau, then where had she come by the information regarding Napoleon?

For the moment Zachary's instructions were clear; he was to continue to keep Georgianna Lancaster imprisoned in his home and continue questioning her until such time as he was notified otherwise.

For all that Zachary had earlier today taunted Georgianna with the possibility of her continued incarceration, he was not best pleased at receiving orders to do exactly that.

And one of the main reasons for that was Georgianna herself.

The previous year she had been an inexperienced and idealistic young girl, that plump and desirable pigeon that Zachary had decided to marry, bed and subsequently mould into being his undemanding duchess.

Just a few minutes in her company earlier this morning and Zachary knew that Georgianna's ten months in France had wrought more changes in her than just the physical ones.

That bright-eyed young girl, eager for life, was no more. And in her place was a coolly dignified, capable and stubborn woman. One who had lived in Paris, by all accounts, completely alone for some months, before arranging her own passage back to England. Who had then managed to follow him without his knowledge, until such time as she was able to speak with him privately. Moreover, Georgianna had shown him that very morning she was not a woman who intended to ever be cowed, by him, or anyone else.

If anything, that air of dignity, her independence and intelligence, appealed to and aroused Zachary even more than that naïve young woman he had intended to make his wife.

And whatever else Georgianna might claim to be now, she had eloped with André Rousseau ten months ago. She had been the Frenchman's lover for a number of weeks, if not months, before and following that elopement.

For Zachary to feel desire and admiration for such a woman, a woman he had every reason to distrust, was not only rash on his part, but it could also be dangerous.

Zachary drew in a deep breath as he came to a halt outside the door to his bedchamber, noting there was no sound coming from within. He had questioned his butler on his arrival, and been informed that all had been silent above stairs all morning. Georgianna had obviously taken Zachary's advice to heart and refrained from screaming, or banging on the door, demanding to be set free.

And perhaps that had just been a ploy and she was even now poised behind the silence of that door, candelabrum in hand, ready to knock Zachary senseless before making good her escape?

His smile was grim as he quietly unlocked the door to his bedchamber. He entered softly and saw the room was in semi-darkness, the curtains pulled halfway across the two picture windows, nevertheless allowing him to see that the breakfast tray still sat on the table near the door where he had placed it earlier.

The untouched breakfast tray.

A single glance was enough to show him that none of the food on the plates had been eaten. Only the dregs left in the bottom of the delicate china cup to show that Georgianna had drunk her tea at least.

The half-drawn curtains allowed the weak February sunshine to shaft across the room to where Georgianna lay asleep on top of his bed. She was still dressed in that unbecoming black gown. The curling ebony hair had been loosened, however, and now flowed thick and silky over the pillows behind her and across her breasts down to her tiny waist.

Zachary put down the bag he carried to cross softly to the bedside and look down at her. Her face appeared as a beautiful pale oval in the weak light. Long lashes fanned silkily against ivory cheeks as she continued to sleep, her rosy and sensual lips slightly parted as she breathed softly and evenly.

A deceptive picture of innocence, if not beauty.

So she might once have looked in their marriage bed, Zachary acknowledged with annoyance as his traitorous body stirred, hardened, as he continued to look down at her. And he had no doubt that until a year ago she had been an innocent, those violet-coloured eyes full of joy, of the expectations of life, rather than swirling with dark shadows as they had been earlier today.

Feeling any sort of empathy, sympathy, for this woman would be a mistake on his part. Most especially when he still questioned her real motives for seeking him out.

Zachary's mouth thinned as he turned away impatiently and walked determinedly from the bedside with the intention of pulling the curtains completely across the windows. He had no time to rest himself—he had Wilding's wedding to attend—but Georgianna might as well continue to sleep peacefully.

Zachary was in need of a bath and a change of clothes after his own sleepless night, before he then attended the wedding in just a few hours.

'Leave them. Please.'

Zachary gave a start at the sound of Georgianna's voice. A voice that sounded as if it were underlined with panic. Or possibly fear? Simply because he had been about to draw the last of the curtains fully across the windows to shut out the daylight?

He turned to see that Georgianna had moved up on to her elbows, those ebony curls falling past her shoulders and cascading back on to the pillows behind her.

Her face was still that ghostly oval, her eyes so

dark they appeared almost purple as she looked across at him pleadingly. 'Please,' she beseeched earnestly.

'What is it, Georgianna?' Zachary prompted sharply as he crossed, frowning, to her side.

Her breasts quickly rose and fell. 'I—I am afraid of... I do not like complete dark.' She sat up abruptly to curl her arms defensively about her drawn-up knees, looking for all the world like that frightened deer of earlier.

'What foolishness is this, Georgianna?' Zachary chided impatiently. 'If you think to appeal to my softer side with exhibitions of feminine—'

'How could I possibly do that, when we both know you do not have a softer side for me to appeal to!' she came back sharply as she moved swiftly to the side of the bed before standing up and crossing to the window on stockinged feet. There she pulled back the curtains to allow in the full daylight. 'And I assure you I speak only the truth.' Her hands, no longer hidden in those black lace gloves, were clasped tightly together in front of her, the knuckles white as she looked up at him. 'I do not like to be in the complete dark. Ever.' Her lips firmed as she raised her chin in challenge.

Zachary ignored Georgianna's insult as he continued to study her through narrowed lids. Her face was ashen, but that could be because she had not slept for long enough, nor had she eaten the breakfast he had had brought to her.

No, it was those tightly clasped hands, and the defiance in her stance, which now convinced Zachary that she was sincere in her dislike, even fear, of the complete dark.

'And why is that?' he prompted softly.

Georgianna swallowed, hating that she had shown any sign of weakness in front of Zachary Black, the mocking Duke of Hawksmere. She hated him for dwelling on that weakness, whereas before she had merely feared him.

Nor did she have any intention of telling this hateful man of the head injury she had suffered and which, for two weeks, had left her blind. For that short time she had been caught in eternal darkness, afraid that she would never be able to see again.

It had been fear unlike anything Georgianna had ever known before, including the bleakness of those hours after André had attempted to murder her, leaving her body in the woods for the wild animals to devour.

She accepted she had wronged Zachary Black in the past and had apologised for it, but surely, surely she did not have to now reveal all of her humiliations so that he might taunt her further?

She hoped to keep some dignity.

'How did you get that?' she demanded sharply, eyes wide as she saw and recognised her travelling bag sitting on the floor just inside the door of the bedchamber.

Hawksmere gave it a cursory glance before turning back with a dismissive shrug. 'It was collected from your lodgings this morning, of course.'

'I— But— How did you know where...? I told you

earlier the name of the street where I had taken lodgings,' Georgianna confirmed heavily.

'You did, yes.' Zachary gave a hard smile of satisfaction. It had not taken long at all for one of his footmen to be sent to Duke Street to discover in which lodging Georgianna was staying. 'It was not too difficult to guess that the Anna Smith, who arrived in London yesterday, was in fact Georgianna Lancaster,' he added coolly as she seemed to have been struck momentarily dumb. 'And the two small portraits on the dressing table of your mother and father together, and another of your brother, confirmed it was so.'

Those violet eyes rose quickly to meet his. 'You went to Mrs Jenkins's house yourself?'

He shrugged. 'I did not think you would appreciate having one of my footmen pawing through your more personal items.'

She bristled. 'Obviously you did not hesitate to do so yourself.'

'Obviously not.' Zachary gave a mocking nod. 'We may have fought a war with France, but I have always considered that they do make the most sensual of ladies' undergarments.'

Two spots of colour appeared in the paleness of Georgianna's cheeks. 'And no doubt you have seen enough of them to be an expert on the subject?'

'No doubt.' Zachary's mouth quirked in amusement. 'Is it not a little late for you to be exhibiting such maidenly outrage, Georgianna?' he added hardly.

He was right. Of course he was right, Georgianna

acknowledged heavily. She knew she had forfeited any right to feel outrage, maidenly or otherwise, in Hawksmere's eyes, as well as those of all decent society, the moment she left her home in the middle of the night and eloped with André.

Except, unbelievable as it would undoubtedly be for others to learn, she was still a maiden…

She and André had spent the first night and day of their elopement travelling by coach to the port where they intended to board the boat bound for France, their intention being to marry there rather than linger overlong in England. And André had explained, once they reached that port, that they stood more chance of remaining undetected if they travelled as brother as sister. A logic for which Georgianna had been exceedingly grateful.

Not least because, by that time, she had begun to doubt the wisdom of her actions.

It had all seemed so romantic, so exciting, when she and André made their plans to elope together in the middle of the night. But the long hours spent in the coach together, the rattling and jostling too severe to allow sleep or even rest, and fraying both their tempers and patience, had enabled Georgianna to see André as rather less than the romantic hero she had thought him to be.

To realise that, by running away with André in the middle of the night, she had cut herself off completely from her family, from society, in a scandal so shocking she would never be able to return.

The respite of travelling on the boat together as

brother and sister had been something of a balm to her already frayed nerves.

To accept that she was no longer as sure that she wished to become André's wife at all.

Considering the nightmare that had followed, it was perhaps as well she had already begun to have those doubts.

She drew herself up to her full height of just over five feet as she now met Hawksmere's gaze unflinchingly. 'I trust you are not expecting me to thank you for something that was unnecessary in the first place?'

'Oh, it was very necessary, Georgianna,' he corrected harshly. 'As I informed you earlier, you are to remain here for the next few days. And I thought you might feel more comfortable if you had your own things with you.'

Georgianna's head ached from having awoken so suddenly, in response to Hawksmere shutting out the daylight. The same response, panic and fear, she always felt now at finding herself in complete darkness.

Nevertheless, headache or no, she could not allow Hawksmere's words to go unchallenged. 'We both know your only concern was to allay Mrs Jenkins's suspicions when I did not return there later today. No doubt she was suitably impressed at the presence of the illustrious Duke of Hawksmere in her modest home?'

He gave that derisive smile. 'No doubt.'

Georgianna gave a disgusted shake of her head.

'You really do mean to keep me a prisoner here, then?'

His jaw tightened. 'For the moment, yes.'

She sighed. 'An occurrence which I can see does not suit you any more than it does me.'

He shrugged his wide shoulders. 'It would seem that neither one of us has a choice in the matter. But there is a bright side to all of this, Georgianna,' he added softly as he crossed the bedchamber with those soft and predatory steps. 'Just think, you did not have to marry me in order to share my bedchamber.'

Georgianna refused to be intimidated as Hawksmere now stood just inches away from her. So close, in fact, that she could see every detail of the livid scar upon his throat, as well as the dark stubble on his jaw, evidence that he had not yet had time to shave today. Indeed, his evening clothes from the night before showed that he had not so much as taken the time to change his clothes yet this morning.

Because, despite his scepticism towards her earlier, he had believed enough of what she told him to not waste any time in sharing that information?

Georgianna certainly hoped that was the case.

She could bear any amount of Hawksmere's mockery, as well as his scorn and disgust, if at the same time he helped to thwart this latest plot to liberate Napoleon from Elba.

She gave a humourless smile. 'We must all be grateful for small mercies, your Grace.'

Zachary's bark of laughter was completely spontaneous. A genuine appreciation of Georgianna's continued feistiness, despite the direness of the situation in which she now found herself.

And not much succeeded in amusing Zachary any more.

As an only child, he had inherited the Hawksmere title eleven years ago, upon the death of both his parents in a carriage accident. The years that followed had been lonely as well as busy ones, mainly filled with the responsibilities of his title, and fighting against Napoleon, in open battle, and secretly as an agent for the Crown.

Those same years had shown him that women, young and old, thin or plump, fair or dark, single or married, were willing to do almost anything for the attentions of a duke. This had resulted in a jading, a cynicism within him, beyond Zachary's control.

It appeared Georgianna Lancaster was the exception.

Not only had she chosen to run away from becoming his duchess ten months ago, but even now she continued to defy and challenge him in ways that no other woman ever had.

'I believe I prefer you feisty and defiant, Georgianna, rather than the naïve ninny you were ten months ago,' Zachary murmured appreciatively as he looked down searchingly into the pale face she held up to challenge him. The arching of her slender neck allowed those ebony curls to fall silkily down the length of her spine to her pert little bottom.

'A naïve ninny you nevertheless intended to make your wife,' she reminded scathingly.

He shrugged. 'I believed you to be a malleable ninny then.'

Her brows rose. 'And now?'

Zachary gave a slow and appreciative smile. 'Now I believe this added fire makes you more appealing than I might otherwise have expected.'

Georgianna shuddered, keeping a watchful eye on Hawksmere as she instinctively took a step back from him. She was wary of the way in which his eyes now glittered down at her so intently, almost as if a white light had been ignited in those silver depths. Georgianna was unsure of precisely what that flame might mean, but she did know that she no longer wished to stand quite so close to him.

Hawksmere took that same step forward before raising his hand to gently cup one side of her face, the soft pad of his thumb moving in a soft caress across her parted lips. 'There is nowhere you would be able to run this time, Georgianna, that I would not find you.'

Her heart was beating rapidly in her chest: at Hawksmere's threats, his proximity, and the effects of that caressing thumb against her lips. A sensuous caress, much as Georgianna might wish it otherwise, which caused a heat to course through her whole body, leaving her skin feeling flushed and tight and her breasts swelling uncomfortably beneath her gown.

Because, as Hawksmere had claimed earlier, she was aroused by his touch?

How could that possibly be, when she disliked this

man, when she had run from him, from the very idea of becoming his wife, less than a year ago?

Perhaps it was just that she had been alone, and lonely, for so very long? Too long without the gentle touch of another? Since she had been held by another? Looked at with warmth, if not affection?

Except the warmth in Hawksmere's gaze was so clearly predatory rather than affectionate.

Georgianna pulled back sharply from the mesmerising effect of that silver gaze. 'I have no intentions of running anywhere,' she assured him decisively. At least, not until this matter of Napoleon's liberation was settled. 'Did you go to your superior this morning and report my information?'

Zachary continued to look down at Georgianna for several long moments more. His response to her was undeniable. To her beauty, her proximity, to having touched and caressed those soft and pouting lips. Totally undeniable, when his erection pressed so insistently against the front of his breeches.

'And what business is it of yours whether I did or I did not?' He arched a challenging brow.

'But...' she blinked her bewilderment '...I am the one responsible for giving you that information.'

He nodded abruptly. 'All the more reason for it to be mistrusted, surely? What did you expect, Georgianna?' he taunted as she looked pained. 'Did you think that by returning to England, by twittering about some ridiculous plot of how Napoleon intends to leave Elba before the end of the month, that all would be forgiven? That you would be a heroine, and could then return to your family, to society?' he prompted cruelly.

Those striking eyes became misty with unshed tears. 'I am well aware there can be no forgiveness, in any quarter, for the way I have behaved,' she spoke so softly Zachary could barely hear her, as her tears fell unchecked down the paleness of her cheeks.

Zachary felt instant regret for his deliberate cruelty. Whatever this woman might have done to him personally in the past, there was an undeniable vulnerability about her now, an aloneness, that Zachary knew he could relate to.

He breathed deeply through his nose. 'Perhaps that situation is not quite so bleak as you think it is.'

She tilted her head curiously. 'What do you mean?'

He owed this woman nothing except his contempt and distrust, Zachary reminded himself impatiently. Certainly not absolution for her deeds of ten months ago.

And yet…

He was not a deliberately cruel man, no matter what others might say or think to the contrary. He considered their past association.

Could Georgianna really be blamed for what had happened in their past? She was a young girl of only nineteen who'd feared, to the extent of running away from marriage to a man who had not even troubled himself in getting to know her before offering for her. He'd been a man who had not even spoken to her before making that offer. And once made, she'd had that offer accepted by her father without knowing a thing about it—or him.

Much as it galled him, Zachary knew he must accept some of the blame for the way in which Georgianna had run away back then.

But not for what had happened since that time, or the possible depth of her continued involvement with Rousseau.

He hardened his heart against the idea of telling Georgianna of the way in which he and her father had, between them, managed to salvage her reputation at least, if not their own embarrassment.

'A place can always be found in a gentleman's life for a beautiful woman,' he rasped insultingly.

Her throat moved as she swallowed. 'As his mistress, you mean?'

Zachary bared his teeth in a humourless smile. 'But of course.'

'I believe I should rather become an old maid,' she answered with quiet dignity.

'Do not make your decision based on your experience with Rousseau, Georgianna,' he advised coldly. 'Being the mistress of a gentleman would not be like it was with him. You would have a house of your own. Servants. An elegant carriage. A generous allowance, for clothing and such.'

Her chin rose. 'You, of course, would know of such things.'

In actual fact, Zachary had no personal knowledge of such an arrangement. He had never been enamoured enough of any of the women he had bedded in the past to have so much as ever considered making any his permanent mistress.

What sort of mistress would Georgianna make? The depths to those violet-coloured eyes, the sensual pout of her lips, and the uncontrollable response of her breasts to his lightest touch, all spoke of a passionate nature. Of a woman who was more than capable of meeting his physical demands with an equal fire.

And that she was untrustworthy?

Perhaps that might even add to the excitement, the danger, of such an arrangement?

He was a fool for even considering taking Georgianna Lancaster as a mistress, when there was no question that she had been mistress to Rousseau. Might still be so, for all Zachary knew of that situation.

'Not recently, no,' he answered bitingly. 'Which means the position is currently available, if you are interested in applying?' He raised goading brows.

Georgianna drew herself up proudly. 'So that you might insult me by refusing, no doubt?'

'No doubt.'

She gave a shake of her head. 'I am not, nor will I ever be, interested in such a role, in your life or any other man's.'

Zachary gave a hard smile. 'It is the only one still available to you.'

'I said I am not interested,' she repeated firmly.

'Then I will see that the bedchamber adjoining this one is prepared for your use. Yes, I too appreciate the irony of having you now occupy the bedchamber intended for my duchess,' he drawled as Georgianna's eyes widened. 'But it would seem that for the moment, at least, I am to have little choice in the matter.'

'You have the choice of releasing me—you just refuse to take it,' Georgianna pointed out sharply.

'I do, yes.' The duke gave a haughty inclination of his head. 'But I do not intend to keep you prisoner all the time, Georgianna. When I return later this evening you will join me downstairs for dinner. And I wish you to wear the lilac gown I brought from your lodgings rather than the black.'

'I will not be told by you what I shall do or what I shall wear.'

'You will if you do not wish to find yourself face first over my knee, with your skirts thrown up to your waist, whilst I thrash your bare bottom a rosy red for daring to disobey!' Hawksmere assured harshly.

Georgianna gasped at the crudeness of the threat. A threat she knew this man to be more than capable of carrying out. 'You are a barbarian, sir.'

He bared his teeth in a smile. 'All men are barbarians at heart, my lady.'

Georgianna repressed a shudder as the conversation brought back the painful memory of the violence she had suffered at André's hands. A violence she would not have believed possible of the once gentle man she had thought she knew and loved. A violence which had left her both blind and fighting for her life.

Again she wondered if Hawksmere would believe her, trust that she only spoke the truth, if she were to tell him of that terrible night when André had tried to kill her. When he thought he had killed her. It was only luck, and the arrival of a local farmer who had heard the shots being fired and feared for his live-stock, that had ensured she had not died that night.

'What are you thinking about?' Hawksmere de-manded shrewdly.

Would he believe her if she were to show him the scars her body carried from that night?

They were undoubtedly the scars left by a bullet wound, but there was no guarantee, even if Georgi-anna were to bare her flesh, that Hawksmere would any more believe it was André Rousseau himself who had inflicted them than the duke believed the infor-mation she had brought to him regarding Bonaparte's intended escape from Elba.

Georgianna had little in her life now except the small amount of pride left to her. She feared she might lose that, too, if Hawksmere were to both ridicule and scorn, and to disbelieve the physical scars she bore as proof of André Rousseau's complete disregard for her.

Hatred was far too strong a word to use to de-scribe the calculated way in which André had come to the conclusion that she had outlived her purpose. He had been completely unemotional that night in the woods before he shot her, having assured her it was not a personal action, rather it was that he had no more use for her.

She could not bear to now have Zachary Black, the scornful Duke of Hawksmere, prod and poke at the even deeper wound that had been inflicted that night upon her heart and soul.

She raised her chin. 'I do not care for your threats.'

'No?'

'No!'

He shrugged wide shoulders. 'Then do as I say and wear the lilac gown for dinner this evening.'

'I am not hungry.'

'You will eat, Georgianna,' Hawksmere bit out determinedly. 'As I also have to eat. And I have no intentions of looking across my dinner table at the unpleasant sight of a scarecrow in a black mourning gown.'

She drew in a sharp breath. 'You are exceedingly cruel.'

'I am, yes,' he acknowledged unapologetically. 'Perhaps if you had eaten your breakfast, as I instructed you to do…' He shrugged. 'But you did not, so there it is.'

'I told you then, I was not hungry.'

'And I distinctly recall telling you that you are too thin,' he countered forcefully. 'You look as if a stray breath of wind might blow you away. It is a fact that most gentlemen prefer a little meat on their women.'

'It is not my intention to be attractive to any gentleman.'

'Then you have succeeded. Admirably so, in fact,' Hawksmere added grimly.

'And most especially to you,' she concluded fiercely.

'Most especially me?' he repeated softly, dark brows raised speculatively.

'Yes.' Her cheeks were flushed.

Hawksmere gave a slow smile. 'Then I am sorry

to inform you that I do not appear to find the loss of your curves to have affected my own physical ardour in the slightest.'

'And I am sorry to inform you that I am not in the least interested in a single one of your likes or dislikes,' she replied heatedly.

'I believe you made that more than obvious when you broke our betrothal to elope with another man.'

Georgianna blinked at the harshness of his tone. As if he might actually have cared about her ten months ago?

But of course he had cared, she reminded herself heavily. Oh, not about her, but he most certainly cared about the blow she had dealt him by running away with André. But it was Hawksmere's pride which had been injured, not his heart. Because he had no heart to injure?

He drew in an impatient breath. 'I do not have the time to discuss this any further just now, Georgianna. I have a wedding to get to.' He eyed her irritably. 'If you were to stop being so damned difficult, then I might arrange for a bath to be brought up to you later this afternoon. You would like that, would you not?'

Georgianna had no interest in dining with this cold and insulting man, no interest in eating, nor being in Hawksmere's company any more than she had to be.

But if agreeing to wear the lilac gown, and sitting down to dinner with him this evening, also ensured she was allowed the luxury of a bath, then perhaps it would not be so bad? She might even find the chance to escape this house some time during the evening.

'You obviously know something of a woman's weaknesses, your Grace.'

He gave another of those humourless smiles. 'You have the honour of being one of the women from whom I have learnt that particular lesson, Georgianna.'

Her gaze dropped from meeting his at the obvious reference to her elopement with André. 'Very well, I will wear the lilac gown and sit down to dinner with you,' she conceded quietly. 'But I warn you again, I have little appetite.'

Her breath caught in her throat at the intensity of Hawksmere's gaze as he now crossed the distance between them on stealthy feet, her heart fluttering wildly in her chest as she refused to give ground when he came to a halt in front of her.

He smiled slightly at her defiance as he raised his hand and once again cupped the side of her face. He ran the soft pad of his thumb across the swell of her bottom lip. 'Not to worry, Georgianna, I believe I can find appetite enough for the both of us this evening,' he promised gruffly, his gaze continuing to hold hers for several long seconds, before he abruptly lowered his head to sweep the firmness of his lips across hers. 'So soft,' he murmured appreciatively, his breath warm as those lips now trailed caressingly across the paleness of her cheek to her earlobe, teeth gently biting.

Georgianna was too stunned by the unexpected intimacy to be able to move, could barely breathe, as her heart pounded erratically in her chest.

Hawksmere raised his head to look down at her for several long seconds, silver eyes glittering, before he straightened abruptly and turned on his heel to cross the room and depart, followed seconds later by the sound of the door locking behind him.

Leaving Georgianna in a state of complete emotional turmoil.

Chapter Five

'You see how much pleasanter it is when you do as I ask, Georgianna?' Zachary mocked several hours later as he pulled back a chair for her to sit down at the dinner table before taking his place in the chair beside her.

He had left instructions that he and Georgianna would be dining together in the smaller, more intimate dining room. A fire crackled merrily in the hearth, and two three-pronged candelabra illuminated the crystal glassware and silver cutlery. A bowl of pale pink roses had also been placed in the centre of the small round table.

To her credit, Georgianna had been ready and waiting for Zachary when he'd unlocked the door and entered the bedchamber adjoining his own, her expression one of cool composure as she stood in the middle of the room.

The darkness of her hair was smooth and shining and once again secured at her crown, with those tantalising bunches of curls at her temples and nape. The lilac gown had darkened her eyes to that deep violet. Her face was a pale ivory, her lips a full and rosy pout against that pallor.

Zachary shifted uncomfortably now as he realised he was once again aroused by the sight and scent of her.

No other woman had ever physically aroused him as easily as this one appeared to.

Zachary's gaze narrowed on her critically as she smiled her thanks up at Hinds as he poured wine into her glass. What was it about this woman in particular that she managed to hold him in a constant state of arousal?

She was undoubtedly a beautiful young woman, her hair so dark and silky, and her delicately lovely face dominated by those violet-coloured eyes. And the lilac gown was certainly an improvement on that unbecoming black. But even so the style of the new gown still left a lot to be desired. It was not particularly fashionable, with its high neckline buttoned all the way up to her throat, revealing none of the tempting swell of her breasts as so many other women did nowadays, some of them to a degree of indecency.

Zachary had seen, and bedded, many beautiful women in his lifetime and all had been more fashionable and some more beautiful than Georgianna. So why was it that she affected him in a physical way he appeared to have absolutely no control over?

He should not have kissed her earlier, of course. Certainly should not have enjoyed the softness of her lips quite so much as he had, to the point that he had almost said to hell with attending Worthing's wedding and carried Georgianna back to the bed instead. It was not a pleasant realisation for a man who had always put duty, and the well-being of his close friends, first.

'I should have worn the lilac gown this evening in any case.'

It took Zachary several moments to pull out of the bleakness of his thoughts and realise that Georgianna was now answering his own earlier comment. Defiantly. Challengingly.

And there he had it.

This was the way in which Georgianna differed to every other woman Zachary had ever met. Because no man, or woman, had ever dared to defy or challenge the will of the Duke of Hawksmere.

That plump pigeon of ten months ago had undoubtedly feared him, as much as she had feared becoming his wife, but this Georgianna gave the impression that she feared nothing and no one. Except...

'Have you always disliked being in complete dark?'

Georgianna had not been expecting the question. Although perhaps she should have done; Hawksmere was a man who liked to disarm his adversaries rather than put them at their ease. As he had just done by unexpectedly mentioning her fear of darkness.

As he had disarmed her a short time ago, when he had unlocked and entered her bedchamber through the door which adjoined that room to his own. Looking every inch the handsome and highly eligible Duke of Hawksmere, dressed in impeccably tailored black evening clothes and snowy-white linen, his fashionably overlong hair a damp and ebony sheen about that saturnine face. A face dominated by those piercing silver eyes.

As sitting beside him now at the dinner table, the warmth of his thigh almost touching her own, was also disarming her.

Only because he had unexpectedly kissed her earlier, she reassured herself impatiently. A totally unwelcome kiss.

A kiss she had nevertheless been unable to forget in the hours that followed.

Instead of the suppressed violence she might have expected, Hawksmere's kiss had been gentle, searching, as if seeking a response from her rather than demanding one.

And all these hours since Georgianna had questioned if in fact she had responded.

It had been such a fleeting kiss, a mere brushing of Hawksmere's lips against her own, and Georgianna had been so surprised by it that she had no memory of whether or not she had returned the pressure of those firm lips. She certainly hoped not, but still she could not be sure.

She turned to him with cool eyes. 'I have been wondering about that wound to your throat, and the possibility it was inflicted by another female who was equally as unwilling to become your duchess?'

And there he had it again, Zachary acknowledged,

as he began to smile and then to chuckle openly; not only did Georgianna challenge him, but she also had the ability to make him laugh, at himself as much as others. 'There have been no others females, unwilling or otherwise, whom I have asked to become my duchess.' He finally sobered enough to answer her.

'You surprise me.'

He gave a mocking inclination of his head. 'My only unsatisfactory venture into contemplating the married state has made me wary of repeating the experience.'

'Then your wound really was, as it is rumoured, inflicted by a French sabre?' She was barely able to suppress a shiver.

Zachary's humour faded, his expression darkening as he ran his fingertips along the six-inch length of the scar. It had been with him for so long now that he rarely thought about it any more. Or the effect it might have upon others. Upon Georgianna. 'You find it repulsive?'

'I find the idea of the violence behind it repulsive, yes,' she answered him carefully.

'Indeed?' he rasped.

'I did not mean you any insult,' Georgianna assured hastily. 'I—I am sure we all have our scars to bear, some more openly than others.' Her gaze moved to the fireplace as she picked up her glass and took a sip of her wine.

'Do you?' Zachary continued to study her profile through narrowed lids.

She straightened her spine but continued to look

towards the fireplace rather than at him. 'Of course. How can I not after the events of this past year?'

'Tell me where you have been these past nine months, Georgianna?' he prompted softly.

She gave a start—a guilty one?—as she now looked down at the food in front of her, as if seeing it for the first time. 'Should we not eat our soup before it becomes cold?'

'By all means.' Zachary nodded. 'But there is no reason why we cannot continue talking as we eat,' he added once Georgianna had raised the spoon to her lips. A spoon that shook precariously as her hand began to tremble, until she placed it carefully back beside the soup bowl. 'What are you hiding, Georgianna?' Zachary demanded sharply as he saw that nervousness.

'Nothing.'

'Do not lie to me, Georgianna.'

She drew in a ragged breath as she now looked down at the tablecloth. 'I am not hiding anything. Or rather, I am hiding, but it is not from a what but a who,' she continued so softly it was difficult for Zachary to hear her.

'Who?'

Her eyes closed. 'Rousseau, of course.'

'Why?'

She gave another involuntary shudder. 'Because I fear what he would do if he were to ever find me again.'

Zachary had absolutely no doubt that Georgianna's fear was real. He could feel it in the tension of the air surrounding them. As he could see it, in the trembling of Georgianna's body and the quivering of her lips. 'What do you have to fear from that, Georgianna?' he prompted gruffly.

'What do you care?' She turned on him fiercely, two spots of angry colour in her cheeks. 'You have not believed a single word I have said to you so far today, so why should you think I might now bare my soul to you? Just so that you might have the pleasure of ridiculing me again?'

She had a point, Zachary conceded impatiently. But could she not see how difficult it was for him to believe the things she had told him, a woman who had eloped with a known French spy?

Except it had not been confirmed that Rousseau was a spy when Georgianna eloped with him, that certain knowledge only having come later, he reminded himself.

'This conversation is not at all conducive to our digestion.' She gave a weary shake of her head. 'Perhaps it would be best if you were to lock me back in the bedchamber.'

'You have to eat, Georgianna, or you will starve yourself to death.' Zachary scowled.

Her laugh sounded bitter. 'I am harder to kill than you might imagine!'

He was taken aback by the vehemence of her tone. 'What?'

'How went your friend's wedding today?' Once again she avoided answering his question.

The whole conversation of this past half an hour

had resembled that of a sword fight, Zachary realised irritably. He would thrust. Georgianna would parry. Georgianna would thrust. He would then parry. It was frustrating, to say the least.

But her question as to how Worthing's wedding had proceeded earlier today brought forth memories of the love and pride that shone in Worthing's face as he turned to watch his beautiful bride walk down the aisle towards him. Of that same love and pride shining in Julianna's eyes as she walked without hesitation to join her handsome bridegroom at the altar, before they spoke their vows to each other. Declaring loudly and clearly, sincerely, to love and to cherish each other from this day forward.

A bittersweet reminder to Zachary that he could never hope to have that love and devotion bestowed upon him.

And bringing into sharp contrast the wedding which should have taken place the previous year. Between a bridegroom who was only marrying because he was in need of a wife to provide his heir and to retain his fortune. And the young and romantic woman who had feared her bridegroom so much she had eloped with another man.

Zachary looked at that young woman now, once again acknowledging that he was partly, if not wholly, to blame for Georgianna having run away from her family and her home.

And for the things that had happened to her since.

Whatever they might be.

Whatever they might be?

He drew his breath in sharply. 'I believe I owe you an apology, Georgianna.'

She gave him a startled glance. 'I don't…?'

'For the manner of my proposal to you last year,' Zachary continued grimly. 'Worthing's wedding today made me see that I was unfair to you then. That I should never have spoken to your father regarding a marriage between you and I before we knew each other better.'

'We did not know each other at all!'

He nodded. 'And for that I apologise.'

Georgianna stared up at him wordlessly for several seconds, those violet-coloured eyes searching his face. 'Do not be kind to me, Zachary, please,' she finally choked out. 'I believe I can bear anything but your kindness.' She stood up to cross the room on slippered feet, coming to a halt beside the fireplace, her head bowed, revealing the vulnerable arch of her nape.

Zachary rose more slowly to his feet, more inwardly pleased than he cared to contemplate, at hearing Georgianna use his name for the first time.

He crossed the room silently until he stood just behind her, not quite touching, but enough to feel the warmth of her body just inches away. 'My actions then were selfish and totally without thought for how you might have felt in regard to marrying me. For that I am deeply sorry.' His apology still sounded awkward. As evidence, perhaps, that it did not come easily to him?

As it did not. Zachary was unable to remember the

last time he had apologised to anyone for anything he had said or done.

Georgianna's shoulders moved as she sobbed quietly. 'It does not matter any more, Zachary.'

He reached out to lightly grasp the tops of her arms. 'It does matter if it forced you into unnecessary anger towards your father and consequently into a course of action you might otherwise not have taken—' He broke off as the door opened quietly and Hinds stood uncertainly in the doorway. 'I will ring when I need you.' Zachary dismissed him grimly, waiting until the butler had left again before resuming the conversation. 'Is that what happened, Georgianna? Was it my selfishness that pushed you into taking the step of defying your father, leaving your family, and eloping with Rousseau?'

'What does it matter?' She shook her head. 'What is done cannot now be undone.'

'Georgianna.' His hands slid down the length of her arms until he clasped the bareness of both her hands in his. 'What the—?' Zachary turned her to face him before looking down to where he held her hands palms up in both of his, noting how red and roughened the skin was, with several calluses at the base of her fingers on both hands.

Georgianna almost laughed at the shocked expression on Hawksmere's face as he looked down at her work-worn hands. Except it was no laughing matter. 'They are not as pretty as they once were, are they?' She grimaced, knowing her hands were no longer those of a pampered and cosseted lady.

Zachary ran his thumbs across the calluses. 'How did this happen?'

Georgianna had learnt this past few dangerous months that it was best, whenever possible, to keep to the truth as much as possible. Far less chance of making a mistake that way. 'After André had... After he made it clear he did not want me any more, I left Paris for a while.' She raised her chin determinedly as she pulled her hands from his. 'I was lucky enough to be taken in by a kindly farmer and his wife.'

'And they obviously used you like a workhorse.' Hawksmere scowled his displeasure.

'Not at all.' Georgianna smiled slightly. 'I did work for them, of course; I could not accept their hospitality without repaying them in some small way. But it was never hard labour, just—just milking cows and feeding chickens and such. And Madame Bernard taught me how to cook. Stews, mainly. I think because...' Georgianna drew in a breath. 'They had a daughter, but she had married the year before and gone off with her soldier husband. I think they were pleased to have a young woman about the place again. In any case, they allowed me to stay with them for almost two months, after which time I decided I should return to Paris.'

'Why, when you were so obviously safe and with people who cared for you?'

She shrugged. 'I decided that I was behaving the coward by hiding away in the countryside and might be of more help to England if I were to return to the city and keep my ears and eyes open to the plots and intrigues that so abounded there. I found a job working in a tavern.'

'A tavern!' Hawksmere repeated, obviously more shocked than ever.

'In the kitchen, preparing food, rather than the tavern itself,' Georgianna assured ruefully. 'The lady who owned the tavern assured me I was not...was not buxom enough to work in the tavern itself.'

The duke raised dark brows. 'You are thinner than you were, certainly, but that does not detract... Never mind,' he said dismissively. 'I suppose this is another of those occasions when we must be grateful for small mercies?'

Georgianna smiled slightly. 'Indeed.'

'The name of this tavern?' he prompted sharply.

Georgianna had no doubt that, as she had suspected might be the case, Hawksmere would make it his business to check as to the truth of what she was now telling him. That he would not simply take her word for any of it. So, yes, better by far that she had kept to the truth as much as was possible.

Her gaze met the duke's unflinchingly. 'It was the Fleur de Lis.'

'And?' Hawksmere stilled as he looked down at her between narrowed lids. 'Surely that is the name of the tavern owned by...'

'Helene Rousseau, the sister of André Rousseau,' Georgianna confirmed evenly as she turned away to once again stare down at the fire. 'I did not go there as Georgianna Lancaster, of course, but assumed the identity of Francine Poitier, the married daughter of the farmer and his wife.' Again, she had kept to the truth as much as possible when she returned to Paris, knowing that if her identity were to be checked by Helene Rousseau, that the other woman would learn that the Bernards' did indeed have a married daughter called Francine.

Zachary released her hands to step back, not sure if he dared believe this fantastical tale. But he wanted to. Oh, yes, he found that he dearly wanted to believe it.

But, in truth, it seemed too much to accept that the young and flirtatious Georgianna Lancaster, that indulged and plump pigeon, the daughter of the Earl of Malvern, could possibly have worked as a labourer on a farm for several months, and then in the Paris tavern owned by Helene Rousseau, albeit in the kitchen. 'And how did you manage that?' he prompted in perfect French.

'I managed it very well, thank you,' Georgianna replied just as fluently. 'My father was unaware of it, of course...' she grimaced ruefully as she reverted back to English '...but during the winter months we spent at Malvern Hall before I...before I left, I had attended all of Jeffrey's French lessons with him.'

Zachary's mouth twisted humourlessly. 'No doubt drawn more by the charming and handsome Frenchman teaching the subject, than an interest in the language itself.'

'No doubt,' she conceded quietly. 'But, as you now hear, I did learn it.'

'That must have made it doubly choking for you

when the duke who offered for you was neither charming nor handsome,' he rasped harshly.

Georgianna's eyes widened incredulously. Hawksmere could not be serious, could he?

Oh, he definitely lacked the charm, was too forthright and forceful to ever be called charming, but as any woman of the *ton* would be only too happy to confirm, he was most certainly handsome. And it was a handsomeness that would cause most women to willingly overlook his lack of charm.

Even Georgianna admitted to having been taken with his dark and dangerous good looks during her first two Seasons. Indeed, he was a man it was impossible for any woman, young or old, to ignore. His arrogant bearing was always shown to advantage in his perfectly tailored clothes and she had never been able to decide whether his face was that of a fallen angel or a devil. André had possessed the face and golden hair of an angel, of course, but as Georgianna knew to her cost, he was most certainly a devil.

Whereas Zachary Black had long been considered the catch of any Season.

It had been the fact that Georgianna had been the unlikely one to 'catch' him which had come as such an unpleasant shock to her ten months ago.

Gazing at such a handsome and unobtainable duke from afar was one thing—being informed he was to become her future husband was something else completely. Even the thoughts of becoming the wife of such a cynical and experienced gentleman had thrown

Georgianna into a turmoil of doubt and fears. Mainly fears, she now realised.

What could a young girl of nineteen know of being married to a jaded gentleman of one and thirty? How would she even know what to talk to him about, let alone perform any of her other wifely duties? Georgianna had shied away from even thinking of the two of them in bed together, she plump and inexperienced, he as sleek and beautiful as a Greek god, with a legendary number of women known to have shared his bed.

Nor did she understand why he had chosen her at all, when he had never so much as even spoken or danced with her. The reason had become obvious, of course, and Hawksmere had confirmed it earlier today when he admitted he had believed her to be young enough, malleable enough, to make him an undemanding duchess.

She clasped her hands tightly together as she forced her gaze to meet his. 'So there you have the answer to your earlier question. Working in Helene Rousseau's tavern was inadvertently the way in which I gathered the information I gave you earlier.'

Impossible as it seemed, Zachary had already guessed that might be the case. Although he still had to question whether the delivery of that information had been deliberate or accidental. 'And why did you find it so difficult to confide that to me earlier?'

She drew in a deep breath. 'Because I feared you would not believe me.'

He raised dark brows. 'But you no longer fear that might be the case?'

She grimaced. 'Whether I do or I do not is no longer relevant—having now lost my liberty, I consider I have nothing else left to lose, and everything to gain, by confiding all to you.'

His eyes narrowed. 'And you expect me to believe that Helene Rousseau confided in you, a young woman she had employed to work in her kitchen?'

'Of course I do not.' Georgianna gave him an impatient glance for the derision in his tone. 'The truth is that I eavesdropped on the conversation in which Napoleon's liberation from Elba was discussed.'

'Eavesdropped how?'

'I quickly realised that a group of men, including André, met upstairs in a room of the tavern several times a week. And I discovered, quite by accident, that a convenient knothole in the floor of that room allowed their conversation to be overheard in the storeroom directly below.'

'You will have to forgive my scepticism, Georgianna.'

'Will I?' she retorted sharply.

Zachary grimaced. 'The Rousseaus, both brother and sister, have been watched constantly since it was discovered that André Duval was actually André Rousseau, a known spy for Bonaparte.'

'I am gratified to hear it,' she responded tartly. 'Indeed, it is a pity his duplicity was not discovered earlier, as it might then have saved me from considerable heartache.'

And Zachary was not in the least gratified to hear that Rousseau's treatment of her had succeeded in breaking Georgianna's heart. 'You speak now of having a fear of meeting Rousseau again; how is it that you did not fear meeting him again at his sister's tavern?'

She shook her head. 'He was present at all of those meetings, but ordinarily he had no reason to ever enter the kitchen.'

'Even so, you were taking a huge risk, Georgianna.'

'Have you never heard that it is easier to hide in full view than it is to run away and attempt to hide?' She sighed heavily.

It was a ploy Zachary had used several times himself these past four troubled years. 'I have, yes.'

'Besides, you only have to look at me now...' Georgianna glanced down ruefully at her slenderness '...to see I am nothing like the girl I once was.'

Because she was no longer a girl but a woman, Zachary conceded grimly. Beautiful, intelligent, confident, capable, but most of all, in spite of everything, utterly desirable.

And nothing Georgianna had told him this evening had lessened the pounding of the relentless desire Zachary had felt for her since meeting her again. Was it only a matter of hours ago? It seemed as if he had been in this state of constant arousal for days rather than just hours.

He gave a shake of his head in an attempt to clear his head, at least, of that desire; his body was another matter entirely. 'You understand I shall need time to confirm this new information?'

She held herself up proudly as she nodded. 'I expected nothing less.'

Zachary gave an inward groan at the way the straightening of Georgianna's spine had now pushed her breasts up against the soft material of the lilac gown. They were full and pert breasts, the nipples resembling ripe berries. As her waist would be slender, her hips gently curving, with a tempting triangle of dark curls hiding the succulent fruit between her...

'Zachary?'

'Say my name again,' he encouraged gruffly.

Georgianna blinked, taken aback by this sudden change of subject.

More than taken aback when she realised Hawksmere was now standing so close to her she could once again feel the heat of his body through the material of her gown.

Her heart began to pound rapidly in her chest as she found herself unable to look away from the fierce intensity of those mesmerising silver eyes.

Chapter Six

'Zachary, I do not…'

'Yes,' he murmured with satisfaction, his eyes glittering down at her intently as he stepped even closer to her, his thighs almost touching hers as he raised a hand to cup one of her cheeks. 'Say it again, Georgianna,' he encouraged huskily as his thumb moved caressingly across her lower lip.

She flicked her tongue out with the intention of moistening her suddenly dry lips, quickly withdrawing it again as she inadvertently caught the edge of Zachary's thumb, instantly able to taste the tangy salty sweetness of his skin. 'Zachary,' she protested weakly.

His thumb was a rousing caress in the tiny indentation in the centre of the fullness of her bottom lip. 'Are you wearing the white silk drawers tonight, Georgianna? The ones with the little lilac bows?'

Georgianna was so lost in the burning heat of that silver gaze that it took several seconds for her to realise exactly what Zachary had said. Her cheeks blushed a fiery red as she acknowledged the intimacy of his question. 'How did you know about…? You were responsible for packing my things earlier,' she said, remembering in embarrassed consternation.

He gave a feral grin. 'And I have been imagining you wearing those drawers ever since.'

Georgianna breathed shallowly. Zachary's close proximity, and that caressing thumb against her lip, made it difficult for her to think, let alone breathe.

'And the matching camisole,' he continued softly, his breath a warm caress as he lowered his head, his lips a light caress against the warmth of her throat. 'Are you wearing them both tonight, Georgianna?'

His feather-light kisses burned an arousing path down the length of her throat to the sensitive hollows beneath. Georgianna was barely breathing at all now, her hands moving up to grasp his muscled shoulders even as she arched her neck into that sensuous caress. 'Zachary, you have to stop,' she attempted half-heartedly.

'Why must I?' His hands moved down to her hips, moulding the softness of her curves against his much harder ones as his tongue dipped moistly and then withdrew from those hollows at the base of her throat, sending shivers of pleasure down the length of her spine. 'We are neither of us is involved with anyone else. Are we?'

'No.' The heat coursed through her body, tightening her breasts under her gown and camisole, warming between her thighs beneath her drawers, only the soft sighs of their ragged breathing now to charge the air. It made it impossible for Georgianna to think of a single reason why Zachary should stop.

That Zachary was equally affected was apparent by his ragged breathing and the throbbing length of his desire as his thighs pressed along the welcoming softness of her abdomen.

'Are you wearing them, Georgianna?' he pressed gruffly.

'I am, yes,' she confirmed softly, her legs feeling so weak now she was sure that if she were not clinging to the firmness of Zachary's shoulders she might find herself sinking down on to the carpeted floor at his feet.

She truly felt in danger of doing exactly that, as Zachary continued to lick and taste the length of her throat even as one of his hands slowly skimmed along the length of her hip and waist before cupping beneath the firm fullness of her breast. Her nipple instantly responded, swelling, engorging beneath the thin material of her gown and camisole in reaction to that caressing heat.

This was madness.

Complete madness.

And yet Georgianna had no strength to stop it. No will to pull away from Zachary. From the pleasure created by his lips and hands. From the closeness of him. From feeling wanted, held, for the first time in months.

And that was all this was, Georgianna told herself firmly. A need, an ache, to feel wanted and to be held. 'Have you forgotten I might be a spy?' She sought desperately for a return to sanity.

Zachary raised his head to look at her with mercurial grey eyes. There was a flush to the hardness of his cheeks and the darkness of his hair was dishevelled. 'I have forgotten nothing, Georgianna,' he assured huskily. 'If anything, I find that edge of danger only makes you more intriguing. Besides which, if you are a spy, then you are currently an imprisoned one. My imprisoned spy.' He smiled his satisfaction with that fact.

Georgianna drew her breath in sharply as she once again felt the soft pad of his thumb caress across the hardened tip of her breast.

'Perhaps that was my plan all along?' She tried to fight the sensations currently bombarding her senses: pleasure, arousal, heat. 'Has it not occurred to you that maybe my plan is to stab you at the dinner table with a knife from your own ducal-silver dinner service?' she persisted breathlessly even as she found it impossible not to arch once again into that marauding mouth as it continued to plunder the sensitive column of her throat.

'No.' Zachary smiled against the fluttering wildness of the pulse in her throat. He might have become slightly blasé this past few months, but he was nevertheless positive his self-defence skills were still as sharp. 'Because I very much doubt you will find the opportunity. Or, if you did, that my strength would not far outweigh your own.'

'Then perhaps it is my intention to hide one of the

knives and take it back upstairs with me, so that I can stab you later, while you sleep?' There was now an edge of desperation to Georgianna's voice; she simply couldn't allow this to continue.

Zachary deftly released the first button at the throat of her gown. 'Then I will have to ensure that the door between our two bedchambers remains locked at night.'

'I do not believe you are taking me seriously.'

'When I am holding you in my arms and about to kiss you? No, you may be assured I am not taking your threats seriously at all, Georgianna,' he acknowledged gruffly.

'Zachary!'

'Georgianna,' he chided gently as he released the second button and revealed the top of the silky smooth skin above the swell of her breasts.

'I cannot... This is not—' She broke off abruptly as Zachary claimed her mouth with his and silenced her protest.

She tasted as delicious as she smelt, of honey and roses, and everything that was so sweetly, temptingly Georgianna.

Zachary groaned low in his throat as he deepened the kiss, his hands sliding down the length of her spine to cup the sweet curve of her bottom and pull her closer against him, the length of his arousal nestling into the heated welcome of her abdomen.

Georgianna could not think, could only continue to cling to the strength of Zachary's shoulders as the firmness of his mouth now claimed, devoured, her own.

She felt dizzy, light-headed, as her body burned, a heated dampness moistening between her thighs as Zachary cupped the rounded globes of her bottom and held her firmly into and against him. Her breasts were crushed to the hardness of Zachary's muscled chest, the length of his erection pounding, pulsing, to the same rhythm as his heart beating so erratically against hers as his hands now roamed restlessly up the length of her spine.

A need, a want, a desire Georgianna became totally lost in. Until she felt the warmth of one of Zachary's hands against the bare skin at her throat and then lower still as he cupped the bareness of her breast beneath the material of her gown.

Her emotions immediately turned to one of panic as she realised that Zachary must have unfastened all the buttons down the front of her gown as they kissed, the material now gaping wide and revealing everything.

She wrenched her mouth from beneath his, both her hands moving up to push him aside as she pulled the sides of her gaping gown back over her chest, before glaring up at him accusingly. 'You will stop this immediately!'

His eyes narrowed to silver slits, that flush still to his cheeks and his hair dishevelled on his brow. 'Why?'

'Because I cannot allow this. It is…' Georgianna gave a shake of her head, feeling as if she were floundering, much like a fish newly hooked on the line and brought to shore. A fact Zachary was wholly aware of, if the mocking challenge in those silver eyes was any indication. And she had no doubt that it was. 'Because I do not want you,' she spat out determinedly as she hastily refastened the buttons on her gown.

'All evidence to the contrary, my dear Georgianna.' Zachary's insolent gaze moved slowly over her flushed face, slightly swollen lips, and then down the length of her throat and chest to where her nipples still pushed against the fabric of her gown.

Geogianna's lips firmed as she determinedly refused to follow the direction of that insolent gaze. 'That is purely a physical reaction to a man's touch. Any man's touch,' she added defiantly as he appeared satisfied at the admission. 'I assure you, my intellect tells me something else completely.'

'Intellect has very little to do with physical arousal,' he allowed disgustedly, all humour now gone. 'If it did, then I should not find myself in the least aroused by you, either.'

Georgianna flinched inwardly at the deliberate insult. 'Then we are in agreement on the subject, because my head tells me I should not allow a man such as you to take liberties.'

'A man such as me?'

She met his gaze defiantly. 'A libertine who is not to be trusted.'

Humour lit Zachary's eyes as he stepped back to regard her through narrowed lids. Admiration, too, because Georgianna Lancaster was, without a doubt, now a woman he could admire. Oh, not for her political beliefs, if indeed she should turn out to be a Trojan Horse for Rousseau's cause, but most definitely for the courage she had shown in the face of her present dilemma.

She was a woman who believed herself disgraced in English society. A woman who had nevertheless returned to England, only to now find herself a prisoner of the very gentleman she had once been betrothed to. Her suggestion earlier that it might have been deliberate on her part was, Zachary was sure, completely untrue; Georgianna had been far too genuinely shocked and outraged at finding herself incarcerated in his home for it to have been her intention all along.

And this, taking advantage of Georgianna, making love to her, when she was a prisoner in his home, was not a gentlemanly thing for him to do.

Georgianna's past behaviour might render her undeserving of such consideration on his part, but that did not mean he had to lose all honour.

Most especially when he still had no idea, as yet, as to whether or not Georgianna was merely Rousseau's minion, sent to England, to Zachary, at the other man's bidding.

The fact that she was now repelling his advances was, perhaps, a mark in her favour; a devious and manipulative woman would surely have used his obvious attraction to her own advantage?

Georgianna Lancaster was more than just a fully mature woman now, Zachary acknowledged, she was also an intriguing one. One who appealed to him on several levels. In her character. Intellectually. And certainly physically.

Which was all the more reason for him to keep his distance, at least until after he had confirmed, one way or the other, as to whether or not she was telling him the truth.

And if her information should prove correct, then he might no longer be given a choice about keeping his distance, because Georgianna would want nothing more to do with him after the way he had treated her whilst holding her prisoner.

His mouth twisted mockingly. 'It takes one to know one, my dear Georgianna.'

Georgianna gasped, her face paling at what she knew to be another deliberately delivered insult and a direct reference to her scandalous behaviour the previous year. 'I believe I will go back upstairs to my room now.'

'You have not eaten any dinner.'

'I am not hungry.'

The duke's lips firmed with his displeasure. 'It is no wonder you are now thin as a stick, if you do not eat.'

Georgianna refused, absolutely refused, to spill the heat of tears that now blurred her vision. 'You did not seem to have any complaints a few minutes ago, your Grace,' she reminded stiffly.

He shrugged wide shoulders. 'Thankfully the size of your breasts does not seem to have suffered in the process.'

Colour now burned Georgianna's cheeks. 'You are truly insufferable.'

He raised dark brows. 'Was that ever in any doubt?'

'Obviously not.' She blinked back those tears as she lowered her lashes before turning away, no longer willing to even look at that triumphantly mocking face. 'If you would care to act the turnkey again, I am more than ready to return to my room.'

Zachary cursed himself for feeling every kind of monster as he gazed upon the stiff slenderness of Georgianna's back and the vulnerability of her exposed nape, knowing he could not give in to the impulse he felt to take her back into his arms and apologise for having deliberately insulted her.

For having hurt her?

Her eyes had looked awash with tears again before she lowered those long, protective lashes, as if his cutting words really had injured her feelings.

Damn it, how long could it take to confirm or deny Georgianna's information? Zachary wondered impatiently. How much longer did he have to wait before he…?

Before he what? Exactly what difference was it going to make to Zachary's dealings with Georgianna once he did know the truth?

Georgianna might have responded to him a short time ago, but she also so obviously despised him, and herself, for that response. He could not see anything, even the unlikely confirmation of her information being true, ever changing that.

'Very well.' Zachary nodded abruptly, having no

appetite himself now. For dinner, at least. 'But a dinner tray will be brought up to your room.'

Her head remained bowed as she nodded. 'Thank you.'

'And you will eat its contents,' he added sternly.

Humour glinted in her eyes as she looked across at him. 'Must I remind you that your dictates to me so far have not proved in the least successful?'

No, Zachary needed no reminding of Georgianna's wilfulness. Or of his own response to those displays of stubbornness. 'That is because you are contrary in the extreme.'

'That being the case, perhaps you should have instructed me not to eat the food on the dinner tray rather than to eat it?'

'That would be a useless exercise now that we have discussed the possibility,' Zachary dismissed impatiently. 'Eat, or do not eat,' he advised wearily. 'Personally, I grew bored with the subject some minutes ago.'

As Georgianna had no doubt he was bored with having her in his home. With her. And who could blame him? It was so obviously not his choice, but had been foisted upon him by his superior. As she had been foisted on him.

Zachary could not really be blamed for having tried to lighten that burden by entertaining himself in making love to her. A woman whose intimate association with another man put her well beyond the need for either respect or maidenly consideration from the top-lofty Duke of Hawksmere.

She straightened her shoulders. 'Then I will relieve you of the necessity of suffering any more boredom by removing myself from your presence, so allowing you to go out and seek more entertaining and exciting company.'

Frustration surged inside Zachary as he eyed her impatiently, knowing he did not find Georgianna in the least boring. Indeed, she continued to intrigue and entertain him in a way he could not remember feeling with any other woman. Nor could he recall ever being anywhere near as 'excited' by another woman, as he had been just from kissing and caressing Georgianna.

He gave a mocking inclination of his head. 'That is very considerate of you.'

'I thought so, too,' she riposted drily.

Georgianna's sense of humour so appealed to his own that Zachary knew if he did not have a care he would find himself laughing once again, a move guaranteed to completely nullify the distance that he had deliberately put between them this past few minutes. It was a distance Zachary knew he desperately needed to maintain if he were to continue to keep the upper hand with this particular woman. If, indeed, he still had it. If he had ever had it?

Georgianna's flight from a marriage to him ten months ago would seem to imply, that even as the flirtatious and slightly immature Lady Georgianna Lancaster, she had possessed a wilfulness that had been strong enough to at least ensure the unwanted marriage did not take place. The Georgianna who had returned from France was even more determined to defy, and alternately beguile, him at every turn.

Zachary held himself stiffly. 'Luckily I do not need your permission to do anything I wish, or go anywhere I please, whereas the same obviously cannot be said of you.' He eyed her challengingly.

Rebellion glowed in those violet-coloured eyes. 'The bedchamber you have allocated for my use is far superior to my lodgings at Mrs Jenkins's house. It also has the added advantage of being given to me completely free of charge.'

Experience, so far in their reacquaintance, had served to show Zachary that it was doubtful he would ever manage to have the last word in a conversation with this particular woman. 'That could change at any moment,' he drawled challengingly in an attempt to do so.

Her chin rose stubbornly as she met that challenge. 'Your threats grow as wearisome to me as my company has become boring to you.'

The smile refused to be denied this time as Zachary gave a weary, defeated shake of his head. His lack of sleep the night before was certainly taking its toll on him now. A disadvantage Georgianna obviously did not suffer from. 'I do believe your tenacity of will has worn me down for this evening, Georgianna.'

'I am glad to hear it,' she replied pertly. 'Now, if you will excuse me? I really would prefer to return to my room.'

And Zachary, much as he might prefer to go out for the rest of the evening, well away from the temptation of knowing Georgianna was in the bedchamber adjoining his own, now knew himself to be so tired, from lack of sleep and the exhaustion of constantly crossing verbal swords with Georgianna, that he wanted nothing more than to go to his own bedchamber and sleep like the dead for a dozen hours or more.

He nodded abruptly. 'I will arrange for Hinds to bring you up a tray of food shortly.'

She arched one dark brow. 'Do you not intend to lock me in again first?'

He smiled slightly. 'I believe Hinds may find it rather difficult to deliver your tray if the door is locked.'

'And if I should attempt to escape in the meantime?'

Zachary took two predatory steps forward, coming to a halt just inches in front of Georgianna and forcing her to tilt her head back in order to look up at him.

'If you were to escape, Georgianna, then I should then have the pleasure of tracking you down,' he told her softly. 'And when I had, you may be assured I should extract the necessary revenge for your having dared to defy me.'

Georgianna repressed a shiver of apprehension as she saw the raw intensity of emotion glittering in the hard depths of Zachary's eyes. Challenge. Confidence. Amusement.

It was the latter emotion that caused her to straighten resentfully. 'You would have to find me first. Something I believe you were not too successful in doing ten months ago,' she added with deliberate sweetness.

His lids narrowed about those silver eyes. 'Perhaps that is because I did not bother to look too hard for my obviously reluctant bride?'

Colour warmed her cheeks. 'As you had never so much as bothered even speaking to her, I am not surprised. Indeed, as I have already told you, my only surprise is that you haven't found my replacement and married since.'

Zachary looked down at her coldly, only too well aware that his time for marrying, and producing an heir, was ticking by faster than he would have wished. 'Perhaps that is because I have decided to be more cautious in my second attempt at matrimony.'

'How sad to know you were the second choice for the Duke of Hawksmere's duchess!' she retorted tartly.

He drew in a sharp breath. 'My wife will not be my second choice, but the correct one. Which you, most assuredly, were not.'

The colour deepened in Georgianna's cheeks. 'Then it appears we may both be thankful for having escaped such an ill-matched union.'

'Indeed, we can,' Zachary bit out harshly.

They stared each other down for several more long seconds before Georgianna turned sharply on her heel and walked hastily from the room.

Much as he might wish to, Zachary did not trouble himself in following her, knowing he was in no mood at the moment to deal with her gently. Besides, he had meant it when he said he would very much enjoy the pleasure of recapturing her, and extracting payment, if she should try to escape Hawksmere House.

And him.

Chapter Seven

'It is past time you woke up, Georgianna.'

Georgianna roused slowly from the deepness of her slumbers at the sound of that intruding voice. She'd been sleeping so deeply, lost in a most wonderful dream. A dream where she had felt both safe and warm, something she had not been for so very long.

'Georgianna!'

She frowned as the impatient voice rallied her for a second time. She was so very reluctant to relinquish those feelings of safety after months of fear and the nervousness of discovery.

'If you do not open your eyes in the next few seconds, Georgianna, then you will leave me with no choice but to throw this jug of cold water over you.'

It really was Hawksmere talking to her, she realised with a groan.

For surely only Zachary Black, the forceful Duke of Hawksmere, could be so very demanding? So impatient for her to obey his every instruction, he threatened to douse her in water?

She forced her lids to open before going up on her elbows to seek his exact location in the half gloom of the bedchamber. 'What? That was deliberately cruel.' She glowered across the room at the duke as she saw he stood beside where he had just thrown back the curtains fully in order to let in the brightness of the morning's sunshine.

He gave a hard and unapologetic smile. 'But no doubt preferable to the dousing in cold water. Of course, the water for washing was not cold when it was delivered to your room three hours ago,' he added scathingly. 'But it most certainly will be now.'

Three hours ago? 'What time is it?' Georgianna pushed the silky curtain of her hair over her shoulders.

Hawksmere strode impatiently to the bedside, revealing he was already dressed for the day, in a dark grey superfine, silver brocade waistcoat over white linen, with pale grey pantaloons and brown-topped Hessians. 'After eleven.'

Georgianna blinked up at him. After eleven o'clock in the morning? Then she had must have slept for a dozen hours or more after eating a little of the food from the tray that Hinds had delivered to her room last evening. How could she have slept for so long? It had been weeks, months, since she had been able to sleep so deeply.

She recalled her dream. The safety and the warmth she had felt cocooning her. Implying she felt safe in

Hawksmere's home? With Hawksmere just feet away in the adjoining bedchamber? The same gentleman who had threatened and imprisoned her? Impossible!

And yet...

Georgianna could not deny that she had felt that sense of safety and warmth as she awoke, as if nothing and no one could harm her whilst she was in Hawksmere House.

A feeling she had no intentions of sharing with Hawksmere himself.

'Obviously you slept well,' he added mockingly. 'No doubt you will claim it was the sleep of the innocent.'

Georgianna frowned at his harshness, checking that her nightgown was securely fastened up to her throat before sitting up in the bed to glare accusingly at her tormentor. 'You should have woken me earlier if my sleeping late displeases you.'

He raised dark brows. 'I do not believe that is included in my duties, as your gaoler.'

'Then perhaps in future it should be,' she snapped irritably.

Hawksmere frowned grimly. 'I have had other things to occupy me this morning, other than troubling myself to wake you from your lazy slumbers.'

Georgianna almost laughed at his words; there had been no lazy slumbers for her since she'd left England for France the previous year!

The time she had spent with André had been rife with tension and the days had started early on the Barnards' farm. The tavern had been even worse, with late nights cooking food followed by early mornings spent cleaning in readiness for the next influx of customers.

All so very unlike her previous pampered and privileged life as the only daughter of the Earl of Malvern.

She looked up at Hawksmere searchingly now, immediately noting the grimness about his eyes and the firmness of his mouth. His expression was altogether one of harshness this morning, rather than the lazy mockery he had shown towards her yesterday evening. His movements were restless as he turned away from the bed and began to pace the bedchamber.

'What other things have occupied you this morning?' she prompted warily.

Zachary shot her an impatient glance, not sure how much he should reveal to Georgianna, how much he needed to reveal to her, when the information delivered to him earlier this morning was not confirmed, only suspected at this point in time. When his instructions were still to keep her a prisoner here.

He drew in a controlling breath. 'I shall be leaving London later today and I am uncertain when I shall return.'

'You are leaving London?' she echoed sharply. 'To go where?'

Zachary had known that Georgianna was too intelligent, had grown too unconventional in her ways, to accept his statement without suspicion or question, as most women in society would have done. To most women a gentleman's activities outside their home were his own affair and definitely not to be questioned too deeply. Not so with the forthright Georgianna, unfortunately.

He glowered down at her, wishing she did not look quite so delectable this morning, her face soft and flushed from sleep, that silky dark hair once again loose about her shoulders and down her spine. The white cotton nightgown also did little to hide the fact that she was naked beneath it, her breasts jutting out firm and tempting against its voluptuous folds.

'What will you do with me while you are away?' she added slowly.

Zachary scowled. 'You will remain here, of course.'

Her eyes widened. 'You intend leaving me a prisoner in this bedchamber indefinitely?'

'I see no alternative.' Much as he might wish it were otherwise. And the thought of keeping Georgianna cooped up in this bedchamber was not a pleasant one. Especially when he had no idea how long her incarceration would last. Or when he would return to England.

'Where are you going, Zachary?' she demanded sharply. 'Tell me,' she insisted determinedly as his mouth thinned.

He sighed his impatience as he once again wished for a less intelligent and astute woman than Georgianna. 'As you are to remain incarcerated here, I can see no harm in your knowing that rumours have reached our shores that Napoleon is on the move.'

'I knew it!' Georgianna announced, her face aglow with triumph as she threw back the bedcovers before climbing out of the bed and revealing that her nightgown covered her from her throat down to her slender ankles.

Or it attempted to do so, because Zachary could clearly make out the shadowy outline of the rosy tips to the fullness of her breasts, as well as the dark shadow of the curls nestled so seductively between her thighs.

He gave an inward groan as his own body instantly reacted to those tantalising glimpses of the shadowy outline of Georgianna's body, his arousal hardening to pulsing need inside his pantaloons.

'Did I not tell you it would be so, Zachary?' she continued excitedly, her face glowing with that excitement as she paced quickly to one of the windows, unknowingly allowing the sun, as it shone through the glass, to instantly turn her nightgown diaphanous.

Zachary closed his eyes briefly in order to shut out the sight of Georgianna's slender nakedness so clearly outlined through the white material. A brief visual respite that made absolutely no difference to the engorging of his erection as it continued to pulse, to lengthen and thicken, with impatient need.

He gave a shake of his head as he opened his lids to look across at her guardedly. 'Has no one ever told you it is most unattractive to say *I told you so* in that triumphant manner?'

'Hah to that.' Georgianna was too excited at being proved right to behave in the least ladylike about it, despite Hawksmere's rebuke. 'I was right, Zachary, and you were wrong, and you may mock all you like, but…' She stilled, excitement dying as she took in the full import of Hawksmere's statement. 'He is already on the move, you say?'

The duke gave a haughty inclination of his head. 'So it is reported, yes.'

'Then I was too late to be of help, after all.' Georgianna groaned, shoulders slumping in defeat. 'I delayed too long and arrived too late, Zachary.' She buried her face in her hands. 'Too late.'

Zachary was instantly torn between the need to go to Georgianna and comfort her by taking her into his arms, and the certain knowledge that if he did so he would be unable to stop himself from making love to her again. Last night had been a tortuous hell for him after he and Georgianna had parted so ignominiously. Knowing Georgianna was in the adjoining bedchamber, that silky ebony hair no doubt once again loose about her shoulders and breasts, and wearing nothing more than one of the two white nightgowns he had packed into her bag earlier in the day at her lodgings, had played havoc with his efforts to find rest, let alone sleep.

So much so that he had quickly worked himself up into a fine temper, his annoyance with both Georgianna, and his own weakness in desiring her, making it impossible for him to relax.

He had finally given up all attempt of sleeping just before two o'clock in the morning. He'd thrown back the bedcovers to get out of bed and pull on his brocade robe over his nakedness before pacing about his bedchamber instead. All the time aware, so totally aware, that Georgianna was just a door-width away from satisfying the lust that coursed so hotly through his body.

A lust Zachary could not, dare not, allow to rule him, when he still distrusted the woman responsible for that emotion.

Only to then realise, when Georgianna had slept in so late this morning, that while he had been suffering the torments of the damned the night before, she had been perfectly at peace in the adjoining bedchamber, sleeping like the dead—or innocent?—and so totally unaware of his own tormented longings.

His visitor earlier this morning, bearing news of Napoleon's possible flight from Elba, had done nothing to improve the already short fuse on his over-stretched temper. To so much as touch her now would be insanity on his part.

Oh, to hell with his caution, Zachary dismissed as he took the two long strides that brought him to her side, before reaching out to take her in his arms. He wanted this woman, to kiss her, to caress her, and God knew when he would have the opportunity to do so again.

She was so very slight, in both height and stature. Her head rested against his chest just beneath his chin. So slender, it was almost like holding a child in his arms.

Almost.

Because it was a certainty that Georgianna did not bring out even a spark of paternal instinct in him.

'I should not have delayed my departure from France for so long.' Her voice was muffled against his chest, her breath a warm caress through the thin material of his shirt. 'Should not have been so cautious, so worried, that I might be discovered attempting to leave. And now Napoleon will return to France and— My God—' she lifted her head to look up at Zachary searchingly, her face paling as realisation dawned '—that is where you are going, is it not?'

It so happened that that was exactly where Zachary was going.

But he was not allowed to discuss his mission. Even with the woman who was responsible for bringing him the news that it was Napoleon's intention to leave Elba. If, as was suspected, the Corsican had not already done so.

Zachary gave a mocking smile. 'I had not realised you had such a vivid imagination, Georgianna.'

'Do not even attempt to treat me like the foolish young girl I once was, Zachary,' Georgianna warned fiercely.

His expression was grim. 'Oh, I assure you, I am only too well aware that you are no longer that young innocent, Georgianna, foolish or otherwise.'

'Then do not... Umph!' The last came out as a protesting squeak as Zachary silenced her by claiming her mouth with his own, his arms like steel bands about her waist as he held her so tightly to him her body was melded close against his own.

Georgianna fought against the confinement of those arms as she also tried to wrench her mouth from beneath his. All to no avail, as Zachary merely tightened his arms and deepened the kiss by parting her lips beneath his with the invasion of his tongue into the moist heat of her mouth.

His marauding tongue that explored every sensitive and heated contour of her mouth, before stilling her as that tongue stroked against her own in a slow and sensuous caress, claiming, possessing, and sending rivulets of pleasurable heat coursing through the whole of Georgianna's body.

She had never... No one had ever made her feel like this before.

The sheer carnality of Zachary's kiss was beyond anything Georgianna had ever experienced before, beyond anything she had ever imagined, and she had no defences against it.

No defence against Zachary as he continued to plunder and claim her mouth even as he lifted her up into his arms and carried her across the room to lay her down upon the bed before joining her there. He draped one of his legs across her thighs to keep her in place beside him as he continued to kiss and taste her even while one of his hands began to roam restlessly along the length of her body.

Her neck arched as Zachary broke that kiss to explore the column of her throat. She gasped as his hand cupped beneath her breast, instantly seeking out the sensitive berry at its tip, caressing, stroking and causing a tingling ache that spread like wildfire from her nipple down to between her dampening thighs.

Nevertheless, she knew she must seek some semblance of sanity, to put an end to the madness that had so rapidly overtaken them. 'Zachary.'

'Do not deny the desire that exists between us, Georgianna.' He raised his head to look at her, his eyes glittering fiercely, a flush across the sharp blades of his cheekbones, his lips thinned.

As evidence that his own desire for her angered him rather than pleased him?

No doubt it did, when Zachary had every reason to believe she had been André Rousseau's lover.

'I will allow you to think of nothing and no one else whilst you are in my arms, Georgianna,' he warned harshly, as he seemed to guess some of her thoughts. 'And I fully intend to have you before I leave,' he continued determinedly as he rose above and then over her, pushing her nightgown up her thighs as he settled between her legs. 'All of you.'

She swallowed at the lustful violence she now saw in the fierceness of Zachary's gaze. A violence of emotion that threatened to overwhelm completely Zachary's previous cautions where she was concerned.

Georgianna ran the moistness of her tongue across the dryness of her lips. 'You will only regret it.'

'As you warned me yesterday I should regret having insisted you remove your veil?' he retorted harshly as he slid slowly down the length of her body, able to smell the sweet lure of her arousal once he was comfortably settled between her thighs.

'Yes.'

'And I did regret it. I regret it still. But it seems that regret does little to change the fact that I also desire you.' Zachary gave a shake of his head, his endurance, and his patience, pushed beyond his control after his second sleepless night in succession. Because of this woman. Because of the desire he felt for her. A desire he had every intention of satisfying before he left England later today.

'Please, Zachary.'

'Oh, I intend to please you, Georgianna.' He looked down as his hands moved up her thighs, pushing her nightgown up to her waist, revealing smooth, ivory skin and the dark thatch of curls nestled between her thighs. 'And by pleasing you I also intend to please myself,' he promised darkly, even as his fingers parted those curls to reveal the lushness of her rosy red folds with the little nubbin peeking out temptingly from beneath the hood above. 'Open your legs wider and let me in, Georgianna,' he encouraged gruffly.

'I cannot.'

'You can.' Zachary moved even lower, the width of his shoulders pushing her thighs further apart, and allowing the heat of his gaze to feast on the slickness of her folds. So deep and rosy coloured, the lips there already swollen, moist, with Georgianna's own arousal. 'You are so beautiful, Georgianna,' he murmured as his thumbs moved to part those folds, revealing the moist and welcoming centre. 'Like a flower unfurling petals touched by the morning dew.'

Georgianna was not sure which mortified her the most, the suddenness of this intimacy, or her unmistakable arousal. Certainly she could not deny she was aroused, but at the same time she felt embarrassed by that response. At having a man, any man, look at and touch her so intimately. To have Zachary look and touch where she had never even looked or touched herself.

'I had not taken you for a poet, Hawksmere.'

'You and this lush bounty make me one,' he assured gruffly as his fingers lightly caressed the delicacy of her skin.

'I…'

Georgianna's protest died in her throat, her back arching off the bed at the first pleasurable sweep of the heat of Zachary's moist tongue against that very private place, before he commenced a slow and sensuous licking of those sensitive folds. He greedily lapped up the moisture now flowing between her thighs.

'I do not…' Georgianna halted with a gasp as the pleasure became so intense it threatened to totally overwhelm her.

Zachary felt the deepening of Georgianna's response as his tongue now probed beneath the hood above her folds, seeking out that erect nubbin, lathing and then sucking it fully into his mouth as he felt it pulsing against his tongue as evidence of her rapidly approaching climax.

His senses were filled with the taste and smell of her, like the sweetest of nectars, and just as addictive. 'Yes, Georgianna,' he encouraged hotly as she now arched up into the stroking of his tongue. 'Find your rhythm, love. Move with me. Into me. Yes,' he muttered fiercely as she found that rhythm with the undulating arching of her hips.

He slipped a finger between the slickness of her folds, stroking the edge, before sliding slowly inside, groaning low in his throat as he added a second finger and felt her muscles tighten about him. Imagining, craving, those same muscles tightening snugly about his erection in exactly the same way they gripped his fingers.

But first he intended to pleasure Georgianna, to obliterate from her memory any other lover she had ever known.

He continued that slow thrusting with his fingers even as he lowered his head and his tongue once again stroked the erect nubbin above, suckling it into his mouth before closing his teeth gently about it.

Georgianna gasped and then cried out as the pleasure rose up to an unbearable height before crashing, streaking through her in hot, burning flames, threatening to consume her with their intensity. Wave after wave of mindless, all-consuming pleasure, tossing her higher, and then higher still as Zachary continued to stroke and thrust her to a second, even more exquisitely powerful climax with the merciless strokes of his tongue. Her body contracting as he continued to thrust his fingers deep inside that flooding heat.

'No more. Please, Zachary,' she finally cried out weakly, so sensitive now that every touch, every stroke threatened to send her over the edge of falling into yet another exquisite climax.

'Why not?' Zachary's eyes were dark as he raised his head to look up at her, his cheeks flushed.

Georgianna felt the heat burn her cheeks as she saw how glistening wet his lips were, and realised it had to be from the copious flowing of her juices. 'I had not realised... I did not know. Do men enjoy doing that?'

'I do,' Zachary assured gruffly, pleased beyond measure that he was obviously the first man to have introduced Georgianna to this intimacy. 'You taste divine, Georgianna,' he added huskily as he licked the juices from his lips and had the pleasure of watching her cheeks blush an even deeper red.

'And I—' He broke off with a scowl as a knock sounded on the door of the bedchamber. 'What is it?' He turned to direct that scowl towards that closed door.

'The Duke of Wolfingham is awaiting your presence down in the blue salon, your Grace,' Hinds informed him stiffly through the closed door.

Damn it. Zachary had completely forgotten that Wolfingham was joining him here this morning.

Forgotten everything but his need to make love to Georgianna.

Chapter Eight

Georgianna washed, and dressed herself in the black gown, then arranged her hair neatly at her crown in record time after Zachary left her bedchamber. She was determined that when, and if, the duke should return, her appearance would at least be respectable.

The only thing she now considered 'respectable' about herself.

She had no idea what had happened with Hawksmere just now. One minute they had been talking, and the next…

Oh, dear lord, the next.

Just thinking about Zachary possessing her with his mouth was enough to make Georgianna quiver with embarrassment.

Or possibly remembered pleasure?

Unimagined, indescribable, out-of-this-world pleasure.

She had not known such intimacies, such pleasure, as that existed.

The attentions of Zachary's mouth, tongue and fingers had been centred between her thighs, but the pleasure had been felt everywhere. Radiating out from between her and consuming her every sensation, as it coursed, burned through her torso and throat, and into all of her limbs to the very ends of her fingers and her toes. And not just once, but twice! That pleasure building again, carrying her along on a tide of sensation. By the time Hinds had knocked on the door of her bedchamber...

Hinds!

What must he think? What conclusion could the butler have come to, in respect of the time his employer had spent in Georgianna's bedchamber this morning?

Considering the reason Zachary had informed his household staff for her being here at all, no doubt the butler had drawn the correct conclusion regarding their activities this morning.

Georgianna was genuinely shocked at her own behaviour. Mortified. She had no idea how she was going to face Zachary again when he had looked at her and touched her so intimately.

However, this personal mortification paled into insignificance in the face of Napoleon's move from Elba.

If it was true, and if Napoleon should indeed return to the shores of France, then there was sure to be another war. England and her allies could not just sit back and allow the Corsican to retake the French crown for his own. And if, when, that happened, more Englishmen would die.

And to think, Georgianna might have prevented it if she had been more courageous. If she had not wasted so much time seeking safe and undetected passage for herself from France.

Zachary might be one of the ones to die.

Sooner rather than later if, as she suspected, he was leaving for France later today.

If Napoleon should make it back to France in the next few days, as he was bound to do, then the next few weeks, as he marched towards Paris, would be dangerous indeed. Having lived there for the past few months, Georgianna knew, perhaps better than most, that the people of France were not all enamoured of having their king returned to them. And that many, given the choice, would far rather that Napoleon return as their emperor.

The thought of Zachary deliberately placing himself in the midst of that turmoil was a frightening one.

Georgianna shied away from admitting why she found the idea of Zachary in danger so disturbing. Shied away from facing that truth. Even to herself.

She should hate Zachary Black. For having imprisoned her here. For disbelieving the things she had told him about André, as well as Napoleon's plans to leave Elba. Most certainly for the liberties he had taken with her this morning.

And yet she found she could not bring herself to hate Zachary. Certainly not enough to wish him ill. To wish him dead.

Surely she had not come to care for him this past day or so? To feel something, some nameless, softening of emotion, for the very man she had run away from marrying in the first place?

What other explanation was there for her response to him such a short time ago?

It would be worse than ironic if that should be the case.

'What are you thinking about so intently?'

Georgianna spun sharply to face the man standing in the doorway of the bedchamber. The same gentleman, who now occupied so much of her thoughts.

Her face was instantly ablaze with embarrassed colour, as she found her gaze drawn to those beautifully sculptured lips. Lips, that such a short time ago, had been kissing and suckling her intimately.

'I was merely wondering exactly when you intended leaving for France, so that I might know when I will, most thankfully, be relieved of your company,' she replied tartly, her gaze now meeting his boldly.

Zachary gave a slow and mocking smile at that now-familiar sharpness; ridiculous of him to have expected that their earlier intimacies might have in any way softened Georgianna's feelings towards him.

The fact that she had once again dressed in the unbecoming black gown in his absence was evidence enough, surely, that she regretted those intimacies?

At the same time as Zachary acknowledged he now had no choice but to believe that the information Georgianna had given him about Napoleon's movements was, in fact, the truth.

As had been her claim not to have seen Rousseau for many months?

The intelligence report that Zachary had read on Rousseau would seem to indicate that also was true.

Which, taken to its logical conclusion, must also mean that Georgianna had indeed parted from Rousseau only a week or so after arriving in France, and that she had then worked on a farm for several months, before going to back to Paris to work as a kitchen maid in Helene Rousseau's tavern.

Zachary found himself scowling at the thought of this beautiful young woman wandering alone about the French countryside, let alone returning to Paris to work in such a lowly tavern as the Fleur de Lis, leaving herself prey to any and all of that inn's patrons.

'Never mind my own plans for now, what on earth did you think you were doing by remaining in France once Rousseau had finished with you, and so putting yourself in danger for so many months?' He scowled his displeasure.

Oh, yes, André had certainly finished with her, she reflected bitterly. Indeed, as far as she was aware he still believed he had finished her off completely and that her stripped and bleached bones now lay scattered about a forest outside Paris.

She gave an uninterested shrug. 'Why not stay, when I had nothing to return to in England?'

'Your father was still alive then, and your brother...'

'A father and a brother who had quite rightly disowned me,' she responded tautly.

The duke scowled.

'Why did the Duke of Wolfingham need to speak with you so urgently?' she prompted shrewdly.

Zachary raised dark brows. 'I do not recall Hinds indicating that Wolfingham's visit was urgent in nature.'

'I assumed, from the haste with which you left earlier… Silly me.' Georgianna gave a discomforted grimace. 'No doubt the urgency was for you to leave my bedchamber, rather than your need to rush to Wolfingham.'

'And yet here I am, back again,' he drawled.

'Only because you had not finished our earlier conversation, I am sure.' Georgianna turned away to walk over to one of the windows. 'You cannot seriously intend to leave me a prisoner here whilst you go to France?'

'I do not believe I have ever confirmed my intention of going to France.'

'But we both know that you are.' Georgianna glanced back at him as he did not deny it a second time. 'And you would have admitted it was so earlier if we had not been…' Her face flushed fiery red as she remembered the reason for their earlier distraction.

'No, I would not, Georgianna, and for the simple reason I do not consider my immediate plans to be any of your concern,' Zachary bit out harshly.

Georgianna recoiled at the disdain underlying his dismissal. It was as if he had physically struck her. As if, despite everything, Zachary still distrusted her.

She turned stiffly to face him. 'Nevertheless, you

cannot expect me to continue to remain here whilst you are away.'

'And yet that is exactly what I expect.' Hawksmere eyed her challengingly.

'And if I should choose to make my presence here a difficult one?'

'Then do so by all means. It will make no difference to the outcome.' Zachary was no happier than Georgianna about the arrangement, and as such, his patience had worn beyond thin on the subject.

She raised haughty brows. 'You may be lord and master of all you survey in your own world, Zachary, but I assure you, you are not my lord or master, in this world or any other.'

No, because if he were, Zachary would have put her over his knee by now and spanked her obstinate little bottom into obedience. As it was, he was so angry with her, not just for her stubbornness now, but because he now knew she had deliberately placed herself in danger these past months. So angry that he might still be driven to that action, if Georgianna didn't cease arguing with him at every turn.

Not that he had really expected their earlier intimacy to have changed that stubbornness in any way. Georgianna had shown him only too clearly that this wilfulness was part and parcel of who she was. Or, at least, who she had become.

No doubt those weeks and months she had spent alone in France, fearing for her safety, for her life, were in part responsible for her present independence of nature.

The truth was, after the information Zachary had received this morning, he now believed the things Georgianna had told him about the time she had spent in France. And knowing that she had wilfully chosen to put herself in harm's way by working at the tavern of Helene Rousseau was enough to turn the blood cold in Zachary's veins. Anything might have happened to her; a young and beautiful woman, so obviously alone and without male protection.

As perhaps anything had?

His eyes narrowed. 'Where did you live while working in the kitchen of Helene Rousseau's tavern?'

Georgianna eyed Hawksmere warily as she heard the steely edge beneath the softness of his tone. 'I do not see that is any of your concern.'

'Answer the question, damn you.' He strode forcefully across the room.

She blinked up at him as he now stood just inches in front of her. 'I was given a room in the attic.'

'You lived on the premises?'

She nodded. 'So I was about to tell you, if you had let me finish.'

He drew in a slow and deliberate breath. 'You, Lady Georgianna Lancaster, daughter, and now sister of the Earl of Malvern, lived in the attic of a common French tavern?'

Georgianna had no idea why Hawksmere was so obviously angry on the subject. Living in the attic of the Fleur de Lis paled into insignificance when she considered the other dangers she had faced during those months in France. 'Mademoiselle Rousseau allowed me to stay there as part of my payment.'

'So that you might entertain men there?'

Georgianna gasped in shock. ' Of course not! How dare you imply—?' She broke off as Hawksmere took a painful grasp of the tops of her arms, his face tight with anger as he towered over her.

'I was employed as a kitchen maid, not a whore, Hawksmere.'

'I very much doubt that the men who frequented the tavern were capable of making that distinction.' he said scornfully.

She frowned. 'You are obviously more familiar with the practises of such places than I.'

His hands tightened painfully as he shook her. 'It is not a question of what I am familiar with.'

'Is it not?' Georgianna challenged scathingly. 'I worked in the kitchen of the tavern, Hawksmere,' she maintained firmly. 'And that is all I did.' She looked up at him defiantly.

Zachary looked down at her searchingly, seeing the challenge glittering in those violet-coloured eyes, the unmistakable pride in the tilt of her chin, indignation in the stiffness of her body. As proof of her innocence? In regard to the months she had spent working at the tavern, perhaps; the weeks she had spent as Rousseau's mistress were a different matter entirely.

'What more is it going to take for you to trust me, Zachary?' She looked up at him with pained eyes. 'You now have information that confirms Napoleon is to leave Elba, if he has not already done so. What more do you need from me to be convinced that I have told you nothing but the truth since we met again yesterday?'

His jaw tightened. 'You have yet to tell me how you escaped from Rousseau once your association was over.'

Her gaze avoided meeting his. 'Is that really necessary?'

'It is if you truly wish for me to trust you.'

She moistened dry lips. 'And if I tell you, will you then consider allowing me to leave this house at the same time you do?'

'To go where?'

'Anywhere I am not a prisoner.'

'I will consider the idea, yes,' he bit out tautly.

'That is not good enough.'

'It is all the concession I am willing to make at this point.'

Georgianna stared up at Hawksmere's hard and unyielding expression, his eyes that glittering remorseless silver. As evidence that he would not relent without that last irrefutable proof from her as to her innocence.

She had hoped to spare herself this final humiliation, but saw now that it was not to be, that the time for such prevarication was now at an end.

'Release my arms, if you please,' she instructed softly.

Zachary looked down at her searchingly for several long seconds before his fingers slowly loosened, his hands dropping back to his sides as he took a step back.

Georgianna averted her gaze from meeting his own, her hands shaking as she raised them to the neckline of her black gown, fingers fumbling as she began to unfasten the tiny buttons.

'Georgianna, I do not have the time now to finish what we started earlier,' Hawksmere dismissed impatiently. 'Nor will you succeed in distracting me by attempting to seduce me,' he added scathingly.

'You are arrogance personified.' Georgianna's fingers paused on the buttons of her gown as she gave him a pitying glance. 'I have absolutely no intentions of distracting or attempting to seduce you.'

He raised dark brows. 'Then why are you unfastening your gown?'

She sighed heavily. 'Because it is the only way I know of to show you how I escaped from Rousseau.'

'I do not see how the unfastening of your gown will help convince me of anything.'

'Will you please cease your sarcasm for just a few moments, Hawksmere?' Georgianna's voice shook with emotion, her vision blurred by unshed tears as she looked up at him. 'I cannot—' She bit her bottom lip as she gave a shake of her head. 'I believe if I have to suffer another one of your insults then I might begin to scream and never stop.'

Zachary could see that by the strained expression on Georgianna's face. Her eyes were a dark purple and shimmering with tears, her cheeks pale and hollow, all the colour seeming to have drained even from the fullness of her lips. She was seriously distressed. Enough to scream? He believed so, yes.

'In that case, please continue,' he invited in a bored voice as he moved to slowly lower his length comfortably down on to the chair placed in front of the dressing table.

Her eyes narrowed as she glared across at him. 'I only intend to unfasten a few buttons of my gown, Hawksmere, not provide a striptease show with you as the audience.'

'That is a pity,' he drawled as he crossed one elegant leg over the other.

Georgianna closed her eyes briefly in an attempt to dig deep inside herself for the courage needed for her to continue along this course.

Not an easy feat when Hawksmere continued to treat her with such disdain. Nor was there any guarantee, having literally bared her scarred soul to him, that he would dispense once and for all with the distrust with which he continued to treat her.

But she had to at least try.

Her fingers trembled even more than before as she recommenced unfastening the buttons down the bodice of her gown, causing her to fumble several times before the last button was finally unfastened.

She hesitated, holding the two sides of her gown together, as she forced herself to look across at Hawksmere. 'Please attempt to hold your derision and scorn at bay, if only for a few minutes, if you please, Hawksmere.' Her voice shook with emotion.

Zachary frowned as he looked across at her searchingly, having no idea what it was that Georgianna was hiding from him. He was nevertheless aware that, whatever it was, it affected her deeply. 'Show me,' he encouraged gruffly, shoulders tensed.

Georgianna kept her eyes closed, her lips clamped firmly together, as she slowly parted the two sides of her gown before her fingers pulled down the soft material of her camisole, fully exposing her breasts to him.

It was impossible for Zachary to hold back his sharply indrawn breath as he saw the discoloured and livid scar between the swell of Georgianna's breasts for the first time.

Even from across the room he could see that the redness of the puckered and scarred skin now exposed to him was recent and several inches around. It was the same type of wound and scarring he had unfortunately seen many times during his years of battle against Napoléon's armies.

His gaze moved sharply back up to the pallor of Georgianna's face. Her eyes were once again open as she looked back at him with a flat and unemotional expression. He moistened lips that had gone suddenly dry.

'Is that...?'

'The result of a bullet wound?' Georgianna finished dully. 'Yes, it is.'

Zachary stood up, too restless, too disturbed by what he was seeing to remain seated for a moment longer. He crossed the room in long strides before gently pushing her fingers out of the way so that he might better see the livid red scar. 'How is it you did not die from such a wound?'

She gave an emotionally choked laugh. 'As it was so obviously intended that I should?'

'Yes.'

'How typical of you, Hawksmere, to cut straight to the point.' She looked up at him coldly. 'It was pure chance that I did not die, that the force of the bullet was deflected slightly by the locket I wore about my neck at the time.'

Zachary gave a dazed shake of his head, unable to stop looking at the terrible scarring that had been inflicted on Georgianna's otherwise beautiful and flawless skin. He was unable to stop himself from imagining a bullet entering Georgianna's smoothly perfect flesh, and the agony she must have suffered as it ripped through that delicate tissue, no doubt taking her down. Miraculously the locket prevented it from actually killing her.

He looked up, eyes narrowed. 'Who did this to you?'

Her smile turned humourless. 'Ah, and now comes the intelligence beneath the scorn and derision.'

'Georgianna.'

'Have you seen enough that I might refasten my gown now?' she challenged tensely.

His jaw clenched tightly as he demanded again, 'Who did this to you?'

Her eyes hardened to glittering violet jewels. 'Who do you imagine did it to me?' She refastened her gown without waiting for his permission. 'Who was it that you yourself said could not allow me to live once I had left him?'

'Rousseau,' he breathed softly.

'Exactly. Rousseau,' she confirmed flatly. 'Have you seen enough yet to believe me, Hawksmere?' she challenged tautly. 'Or would another scar help to finally convince you that everything I have told you is the truth?' She lifted a hand to move back the cluster of curls gathered on her left temple, revealing a long scar where a second bullet appeared to have grazed and broken her skin without actually penetrating it. 'This one was to be the coup de grâce, I believe. Unfortunately for André it was dark that night and I must have turned my head away at the last moment, because the second bullet only succeeded in rendering me unconscious rather than killing me outright.'

A single bullet to the heart and another to the head.

'An assassin's method,' Zachary acknowledged gruffly.

'Because André killed me,' Georgianna confirmed emotionally. 'Or, at least, he believed that he had when he left me for dead in that deserted forest just outside Paris,' she continued flatly. 'Which is where Monsieur Bernard, having heard the two shots and fearing for his livestock, found me unconscious and took me back to his farm.'

'The doctor?'

'The Bernards dare not call in a doctor, because they had no way of knowing who had inflicted such injuries. And, being unconscious, I could not tell them, either.' She smiled ruefully. 'Madame Bernard removed the bullet herself, then she sewed the wound back up as best she could. It could have been worse, I suppose, and *monsieur* might have lived alone and so been the one to attempt to sew the wound.'

'For pity's sake, be silent a moment, Georgianna.' Zachary choked as he finally found the breath to speak.

'Why?' she challenged. 'Did I not tell you yesterday that we all carry scars, some more visibly than others? Or does it sicken you to see such imperfection? It sickened me at the time. Although, in truth, I did not see the scars for some weeks,' she continued conversationally. 'I remained unconscious for several days afterwards and delirious for the better part of a week or more,' she explained flatly as Zachary looked at her sharply. 'And then, finally, when I did awaken it was to discover that I was blind, Zachary. Completely and utterly blind.' She raised her chin as she looked at him in defiant challenge.

'Dear God.'

'Yes.'

Zachary closed his eyes momentarily. 'That is the reason you do not like full dark.' It was a statement rather than a question.

'Yes. The blindness lasted only a couple of weeks, but it was the longest fortnight of my life, as I lay there wondering if I should ever see again. Do you believe me yet, Zachary?' she continued tauntingly. 'Or do you require further proof? If so, I am afraid I have none.'

'Stop it, Georgianna. For pity's sake.'

'Pity?' she echoed bitterly. 'And why should I pity you, Hawksmere? You were not the stupid fool who believed she was eloping with the man she believed herself in love with and whom she believed loved her, only to discover that she had been nothing more to him than a useful pawn. A pawn who was totally dispensable once he was safely returned to his native France and fellow conspirators.'

Zachary gave a dazed shake of his head. 'I meant only that you have had months to grow accustomed to this, Georgianna. I have had only a few minutes. Rousseau truly believes he has succeeded in assassinating you?'

'Oh, yes.'

'That is why you did not fear his looking for you after you had left him? Because he believed you already dead?'

She nodded abruptly. 'And my body then eaten by scavenging animals, yes.'

Now Zachary did feel sickened. But not by Georgianna's scars. Never that.

How could he ever be sickened by those, when they were the scars of the war she had been forced to fight alone, and in a country not her own? Indeed, it was the same evidence of war which he carried upon his own throat.

Georgianna might well have died, but for the kindness of a French farmer and his wife. And she had then placed herself in danger by working in a French tavern for months, followed by days of fearing being discovered at any moment as she waited at the dockside to return to England, so that she might bring back the information she had overheard of Napoleon's intention of leaving Elba.

There had been no father to defend her.

No brother to cherish her.

No husband to protect her.

Chapter Nine

'I demand to know where you are taking me,' Georgianna insisted even as she accepted Hawksmere's hand to aid her in climbing inside the ducal carriage.

Hawksmere waited until she was seated before climbing in behind her and sitting on the seat opposite as the door was closed. His expression was as grimly forbidding as it had been this past hour, since he had informed her she would be leaving Hawksmere House at the same time as he. 'Somewhere you will be safe.' He turned away to look out of the carriage window as it moved forward.

Georgianna had no idea what to expect from Hawksmere after her revelations to him earlier in the bedchamber. She had waited nervously as he went exceedingly quiet, restlessly pacing the room, so deep in thought he seemed almost to have forgotten she was there. Zachary had then come to an abrupt halt and instructed her to repack her bag and be ready to leave within the hour, before he had then departed her bedchamber.

There had been very little for Georgianna to re-pack. The things she had originally taken with her to France had all, apart from what she had carried in her reticule, been left behind when André took her to the forest outside Paris with the intention of killing her.

The Bernards had later provided her with a couple of worn gowns left behind by their daughter when she went off to marry her French soldier. And Georgianna had added two more gowns to that meagre wardrobe with the wages she'd earned at the tavern. She was wearing one of the only two sets of under-garments she possessed. As she had last night worn one of her only two nightgowns. Otherwise she had no other possessions.

Consequently she had spent most of that hour sitting in a chair beside the window, worrying about what Hawksmere intended to do with her now. As his final words had implied, he intended doing some-thing.

'Is there such a place?' she prompted softly now.

Zachary turned back to look at her, his expression unreadable beneath the brim of his beaver hat as he answered her. 'I believe so, yes.'

Georgianna gave a pained frown. 'Is it your inten-tion to foist me off on to one or other of your close friends? Perhaps that was the reason for Wolfing-ham's visit to you this morning?' she asked heavily.

Zachary now had cause to regret many things in his life. The nature of his marriage proposal to Georgianna Lancaster certainly being one of them. But the cruelty of his distrust of her these past two days, in light of the things she had revealed to him this morning, the terrible scars he had seen upon her body, and no doubt a reflection of the scars she also carried inside her, by far and away exceeded any previous regrets.

And Georgianna was as yet unaware of the worst of the cruelties of which he was guilty.

Once she did know then her disgust with him, her hatred of him, would no doubt be complete.

Zachary had consulted with no one on the decision, the change of plans, he had made in regards to what he should do with Georgianna when he left for France. He took full responsibility for that decision. And he challenged anyone to question him on it. If they dared.

As far as he was concerned, Georgianna had suffered enough. For her *naïveté* in regard to love, for her youthful belief and trust in a man who had used her and then attempted to kill her. Damn it, as far as Rousseau was concerned, he had killed her.

As Zachary now wished to kill Rousseau.

His hands clenched on his thighs with the need he felt to encircle the other man's throat and squeeze until no more air could enter Rousseau's lungs. To make him suffer, as Georgianna had surely suffered. First, by her humiliation in the man's duplicity. Then by being shot and left for dead. Regaining consciousness days later, only to find she was blind and in terrible pain. And then the months spent in Paris after that, and still fearing for her life. The latter because of her loyalty to England. A loyalty Zachary had distrusted and mocked her for, again to the point of cruelty.

Zachary was heartily ashamed of his harsh behaviour towards Georgianna these past two days. For having disbelieved her. For taunting her. And for then having made love to her, as if she were no better than that whore she had earlier denied being.

He could only try to make amends for those wrongs and hope that Georgianna might one day be able to forgive him.

And Rousseau deserved to die for his treatment of her.

Zachary intended seeing that it happened. Before too many days had passed, if he had his way. And he would. Because, in his eyes, Rousseau was no more than a rabid dog in need of being put down. Not for his loyalty to Napoleon, but for using an innocent, such as Georgianna had once been, to achieve his ends. For attempting and believing he had killed her when she was of no further use to him.

None of which helped to ease the burden of what Zachary now had to reveal to Georgianna, before then watching the hatred and contempt that would burn in those beautiful violet-coloured eyes towards him.

He drew in a long, controlling breath. 'I am taking you to your brother at Malvern House.'

Georgianna sat forward with a start, her face paling beneath her black bonnet. 'You cannot.' Her eyes were wide in her distress. 'Zachary, how can you be so cruel as to humiliate me further, by having my own brother turn away from me? I told you the truth earlier. I showed you.'

'There will be no humiliation, Georgianna.' Zachary sat forward on his own seat to reach out and grasp both of her tiny gloved hands in his, knowing it was possibly the last time she would allow him such familiarity. 'There will be no humiliation for you, Georgianna, and your brother will not turn away from you,' he assured evenly, 'because there was no scandal.'

She stilled at the same time as she blinked rapidly to hold back the tears now glistening in her eyes. 'I do not understand,' she finally murmured huskily.

And Zachary had no wish to tell her when he knew it would result in those beautiful eyes hardening with hatred for him. But his behaviour towards Georgianna this past two days allowed for no mercy being given on his own behalf. He deserved no forgiveness from her, no mercy. For any of the things he had said and done to her.

He released her hands to sit back against his seat as he looked across at her between narrowed lids. 'The notification of the ending of our betrothal appeared in the newspapers only a week after it was announced.'

Guilt coloured her cheeks. 'I expected no other.'

'That announcement stated,' Zachary continued firmly, 'that Lady Georgianna Rose Lancaster had decided, after all, against marrying Zachary Richard Edward Black, the Duke of Hawksmere.'

'But that is not what happened!'

'It also stated that it was your intention to retire to

the Malvern country estate for the remainder of the Season,' Zachary completed determinedly.

Georgianna now looked at him with wide, disbelieving eyes.

'Your father died in a riding accident only a month later,' Zachary continued evenly, 'at which time it was decided between your brother Jeffrey and myself that he would announce that you both intended to remain secluded at Malvern Hall for your time of mourning.'

She swallowed. 'What are you saying?'

Zachary drew in a deep breath before answering softly. 'That there was no scandal. As is acceptable, you were the one to end our betrothal and since then it is believed you have been living quietly at Malvern Hall with your brother.'

'How can this be?' Georgianna gave a dazed shake of her head.

The duke moved restlessly. 'Your father, brother and I discussed it after it was discovered you had eloped with Duval, or Rousseau, as he was later discovered to be. It was your family's hope that you would be found and returned before—well, before any harm might be done to your reputation and without any but the close family, and myself, being the wiser for it.'

Georgianna's cheeks became even more flushed in acknowledgement of the harm to which Hawksmere referred. 'And you agreed with this decision?'

Hawksmere's mouth tightened. 'Yes.'

'Because such an announcement lessened your own humiliation?'

His mouth thinned. 'No doubt that was part of it,' he allowed drily. 'But I hope I also thought of you, and your family, in that decision. I am not a vindictive man, Georgianna,' he assured evenly as she now looked at him blankly. 'No matter the impression I may have given to the contrary these past two days,' he acknowledged heavily.

Georgianna did not believe Hawksmere's behaviour to have been particularly vindictive towards her. She knew that she had fully deserved his anger, for her having eloped with another man so soon after the announcement of their own betrothal, causing him embarrassment. As she also deserved the distrust Zachary felt in regard to her return, when he knew that the man she had eloped with was actually a spy for Napoleon.

But this? Having allowed her to continue to think, these past two days, that she was unforgiven by her father and a pariah to her brother, the only family she had left in the world, as well as ostracised in society, was another matter entirely.

She frowned. 'Does no one in society know of my elopement with André?'

Hawksmere shrugged. 'A few may have guessed at the truth of the matter, but none knows for certain.'

'Then I am not shamed? Or ostracised?'

'No.'

'And does my brother know I shall be returning to him today?'

'I sent him a note earlier informing him so and

have received confirmation back from him, yes,' Hawksmere added softly.

'And does he welcome me back, despite knowing of my past behaviour?'

'He holds Rousseau completely responsible for past events.'

'Then I may return to my brother, my home, into society, without fear of rejection?'

A nerve pulsed in the tightness of Hawksmere's jaw. 'Yes.'

'And you have known this since we met again yesterday, known how much it pains me to think of my father's disappointment in me, to be estranged from Jeffrey? And yet you have continued to let me believe...' Georgianna did not even take the time to consider her next action, merely reacted, eyes glittering angrily as she lifted her hand and stuck Hawksmere across one hard and arrogant cheek.

Zachary had seen the angry spark in Georgianna's eyes, had noted the lifting of her gloved hand and guessed her intent. He'd made no attempt to avoid the painful slap she administered to the side of his face. Knowing he deserved it. That he deserved so much more than a single slap.

So, yes, let Georgianna slap him. Again and again, if that was her wish. Zachary would neither protest nor attempt to stop her.

'You are truly despicable!' Georgianna now glared across the width of the carriage at him. 'A despicable, unprincipled bastard! Oh, yes, Hawksmere,' she declared scornfully as he raised surprised dark brows.

'I assure you, I heard far worse than that during my months of working in Helene Rousseau's tavern. And you—you deserve to hear every one of those words for the way in which you have deceived me.' She blinked back the tears as they now blurred her vision of the arrogantly superior face across from her own.

'Perhaps we should take them as having already been said?' Zachary excused himself gruffly.

She gave an impatient shake of her head, her hands clenched together. 'I have spent months in despair of ever being able to see or speak to my brother again. Of ever seeing my home again. Of knowing that all in English society shunned me. This past few days of believing I would never be able to visit my father's graveside and beg his forgiveness. A despair which you might have spared me, if you had a mind to do so. If you had a heart with which to do so. Which you so obviously do not,' she added coldly.

Zachary had no defence against Georgianna's accusations. He knew he was guilty of everything she now accused him of. Except perhaps the latter.

It was true he had offered for Lady Georgianna Lancaster ten months ago because he needed a wife and an heir before his thirty-fifth birthday. It was true also that he had been more annoyed than concerned at the inconvenience when she had eloped with another man. As he had no doubt also agreed with Malvern's solution to that problem, as a way of saving himself deeper humiliation, as much as he had Georgianna's reputation.

But he had not really known Georgianna at that

time. Had seen only that plump pigeon, whom he'd decided would make him a suitable and undemanding wife, and a mother for his heirs.

The Georgianna with whom he had spent so many hours these past two days was not only a beautiful woman, but one for whom he knew he had felt a grudging admiration even before she had revealed the extent of the scars she bore, as evidence of Rousseau's betrayal of her.

She was also a woman for whom Zachary felt desire every time he so much as looked at her.

Even now, with her looking across at him with such contempt, Zachary was aware that his body pulsed with that same desire beneath his pantaloons.

Perhaps not as proof that he did indeed possess a heart, but enough so that Zachary knew he felt regret for the wide chasm that now yawned between the two of them. Fuelled by the dislike and contempt Georgianna now felt towards him.

His expression was grim as he nodded abruptly. 'I deserve each and every one of your accusations.'

She eyed him scathingly. 'That was never in any doubt.'

'No.'

Georgianna frowned her frustration with the calmness of Hawksmere's acceptance of her anger. What she really wanted was for him to mock or taunt her, as he usually did, so that she might have the satisfaction of slapping him again.

At the same time she felt as if a heavy weight had been lifted from her shoulders. She could see her brother Jeffrey again. Could go to Malvern Hall and visit her father's graveside and offer him her apologies for her behaviour the previous year. Could return to Malvern House if she wished. Take part in the upcoming Season, too, if that was what she decided to do.

Not that she intended telling Hawksmere of any of the lightness and elation she felt; his contemptuous behaviour towards her this past two days did not deserve to be forgiven, or forgotten, so easily.

At the same time as Georgianna knew she could never forget his lovemaking of earlier this morning.

Having believed her to have been André's mistress for several weeks, at least, Georgianna might have expected Zachary to show contempt for her during their lovemaking. Instead he had been poetical in his appreciation of her body. Giving, even gentle, in his caresses, as he introduced her to a pleasure she had never imagined, let alone experienced.

But beneath all of that appreciation and gentleness Zachary had been keeping the secret that she was not in disgrace, after all, Georgianna reminded herself, impatient with the softening of her emotions towards him. Which surely must make him every inch that bastard she had just called him?

'Again, I owe you my heartfelt apologies, Georgianna.'

She looked sharply across at him, unsure what he was apologising for. For not telling her before now that she was not in disgrace in society? Or for the intimacies of this morning?

Zachary sighed heavily as Georgianna made no

response to his apology. 'Except, of course, I do not possess a heart,' he acknowledged evenly. 'In which case, I will instead offer you my sincerest apologies. For having wronged you and hurt you these past two days.'

Deliberately. And without remorse. Each word was like the lash of the whip across the flesh on his back.

Georgianna looked across at him uncertainly. 'And is that supposed to excuse your behaviour?'

'No,' Zachary answered heavily.

'To make you feel better, perhaps?' she added scornfully.

He gave a humourless smile. 'If it was, then I assure you it has failed miserably.'

She raised haughty brows. 'I trust you will understand when I say that I am glad of that?'

How could he have ever thought this young woman was just a plump and malleable pigeon to be taken to the altar, impregnated, and then left forgotten and languishing on one of his country estates?

Even without her terrible experiences of this past year, he very much doubted that Georgianna would ever have been that malleable wife he had deliberately sought, and expected. If he had taken the time and trouble to get to know her, then he would have realised she possessed far too much spirit, was too emotional, to have ever settled for just being his ignored duchess and the mother of his heirs.

A spirit that was now denied him for ever.

Georgianna, quite rightly, would never forgive him for having deceived her. For deliberately allowing her to think she was still in disgrace. For imprisoning her. For making love to her.

'I understand, and completely accept, the anger you feel towards me.' He nodded abruptly just as the carriage drew to a halt outside Malvern House. 'Would you like me to come in with you or would you prefer to reconcile with your brother alone?'

Georgianna felt extremely nervous now that they had actually arrived at Malvern House, the same house she had always lived in whilst in London. The house where her brother Jeffrey now awaited her.

Her brother would be nineteen now and already he had been the Earl of Malvern this past nine months. Without benefit of even his sister to support him, with only that guardian, an elderly friend of her father's, to guide and help him.

'Georgianna!'

She was given no more time for those regrets, or the insecurity of wondering if Jeffrey really would be pleased by her return, as the carriage door was flung open and her brother himself hurtled inside the carriage before pulling her into his arms.

Georgianna gave a sob as she clung to Jeffrey, totally overwhelmed by the eagerness of his greeting, and being with someone she loved and who obviously still loved her. It had been so long since anyone had held her so tenderly, so unconditionally. Hawksmere's lovemaking did not count when she knew his motive had been revenge for her past misdemeanours towards him.

Zachary felt the unaccustomed sting of tears in his

own eyes as he witnessed the emotional reunion between brother and sister. Jeffrey with his usual youthful enthusiasm, Georgianna crying with joy as she clung to the younger brother she obviously adored and had missed so much.

A reunion that Zachary could have allowed her much sooner than this, if he'd had a mind to do so.

Georgianna might never forgive him for that, but Zachary knew he would never forgive himself, either. Or for any of his behaviour towards her these past two days.

Behaviour for which he would happily have got down on his knees and begged for forgiveness if he had thought it would do any good!

He raised a hand to the cheek that still stung from where Georgianna had slapped him just minutes ago. A vehemently delivered slap he had fully deserved.

As he deserved the tearfully accusing gaze she now gave him over her brother's shoulder.

Jeffrey was the one to finally pull back as he continued to beam down at his sister. Their colouring was similar, both were dark haired and blue eyed. 'Perhaps we should take this reunion into the house? Join us, Hawksmere?' Jeffrey prompted lightly as he glanced at Zachary.

Zachary saw the flash of resentment in Georgianna's eyes as she remained tucked beneath her brother's protective arm. 'I think not, thank you, Jeffrey. I have several other things in need of my attention this morning.' He excused himself.

The younger man frowned his disappointment. 'I thought you might at least come in for a few minutes?'

Zachary bit back his impatience. 'As I said, I have other things to do today.'

'I am sure we have taken up enough of Hawksmere's valuable time, Jeffrey,' Georgianna exclaimed without so much as a glance in the duke's direction.

'I did not think.' Jeffrey grimaced. 'Of course you are busy. But perhaps you would like to join us for dinner later this evening?'

'Jeffrey.'

'That will not be possible, I am afraid,' Hawksmere drawled over Georgianna's alarmed protest.

She blinked. 'His Grace is leaving.'

'For my country estate later today.' Once again the duke rudely spoke over Georgianna, his eyes flashing a reproving silver as he gave her a pointed glare. Evidence that Jeffrey was not one of the people privileged to know of Hawksmere's activities for the Crown.

Georgianna felt the warmth of that rebuke in her cheeks as she lowered her gaze. 'Of course.'

'Thank you for returning my sister to me.' Jeffrey grinned his pleasure at the older man as he held Georgianna close to his side.

Hawksmere nodded abruptly. 'I believe you will find that it was Georgianna who has returned herself to us all.'

She looked up at him sharply, searching that hard and arrogant face for some indication of Hawksmere's signature sarcasm and finding none. Instead he gazed across at her guardedly, as if unwilling to reveal his emotions. Which, no doubt, he was.

She straightened before speaking formally. 'I trust you will have a safe journey, your Grace.'

'As do I,' he drawled before turning to Jeffrey. 'I will be in touch when I return to town, Malvern.'

'We shall look forward to it, shall we not, Georgianna?' Jeffrey beamed enthusiastically.

'Of course,' Georgianna concurred softly, purposefully not looking at Hawksmere, knowing she would see only mockery for her there, both of them aware that if they never saw each other again it would be too soon for either of them.

And yet...

Once Georgianna had alighted from the carriage and begun slowly walking up the steps to Malvern House beside her brother, she was aware of a feeling of discomfort as she heard Hawksmere's carriage move on down the cobbled street. Of feeling slightly bereft at not knowing when, or if, she would see ever him again.

She was angry with him, yes, as her slap to his cheek had demonstrated. But what if he did not return from France? She was not angry enough, did not dislike him enough, to never wish to see him again.

Georgianna came to a halt on the top step into Malvern House before turning to gaze after Hawksmere's carriage, catching a brief glimpse of his profile inside the carriage as it turned the corner before disappearing from view.

'Are you well, Georgianna?'

She turned to find Jeffrey looking down at her with concern, his eyes bluer than her violet-coloured ones, his boyish face having grown handsome, chiselled, this past year. No doubt from his added responsibilities as Earl of Malvern. 'I am very happy to be home, thank you, Jeffrey,' she assured him warmly.

'You looked a little wistful for a moment. We shall see Hawksmere again very soon, I am sure,' he added reassuringly. 'He has become a regular visitor at Malvern House these past few months.'

'He has?' Georgianna looked up at her brother curiously as the two of them entered the house together, warmly accepting the butler's beam of pleasure and kind words at seeing her returned to Malvern House.

Jeffrey nodded. 'I have found his guidance invaluable these past months.'

'But what of your guardian? I would have thought that he would have been your mentor rather than Hawksmere?' Georgianna handed Carter her bonnet and gloves.

'Perhaps we should discuss this in the library,' Jeffrey requested before turning to the butler. 'Lady Georgianna and I would like hot chocolate and crumpets beside the fire, if you please, Carter.'

Georgianna's heart melted at the reminder of the way in which she and Jeffrey had passed many an afternoon together in the schoolroom when they were younger. 'Oh, yes, please, Carter.' She squeezed her brother's arm as they walked companionably to the library. 'It is so good to be back with you, Jeffrey,' she spoke emotionally once they were seated opposite each other beside the warmth of the fire.

Her brother sat forward, looking quite the dandy in his blue superfine and high-collared shirt. 'And you will tell me all about your adventures in a minute,' he promised. 'But first, did Hawksmere not talk to you of our guardian?'

'He mentioned that you have one,' Georgianna answered carefully, not sure of exactly what Zachary had told Jeffrey in his note in regard to when, how and why she had returned to England.

'We both have one, the same one, until we are both one and twenty,' Jeffrey corrected ruefully.

Georgianna's eyes widened. 'But...' She had a guardian? After all she had been through this past ten months, the independence, the decisions she had been forced to make for herself, she now had to suffer having a guardian until her birthday in three months' time? 'Who is it?' she demanded as a terrible foreboding began to wash over her.

Jeffrey grinned. 'Hawksmere, of course.'

That was the very answer Georgianna had begun to suspect, and dread.

Chapter Ten

'Would you care to tell me exactly what we are still doing in Paris, Zachary, when our mission was to sound out public feeling here, in regard to Napoleon's imminent arrival in Paris, before returning to England with our report?'

Zachary did not so much as glance at his companion as he kept his narrowed gaze levelled upon the establishment across the street from where the two of them stood, dressed as middle-class citizens of Paris.

'Do you remember Bully Harrison from Eton?'

There was a slight pause. 'How could I forget him, when he took such pleasure in beating the younger boys at every opportunity?' Wolfingham confirmed impatiently, green eyes hard. 'I also remember you taking an even greater delight in giving him a beating of your own, as a warning for him to instantly cease those unpleasant activities. Which he did. But I do not see what Harrison has to do with us being here in Paris.'

'There is an even worse bully inside that establishment.' Zachary nodded in the direction of the Fleur de Lis tavern across the street. 'A monster who took delight in hurting a woman.'

'Ah.'

'Indeed,' Zachary confirmed grimly.

'A woman of your acquaintance?'

'Yes.'

'Is she—? Did he hurt her very badly?'

Zachary's jaw tensed. 'He lied to her. Seduced her. For his own selfish reasons. And, when she was of no further use to him, he shot her. Twice. Once in the chest and then in the head.'

'Assassin!' Wolfingham hissed.

Zachary nodded. 'Miraculously she did not die. But she now lives in daily fear of the monster discovering his failure. Of him seeking her out and completing the assassination.'

Wolfingham glanced across at the tavern. 'And he is in there now?'

'I saw him enter a short time ago, with half-a-dozen cohorts.' Zachary nodded.

'Knife or pistol?'

'I believe I told you that he shot her.'

'I enquired as to whether you intend to use knife or pistol?'

Zachary's brow cleared slightly as he turned to look appreciatively at one of his closest friends. 'I apologise for underestimating you, Wolfingham,' he drawled ruefully. 'And I shall use my pistol. I believe I should like him to know what it is like to stare down the barrel of a gun and know you are about to breathe your last,' he added with grim satisfaction as he thought of how Georgianna must have suffered the night Rousseau attempted to kill her. And he wasn't just thinking of her physical wounds, but the emotional ones he doubted would ever completely heal.

There was little enough he could do to make amends for the emotional wounds he had inflicted on her since, but dispatching Rousseau was certainly a start.

'I should warn you, though, I have reason to believe the man may recognise me,' Zachary warned, unconsciously touching the definitive scar upon his throat.

Wolfingham nodded. 'What would you like me to do in order to divert his cohorts?'

Zachary gave a hard grin. 'Succinct and to the point—I have always liked that about you.'

'A man who would treat a woman in such a despicable way does not deserve to live.'

A sentiment exactly matched by Zachary's feelings on the matter.

Georgianna paced restlessly up and down the yellow salon at Malvern House, totally unaware of the luxuriously appointed room she had so enjoyed choosing the décor and furnishings for just two short years ago.

Those two years might just as well have been twenty.

Because she was not that same person who had

once so painstakingly pored over swatches of materials for curtains and furnishings for weeks on end, voicing a complaint when the material on one of the chairs proved to be the merest shade darker than its twin.

It all seemed so unimportant now, so petty. As had the ordering of the new gowns Jeffrey had insisted upon, in preparation for their return to society, when it was discovered that all of last year's gowns were far too big for her now-slender figure.

A society with its rules and strictures upon behaviour and speech, which she had so long believed she wished to be part of again, but now found totally stifling.

As she did the fact that those calls and entertainments continued, as if Napoleon and his ever-increasing army were not even now marching doggedly and triumphantly towards Paris.

Indeed, the majority of the *ton* seemed far more interested in the fact that Lady Georgianna Lancaster was returned to town, inciting an avalanche of calls and invitations from those of the *ton* who had already returned in preparation for the full Season.

Polite calls and invitations, which had nevertheless possessed an underlying curiosity to know as to how she had spent the past year. Georgianna had answered all of those queries with the same reply Jeffrey had given at the time of her disappearance; she had spent her time quietly at Malvern Hall, initially following the breaking of her betrothal, and then in mourning for the death of their father.

As Hawksmere had said, some might suspect otherwise, but none dared question the word of either the Duke of Hawksmere or the new Earl of Malvern.

Hawksmere.

As might be expected, there had been neither sight nor sound of Zachary Black and Georgianna could only presume, having heard nothing to the contrary, that silence must mean he was still in France. Perhaps he was even now witnessing Napoleon's triumphant march towards Paris.

If not, then he would no doubt have made a point of calling upon his two wards before now.

Georgianna had far from forgiven Hawksmere for that deception!

As no doubt Hawksmere, in his turn, did not believe he had any need to explain himself to anyone, least of all the two young people who were now under his guardianship.

Georgianna could only wonder what on earth had possessed her father to choose such a man as guardian to his young son and daughter, most especially when that daughter had eloped in order to escape marriage to that same gentleman.

Which was perhaps answer enough as to why Hawksmere had been chosen. As he already knew of the scandal behind the breaking of their betrothal, making him their guardian had meant there would be no need for Georgianna's absence to be explained to a third party after her father's death.

Which did not make the unpleasant fact of being under the guardianship of Hawksmere, of all men, for another three months, any more acceptable to Georgianna.

Something she intended informing him of at the earliest opportunity.

In the meantime, Georgianna was returned to her family, to her home. She already had a whole new wardrobe of gowns, deliberately designed to hide the unsightly scar upon her chest, in which she could receive guests, as well as drive out in the family carriage in the afternoons. She and Jeffrey had also spent some time in deciding which social invitations they could or should accept, when their year of mourning was not quite at an end.

And it all seemed so pointless to Georgianna. So uninspiring. So unexciting after her months of freedom from those strictures.

Oh, she could not deny that they had been terrifying, uncertain months, too. Days and nights when she had feared for her very life. Which was perhaps one of the reasons she was so restless and bored by the tedium of her life now?

And the other reason?

Again that was down to Hawksmere.

Angry as she was with him—furious, in fact—Georgianna could not deny that everything seemed so much duller, flatter, without Hawksmere's arrogantly powerful presence.

Which was utterly ridiculous on her part, when she should be relishing that dullness after so many months spent in fear and torment.

A fear and torment that was not over and never

could be whilst the danger of André Rousseau lurked so ominously in the shadows of her life.

'Is it time for hot chocolate and crumpets beside the fire again?'

Georgianna turned with a smile as her brother quickly crossed the room to kiss her warmly upon the cheek.

'What makes you say that?'

Jeffrey looked down at her quizzically. 'You looked very forlorn and wistful when I entered the room.'

Forlorn and wistful?

Because of her thoughts of Hawksmere?

No, of course it had not been because of thoughts of Hawksmere; she had been thinking of André, not Zachary, when Jeffrey entered the salon. 'I believe I am still adjusting to being back in England and society,' she excused lightly.

'But you are pleased to be, surely?' he cajoled.

Barely a year separated them in age and Jeffrey had certainly matured exponentially during his months as the Earl of Malvern under Hawksmere's guidance. But still Georgianna felt so much older than her brother now, in her emotions as well as her interests.

Not that she could explain to Jeffrey without fear of revealing too much of her experiences over the past year.

They had necessarily talked of her elopement, her parting from André, her months of working, though she had not revealed exactly where she had worked, only that it was in a kitchen, to earn the money for her boat passage back to England. Not once during their conversations had Georgianna told Jeffrey the complete truth about the months she had spent in France. How could she, when that truth was so horrible, so demeaning, so frightening?

It was a truth which only Hawksmere knew for certain.

Such was her brother's obvious admiration and liking for the older man, and oblivious of their guardian's work for the Crown, Jeffrey had so far not questioned why she had chosen to go to Hawksmere, of all people, immediately upon returning to England. Nor had Georgianna chosen to enlighten her brother as to the exact day of her return, or that she had been kept a prisoner in Hawksmere's home for two days and nights.

She might be angry with Zachary, resentful even, but it served no purpose for her to confide in her brother, when he obviously admired Hawksmere so. The older man was to be his guardian for some time to come. Also, it could endanger the work Zachary even now carried out for the Crown.

'Of course.' She gave her brother a brightly reassuring smile. 'I am merely finding it strange, after so many months away.'

'In that case, a dinner party is exactly what is required.' Her brother moved to the fireplace to warm his hands, the darkness of his hair appearing blueblack in the firelight.

'A dinner party?' Georgianna's pulse jumped in nervousness, her heart leaping in her chest, as she joined Jeffrey beside the fire. 'But I thought tomorrow evening at Lady Colchester's musical soirée was to be our first appearance back into society?' Individual calls by members of society was one thing, as was riding in her carriage in the afternoons, but Georgianna was dreading having that society staring at her *en masse* and wondering if any of the rumours that so abounded about her were true.

'I should have said a dinner party *en famille*,' Jeffrey corrected cheerfully. 'Hawksmere has sent word he is returned from the country and wishes the two of us to join him at Hawksmere House for dinner this evening.'

Hawksmere?

Georgianna moved to sit down abruptly on the chair beside the fireplace, her knees feeling suddenly weak at the knowledge that Zachary was returned from France. And safely, too, if he was inviting the two of them to join him for dinner this evening.

'You have seen him?' she prompted huskily.

'He sent for me this afternoon.' Jeffrey nodded.

But not her, Georgianna realised. Because she would be his ward for only a matter of months more? Or because he had no wish to see her again? Including her in this evening's dinner invitation was, after all, what Jeffrey would have expected of their guardian.

'Hawksmere is hardly family, Jeffrey,' she remonstrated stiffly.

'As good as,' he dismissed unconcernedly, seeming completely unaware of Georgianna's reaction to the news of Hawksmere's invitation.

Georgianna had not realised until that moment how worried she had been about Zachary's safe return from France.

A concern she was starting to fear might be based on something other than the anger she bore towards him, for once again having omitted to tell her the full truth.

'It really was not necessary for you to include me in this dinner invitation, Hawksmere!'

Zachary found himself smiling for the first time in days as Georgianna attacked him with her acerbic tongue the moment she entered the blue salon of his home on her brother's arm, rather than offering the expected polite greeting.

'And how gratified you must be to know that there is only the matter of three months before you will be relieved of my guardianship,' he continued haughtily even as she sketched him a polite curtsy.

'Georgianna?' Jeffrey looked nonplussed by his sister's sharpness towards their guardian.

Zachary, on the other hand, found himself highly entertained. 'The history between your sister and me necessarily means that we are still working on acquiring an acceptable politeness between the two of us, Jeffrey,' he excused to the younger man, even as he stepped forward to take Georgianna's gloved hand in his, his own gaze meeting her glittering violet one as he raised that hand to his lips. 'You are looking exceptionally lovely this evening, Georgianna,' he drawled as he straightened before slowly relinquishing her hand.

She did indeed look very beautiful, the darkness of her hair fashionably styled so as to conceal the scar at her temple. Her fashionable gown was the same violet colour as her eyes, with a swathe of lace artfully fashioned across the top of her bosom, so concealing the scar Zachary knew she also bore there.

'I am sure there is no need for false politeness between the two of us in the privacy of your home, Hawksmere,' she dismissed offhandedly as she moved away, at the same time reminding Zachary, at least, that he had not felt the need for this same politeness the last time she had been in his home. 'Jeffrey cannot help but be aware of the reason for our strained relationship.'

Zachary raised dark brows. 'I had hoped we had come to a different understanding of each other since your return?'

Those violet coloured eyes flashed darkly. 'Only in as much as I believe that we have come to an acceptance of our hearty dislike of each other.'

'Georgianna!'

'Do not be alarmed, Jeffrey.' Once again Zachary soothed his younger ward's shock at his sister's rudeness. 'Georgianna and I understand each other perfectly. Do we not, Georgianna?' The hardness of his tone was a warning for her to temper her anger and dislike of him. Her behaviour was not only alarming her brother, but also implied that they knew each other far better than their previously known acquaintance might imply.

Which they obviously did.

Zachary had thought of Georgianna often these past two weeks, whilst he was away in France. More often than he might have wished, if truth be known, and not just because of his dealings with Rousseau.

Georgianna had only been a prisoner in his home for a matter of thirty-six hours, but they had been intensely intimate hours. Hours, when Zachary came to know Georgianna rather better than he had ever known any woman. Hours, when he had come to admire her, for her spirit and determination. Hours, when he had come to like, even appreciate, her outspokenness and the way that she refused to be cowed by anything he did or said to her. Hours, when he had come to desire her more than any woman of his acquaintance.

As he desired her still, Zachary acknowledged as he studied her through narrowed lids.

Georgianna appeared less strained than she had been two weeks ago, the lines smoothed from her forehead and beside her eyes and mouth, and there was a becoming colour in the smoothness of her cheeks and full, pouting lips. But she still looked too slender in that violet-coloured gown. Perhaps more so, her unadorned neck and throat appearing delicately vulnerable, as did the slenderness of her arms.

And Zachary's desire to possess all that loveliness was almost painful.

Damn it, it was painful.

His body throbbed with desire for her even more after their two weeks apart.

'Yes, Hawksmere, I believe we do indeed understand each other. Perfectly.' She lifted her chin in challenge.

Zachary very much doubted that Georgianna's understanding of that statement was the same as his own. Because, without the strictures Jeffrey's presence necessarily put on his behaviour, Zachary very much doubted he would be able to control the desire he now felt to make love to Georgianna again.

And not just physically. He ached to possess all of her. Her spirit. Determination. Her outspokenness. Along with her often sarcastic sense of humour, the latter more often than not at his own expense.

Georgianna had shown him this evening, with just a few brief words, that she disliked him as much now as she ever had.

Which was no doubt a fitting punishment for his having proposed marriage to her so shabbily the previous year. And Zachary knew he had again treated her abominably when she returned from France so unexpectedly.

Was it any wonder that she now disliked him so intensely?

Or that he, having thought about her so much, remembering over and over again making love to her, touching her, kissing her, bringing her to completion, desired her more now than he had two weeks ago?

'Are you ill, Hawksmere?' she now taunted mockingly. 'You have gone exceedingly quiet for someone who I believed always had an answer for everything.'

'I say, Georgianna…' cautioned Jeffrey.

Zachary held his hand up to prevent Jeffrey from continuing to chastise his sister on his behalf. 'I do not believe I as yet have the answer to you, dearest Georgianna,' he assured softly.

Georgianna felt the burn of colour in her cheeks, knowing she had brought Hawksmere's taunt upon herself by her challenging and rude behaviour. Except she could not seem to behave in any other way when in his company, her hackles rising, defences instantly up, as she verbally attacked him. Before she was attacked herself?

Maybe so, but she certainly did not appreciate his sarcasm in addressing her as 'dearest Georgianna', when they both knew she was here on sufferance only. Because it would have appeared odd to Jeffrey if his sister had not been included in the dinner invitation from their guardian. A guardianship, in regard to herself, that Georgianna had no doubt Zachary found tiresome, to say the least.

'It is a woman's prerogative to remain something of a mystery to a gentleman, is it not?' she dismissed airily, very aware that this man knew her far better than any other, physically as well as emotionally.

Challenging Zachary the moment the two of them met again had been Georgianna's only way of dealing with those memories of their previous intimacy, her only defence against the rush of emotions and the memories, which had threatened to overwhelm her the moment she looked at him. Of him kissing her, caressing her, pleasuring her, with those sculptured lips and large, and wholly seductive, hands!

There was no denying that Zachary looked very handsome this evening, in his black evening clothes and snowy white linen. His hair had grown longer this past two weeks and now curled silkily about his ears and nape. He appeared slightly thinner in the face, too, no doubt from the weeks he had spent in the turmoil of France, bringing into stark relief his handsome features.

Just to look at him caused Georgianna's heart to beat faster and the palms of her hands to dampen inside her lace gloves.

'So it is,' he drawled in answer to her comment as Hinds appeared discreetly in the doorway. 'Shall we go into dinner now?' He offered Georgianna his arm.

Georgianna hesitated at the offered intimacy, having no desire to touch Zachary, to be made so totally aware of him, and of those memories that had haunted, and so bedevilled, her these past two weeks.

Nevertheless, she forced herself to show no emotion as she placed her gloved hand upon his arm and walked beside him to the dining room.

The same intimate dining room in which she and Zachary had dined alone together two weeks ago.

Chapter Eleven

'I'm sure you will have received many visitors and invitations now that you are returned to society?'

'Hawksmere, I give you permission to cease all attempts at this strained politeness between the two of us for the time my brother is out of the room,' Georgianna dismissed impatiently, Jeffrey having excused himself on a call of nature just a few short minutes ago.

Zachary smiled at her customary straightforwardness. Georgianna was right: their efforts at maintaining that imposed social politeness, because of Jeffrey's presence, had become more and more difficult as dinner progressed, to the point that even the boyishly enthusiastic Jeffrey had seemed to become uncomfortable in their company.

'I am far more interested in knowing how things progress in France than in the two of us being socially polite to each other,' Georgianna prompted interestedly as she sat forward eagerly.

Zachary gave a guarded shrug. 'As you say, they progress. At least, Napoleon does,' he added grimly.

She gave a soft gasp. 'And do you believe he will be successful in his endeavour?'

Zachary did not bother in so much as attempting to dismiss Georgianna's concerns. She was far too intelligent to be fobbed off. Besides which, the months she had spent in France had given her an insight into the turmoil which had once again beset that country. 'I do not believe I am breaking any confidences by revealing that his army grows bigger by the day and that he will soon enter Paris itself.'

'And the king?'

'I believe Louis is preparing to flee.'

Georgianna's cheeks grew pale. 'Then there will most certainly be another war.'

'Undoubtedly.'

She flicked him a glance beneath long silky dark lashes. 'You will be a part of that war?'

'Most certainly.' Zachary gave her a mocking grin. 'Just think, Georgianna, I might even manage to get myself killed, and in doing so relieve you of the burden of suffering both my guardianship as well as my company.'

Georgianna frowned across at him darkly. 'You are being unfair by inferring that I have ever wished you dead, Hawksmere.'

'Just consigned to Hades.'

'Well, yes, there is that.' A beguiling dimple appeared in her cheek as she smiled genuinely for what seemed to be the first time this evening. 'A little singeing by those hellish fires, at the very least, might succeed in stripping you of some of your irritating arrogance.'

Zachary found himself chuckling. 'I do believe I have missed both you and your insults, Georgianna.'

She raised dark brows. 'Somehow I doubt that very much!'

Then she would be wrong, Zachary acknowledged. Georgianna was a woman with whom he now spoke almost as freely, and on similar subjects, as he did his closest male friends. Something he had not believed possible with any woman in society.

It had long been his experience that the women of society preferred not to know of the more unpleasant facts of life, their main topics of conversation seeming to be fashions, gossip, and the managing of their household and family. Georgianna's experiences this past year had taken her far beyond being interested in such trivialities.

Reminding Zachary only too forcibly that there was something he needed, rather than wished, to discuss with her in private.

'You will not allow Jeffrey to fight?' Georgianna looked at him anxiously now.

Zachary frowned. 'He is a man grown, Georgianna.'

'And you are his guardian.' Her eyes glittered a deep, emotional violet.

'And, no doubt, you will never forgive me if something should happen to him.' It was a statement rather than a question.

'And I doubt my forgiveness is of the least interest, or importance, to you.'

'You might be surprised,' Zachary murmured softly before sighing as Georgianna continued to look at him expectantly. 'I make no promises, but I will see what can be done to prevent Jeffrey from rushing headlong into the coming war,' he added grimly.

She sighed. 'He admires you tremendously, you know.'

'Unlike his sister,' Zachary drawled drily.

She gave him a brief glance. 'It is not a question of not admiring you, Hawksmere. Indeed, I admire your endeavours on behalf of the Crown enormously.'

'That is something, I suppose,' he drawled.

'The rest of your personality leaves a lot to be desired, of course,' she added caustically, 'but one cannot have everything.'

'As usual, the sword thrust in the velvet glove.'

Georgianna eyed him mockingly. 'At least I am consistent.'

'Oh, you are most certainly that, Georgianna,' Zachary allowed before sobering. 'Is it convenient for you to come here tomorrow afternoon?'

'Why?' She eyed him warily now.

He grimaced. 'I would prefer to discuss that with you tomorrow.'

And Georgianna would prefer to know now what that discussion was to be about.

Unfortunately, Jeffrey chose that moment to return to the dining room, so putting an end to their own conversation as they all began to talk instead of the invitations they had accepted for the coming season.

'Thank you, Hinds.' Georgianna smiled politely at the butler as he showed her into the blue salon of Hawksmere House the following afternoon.

After she had spent the night, and all of this morning, fretting and worrying as to what it was Hawksmere could possibly wish to discuss with her today in private.

Hawksmere himself had his back turned towards her as he stood in front of one of the large bay windows, looking out of into the garden beyond. He turned the moment the door closed as evidence of his butler's departure.

'I did not think, when I asked you to come here.' He frowned darkly. 'You do at least have a maid with you, I hope?'

Georgianna nodded. 'She is waiting out in the hallway.'

'Would you care for refreshment?' the duke offered politely. 'Tea, perhaps?'

She eyed him scathingly. 'The only time I have been in this house, apart from that surreal dinner with Jeffrey yesterday evening, was as your prisoner, so, no, I do not require the nicety of tea, thank you, Hawksmere.'

'The time for social politeness between the two of us really is over then, hmm?' he guessed drily.

'I am not sure it ever began.'

Once again Zachary found himself chuckling at

Georgianna's honesty. 'Let us at least sit down,' he invited ruefully.

'You consider I might feel a need to do so, once you have spoken with me?' she murmured concernedly as she moved to perch demurely on the edge of one of the armchairs.

Zachary had debated with himself long and hard as to what he should tell Georgianna about Rousseau. And still he had no real answer, only knew that she needed to know that the other man no longer posed a threat, to her liberty or her life.

She looked so lovely today, dressed in a gown of pale silver, the darkness of her curls peeping out from beneath the matching bonnet, her face youthfully flushed by the freshness of the breeze outside, that Zachary baulked at even introducing the subject of her previous lover.

Her previous lover?

Well, yes, because the intimacies the two of them had shared two weeks ago meant that Zachary had certainly been Georgianna's most recent lover.

And now that he was alone with her once again, he found that the last thing he wished to do was talk of Rousseau.

'Have you thought of me at all this past two weeks, Georgianna?' he found himself prompting huskily.

She blinked at the unexpectedness of his question. 'Politely or impolitely?'

'Oh, impolitely, I am sure,' he allowed with another laugh.

'Then, yes, I do believe I have thought about you. Often,' she added pointedly.

Zachary smiled ruefully. 'And were all these impolite thoughts unpleasant ones?'

Georgianna was uncertain where Zachary was going with this line of questioning. They were two people who had once been betrothed to each other and now found themselves thrust into a situation not of their choosing. She very much doubted that Zachary had wished to become her guardian, any more than she now wished him to be. And that was without the awkwardness of the intimacies which had taken place between the two of them two weeks ago. That certainly made for a very strained relationship between the two of them.

To a degree that Georgianna had found herself wondering many times since how such a thing could ever have happened between two people who could not even claim a liking for each other?

And then she remembered the touch of Zachary's hands upon her, his lips, his tongue, and she knew exactly how such a thing had occurred between them. They were a man and a woman, who had been forced into a situation of close proximity. Factor in Zachary's feelings of anger towards her for past wrongs, then making love to her, ensuring that she enjoyed having him make love to her, and those intimacies had become inevitable.

Her own response to them she found harder to explain.

'Unpleasant enough,' she answered him sharply as she stood up restlessly. 'Now…?'

'I thought of you, too, whilst I was away, Georgianna.'

She stilled, once again eyeing him warily. 'Oh, yes?'

Zachary nodded, his expression intense. 'They were not unpleasant thoughts at all.'

Georgianna's heart began to beat loudly in her chest, her cheeks suddenly warm. 'You surprise me.'

'Do I?' He crossed the room silently until he stood only inches away, looking down at her. 'Does it really surprise you that I remember our time together here so vividly and so pleasantly, Georgianna?' he repeated huskily.

It did, yes. Hawksmere had not earned his reputation, as one of the five Dangerous Dukes, solely on his war record. No, his exploits in the bedchamber were also lauded by the ladies of England and much envied by the gentlemen. Georgianna did not imagine that someone as inexperienced as herself would have been in the least memorable amongst the dozens of beauties who were reputed to have shared a bed with Hawksmere.

As she had done. However briefly.

Her legs trembled slightly, hands clasped tightly together, as she looked up at him. 'It would surprise me very much,' she answered stiltedly.

'And yet?'

'I really would rather not talk about that particular subject, Hawksmere.' She had meant the words to come out as a set-down, but instead they sounded wistful and yearning.

Yearning?

Could it be that she secretly wanted there to be a repeat of the events, the intimacies, they had shared that morning in the bedchamber above them?

That would be madness on her part.

Georgianna's thoughts were broken off abruptly, indeed, her mind went a complete blank, as Zachary took her in his arms and claimed her lips firmly with his own.

The passion and desire were instantaneous, as Zachary's arms tightened about her even as his mouth devoured hers hungrily. It was all that Georgianna could do to remain on her feet, by clutching tightly to the tops of his muscled arms as she returned the heat of those kisses.

Zachary broke the kiss to graze his lips against the softness of Georgianna's cheek. 'I have thought this past two weeks—' he kissed her earlobe '—of doing this again.' He tasted the delicate column of her neck. 'Constantly.' His tongue sought out the hollows at the base of her throat, the creamy softness of the tops of her breasts through the silver lace. 'And none of those thoughts matched up to this reality,' he acknowledged gruffly, his body throbbing and achingly engorged. 'God, how I want you, Georgianna!'

She gasped. 'Zachary, we cannot. We must not.'

'I must,' he rasped fiercely as he lifted her up in his arms and carried her over to the chaise. He lay her down on its softness and sat down beside her, his gaze holding hers as he untied her bonnet before re-moving it completely.

'You have the most beautiful hair, Georgianna, so soft and silky.' He removed the pins as he spoke, before gazing down at her appreciatively as he loosened those curls about her shoulders.

'Zachary,'

'And your skin is like the finest ivory.' His gaze followed the path of his hand as it trailed down the column of her throat to the swell of her breasts. 'So pale and so soft to the touch.' He pushed the lace aside to reveal the scar between her breasts. A scar Zachary did not find any more repellent than she appeared to find the one upon his own throat. No, he considered this scar to be Georgianna's own, very private, war wound.

A sign, a remembrance, of the battle she had fought, and won, and which now only he and she had knowledge of.

'You can have no idea how much I have thought of making love to you again, Georgianna,' he groaned achingly.

Georgianna thought, from the intensity of his kisses and the fire now gleaming, burning, in the silver depths of his eyes as he slowly lowered his head, that she might hazard a guess.

And the thought that this man, that Zachary, wanted her so deeply he had thought of her even whilst he was away in the turmoil of France, filled her with an elation, a happiness Georgianna had not even known she secretly longed for.

She gasped as she felt the warmth of his lips against the scar on her chest. 'Zachary, don't.'

'Let me, Georgianna.' He breathed hotly against her even as his lips continued to kiss every inch of that scarred flesh.

'It is unsightly.' It took every effort of will Georgianna possessed to stop herself from pulling that lace back over the disfiguring scar on her chest, her jaw tight, her hands clenched at her sides.

'No more so than my own scar. Does that repulse you?'

'How could it, when it is evidence of your bravery?' she assured unhesitatingly.

He looked up at her darkly. 'As your own scar is a part of the brave and beautiful woman that you are. One who has suffered and yet survived.'

'I barely survived, Zachary,' she reminded weakly.

'And you are all the braver and stronger for it.'

Was she braver and stronger? Stronger, certainly, but she did not think herself braver. She still suffered nightmares in her bed at night. Dreamt constantly of that night in the woods. The pain, both emotional and physical, that she had suffered. The terror of waking up blind and in so much pain. The months afterwards when she had continued to fear for her life.

Of still suffering from that same fear.

Georgianna's limbs turned to water, all other thoughts fleeing her mind, her hands moving up to entwine her fingers in the darkness of Zachary's hair as he unfastened the buttons at the front of her gown and she felt the warmth of his lips against the bare swell of her breast.

She cried out achingly as his lips parted and he took the aroused and aching tip of that breast into the heat of his mouth, before suckling, gently at first, and then more deeply, hungrily. She arched up into him, instinctively seeking, wanting more, receiving more as Zachary's hand cupped beneath her other breast and he began to roll and squeeze the second nipple to the same arousing rhythm.

The sensations were overwhelming. An all-consuming heat and a glorious pleasure that radiated out from her breasts and coursed through the rest of her body, her nipples both hard and aching, the folds between her thighs swelling and moistening, the muscles deep inside her contracting and squeezing hungrily.

And it was a selfish need.

'Zachary?' She breathed weakly as she felt his hand trailing along her calf, pushing up her gown to above her knees and then higher still, until she felt the warm brush of air against those heated and swollen folds between her thighs.

'Allow me to pleasure you again, Georgianna,' he groaned, his breath a hot caress against the dampness of her nipple. 'Grant me that, at least.'

'But what of your own pleasure?' She knew very little about men, but she knew enough to know that Zachary's erection was both hard and demanding as it pressed, pulsed, against her hip.

'I am happy in the knowledge that I please you, Georgianna.'

'No.'

'I am not pleasing you?' Zachary pulled back slightly, his expression one of concern. 'Did I hurt you? Was I too rough with you just now?'

Delicate colour warmed her cheeks. 'I did not say that.'

'Then what?'

'Zachary…' Her gaze could no longer meet his, aware as she was of the fact that the top of her gown still gaped open, revealing the fullness of her breasts. The bare fullness of her breasts. 'Pleasure is surely to be given as well as received?'

'Yes.'

Georgianna moistened stiff lips. 'Then of course I should like to give you pleasure, too. If you will teach me, show me, what pleases you,' she added uncomfortably, knowing that she was far less experienced, make that lacking in experience at all, than all those other women Zachary was reputed to have made love with.

Zachary looked down at her searchingly. It had been his experience in the past that there was no *of course* about it, when it came to a man's pleasure during lovemaking. Whores were one thing and would do what they were asked for with the giving of coin. Wives, he had heard, preferred the act to be without embellishment and over with as quickly as was possible for the begetting of an heir. Other women in society, those married women who took a lover once the heir and spare had been provided, usually considered it enough that they were giving carte blanche with their body and, as such, had no interest in what she might do to please the man in her bed.

Obviously Georgianna was different from all those other women, being neither whore, nor wife, nor a married woman in society looking for a lover. As he could only assume she also meant she wanted him to show her, to teach her, what best pleased him in particular, rather than...

No, he refused to think of Georgianna's relationship with Rousseau now. He would not allow anything or anyone else to intrude upon their stolen time together. 'Are you sure you wish to pleasure me, Georgianna?' he prompted huskily.

She flickered a glance up at him before looking down again.

'It seems only fair I should do so, after—after you gave to me so unselfishly when—when we were last together.' The colour flooded her cheeks once again.

'That did not answer my question.'

Because Georgianna had no idea how to answer his question! She knew nothing of lovemaking, be it man or woman. She only knew, from these times with Zachary, that she could not be a selfish lover, that she wished to please Zachary as he had pleased her. As her own achingly aroused body said she now must.

'What would you be willing to do to give me pleasure, Georgianna?' he prompted huskily at her silence.

'Whatever you wished me to do.'

'Anything?'

She swallowed at the intensity of his silver gaze fixed unblinkingly on her blushing face. 'I believe so, yes.'

He smiled ruefully. 'Words are easily spoken, Georgianna.'

'Then I shall answer in deeds rather than words.' She sat up before sliding down to the base of the chaise to swing her feet on to the floor, before standing up and turning to face Zachary.

His eyes widened in surprise as she put her hands on his shoulders and pushed him down on to his back on the chaise before sitting beside him; obviously Hawksmere was not a man used to a woman taking charge in the bedchamber. Or in this case, the blue salon of his London home.

Georgianna was not a woman used to taking charge in lovemaking, either, but in this case it seemed completely desirable.

Besides, she had not spent all of her time in the kitchen, or the storeroom, at Helene Rousseau's tavern. She had occasionally ventured out to help serve behind the bar if they were especially busy; some of the surprising acts she had witnessed between the male and female customers when she did so had made her blush to the roots of her hair. There had been one act in particular that the gentlemen had seemed to enjoy very much.

If Georgianna only had the courage to now put into practise all that she had witnessed.

'I believe I should like to kiss you as you once kissed me.' She licked her lips in anticipation.

'Georgianna?'

She glanced up enquiringly from where she had already unfastened the buttons on Zachary's pantaloons and was now in the process of untying his drawers. The bulge beneath the linen, stretching and tightening that material, was making that task more difficult than it ought to be and was certainly causing a lack of sexual prowess on her part.

'What are you doing?' He looked pained as she at last managed to unfasten his drawers and reached inside to withdraw the pulsing and throbbing hard length beneath.

Georgianna's fingers stilled as she looked down at him uncertainly. 'You do not like it?'

'Oh, I most assuredly do like it, Georgianna!' he breathed shakily. 'I am just— Are you sure you wish— Do you know what you are doing?'

Colour burned her cheeks. 'I am sure I shall not be as experienced as some of your other ladies, but…'

'That is not at all what I meant,' he grated from between gritted teeth, his fingers having curled about the slenderness of her wrists to halt her movements. 'And I have said there will be no talk between the two of us of any others. I merely wanted to know if you are sure this is what you want. What you would enjoy.'

She glanced down at the thick length of his arousal as she slowly curled her fingers about it, the skin feeling surprisingly soft as velvet.

Georgianna swiped her tongue over her lips. 'It

most certainly appears to be what a certain part of you wants,' she murmured with satisfaction at Zachary's obvious response to her touch.

Zachary could not deny that. Had no desire to deny it. Indeed, just seconds ago he had feared he might spill at the first touch of the softness of Georgianna's fingers closing about him.

He had managed to hold, thank goodness, but he could not deny that his instinct was still to thrust into those encircling fingers, to bid her grip him tighter, stroke him faster, harder, as they worked together towards his release.

'I merely want you to be sure—' Zachary broke off with a strangled groan of pleasure as Georgianna lowered her head, her long hair falling in a soft caress against his thighs as she licked the silken tip. A long and rasping lick that caused him to arch up off the chaise.

'You like that.' She repeated that slow and agonisingly pleasurable rasp.

Liked it? Zachary had thought of this woman constantly this past two weeks, had imagined time and time again making love to her again, pleasuring her again. And in none of those imaginings had he thought of Georgianna pleasuring him, as she was now doing with each slow and delicious swipe of her tongue, the pleasure so intense he could already feel the start of his climax in the tightening, drawing up of his balls.

His gaze dropped to her bared breasts visible through the silky curtain of her hair as they jutted free of her unfastened gown as she bent over him. He wanted to hold them. To caress and squeeze them.

As he came and came!

'Come up here, Georgia,' he groaned urgently even as he lifted her up and over him so that she now had a leg either side of his thighs on the chaise. He pushed her dress up to her hips before lowering her down on top of him, not penetrating her, but arching into her in a slow rhythm as her moist and heated folds rubbed caressingly along the sensitised length of his erection.

'Zachary.'

'Do not worry I shall put you at risk, Georgianna,' he assured gruffly, eyes feeling hot and fevered. 'I merely wish to feel your heat upon me. Oh, that feels so damned good!' The hardness of his length moved easily against the slickness of her juices. 'So, so good!' He reached up to cup and squeeze her breasts, to caress and flick his fingernails against those jutting and sensitive nipples.

Georgianna clutched on to Zachary's chest for support, her head feeling dizzy with her own pleasure as Zachary continued to arch and thrust beneath her, even as he caressed and pinched her engorged and sensitive nipples to the exact same rhythm as the hard length of his erection rubbed against her folds and that sensitive nubbin above.

'Harder, Georgia. Faster. Harder again,' he urged, his eyes glittering, a flush to the hardness of his cheeks. 'Come with me, Georgia. Now!' he urged fiercely, sculptured lips parted as his hips surged up in the most powerful thrust of all.

Georgianna had no time to think about what he meant by that as her own pleasure ripped through and over her as the heated jets of Zachary's release pounded against her own sensitive nubbin, prolonging that pleasure until she screamed his name as he now hoarsely shouted hers.

Chapter Twelve

'Georgia?' she questioned Zachary as she lay on the chaise in his arms in the aftermath of their love-making. She felt physically sated and still inwardly moved at the way in which Zachary had kissed that unsightly scar upon her chest.

'You do not like it?' He played absently with the long strands of her loosened ebony hair as he turned to look at her.

No one had ever shortened her name in quite that way before now. Jeffrey often called her Georgie when they were alone together, in remembrance of their time together in the nursery. Her father, when he was alive, had occasionally addressed her affectionately as Anna, which had been her mother's name. But she could not recall her name ever being shortened to Georgia before now, no.

Before Zachary.

And she did like it. Coming from this man, she

found she liked that familiarity. A lot. That she liked, even loved, Zachary a lot, too.

She had no idea when the liking, the admiration, for the strong and determined man that he was, had happened, let alone whether or not she loved all of him. Or how it could possibly have happened, if that was the case.

Zachary had more or less kidnapped her, then kept her a prisoner in his home.

He had ridiculed and insulted her.

And then he had made love to her.

Which was when the liking had begun, Georgianna now realised.

Because when Zachary made love to her he forgot to insult and ridicule her. To dislike her. Most of all, he was a generous and fulfilling lover. Oh, that first time might have begun as a punishment for her, for daring to elope with another man when she was betrothed to him. But Zachary's generosity of nature, his own physical enjoyment of her, had quickly overcome that emotion.

And today, despite knowing of that disfiguring scar, he truly had made love to her, had kissed and caressed that scar as if it were something to admire rather than be disgusted by.

As Georgianna had made love to him?

She shied away from so much as thinking of that emotion in connection to Zachary Black, the Duke of Hawksmere—the very same man whom she had once shied away from marrying—knowing that to love him would lead to even more heartbreak than had her ill-fated and humiliating elopement with André Rousseau.

'I do not dislike it,' she answered Zachary non-committally, only to look up at him quizzically as he began to chuckle softly. 'What is it?'

'I laugh because, as usual, your thoughts and emotions remain a mystery to me, Georgia.' He gazed down at her indulgently.

She frowned her puzzlement. 'I do not mean them to be.'

'Any more than I believe just now to have been my finest hour.' He had sobered slightly, a teasing smile now curving those sculptured lips.

'I do not understand?' Everything had seemed more than satisfactory to Georgianna. Very much so. 'Did I do something wrong?' she prompted anxiously.

'Lord, no.' He groaned his reassurance. 'If you had done anything more right, then I believe I might now be lying here dead from a heart attack.'

She blushed at his effusive praise for her lovemaking. 'Then I still do not understand.'

Zachary could see that she really had no idea what he was talking about. Had Rousseau been such a uninterested and unsatisfactory lover that even Zachary's hasty lovemaking just now was preferable? Hasty, because his thoughts of Georgianna these past two weeks had caused him to hope, to anticipate, the worshipping of every inch of her delectable and responsive body. To kiss and caress her. To give her pleasure again and again.

Instead Georgianna had taken control of the situation, of him, and made love to him in a way that had surpassed all and any of his fantasies of being with her again.

He grimaced. 'We might have expected our love-making to last for longer than a few minutes,' he explained gruffly. 'I had expected my own control to last for longer than a few minutes,' he added ruefully. 'I wanted it to be enjoyable for you, too.'

'How could you ever imagine it was not enjoyable for me, too, when I cried out my pleasure?' Her cheeks blushed a becoming rose.

'Because I know it could have been better.' He caressed that blush upon her cheeks. 'I could have been better. Instead, I was as out of control as a callow youth being touched by a woman for the first time.' Indeed, he had been lost the moment he had felt the soft fullness of Georgianna's lips upon him, and the soft rasp of her tongue as she licked and tasted him; at that moment he'd had no more control than the night he had lost his virginity fifteen years ago.

'What was your finest hour?' Georgianna now prompted almost warily.

Zachary knew she was questioning him about his previous physical experiences. Unnecessarily, as it happened, because enjoyable as those past encounters might have been, none of them had affected him in the way that making love to and with Georgianna did. And that was without his having as yet fully made love to her, because he had yet to bury himself in the heat and lushness of her.

Even this, their closeness now as they cuddled in

each other's arms in the aftermath of that lovemaking, was an unusual occurrence for Zachary. Usually he could not vacate a woman's bed quickly enough once the deed was done.

This closeness with Georgianna was one he cherished rather than wished to avoid.

At the same time he knew that he must now put an end to that closeness. That he had yet to tell Georgianna of his encounter with Rousseau in Paris.

And he had no idea how she would react, what she would say, once she knew her previous lover was now dead.

Admittedly, Rousseau had treated her abominably, had seduced her, deceived her, betrayed her, before believing he had killed her.

But love, the emotions of a woman's heart, were not things Zachary was familiar with, either. Despite all that Rousseau had done to her, Georgianna might still feel some vestige of that emotion for the other man. Knowing that Zachary had been instrumental in his demise might shatter this unique, and highly enjoyable, time between the two of them.

Did he want to risk that, put an end to this time of harmony between the two of them, for the sake of honesty?

No.

But if he chose not to, then how could he ever reassure Georgianna that she no longer had anything to fear from Rousseau? Or expect Georgianna's forgiveness, when she eventually learnt, as she surely must, that he had kept this information from her and for such selfish reasons?

No, he could not keep Rousseau's death to himself. He knew he must share that news with Georgianna.

Even at the risk of bringing an end to the fragile intimacy that now existed between the two of them.

Reluctantly he pulled his arms from around her, removing his handkerchief from his pocket and gently mopping up the worst of the evidence of their love-making, before standing up to turn away and refasten his clothing. He ran agitated hands through the tousled length of his hair as he contemplated how to begin this next conversation.

'Zachary?' Georgianna eyed him uncertainly as she slowly sat up, continuing to look at him even as she absently refastened the buttons on the front of her gown. Her hair was beyond repair at this moment, the pins scattered about the floor from when Zachary had released it earlier.

The lover of just moments ago was gone. Zachary's expression was guarded when he turned back to face her and flatly announced. 'Georgianna, there is no other way for me to tell you this. My dear, Rousseau is dead.'

She felt the colour leach from her cheeks even as she swayed slightly where she sat, unable to believe, to process the enormity of what Zachary was saying to her.

André was dead?

How was such a thing even possible?

André was still a young man, aged only seven and twenty, and in the best of health when she had last seen him just weeks ago, so his death could not possibly have been through natural causes.

Her gaze sharpened on Zachary, his own eyes, as he met her horrified gaze, a pale and glittering silver in his harshly forbidding face. 'You killed him.' It was not a question, but a statement.

Zachary's expression was grim. 'Unfortunately I did not have that particular honour.'

'But you were responsible for ordering his death?' She could see the answer to that accusation in the tightening of Zachary's jaw and the arrogant challenge now in those eyes, as he looked down at her through narrowed lids.

Zachary had instructed André should be killed.

The question was, why had he done so?

Because the other man had been shown to be Napoleon's spy and in part responsible for the Corsican's escape from Elba?

Or because of a reason more personal to Zachary, in that the other man had taken something of his, had taken Georgianna, when he eloped with her?

She somehow doubted very much it had anything to do with the other man hurting and having attempted to kill Georgianna after they had arrived in France.

The first of those reasons, at least, would be honourable. To have someone killed out of a sense of personal vengeance would not.

She looked up at Zachary searchingly, but could read nothing from the harshness of his expression, could only see the challenge in the set of his shoulders beneath his superfine and his stance: legs slightly parted as he stood on booted feet, his hands clasped together behind the broadness of his back.

Leaving Georgianna in absolutely no doubt that whatever his reason for having André dispatched, Zachary did not feel a moment's remorse over it.

And nor should Georgianna.

But, no matter how cruel and deceitful as André had been, murderously so, and despite the freedom from future fear his death now gave her, Georgianna still could not find cause for celebration. Not for André's demise, nor the fact that Zachary was tacitly admitting to being the one responsible for ordering that death, if not the reason for it.

His mouth twisted derisively now. 'I had expected a happier response from you upon hearing this news?' he drawled mockingly.

Georgianna drew in a ragged breath before speaking. 'Why did you wait until now to tell me?'

'Sorry?' Zachary frowned darkly at the question.

Georgianna lifted her shoulders. 'Why did you wait, until after we had made love, to tell me?'

'It was not a conscious decision.'

'Are you sure of that?' she scorned. 'Could it be that the delay was because you knew I would not wish, or have the inclination, to make love with you once I knew?' she guessed shrewdly.

He gave a shake of his head. 'Georgianna—'

'Why did you do it, Zachary?' Georgianna pushed determinedly, deciding she could not think of Zachary's duplicity now. That she would think of it later. Much later.

'I do not recall admitting that I am the one responsible for Rousseau's death.' He arched arrogant dark brows over those now arctic-grey eyes.

No, he had not. And yet, still, Georgianna knew instinctively that he was. That the Zachary standing before her now, every inch one of the cold and remote Dangerous Dukes, was more than capable of killing if called upon to do so. That he had no doubt killed many men during his years as an agent for the Crown. And lived with the consequences of those deaths without regret or remorse.

But having André Rousseau killed was different to those other deaths. For one thing, they were not yet again at war with Napoleon. And no matter how much Zachary might have assured himself it was necessary to have André killed, it could not change the fact that he had also despised the other man on a very personal level. To the point of seeking out the other man and personally seeing to his demise?

Whatever Zachary's reasons for having dispatched André, Georgianna found she was not as capable as he of placing the events of her life into neatly labelled boxes. She needed time, and solitude, in which to come to terms with what she knew was Zachary's involvement in André's death. 'Were you there when he died?' She looked at Zachary searchingly.

His jaw was tightly clenched. 'Yes. Damn it, Georgianna, the man was a spy against England.'

'And I remind you we are no longer at war with France!'

'We very soon will be again.' A nerve pulsed in that tightly clenched jaw. 'Have you forgotten that just last night you asked that I do all that I can to prevent Jeffrey from becoming embroiled in that war?'

'Do not turn this conversation around on me in that way, Zachary,' she warned through clenched jaw as she stood up abruptly before collecting up her bonnet and gloves. Zachary's words confirmed that at least part of his reasoning for having André killed was because the other man had spied upon England.

Selfishly, perhaps, had she secretly wished that it might have been out of defence of her? She might, with time, have forgiven that. Because it might also have meant that Zachary had perhaps come to care for her as she cared for him.

But the thought that Zachary could have ruthlessly ordered the other man be killed, because of a personal slight against himself, as much as because he was considered to be an enemy of England, was a side of Zachary, that cold and dispassionate side, from which she had run just eleven short months ago.

And from which she must run away again now.

'Where are you going?' Zachary demanded as he watched Georgianna walk to the door of the salon without saying so much as another word to him, her hair a bewitching dark waterfall of curls down the slenderness of her defensively straight spine.

He had half expected this might be Georgianna's

reaction to the news of Rousseau's death. Expected it, but hoped that it would not be so.

Because, he had also hoped, prayed, that she had no softer feelings left inside her for the other man after the abominable way he had treated her. For having attempted to kill her.

Georgianna's reaction now to the news of Rousseau's death, and her obvious disgust with Zachary for what she believed to have been his part in it, now showed him how wrong he had been to harbour even the smallest hope in that regard.

Stupidly, naïvely, because of the warmth of her responses to him earlier, Zachary had harboured another hope, a dream, that all of her softer feelings were now reserved for him.

He had been wrong not to have told her of Rousseau's death immediately—he accepted that now. But he had wanted to hold her in his arms once more at least before he did so, and once he held her in his arms, he'd had no thought for anything else!

An omission for which Georgianna obviously now despised him, as much as she was so obviously distressed at Rousseau's death. She was disgusted, too, with Zachary for what she perceived to be his part in that death.

Because, despite his intentions, he really could not claim to be the one who had delivered the death blow to Rousseau.

Oh, he and Wolfingham had faultlessly carried out their plan for Wolfingham to engage Rousseau and his cohorts when they eventually emerged from his sister's tavern in the early hours of the morning. They had selected Wolfingham because he was unknown to Rousseau, as Zachary was not.

His friend had been the one to weave drunkenly past the inn at the exact moment the group emerged, deliberately knocking into one of them without apology and instantly receiving an aggressively challenging response. At which point Wolfingham had delivered the first punch.

In the mêlée and confusion that followed, Zachary was supposed to emerge from his own shadowed hiding place, to separate Rousseau from his cohorts, before taking him somewhere far quieter than the street, so that the other man might learn exactly the reason he was about to die.

All had gone according to that plan until Rousseau had pulled a gun from within his coat, his obvious intention to dispatch Wolfingham. At which point Wolfingham had no choice but to defend himself. There had been a shot fired as Zachary landed several blows on the other fellows in his efforts to reach his friend's side, but within seconds of the gun being fired, it seemed, the majority of the men had scattered, instantly becoming lost to various parts of the city and leaving behind the two men who lay still upon the ground, their life's blood glistening on the cobbles beneath them.

Rousseau and Wolfingham.

Zachary's own heart had ceased beating in his chest as he rushed to his friend's side and had only started again once he had roused Wolfingham and had satisfied himself that his friend's gunshot wound to the shoulder was nasty, but thankfully did not appear to be life-threatening.

Rousseau had been less fortunate, blood pumping from the artery in his slit throat, his eyes already starting to take on that opaque appearance of one about to die. Nevertheless, he had managed to focus enough to recognise Zachary, a mocking smile curving his lips. 'Hawksmere. I should have known. You are too late, I am afraid—your betrothed is dead,' he managed to taunt gruffly.

Zachary's breath left him in a hiss. 'Is she?' he taunted back angrily. 'I assure you that when I last saw Georgianna, just days ago, she still breathed, and walked, and talked. Mainly she talked of how much she hates you for your failed effort to kill her in a forest outside this very city.'

Surprised blond brows rose above those rapidly glazing blue eyes. 'She still lives?' he croaked, the blood still pumping from his slit throat.

'Oh, yes, despite your intentions for it to be otherwise, Georgianna most assuredly still lives,' Zachary had replied grimly. 'And loves.

'And hates. She also told us a pretty tale about your own involvement with the Corsican's recent departure from Elba.'

The other man gave a gurgling laugh as some of the blood gathered in the back of his throat. 'Georgianna ever saw herself as the heroine.'

'She is a heroine, you bast—'

'*Vive Napoleon,*' Rousseau murmured with his last

breath, those blue eyes wide as he stared lifelessly up into the darkness of the starlit sky above.

Zachary had left him where he lay in his own blood as he hurried back to Wolfingham's side, putting a supporting arm about his friend as they made good their own escape. The two of them hid at the dockside until it was time for them to board their ship and set sail back to England that same night.

The satisfaction of being able to tell Rousseau, before he died, that Georgianna still lived became a hollow victory as Zachary now saw the way Georgianna looked across the room at him with emotionless eyes.

'I am leaving, of course,' she answered his earlier question flatly. 'I presume informing me of André's death was the reason you wished to speak with me today?' She arched cool brows.

There was such a coolness about her, a distance, that frustrated Zachary intensely. Had he been wrong, misread the situation completely, and Georgianna did indeed still have feelings for the man who had once been her lover?

'You should know I have absolutely no regrets concerning Rousseau's death,' he assured through gritted teeth. Wolfingham had no cause for regrets in the matter, either, had merely been defending himself when Rousseau met his end. If Rousseau had not died, then Wolfingham assuredly would have, and that was totally unacceptable to Zachary. 'A friend of mine was also grievously wounded that night.'

Georgianna frowned slightly. 'Wolfingham?'

'Yes.'

'But he lives still?'

'No thanks to your friend Rousseau.'

'He was never my friend.' Her eyes glittered, with the fierceness of her anger as well as unshed tears. 'I must go.'

'Georgianna!'

She gave a fierce shake of her head. 'We have nothing left to talk about, Hawksmere.'

Addressing him as Hawksmere was indication enough of how Georgianna now felt towards him, the cold dismissal in her tone only adding to that obvious disdain.

And pride, though a cold bedfellow, was preferable to Zachary having his further pleas for her understanding rejected out of hand. 'I will see you again this evening, when I accompany you and Jeffrey to Lady Colchester's musical soirée.'

Georgianna gave a shake of her head. 'I am not sure I feel well enough to attend.'

'You most certainly will attend, Georgianna.' Zachary grated harshly. 'Not only will you attend, but you will also give every appearance of enjoyment in the enterprise. In appearing at my side, along with Jeffrey, as my two wards.'

She raised her chin in challenge. 'I am sure you know me well enough by now, Hawksmere, to know that I shall not be bullied into doing anything I do not wish to do, by you or anyone else.'

His jaw tightened, eyes glittering dangerously. 'Nevertheless, it was planned for this evening to be your first appearance back into society, following your period of mourning. As such, as your guardian, I must insist that you accompany Jeffrey and me.'

She looked across at him searchingly, knowing by the coldness in Zachary's eyes, the bleakness of his expression and the nerve pulsing in the tightness of his jaw, that he meant exactly what he said. Nor could she deny the importance of her appearance at Lady Colchester's tonight, following what many in society believed to have been the ending of her engagement to Hawksmere and her term of mourning her father. 'We shall see,' she finally answered noncommittally.

This young woman would surely be the death of him, Zachary acknowledged impatiently. Either that, or he might go quietly and completely insane.

How could it be that just a few moments ago the two of them had been so enjoyably making love together, as close as any two people could be—certainly as close as Zachary had been to any woman—and now they were as distant as they had been ten months ago? More so, for then Zachary had not really known what it was to be close to Georgianna, had never so much as even spoken to her; now he knew exactly what, and who, he would be losing when she walked out of his life for a second time.

The woman he had come to admire above all others.

Georgianna.

Georgia.

Chapter Thirteen

'I do believe you are alarming our poor hostess with the darkness of your scowls, Zachary,' an amused voice drawled beside him as Zachary stood near one of the windows in Lady Colchester's music room during a break in the entertainments.

His eyes widened as he turned to look at Wolfingham. 'Should you be out and about when you are still recovering from a bullet wound to your shoulder?'

'It would look decidedly odd if I were absent from society for any length of time. Besides which, needs must, I am afraid.' Wolfingham gave a grimace.

'Oh?'

His friend nodded abruptly. 'I do not suppose you have seen anything of my little brother this evening?'

Zachary's brows rose. 'Should I have done?' As far as he was aware, young Lord Anthony Hunter had been fortunate enough not to have put in even a nominal appearance at Lady Colchester's musical soirée.

Not unless he had arrived and left before Zachary and his party arrived.

'Obviously not,' Wolfingham uttered disgustedly.

'Is there a problem?'

'If there is, then it is for me to deal with,' his friend dismissed briskly. 'What were you scowling at so intently just now?' Wolfingham glanced across the room in the direction Zachary had been scowling earlier. 'Who is the honeypot attracting all the bees?'

Zachary did not at all appreciate hearing Georgianna described as a honeypot. Even if that was exactly what she had been from the moment they arrived at Lady Colchester's home several hours ago.

Georgianna was resplendent in a gown of purple silk, a strip of lace styled discreetly across the tops of her breasts, and so concealing that damning scar, with a matching purple feather adorning the darkness of her curls.

They had barely had time to greet their hostess before the first of the handsome young bucks began to flock about them. Most of them acquaintances of her brother, Jeffrey, eager to be re-introduced to his beautiful sister. But there had been some older gentlemen, too. Single gentlemen, of Zachary's own age and older, attracted no doubt by the air of untouchable remoteness with which Georgianna appeared to have steeled herself in order to endure appearing at this evening's entertainment.

A remoteness, which had thawed throughout the evening until, as now, she appeared to be enjoying the attentions of so many handsome gentlemen. The wariness had slowly faded from her gaze, a becoming blush now adorning her cheeks, and those two familiar dimples having appeared in those same cheeks when she smiled, at what were no doubt flattering and flirtatious comments being made to and about her.

And for the whole of this time Zachary had wished for nothing more than to dismiss the attentions of every single one of those handsome and fawning gentlemen, before whisking Georgianna away somewhere they could be private together.

So, yes, Wolfingham's description of his having been scowling minutes ago—enough so as to have warned off the approach of all and any who were not closely acquainted with him, who were very few— was no doubt an accurate one.

'My ward, Lady Georgianna Lancaster,' he now supplied.

Wolfingham continued to look at Georgianna consideringly. 'This is the same young woman to whom you were so briefly betrothed last year?'

'Yes.'

The other man's brows rose. 'She appears to be much changed from a year ago.'

Zachary's mouth tightened at the reasons for those changes, in both Georgianna's appearance and demeanour. 'She is, yes.'

Wolfingham turned to look at him through narrowed lids. 'I was not just referring to the more obvious changes in her appearance.'

A nerve pulsed in Zachary's jaw, knowing that his friend was able to detect the air of remoteness, and the sophistication, which had been so lacking in Georgianna just a year ago. 'No.'

'Zachary.'

'I would prefer not to discuss my ward any further,' he warned harshly. 'Even with you.'

Wolfingham continued to study him for several long seconds before nodding slowly. 'If you will just answer one more question?'

Zachary scowled his irritation. 'Which is?'

'Does she know that Rousseau is dead?'

'Yes, she knows.' Zachary did not attempt to pretend to misunderstand Wolfingham, knew that his friend had guessed, correctly, that Georgianna Lancaster was the woman whom Rousseau had treated so despicably. The reason the other man had to die.

'You like her?' Wolfingham guessed astutely.

Zachary's jaw clenched at the understatement. 'I do.'

'Enough to consider renewing your betrothal?'

His jaw clenched. 'There is absolutely no chance of that ever happening.'

'None?'

The nerve in his jaw pulsed even more rapidly. 'None whatsoever.'

'Time is passing, Zachary, and the condition in your father's will that states you must marry and produce an heir before your thirty-fifth birthday remains just as pressing,' Wolfingham reminded softly.

'And Georgianna is the last woman who would ever accept a—another—marriage proposal from me.' Zachary grimaced. 'Indeed, I believe Georgianna despises me more now than she did a year ago.'

Wolfingham sighed heavily. 'Life can be complicated at times, can it not?'

'Very,' Zachary grated.

His friend nodded. 'If you will excuse me, I believe I must continue to search for my own complication.'

Zachary frowned. 'Is Anthony in trouble?'

'Only with me,' Wolfingham assured darkly.

'If you should need any assistance in the matter...'

Wolfingham nodded distractedly. 'For the moment just be grateful you do not have a sibling for whom you are guardian.'

Zachary had very much regretted not having siblings when he was very young, but since meeting his four close friends at school he had not felt that same need, those four gentlemen more than filling that gap in his life. As they had all been there for him when he'd lost his parents when he was a child.

As they all remained there for each other as adults. 'Anthony is not in any danger?' He studied Wolfingham closely.

His friend's mouth thinned. 'Again, only from me. No doubt you have a similar headache, since becoming guardian to the two Lancaster siblings?'

Zachary glanced across at Georgianna once again, eyes glittering as he saw her batting her fan playfully in order to ward off the attentions of one of her more ardent suitors. 'If you will excuse me.' He didn't wait for his friend to reply before marching purposefully across the length of Lady Colchester's music room.

'I believe you are crowding the lady, Adams!' He glared down the length of his nose at the younger man.

Georgianna raised her open fan to hide her surprise as Hawksmere took up a protective stance at her side, his expression grimly forbidding as he glared at the gentlemen surrounding her.

Not that she did not appreciate Zachary having joined her; the gentlemen were becoming more and more persistent in their attentions, several of them currently vying for the honour of dancing the first set with her at the Countess of Evesham's ball tomorrow evening. A ball Georgianna was not sure she wished to attend any more than she had wished to attend this soirée.

This evening had been every bit the ordeal Georgianna had thought it might be.

Being with Hawksmere again had proved to be every bit of the ordeal she had imagined it might be!

It seemed incredible to her that she and Hawksmere had allowed themselves more than once to become embroiled in a situation of deep intimacy. An intensity of intimacy that made her blush with embarrassment every time she so much as thought about it.

And, to her shame, she had been unable to stop herself from thinking about it ever since she and Hawksmere had parted earlier today. Of how he had felt beneath the touch of her hands and lips. How he had tasted.

It had not helped that Zachary had looked, and continued to look, every inch the arrogantly handsome Duke of Hawksmere when he arrived at Malvern House earlier this evening. His muscled physique was shown to advantage in his black evening clothes and snowy white linen, the darkness of his hair arranged in tousled disarray as it curled over his ears and nape and about the sculptured perfection of his face.

Georgianna's heart had skipped several beats when she'd first gazed at him earlier this evening, a reaction she'd been quick to hide as she'd turned to thank her brother as he held out his arm to her in readiness for their departure.

She had deliberately seated herself beside Jeffrey in Hawksmere's carriage, very aware of, and avoiding meeting, the steadiness of Hawksmere's gaze as he sat directly across from her. She had kept her face averted as she looked out the window beside her, pretending an interest in the busy London evening streets.

Only to then find herself accompanied protectively by Jeffrey on one side and Hawksmere on the other, as they had entered Lady Colchester's London home together.

A closeness that had allowed her to feel the warmth emanating from Hawksmere's body through the silk of her gown, to smell his familiar smell of sandalwood and citrus, along with expensive cigars and just a hint of brandy upon his breath.

The latter in evidence, perhaps, that Hawksmere had felt in need of some restorative himself, in order to be able to get through the evening ahead?

Somehow Georgianna doubted that Hawksmere had ever needed a restorative, of any kind, to get through anything.

Nevertheless, Georgianna had felt grateful that the interest and conversation of Jeffrey's friends had separated her from Hawksmere, both before and during this break in the entertainments. His close proximity as they had sat together listening to several of the young ladies perform on their various musical instruments, had disturbed Georgianna on a level she had found distinctly uncomfortable. She still had no idea how she felt about Hawksmere's involvement with André's premature death.

That she no longer had anything to fear, in regard to André ever finding her again, was a relief beyond measure. Nor, having had time to adjust to André's demise, did she find she felt the least regret. How could she regret it, when she had lived in fear of discovery by him these past months? No, it was Hawksmere's involvement in the other man's death which still unsettled her.

Frightened her?

No, she was not frightened by the thought of such violence. She was sure that most men, and women, were capable of committing murder if pushed to the extreme. That she had been more than capable, given the weapon to do so, of killing André herself that night in the woods outside Paris, when he had tried to end her life.

But if she had succeeded in killing André, then it would have been an act of desperation on her part, of self-survival, rather than the cold-blooded murder she suspected his death to have been.

'If you gentlemen will excuse us?' Zachary's narrowed gaze precluded there being any objections to his announcement as he took a firm hold of Georgianna's arm to walk purposefully across to the other side of the room, well out of earshot of Lady Colchester's other guests. A frown darkened his brow as he now looked down at Georgianna through narrowed lids.

'You are hurting my arm, Hawksmere.' She gazed up at him steadily, pointedly, while all the time keeping a smile of politeness upon her lips for the benefit of their audience. The curious glances in their direction by the ladies present were surreptitious, but there nonetheless. No doubt due to the fact that the two of them had once been betrothed to be married. To each other.

Zachary lessened his grip, but refused to release her completely, at the same time as his own expression remained one of bland politeness. No doubt also for the benefit of their audience. 'I realise I am not your favourite person, Georgianna, but I do not think that ignoring me is in any way going to help quell the gossip, as this evening was predisposed to do, regarding our past broken betrothal,' he muttered impatiently.

Zachary believed he was not her favourite person?

Georgianna's feelings in regard to Hawksmere were now in such confusion that she no longer had any idea what she felt towards him. Despite the fact that he only had to touch her, it seemed, for her to melt into his arms.

Surely her reaction could be termed as being merely a physical response to a handsome and desirable gentleman?

Merely?

Her responses to Zachary were above and beyond anything Georgianna had ever experienced in her life before him. Not even that imagined love for André had filled her with such longings, such desires, as she felt when Zachary took her in his arms and kissed and caressed her.

Longings, and a desire, she had no right to feel for a man who would never be—could never be anything more to her than her reluctant guardian. And even that tenuous connection would very soon cease to exist.

Her chin rose defensively now. 'Is it not enough that I am here, as you instructed me to be? I do not recall your having said I had to enjoy or like it?' she added pointedly.

Zachary drew in an impatient breath. 'You appeared to be enjoying the attentions of those other gentlemen just a few minutes ago.'

Georgianna arched a brow. 'Was that not what I was supposed to do?'

As far as Zachary was concerned? No, it was not. In fact, he found he did not enjoy having any other gentleman within ten feet of Georgianna.

His jaw tightened. 'I do not think it a particularly good idea for you to encourage a repeat of society's past belief in your reputation as being something of a flirt.'

Her eyes widened with indignation. 'You— I— You are insulting, sir!'

Deliberately so, Zachary acknowledged heavily. And knowing he was not endearing himself to Georgianna in the slightest by acting the part of the jealous lover.

Even if he knew that's exactly how he felt.

He had hated every moment of watching Georgianna being flattered and admired by those other gentlemen this evening. Had wanted nothing more than to sweep her up in his arms and carry her off to a place no other man could look at her, let alone flatter and charm her into possibly falling in love with him.

Quite what Zachary was going to do about the heat of his own emotions in regard to Georgianna he had no idea, when she now gave every impression of disliking him intensely.

Was he, as her guardian, to be forced to stand silently by whilst some other man charmed and flattered her into falling in love with him?

Would he then have to welcome that suitor into his own home, when that gentleman came to ask his permission for seeking Georgianna's hand in marriage?

Impossible.

Just the thought of it was enough to cause Zachary's hand to clench into a fist at his side. He would not, could not, allow it. 'Are you ready to leave this insipid entertainment?' he prompted harshly.

Violet-coloured eyes widened in the pallor of

Georgianna's face. 'If you have somewhere else you wish to go, then I am sure Jeffrey is more than capable of acting as my chaperon for the rest of the evening.'

'The only somewhere else I wish us both to go is far away from here!' Zachary bit out harshly, only to draw in a long and calming breath as Georgianna's face became even paler at his vehemence. 'I believe we need to talk further, Georgianna,' he added softly.

Her brows rose. 'About what, exactly?'

'In private.' A nerve pulse in his tightly clenched jaw. If he did not find himself alone with Georgianna in the next few minutes then he was afraid he was going to do something that would cause them both embarrassment. Not that he cared on his own behalf, but Georgianna was likely to be less forgiving if he caused a scene on her very first evening back into society.

And a Georgianna who felt angry and resentful towards him was not what he wished for at all.

Georgianna eyed Zachary warily, not sure that she wished to be anywhere private with him, when he was in his current mood of unpredictability. Not that he had ever been in the least predictable to her, but there was such an air of tension about him this evening she felt even more wary of him than she had in the past.

'To what purpose?' she persisted guardedly.

A nerve pulsed in his throat. 'Does it matter?'

'Yes, of course it matters,' Georgianna answered irritably. 'As you have already pointed out, this is my first venture back into society, and my leaving with you now, halfway through the entertainments, would seem… It would look improper,' she concluded lamely.

It was possible to hear Hawksmere's teeth grinding together. 'Then let it.'

Georgianna's eyes widened in alarm. 'Can it be that you are foxed, Hawksmere? I seem to recall I thought I could smell brandy upon your breath when you arrived at Malvern House earlier this evening.'

'I am most assuredly not foxed, nor do I have any intentions of being so,' he bit out harshly. 'I am merely expressing a wish for the two of us to leave this hellish torture and go somewhere where we might talk privately together.'

Her brows rose. 'I do not recall your having been so eager, or particularly interested, in anything I had to say to you in the past.' She felt no qualms in reminding him that he had not so much as had a conversation with her before offering her marriage mere months ago. Or of his distrust of her, and of the information she'd wished to impart to him, when she'd first returned to England just weeks ago.

Was it really only three weeks since she had secretly returned to England? So much had happened in that time it seemed so much longer.

Zachary knew that he well deserved Georgianna's criticism. But he wished to remedy those wrongs now. He wanted to make amends for his past arrogance and thoughtlessness. If Georgianna would only allow it.

'I freely acknowledge that I have behaved appallingly towards you in the past, Georgianna.'

'How gracious of you to admit it!'

Zachary closed his eyes briefly as he heard the sarcasm underlying Georgianna's tone. As he inwardly fought to hold on to what little temper he had left. 'I am asking, politely, that you now leave this place with me, Georgianna, in order that we might talk together in calmness and—'

'This hellish place?' she interrupted tauntingly.

It had been hellish for him to have to sit at Georgianna's side and listen to the often painful musical efforts of half a dozen twittering young women, all of them hoping to impress the gentlemen present with their questionable talents. A so-called entertainment which Zachary would never have bothered himself to suffer through in the past and had only done so this evening as an open support of Georgianna's return to society.

But enough was enough, as far as Zachary was concerned; he simply could not sit through another minute of either of those painful entertainments, or Georgianna's coolly distant presence, as she sat silent and unmoving beside him. Nor could he witness further demonstration of the attentions of other men.

'Do not pretend you have the least interest in listening to any more of this unholy caterwauling,' he muttered disgustedly.

Georgianna quickly caught her top lip between her teeth in an effort to hold back her humour at Hawksmere's characteristic, and totally familiar, rudeness. A rudeness she far more readily understood than the intensity of emotions which seemed to be bubbling beneath the surface of Hawksmere's present mood of restless impatience.

'That is very ungentlemanly of you, Hawksmere,' she murmured reprovingly.

'The truth often is,' he came back unrepentantly.

The truth.

What was the truth of her feelings for Hawksmere? Did she loathe him or love him? She had once loathed him with a passion, enough so as to have eloped with another man, rather than become his wife. Her responses to Zachary since her return to England, the way she trembled even now just at his close proximity, said she no longer felt the least loathing for him, that her emotions now moved in another direction entirely.

Towards love?

For Hawksmere?

If that was truly what she felt for him then she must still be as stupidly naïve as she had been in the past. Certainly more so even than she had been eleven months ago, when she had believed herself to be in love with and loved by André!

Until now she had believed that to have been her defining moment of *naïveté*, but it was as nothing compared to the self-inflicted torture if she had indeed allowed herself to fall in love with Zachary Black. There could be nothing but pain and disillusionment from loving a man such as he. A man so cynical, so indifferent to the emotion of love, he had thought nothing of tying himself for life to, of marrying, a young woman he had not so much as had an interest in speaking privately to or with before offering for her.

And yet he was expressing a wish to talk privately with that same young woman now.

Perhaps so, but it was no doubt only because she had brought an abrupt end to their conversation earlier regarding André's death. A subject about which Georgianna had no desire to hear, or learn, any more than she already did. André was dead, by whatever means, and she did not need to know, could not bear to know, any more on the subject.

She straightened her spine determinedly. 'I am afraid it is not possible for me to leave just yet, your Grace.' She ignored the way Hawksmere's mouth tightened at her deliberate formality. 'My friend Charlotte Reynolds is about to play the pianoforte in the second half of the entertainments and I have already promised her I will stay long enough to listen.'

Zachary snorted his frustration with this development. 'And our own conversation?'

She shrugged uninterestedly. 'Will just have to wait.'

Zachary did not want to wait. Did not want to share Georgianna for another minute longer. With her friends. Her brother. Or the dozen or so eager young bucks watching them so curiously from across the room. No doubt all waiting for the moment they could pounce upon Georgianna again. If there was any pouncing to be done, then Zachary wished it to be only by him!

What he really wanted to do was to once again

make Georgianna a prisoner in his bedchamber. To keep her there, making love to and with her, until she did not have the strength to even think of leaving him again.

It was a side of himself Zachary did not recognise. A side of himself which he was uncertain he wished to recognise.

His mouth thinned. 'You are refusing to leave with me?'

'I believe I must, yes.' Georgianna gave him an impatient glance as his scowl of displeasure deepened. 'You are acting very strangely this evening, Hawksmere.'

No doubt. He felt very strange, too. Felt most uncomfortable with the uncharacteristic emotions churning inside him. There was most certainly impatience at their surroundings. That restlessness to be alone with Georgianna. The desire to make love to her again. And that interminable, unacceptable jealousy of the other men, just waiting for the opportunity to fawn over and flatter her.

What did it all mean? This turmoil of emotions, this possessiveness he now felt towards Georgianna?

Until he knew the answer to those questions, perhaps he should not talk privately with Georgianna, after all, but instead go to his club? Perhaps with the intention of imbibing too much brandy? If only as a means of dulling this turmoil of unfathomable emotions that held him so tightly in its grip.

He removed his hand from the top of Georgianna's

arm as he stepped back to bow formally. 'I will wish you a goodnight, then, Georgianna.'

Georgianna blinked her surprise at the abruptness of Zachary's sudden capitulation to her refusal to leave with him, when just seconds ago he had seemed equally as determined that she would do so.

Would she ever understand this man?

Probably not, she conceded wearily. 'Goodnight, your Grace.'

She bowed her head as she curtsied just as formally.

'Georgianna.'

She glanced up at Hawksmere from beneath lowered lashes as she slowly straightened. 'Yes?'

A nerve pulsed in his tightly clenched jaw, his face pale, a fevered glitter in the paleness of his silver eyes as the words seems forced out of him rather than given willingly. 'Never mind,' he muttered, his gaze no longer meeting hers. 'I wish you joy for the rest of your evening.' He gave another curt bow. 'If you will excuse me? I will inform Jeffrey of my early departure.'

She nodded. 'Your Grace.'

Zachary had never felt such heaviness in his chest before as he now felt walking away from Georgianna in search of Jeffrey Lancaster. He felt strangely as if he were leaving a part of himself behind. A very vital part. Almost as if he might never see Georgianna again after this evening. Which was ridiculous, when he was to be her guardian for another three months at least.

'I believe you and I need to talk privately, Hawksmere.'

Zachary turned at the harsh sound of his younger ward's voice, eyes narrowing as he took in the angry expression on Jeffrey Lancaster's youthfully handsome face.

'Is there a problem, Jeffrey?' he prompted warily, wondering if Jeffrey had witnessed the tension just now between his sister and Zachary.

The younger man's face flushed with displeasure. 'I did not mean— It was not done intentionally— I had thought to join you and Wolfingham earlier and…I inadvertently overheard part of your conversation,' he bit out accusingly.

And, as Zachary so clearly recalled, any part of his private conversation with Wolfingham would be considered damning to a third party. Most particularly Wolfingham having spoken of the conditions of Zachary's father's will, as being the reason for his betrothal and intended marriage to Jeffrey's sister eleven months ago.

Chapter Fourteen

Zachary slouched down in the chair beside the fireplace at his club as he stared down morosely into the bottom of his empty glass. A glass which seemed to have been emptied of brandy far too often these past few hours.

The club was much quieter than it had been when he arrived here after leaving Lady Colchester's musical soirée, the group of gentlemen who had been playing cards upon his arrival, having long departed. In fact, the club seemed to have emptied almost completely now that Zachary took the trouble to take stock of his surroundings. Something he had certainly not noticed before now, lost in the darkness of his own thoughts as he had been, and still was.

He continued to frown as he filled his glass again from the decanter on the table beside him. The alcohol dulled his senses, if it had not settled the confusion of his thoughts.

Of one thing he was absolutely certain, however: Georgianna now hated him.

And what reason had Zachary provided for her not to feel that way?

He had not so much as given a thought to Georgianna's feelings when he made his offer of marriage to her father eleven months ago. Had thought only of his own needs then and assumed that Georgianna would be flattered by the offer, and more than content just to become a duchess, as most young women of his acquaintance would have been.

Zachary had not realised, had not known then, that Georgianna was not like other young women and had a definite mind of her own in regard to what she wanted for her future. And duke or not, a loveless marriage to Zachary Black had certainly not been what she had wanted.

Zachary was not the man she had wanted, either.

And he was still not the man she wanted in her life.

To a degree that Georgianna did not just scorn him, but now heartily disliked him.

Why that should disturb him, hurt him, quite so much as it did was still something of a mystery to him.

Zachary had always lived his life exactly as he pleased, answerable to no one since his parents died. He did not understand why Georgianna's good opinion should now be of more importance to him than anything or anyone else.

He gave a shake of his head in an effort to clear his mind. But, damn it, what did it mean, when thoughts of a certain woman haunted his every waking moment? When just to look at her caused a tightness in his chest? When her unique perfume alone succeeded in arousing him?

When wanting Georgianna, desiring her, now consumed him utterly?

It was thoughts of their explosive and satisfying lovemaking which had made Zachary's torment this evening all the deeper. Far better that he had never known the softness of Georgianna's lips against his flesh, the caress of her hands upon his body. How he wished he'd never touched the silkiness of her own skin and enjoyed her own unique taste. Better that than to suffer the torment of remembering the way in which Georgianna had withdrawn from him after he had informed her of Rousseau's death.

The shock upon her face yesterday, when he had informed her of that death, her obvious disgust at his own involvement in Rousseau's demise, her coldness towards him since, was proof enough, surely, that she still had feelings for the other man?

And that she would never feel any of those softer feelings in regard to Zachary.

Even more so, now that Malvern had overheard part of Zachary's conversation with Wolfingham earlier this evening. The damning part: when Zachary had discussed the conditions of his father's will and the reason he had offered for Georgianna at all the previous year.

A disclosure that had been the truth then, even if it was not now, and which Zachary had not felt it was within his power to ask Jeffrey to keep from telling his sister.

Even though that truth would no doubt damn him for ever in Georgianna's eyes.

Bastard.

Cold, unfeeling, arrogant, impossible, selfish, selfish bastard!

Georgianna's ire towards Zachary was so intense this evening she did not feel in the least guilty about her repeated use of that unpleasant word inside her head, even as she had danced and flirted with all of the gentlemen at the Countess of Evesham's ball.

As she now muttered several other, stronger, French epithets she had in her vocabulary, as she edged her way round the ballroom of the Countess of Evesham's London home towards the open French doors and the solitude of the terrace beyond.

How could Hawksmere have done such a thing?

To any woman?

To her?

Her conversation with Jeffrey the evening before had revealed that she had been wholly correct in her previous assumptions concerning Hawksmere having calculated intentions when he'd offered marriage to her eleven months ago.

Indeed, it was worse than she had thought, because the offer had been made only so that Hawksmere might attain a wife and impregnate her, and so ensure that his heir was born before his thirty-fifth birthday. And all so that he might inherit all of his father's estate rather than a portion of it.

Poor Jeffrey was most disillusioned with the man he had previously so looked up to and admired.

To Georgianna it explained so much of Zachary's behaviour eleven months ago, of course. The reason he had offered marriage at all to a woman he did not even know and so obviously did not care to know. Followed by his anger that she had then chosen to elope with another man rather than marry him. And his distrust and punishment of her for that misdeed upon her return to England.

No doubt it also explained the penchant Hawksmere had for making love to her. As an example to her, no doubt, as a lesson to her never to cross a duke.

And Hawksmere had dared to be angry with her when they met again? To punish her?

How she despised him now.

Hated him.

Wished him consigned to the devil.

'Where are you going?'

Georgianna came to an abrupt halt, unable to keep the surprised expression from her face as she now turned to see the man who so occupied her thoughts.

Primarily because Hawksmere was not supposed to be at the Countess of Evesham's ball at all this evening. He had sent a note to Malvern House late this afternoon to inform Georgianna and Jeffrey that he would not be attending. He had offered no explanation, but had ended the brief note by wishing them both a pleasant evening.

That he was now standing before her, after all, caused Georgianna's heart to flutter erratically in her chest as she gazed up at him from beneath the fan of her lowered lashes.

He looked magnificent, of course, in his black evening clothes and snowy white linen, a diamond pin glittering amongst the intricate folds of his cravat, his fashionably tousled hair appearing as dark as a raven's wing in the bright candlelit ballroom.

And yet beneath that magnificence Georgianna noted the lines of strain around Zachary's eyes and etched beside the firm line of his mouth, the skin stretched tautly across the pallor of his chiselled cheeks. His mouth was set grimly, eyes glittering that intense silver as he continued to look down at her intently.

She moistened her lips before answering. 'I was going outside on to the terrace to take the air.'

He nodded abruptly. 'Then I will join you.' He took a firm hold of her elbow before cutting a determined swathe through the other guests towards the doors leading outside.

A determination none present dare question and leaving Georgianna no choice but to accompany him.

She was not sure she wished to be alone on the terrace with Zachary, or anywhere else.

Her conversation with Jeffrey the evening before, the confirmation of Hawksmere's perfidy, had cut into her almost with a pain of the same terrible intensity as when André had shot her. Starkly revealing, to Georgianna at least, that she had been using the anger she felt towards Zachary as a defence to hide what she really felt for him.

Love.

How it had happened, why it had happened, she had absolutely no idea, but during the events of the past year she had promised herself, if she survived, that she would never deceive or lie to herself again. And somehow, in these past three weeks, she had managed to fall in love.

She was in love, deeply and irrevocably, with Zachary Black, the emotionally aloof and coldly arrogant Duke of Hawksmere.

The same man who, it now transpired, had only offered for her the previous year because of his father's will. A man who had made it more than obvious, now as then, that he did not believe in love, let alone have any intention of so much as pretending to ever have felt that emotion in regard to Georgianna.

She glanced across at him now as he stood beside her in the moonlight, her expression guarded. 'Your note said that you would not be attending the ball this evening.'

Zachary gave a humourless smile. 'Obviously it is not only a lady's prerogative to change her mind.' In truth, he had regretted sending the note to Malvern and his sister almost the moment it had left his house earlier today, meaning, as it surely did, that he would now have no opportunity in which to see Georgianna today.

At the time of writing the note, Zachary had been feeling decidedly under the weather, his head fit to burst from the copious amount of brandy he had consumed the night before. Even the thought of attending the tedium of a ball increased the pounding inside his head.

Until Hinds, with his usual foresight, had provided Zachary with one of his cure-alls and, in doing so, managed to alleviate that pounding headache to a more manageable level. At which time Zachary had deeply regretted having ever informed Jeffrey and Georgianna that he would not be attending the ball with them this evening, after all.

'I do not think it altogether proper for the two of us to be out here alone together.'

Zachary scowled. 'I am your guardian.'

'And that distinction surely covers a multitude of sins!' she came back sharply.

One of those sins surely being Zachary having made love to her. 'Georgianna...'

'Could we please not argue again tonight, Zachary?' she requested wearily. 'I fear I am not feeling strong enough to deal with our usual thrust and parry this evening.'

Zachary looked at her searchingly, easily noting the pallor of her cheeks. 'Are you feeling unwell?' He swallowed. 'Perhaps because you are mourning Rousseau's death?'

'No!' Georgianna assured vehemently.

The duke looked puzzled. 'And yet it so obviously distressed you when I informed you of his demise yesterday afternoon.'

She moistened dry lips. 'I am, of course, sorry to

hear of the death of any man or woman, but I cannot in all conscience say I am sorry that André is no longer here to torment or frighten me.'

'But you blame me still for instigating that death.'

She had never blamed him for André's death, only questioned the reasoning behind it. But to reveal that to Zachary now must surely also reveal the depth of her own feelings for him.

A depth of feeling he so obviously did not return, nor would he ever do so.

In the circumstances, it was humiliating enough, surely, that she had now realised she had fallen in love with the man she'd once so passionately despised. Surely she did not need for Zachary to be made aware of her humiliation, too?

'Georgianna?' he prompted softly now.

She gave a dismissive shake of her head as she avoided looking into that searching silver gaze. 'I blame no one for André's death but André himself.'

He let out a shaky breath. 'I wish I could believe that was true.'

'You may be assured that it is. I was shocked to learn of his death, nothing more. But I believe I must go back inside now,' she added quickly as she realised he was about to question her further on the subject. 'It is somewhat colder out here than I had realised.'

'Here, take my jacket.' Zachary began to shrug his shoulders out of the close-fitting garment.

'No.' Georgianna had taken a horrified step backwards at the suggestion. She was already completely physically aware of Zachary, of his closeness, his warmth, his tempting masculinity, without being surrounded by the warmth and smell of him, too, as she would be if he were to now place his jacket about her shoulders. 'I really must go back inside.' She took another step back.

Zachary sighed heavily, as he obviously saw her efforts to put yet more distance between them. 'If it is not Rousseau causing you to now flinch away from me, then I can only presume— Jeffrey lost no time last night in informing you of the conditions of my father's will, I take it?' A nerve pulsed in his tightly clenched jaw.

Her chin rose. 'No.'

He nodded. 'There is no excuse for the selfishness of my actions last year. I deeply regret— I am sorry for— Damn it, would you perhaps consider forgiving me if I were to get down on my knees and beg?' he grated harshly, eyes glittering fiercely in the moonlight.

Exactly what was Zachary asking forgiveness for?

For that cold and cynical offer of marriage he had made for her last year?

For his distrust and mistreatment of her when she'd returned to England three weeks ago?

For having made love to her so exquisitely that just to be near him again now made her tremble with that knowledge?

For being complicit in, if not personally responsible, for André's death?

For having made her fall in love with him?

Georgianna had already forgiven Zachary for

those other things, but the love she now felt for him, a love she knew he would never return, was like a painful barb in her chest. And would, she believed, remain so for the rest of her life.

It was not Zachary's fault she had fallen in love with him, of course, but...

To have Zachary get down on his knees in front of her for any reason? To hear him beg for her forgiveness?

No.

Never!

It was unthinkable in such an aristocratic and proud man.

In the man she now realised she loved with all her heart.

'No,' she answered decisively. 'Can you not see how impossible it all is, Zachary?' she added forcefully as he scowled darkly. 'That apologies between us now are— That on their own they are not enough?'

Zachary had nothing else to offer Georgianna but his sincere contrition for any and all of his past misdeeds to her. A contrition Georgianna now made it obvious she neither wanted nor wished to hear. It was as he had suspected: Georgianna could never forgive him. For any of his actions, in the past, or now.

He had thought long and hard today on his confusion of thoughts at his club the previous night. On what that confusion of feelings, he now felt towards Georgianna, might mean.

The answer had been so shocking that he had sat alone in his study for hours after the truth had hit him

squarely between the eyes, totally stunned, at the realisation that he had fallen in love with Georgianna.

He had come here this evening in the hope that if
Georgianna would at least allow him to apologise, if
he could perhaps persuade her into not hating him,
that he could then be content with his lot in life. That
he could then accept the little she was prepared to
give him, as his ward, and perhaps even as his friend.

Instead he now found he could not. That he wanted
so much more from Georgianna than her forgiveness, or her lukewarm friendship. That he wanted
all or nothing.

And this conversation with Georgianna told him
it was to be nothing.

He straightened abruptly. 'It only remains for me
to bid you goodnight, then, Georgianna.'

She raised startled lids. 'You are leaving?'

Zachary nodded stiffly. 'My only reason for coming here this evening was to talk to you. To ask your
forgiveness. To see if— In the hope that—' His jaw
tightened as he broke off abruptly.

He had been completely serious in his offer to
Georgianna just now, had been fully prepared to get
down on his knees and beg her forgiveness for his
past actions, if it would in any way help to change
how Georgianna now felt towards him. If he could ask
for her friendship, at least. Her definitive reply had
assured him there was no hope even of that.

Better by far, then, that he should now withdraw
and leave Georgianna to enjoy the rest of the evening,
to allow her to blossom and glow under the attentions

of the other gentlemen present. One of whom she would no doubt one day fall in love with and marry.

'I do apologise, Georgianna.' He held himself stiffly, unable to so much as think of Georgianna being married to another man. 'For all and every wrong I have ever done you. And now, pray be assured, I will not bother you again on this, or any other subject you find so unpleasant.' He bowed formally before turning on his heel and abruptly leaving the terrace.

Zachary had spoken with such finality that Georgianna could not mistake his words for anything other than what they were. An end to any hope of there ever being so much as a friendship between the two of them.

'Georgie?'

She was totally unaware of the tears falling down her cheeks as she turned to see that her brother, Jeffrey, had now stepped outside on to the terrace. 'Did you hear any of that?' she asked dully.

'Most of it, I believe,' Jeffrey admitted as he crossed the terrace to her side before taking both of her hands in his. He looked down at her searchingly. 'I saw your expression as the two of you left the ballroom together and I was concerned enough to stand guard at the doors, so that I might be close enough to be of assistance if you should have need of me. Your conversation was not at all what I had imagined. Georgie, am I right in thinking you have fallen in love with Hawksmere?'

'Yes.' Georgianna made no attempt to deny it.

Her brother nodded. 'And he obviously has feelings for you.'

'Desire is not enough on its own, Jeffrey,' she assured heavily.

'Are you so certain that is all that Hawksmere feels for you?'

She smiled sadly. 'I am sure you heard Zachary say goodbye to me just now? Not necessarily in words, but in the cold formality of his manner?'

'I heard him saying a reluctant goodbye to you, yes. Georgie—' Jeffrey frowned '—you are much changed since your return from France. You have suffered through so much, more than I know, I am sure. And yet you have survived. More than survived. You have grown into a beautiful and independent woman. More forthright in your manner. Less patient of society's strictures and more determined where your own wishes are concerned.'

'Yes.' Again Georgianna did not attempt to deny it; she had indeed become all of those things these past months.

Her brother nodded. 'I have no idea how you and Hawksmere can have become so close in such a short time, but I am young still, Georgie, though I am far from stupid,' he reproved gently as she would have spoken. 'And there is most certainly something between the two of you. An emotion so strong, so intense, that it is possible to feel the tension in the air whenever the two of you are in a room together.'

Her cheeks warmed. 'As I said, desire alone is not enough.'

'I do not believe Hawksmere came here this evening with any intention of making love to you, Georgie,' her brother reasoned softly. 'I heard enough of your conversation to know that he wished only to talk to you. To offer to get down on his knees and beg for your forgiveness, for any and all of his past misdeeds to you, if necessary. Can you not give him some credit for that, at least, Georgie? Some understanding of what it must have cost him, such a proud man, to have offered to do such a thing? And to question why he would have made such a self-demeaning offer of apology to you at all?'

She sighed deeply. 'Who is to know why Hawksmere does anything?'

'You know, Georgia,' Jeffrey chided. 'You know Hawksmere better than anyone, I believe. Is it not time you searched your own heart? That you forgo a little of your own pride? Talk with him again, before the distance between you becomes too wide to ever be crossed,' he urged softly.

Georgianna did not need to search her own heart to know that she was in love with Zachary.

Could she dare to hope, to believe, that his actions tonight implied he might love her in return?

'What do you have to lose, Georgie?' Jeffrey cajoled.

Nothing. She had absolutely nothing left to lose when it came to loving Zachary.

Chapter Fifteen

'Good evening, Hinds.' Georgianna handed her bonnet and cloak to the surprised butler as she stepped past him into the cavernous hallway of Hawksmere House. 'Is his Grace at home?'

The butler looked more than a little flustered by having her arrive at his employer's home at eleven o'clock in the evening. 'He returned some minutes ago and has retired to his study.'

'Which is where?' She gazed pointedly at the half dozen doors leading off the entrance hall.

'The second door on the right. But…'

'Thank you.' Georgianna gave the butler a brightly dismissive smile, determined to go through with her decision to speak with Zachary again. 'Perhaps you might bring through a decanter of brandy?' Bravado had brought her thus far—she did not intend to let it desert her now.

'His Grace has just this minute instructed I do so,

my lady.' Hind's brows were still raised in astonishment at her commanding behaviour.

Understandably so, when she considered the butler was fully aware that she had once been held here as Hawksmere's prisoner.

Although she did feel slightly heartened by the fact that Zachary had obviously felt in need of a restorative brandy—or two—upon his return home. 'I will not delay you from your duties any longer then, Hinds.'

'What on earth is going on, Hinds?' Hawksmere came to an abrupt halt in the now-open doorway of his study, his expression one of stunned disbelief as he gazed across at her.

'Georgianna?'

'Hawksmere.' She managed to greet him with the same brightness as she had addressed the butler seconds ago, determined not to lose her nerve now that she found herself face to face with Zachary.

As Jeffrey had gently chided earlier, the situation between herself and Zachary had come to a breaking point, with no going back, only forward. Wherever that might take her. Consequently, Georgianna had nothing left to lose now but her pride. And where Zachary was concerned, she found that she now had none. How could she have, when she knew he had cast aside his own pride earlier this evening, by offering to get down on his knees and beg her forgiveness.

'The brandy, Hinds, if you please?' she reminded, sending Hinds scurrying down the hallway.

Zachary was dressed far less formally than he had

been earlier this evening, having removed his jacket and cravat, leaving him dressed only in his waist-coat over the snowy white shirt open at the throat and black pantaloons, which clearly showed the lean perfection of his muscled legs and thighs.

He looked delicious, Georgianna decided, good enough to eat, in fact. The heated colour warmed her cheeks as she recalled that she had already tasted and devoured Zachary, when the two of them made love together yesterday afternoon.

She held Zachary's wary gaze unwaveringly as she softly crossed the hallway to join him. 'May I come in?' she beseeched huskily, her heart beating errati-cally in her chest as he made no effort to stand aside and allow her entry into his study.

Zachary's hand tightened on the doorframe, where he had reached out to steady himself in his complete surprise at seeing Georgianna standing in the en-trance hall of his London home. 'Is Jeffrey with you?'

'Jeffrey knows that I am here, because he put me into our carriage himself. Otherwise, I am quite alone,' she dismissed huskily.

A scowl darkened Zachary's brow. 'That was most improper of you.'

She gazed up at him quizzically. 'As you stated earlier, we are well past that point.'

Maybe so, but Zachary's concern was on Georgi-anna's behalf, rather than his own. His own reputa-tion was such that her visiting him alone would only add to his reputation as being something of a rake, whereas Georgianna's still bore a question mark, as far as society was concerned.

'Why are you here, Georgianna?' he prompted warily.

'You would rather I had not come?'

He would far rather Georgianna stayed and never left. Ever again. But, as their earlier conversation had seemed to confirm that was not even a possibility, he could not help but question as to the reason why Georgianna had left the Countess of Evesham's ball only minutes after he had done so himself. With the intent, it seemed, of following him here. With her brother's full consent and co-operation, by the sound of it.

His mouth tightened disapprovingly. 'Jeffrey should have known better than to allow it.'

'Jeffrey overheard part of our own conversation on the terrace earlier.'

'I can see I shall have to have words with that young man regarding his habit of eavesdropping on private conversations.' Zachary scowled.

Georgianna shook her head. 'He is far more mature and sensible than either of us have given him credit for,' she assured drily. 'But would you rather I left again, Zachary?' She looked up at him searchingly.

He drew a deep breath into his starved lungs as he realised he had forgotten to breathe. He allowed himself to indulge his senses where Georgianna was concerned, gazing upon her obvious beauty and the dewy perfection of her skin, that begged to be touched and tasted, and now breathing in her unique perfume—

something floral as well as the unique and feminine warmth that was all Georgianna.

'I would rather you had not come here at all,' he maintained harshly, still making no effort to step aside and allow her entry to his study. It was his last bastion of defence, a place where he did not have any visible memories of being with Georgianna. Unlike his bedchamber upstairs. And the bedchamber adjoining that one. And the blue salon.

Her chin rose determinedly. 'I wished to continue our earlier conversation.'

His jaw tightened. 'And I believe we said then all that needs be said to each other.'

Georgianna looked up at Zachary searchingly, as she easily noted his unkempt appearance. His hair was tousled, as if he had run his agitated fingers through it several times since returning home. The lines beside his eyes and mouth seemed deeper, his mouth set in a thin and uncompromising line, and there was a dark shadow upon his jaw, where he was obviously in need of a second shave of the day.

Altogether, he looked nothing like the suave and sophisticated gentleman who had arrived at the Countess of Evesham's ball earlier this evening.

Because of the unsatisfactory outcome earlier of that conversation with her?

That was what Georgianna was here to find out. And, having made that decision, she had no intentions of leaving here tonight until she had done so.

'You know, Zachary, we both have scars that are visible to the eye if one cares to look for them.' Her gaze softened as she reached up to gently touch the livid scar upon his throat, stubbornly maintaining that touch even when he would have flinched away. 'But I, for one, have other scars, ones deep inside me, that are not at all visible to the naked eye.' She smiled sadly. 'They are the scars left by my unhappy experience at André's hands. Of uncertainty. Of questioning my self-worth.'

'The devil they are.'

Georgianna nodded as Zachary scowled his displeasure at her admission. 'Those scars make it difficult for me to believe that any man, any gentleman, could ever, would ever, want to be with me after— Zachary?' she questioned sharply as he reached up to curl his fingers about her wrist before pulling her inside his candlelit study and closing the door firmly behind them. His eyes were a dark, unfathomable grey as he gazed down at her hungrily before his arms moved about her and he lowered his head to crush her lips beneath his own.

It would have been so easy to lose herself in that kiss. For Georgianna to give in completely to the arousal which instantly thrummed through her body. To feel gratified, to revel, in this proof that Zachary still desired her, at least.

But she could not. Dared not. Because she knew it would be all too easy to give in to those desires and for the two of them not to talk at all. And they needed the truth between the two of them, before, or if, there was to be any more lovemaking.

Georgianna wrenched her mouth from beneath

Zachary's even as she pushed against his chest to free herself.

His arms fell reluctantly away as he stepped back, his heavy lidded gaze now guarded. 'I trust that answers your question as to whether or not you are wanted by me?'

She drew in a shaky breath, even more determined, after Zachary's show of passion, to say all the things she knew needed to be said between them. 'I made a mistake last year, Zachary, one for which so many people have suffered.'

'You most of all,' he pointed out gruffly.

She sighed equally as shakily. 'I really was so very young, and even more foolish. I am ashamed to say that at the time I saw it all as a grand adventure, with no real thought for what the long-term consequences of my actions might be.'

'Except to escape being married to me,' Zachary reminded drily.

'Yes.' Georgianna's gaze now avoided meeting his, as she began to pace the rug before the warmth of the fireplace. 'And now I have so many things to thank you for, Zachary.'

His eyes widened. 'What on earth...?'

'I am so grateful for your own efforts, last year and now, to maintain my reputation in society,' she continued determinedly. 'So thankful that Jeffrey has had you to help him through these trying months since our father died. And...' she looked up at him helplessly '...and, yes, I am more gratified than I have cared to admit, until now, that you have helped rid the world of a monster such as André Rousseau.' That last admission was against everything she had been brought up to believe in regard to the sanctity of human life.

It was also, Georgianna now accepted, a large part of why she had been so angry with Zachary when he had informed her of André's death. Because, having lived in fear of discovery by André these past few months, she had wanted him to be dead. Wished him so. And she had inwardly rejoiced yesterday when Zachary had told her André was indeed dead.

It was a reaction, a rejoicing, of which she had felt heartily ashamed.

But that shame and anger were directed towards herself, not Zachary. 'I was ashamed to admit it until now,' she admitted huskily.

'But you loved him. Love him still, damn it.'

Her eyes widened. 'I most certainly do not. I…' She paused, chewing briefly on her bottom lip before continuing. 'I fear I have been less than honest, with myself, and with you, on that matter.'

Zachary gave a grimace. 'Your reaction yesterday, your distress, were evidence enough of how you felt. That you still had feelings for the man,' he added harshly.

'No,' Georgianna denied vehemently. 'Never that. Never,' she repeated with a shudder of revulsion. 'The truth of the matter is—I realised some time ago—Zachary, I do not believe I was ever truly in love with André.' She gave a pained grimace at the admission. 'I was very naïve, flattered by his attentions and desperate to escape a loveless marriage and, I now know, in love with love rather than André himself.'

Zachary stared at her searchingly for long, tense moments, before turning abruptly to cross the room and seat himself behind his imposing mahogany desk. That she had not loved Rousseau after all was no reason to suppose, to hope, she would ever love him.

'I am gratified to you—' he nodded '—for allowing me to know that Rousseau's death has not succeeded in breaking your heart, as I previously believed it to have done.'

Georgianna could hear the *but* in his voice.

But the admission made no difference to the outcome of their own conversation, perhaps?

Whether or not that was true, Georgianna had no intentions of leaving here tonight without there being complete honesty between herself and Zachary. After which, fate, or rather Zachary, could do with her what it would. 'Are you not interested to know how it is I came to be certain I was never in love with André?'

His mouth twisted wryly. 'No doubt it is difficult to continue to love a man whom you knew had attempted to kill you.'

'Indeed.' She nodded ruefully. 'Almost as difficult, in fact, as finding you have fallen in love with the very same gentleman whose hand in marriage you had once shunned so cruelly.'

Zachary rose sharply to his feet. 'Georgianna?' His eyes glittered as he gazed across at her uncertainly.

Her heart was now beating so erratically, so loudly in her chest, she felt sure that Zachary could not help but be aware of it, too, despite the distance between them. 'It is the truth, Zachary.' She forced herself to forge ahead, to not retreat or back down, now that she had come so far. 'Since I returned to England you have shown me a side of yourself I did not know existed. That I did not even dare dream existed. On the outside you are so very much the cool and arrogant Duke of Hawksmere, so very much in control. But inwardly there is a kindness to you, one which you try to hide, but which shines through anyway.'

'And you reached this conclusion by my having locked you in my bedchamber? By my making love to you at every opportunity?' He raised incredulous brows.

'I reached that conclusion by knowing that you could have been so much harsher with me, after the way I had behaved in the past. By knowing that you were complicit in protecting my reputation, despite that behaviour. By your overwhelming kindness to Jeffrey these past months. And by the realisation this evening, the certainty,' she declared determinedly as he would have spoken, 'that your reasons for seeing André dispatched were not, as I had supposed, because of loyalty to England, or because of a personal grudge you held against him, for having dared to elope with your future bride.'

'Dear God, you thought that of me?'

Colour warmed the paleness of her cheeks. 'I am ashamed to say it occurred to me those might be your reasons.'

'I did it because of you, Georgianna. Because

André had attempted to kill you.' Zachary's hands were clenched at his side.

It was as Georgianna had thought earlier when he'd pleaded with her so emotionally.

'Just leave it on the side table there,' Zachary instructed his butler harshly as the man entered after the briefest of knocks, holding aloft the tray with the decanter and glasses. 'And in future, would you please knock and wait before entering any room in which Lady Georgianna and I are alone together?' he added, his gaze remaining intent upon Georgianna.

'Certainly, your Grace.' The butler placed the tray upon the side table. 'Will that be all, your Grace?'

Zachary barely resisted the impulse to tell the man to go to the devil, wishing to be alone again with Georgianna, to continue their conversation. To hear her repeat that she had fallen in love with him.

Something he hardly dared to believe.

'You may retire for the night, Hinds,' Zachary dismissed distractedly. 'And thank you.'

His butler gave him another startled glance before gathering himself and leaving the room. As evidence perhaps that Zachary's temper had been less than pleasant this past few days?

As no doubt it had, caught up in the pained whirlpool of his uncertainty in his own emotions, as he had surely been.

'Is that not a strange request to make of your butler, when there is no reason to suppose that the two of us might ever be alone together in a room in this house again?' Georgianna queried huskily.

Zachary stepped out from behind his desk. 'There is every reason to suppose it, Georgianna.' He strode purposefully towards her before grasping both of her hands in his. 'Believe me, when I tell you, that these past three weeks I have come to love and admire you beyond anything and anyone else in this world.'

'Zachary?' she choked out emotionally.

'Georgia, will you please, I beg of you, consent to becoming my wife?'

Georgianna stared up at him wonderingly, sure Zachary could not truly have told her that he loved her, too. That he had begged her to marry him?

His hands tightened about hers as he obviously mistook her silence for hesitation. 'And not because of any ridiculous clause in my father's will, either. Indeed, if you require it as proof of the sincerity of my feelings for you, I will give away half of the Hawksmere fortune to my cousin Rufus forthwith, as my father's will decrees if I do not have an heir by my thirty fifth birthday. Anything, if you will consent to become my wife immediately.'

Georgianna's mouth felt very dry, and after its wild pounding earlier she was sure her heart had now ceased to beat altogether. 'Is your cousin in need of half the Hawksmere fortune?'

'Thanks to Rufus's business acumen, he is already one of the richest men in London.' Zachary bared his teeth in a brief smile before just as quickly sobering. 'Nevertheless, I will happily give him the money, if it will ensure that you believe I am sincere in my declaration of love for you. If you will only consent to become my wife as soon as it can be arranged?'

Georgianna had no idea what she had expected the outcome of her visit here this evening to be, but she knew she had certainly never expected it to be the complete and utter happiness of hearing Hawksmere declare his love for her and his asking her to marry him.

Her vision was blurred by those tears of happiness. 'You truly love me?'

'To the point of madness,' Zachary assured fervently. 'Indeed, I believe I have been half-insane with the emotion these past few days.' The intensity of his gaze held her. 'I love you so very much, Georgianna Rose Lancaster.'

'As I love you, Zachary Richard Edward Black,' she answered him huskily. 'Completely. And always.'

His face lit up. 'Then put all of the past behind us and consent to marry me.'

She swallowed. 'Are you absolutely sure that is what you want, Zachary? My reappearance in society is still tenuous.'

'What are you suggesting, Georgianna?' Zachary demanded. 'That I should make you my mistress rather than marry you? That I should hide you away somewhere?'

'I am something of a novelty in society just now, Zachary, but if anyone should ever learn of my elopement with André...'

'They will not discover it,' Zachary announced arrogantly. 'And even if they did, none would dare

to question the reputation of the Duchess of Hawksmere.'

It was a name, a title, when used in connection to
herself, that had once filled Georgianna with such
dread. Now it only filled her with a happiness that
threatened to overwhelm her. 'I am so in love with
you, Zachary. So very, very much, my darling. And
if you are serious in your proposal of marriage...?'

'I will accept nothing less,' he assured firmly.

She glowed up at him. 'Then I believe I should
much prefer that you keep the Hawksmere fortune
intact for our children, when they are born.'

'Georgianna?' Zachary had almost been afraid to
hope, to dream, that Georgianna would ever accept
his proposal. 'You truly will consent to become my
wife?' His fingers tightened painfully about hers.
'You will marry me as soon as a special licence can
be arranged?'

She nodded happily. 'And Jeffrey shall give me
away and one of your friends, Wolfingham, perhaps,
shall stand up with you. Oh, yes, I will marry you,
Zachary. Yes, yes, please, yes.' She launched herself
into his arms as his mouth swooped down to once
again claim hers.

'You were very brave to come here alone this evening, my love,' Zachary murmured admiringly some
time later, Georgianna's head resting on his chest as
the two of them lay on the chaise in his study together.
He played with her curls, having once again released
her hair so that it cascaded loosely down her back.

She laughed softly, contentedly, the two of them having professed their love for each other over and over again this past hour or more. 'To confront the fierce lion in his den?'

'To have completely tamed the lion in his den,' Zachary corrected with humour. 'Indeed, I find I am so much in love with you I very much doubt I shall ever be able to deny you anything in future, love.'

Georgianna hesitated, knowing that there was still one thing that she had not confessed to her beloved. The last confession.

When she first returned to England she had been too angry at Hawksmere's incarceration of her, to talk of such things, and since then there had been no right time, no opportunity, for her to do so.

'What is it, Georgia?' Zachary sat up slightly as he sensed her sudden tension. His hands gently cupped either side of her face as he looked down at her searchingly. 'Tell me, my love.'

She chewed on her bottom lip. 'I— It is only— A lady should not talk of such things,' she choked out emotionally.

'Now you are seriously worrying me, love.' Zachary frowned. 'We have talked about so much this past hour. The past, the now, our future together. What on earth is there that still bothers you so much that you look as if you are about to cry?'

Georgianna felt as if she were about to cry. It was all too embarrassing. Too humiliating.

Her gaze dropped from his as she moistened her

lips with the tip of her tongue. 'When I eloped with André…'

'I thought we had agreed earlier that we would not discuss that ever again,' Zachary reminded with chiding gentleness.

'Just this one thing, Zachary,' she pleaded. 'It is important, if we are to be married.'

'We are most certainly going to be married and sooner rather than later.' Zachary had never been as happy as he had felt this past hour of knowing that Georgianna loved him, that she had consented to marry him. He could not bear it if that happiness— if a lifetime with Georgianna as his wife, should ever be snatched away from him.

'Whatever you have yet to tell me, never doubt my love for you, Georgianna. Never. Do you understand?' He held her tightly against him. 'Be assured, nothing you have to say, now or in the future, will ever change that,' he added with certainty.

Georgianna looked up at him wonderingly, moved beyond measure at the knowledge that Zachary loved her so deeply, so unconditionally. The same deep intensity of emotion with which she now loved him. 'It is nothing bad, my love,' she assured huskily as she reached up to stroke his cheek. 'Only embarrassing for me to speak of,' she conceded ruefully.

'I grow more intrigued by the moment, my love.' He eyed her quizzically.

'Where to start?' Georgianna pulled out of his arms before standing up and turning away slightly, her hands clasped tightly together in front of her.

'When I eloped with André—allow me to finish, my love, please!' she begged as Zachary made a noise of protest. 'We spent several uncomfortable days being jostled about in the coach together on the way to the seaport. We passed the sea journey as brother and sister in separate cabins. And once we reached Paris…' She gave a shake of her head. 'You are well aware of what transpired within days of our reaching the French capital.'

Zachary's narrowed gaze remained intently on Georgianna as he slowly stood up to move softly to her side, reaching down to lift her chin so that he might gaze down directly, searchingly, into the frankness of those violet-coloured eyes. 'Are you saying…?' He drew in a sharp breath, hardly daring to believe.

'I am saying that André and I had never shared any more than a few chaste kisses before we eloped and that he did not so much as kiss me during the whole of our journey to France.'

'Georgianna?'

She swallowed. 'The intensity, depth, of our own lovemaking was—is, the first I have ever known.'

'Can it be? Are you a virgin still, Georgianna?' Zachary prompted tensely.

The colour deepened in her cheeks as she nodded. 'I could not bear to tell you before now.' She grasped tightly to the front of his waistcoat as she gazed up at him imploringly. 'The Zachary I met on my return to England would have enjoyed tormenting me with that knowledge. Would have mocked and taunted me as to André's disinterest in me. Would have—'

'Hush, my love.' Zachary placed a silencing fingertip against her lips, his heart having swelled almost to bursting point in his chest.

He had long ago accepted that Georgianna had been Rousseau's lover and it had made no difference to the deep love and admiration, respect, that he now felt for her. But to now realise, to know, that Georgianna had never, would never, belong to any other man but him?

It was a priceless gift. A gift beyond anything Zachary might ever have imagined.

'I took such liberties with you.' He groaned, disgusted with himself. 'I was far too rough in my lovemaking. Too advanced in the things I did to you and demanded from you in return.'

'I loved the way you made love to me, Zachary, and so enjoyed making love to you,' she admitted shyly. 'Indeed, I cannot wait to repeat it.'

'That will not happen until after we are married,' he assured her determinedly.

She chuckled throatily. 'Can it be that Zachary Black, the arrogant and haughty Duke of Hawksmere, has now become prim and respectable?'

'You may take it that Zachary Black, the arrogant and haughty Duke of Hawksmere,' he repeated huskily, 'intends to cherish and love, to make love to, Georgianna Rose Black, Duchess of Hawksmere, and only Georgianna Rose Black, Duchess of Hawksmere, for the rest of their lives together.'

It was so much more, so indescribably, wonderfully, ecstatically more than Georgianna Rose Lancaster, soon to be Black, could ever have hoped or dreamed of.

* * * * *

DARIAN HUNTER: DUKE OF DESIRE

My good friend, Susan Stephens.
What fun we have on our travels!

Prologue

'You wanted to speak to me?'

Having been perusing today's newspaper, whilst seated in an otherwise deserted private room of his club, Darian Hunter, the Duke of Wolfingham, now continued reading to the end of the article before folding the broadsheet neatly into four and placing it down on the low table beside him. He then glanced up at the fashionably dressed young gentleman who had addressed him so aggressively. 'And a good afternoon to you, too, Anthony,' he greeted his younger brother calmly.

Anthony eyed him impatiently. 'Do not come the haughty duke with me, Darian! Most especially when I know it is you who wished to speak with me rather than the other way about. You have left messages for me all over town,' he reminded as Darian raised dark brows questioningly. 'I presumed the matter must be of some urgency?'

'Is that why it has taken you those same two days to respond to those messages?' Darian was not fooled for a moment by his brother's bluster. He knew that his brother always went on the attack when he knew he was in the wrong, but was refusing to admit it.

'I have better things to do with my time than seek out the more often than not elusive Duke of Wolfingham—even if he does happen to be my big brother as well as my guardian. The latter for only another three months, I thank heavens!'

'Oh, do sit down, Anthony,' Darian snapped. 'You are making the place look untidy.'

Anthony gave a wicked grin at having obviously succeeded in irritating Darian as he threw himself down into the chair opposite. He was dressed in the height of fashion as usual, in his jacket of royal blue, with a bright blue-and-green paisley-patterned waistcoat beneath and buff-coloured pantaloons, his dark hair rakishly overlong and falling across his brow. 'When did you get back to town?'

'Two days ago, obviously,' Darian drawled.

'And you immediately sought me out?' Anthony raised mocking brows. 'I am flattered, brother.'

'Don't be,' he advised pointedly.

His brother now raised his gaze heavenwards. 'What have I done to annoy you this time? Overspent at my tailor's? Gambled at the cards a little too heavily?'

'If only it was your usual irresponsible behaviour

then I should not have needed to speak with you at all, but merely dealt with the matter as I always do,' Darian drawled in a bored voice. 'I am sure we are both well aware of why it is I wished to speak with you, Anthony,' he added softly.

'Not the slightest idea.' The fact that Anthony shifted uncomfortably, his gaze now avoiding meeting Darian's as a slight flush coloured his cheeks, instantly gave lie to the claim.

Darian gave a humourless smile. 'Do not force me to mention the lady by name.'

Anthony narrowed eyes as emerald green as Darian's own, the two of them very alike in colouring and looks, and so obviously brothers, in spite of the eight years' difference in their ages; Darian aged two and thirty to his brother's four and twenty. 'If you are referring to the actress with whom I had a liaison last month, then I do not even recall her name—'

'I am not.'

Anthony gave an exaggerated stretch of his shoulders. 'Then give me a clue, brother, because I have absolutely no idea what—or possibly who?—you might be referring to.'

Darian's mouth firmed at his brother's determination not to make this an easy conversation. For either of them. 'It has been brought to my attention that you have been seen in the company of a certain lady, more often than is socially acceptable.'

Anthony stilled. 'Indeed?'

Darian nodded. 'And while it is perfectly acceptable for you to discreetly indulge in a gentleman's diversions, this particular lady could never be considered as being in the least discreet. Indeed, she is—'

'Have a care, Darian,' Anthony warned softly.

'Her associations, past and present, mean she is not a woman with whom it is acceptable for a gentleman of your standing to indulge in these diversions,' Darian maintained determinedly. 'You—' He broke off as Anthony sprang lightly to his feet, hands clenched into fists at his sides as he glared down at Darian. 'I have not finished—'

'In regard to this particular lady, I assure you that you have indeed finished,' Anthony said fiercely. 'And might I say that you have a damned nerve, daring to lecture me about my behaviour, when you have only just returned from spending almost two weeks in the company of whatever doxy it was who had so taken your fancy you might have disappeared off the edge of the earth! Or perhaps it is that you consider a duke is allowed to live by different standards than us mere mortals?'

Darian lowered heavy lids as he flicked an imaginary speck of lint from the sleeve of his jacket, at the same time avoiding meeting his brother's accusing gaze.

Not because he had just spent almost two weeks with his latest doxy. 'Latest doxy'? Darian could not even remember the last time he had spent any length of time in a woman's company, let alone her bed.

No, the reason for his avoidance of Anthony's probing gaze was because he had not been in a woman's company at all, but had spent almost two weeks across the sea in France, acting secretly as an agent for the Crown.

Almost two weeks when he and his good friend Zachary Black, the Duke of Hawksmere, had roamed the French countryside, and then Paris itself, as they endeavoured to gauge how the French people themselves felt about Napoleon's return, the emperor having recently escaped from Elba and currently on his way to the French capital.

Not even Darian's own brother was aware of the work he had undertaken for the Crown these past five years. Anthony certainly had no idea that Darian had suffered a bullet wound to the shoulder just days ago, a souvenir of this last foray into France. And that he was suffering with the pain and discomfort of that wound even now.

Something that had not improved his temper in the slightest. 'Perhaps you would care to lower your voice?'

'Why should I, when there is no one else here to hear us?' Anthony challenged as he looked about the otherwise empty room.

Darian sighed. 'I am well aware that this lady has certain attributes that you—most gentlemen!—might find diverting. But she is not a discreet woman. Far from it, if gossip is to be believed. People in society are starting to comment upon your marked attentions to her.'

'Then let them,' Anthony dismissed with bravado.

He sighed. 'It simply will not do, Anthony.'

'Says who? You?' his brother challenged, aggressive once again. 'I am almost five and twenty, Darian, not five. Nor,' he added darkly, 'do I appreciate your interference in this matter.'

'Even when I have your best interests at heart?'

'Not when I am in love with the lady, no.'

Darian held on to his temper with difficulty, having had no idea that his brother's affections had become engaged to such a degree. A physical diversion, if discreetly handled, was acceptable; a love affair most certainly was not. 'I am sure the lady has certain charms and experience, which you obviously find attractive. But it would be a mistake on your part to confuse lust with love.'

'How dare you?' Anthony challenged fiercely, his face having become a mottled and angry red. 'My intentions towards the lady are completely honourable!'

Then it was worse even than Darian had feared. 'By all means continue to bed her then, Anthony, if that is your wish. All I am asking is that you at least try to make less of the association when the two of you are in public.'

'Continue to—' Anthony looked as if he might now explode with the depth of his fury. 'I have not laid so much as an indelicate finger upon the lady. Nor do I intend to do so until after I have made her my wife.'

Now it was Darian's turn to stand up, his shock at this announcement too great to be contained. 'You cannot even think of making such a woman your wife!'

'Such a woman? You damned hypocritical prig!'

Anthony glared at him, eyes glittering darkly. 'You return from who knows where, after spending days, almost two weeks, in some woman's bed, and you have the nerve to tell me how I might conduct my own life. Whom I may or may not marry! Well, I shall have none of it, Darian,' he dismissed heatedly. 'In just a few more weeks I shall have control of my own life and my own fortune, and when I do I shall marry whom, and when, I damn well please.'

Darian gave an impatient shake of his head. 'This particular woman is—'

'A darling. An angel.' His brother's voice rose angrily. 'And it is as well you have chosen not to so much as say her name, because your conversation today shows you are not fit to do so.'

Darian winced. From all that he had heard of the lady, she was neither a darling nor an angel. Far from it.

Nor did he have any intentions of allowing his brother to marry such a woman.

And if Anthony could not be made to see sense, then the lady must...

Chapter One

Two days later—the ballroom of Carlisle House, London

'Would you care to repeat your remark, Wolfingham, for I fear the music and loud chatter must have prevented me from hearing you correctly the first time?'

Darian did not need to look down, into the face of the woman with whom he was dancing, to know Mariah Beecham, widowed Countess of Carlisle, *had* heard him correctly the first time; her displeasure was more than obvious, in both the frosty tone of her voice and the stiffness of her elegantly clad body.

'I doubt that very much, madam,' he drawled just as icily, as the two of them continued to smile for the benefit of any watching them as they moved about the dance floor, in perfect sequence with the other couples dancing. 'Nevertheless, I will gladly repeat my statement, in that it is my wish that you immediately cease to encourage my brother in this ridiculous infatuation he seems to have developed for you.'

'The implication being that you believe me to have been deliberately encouraging those attentions in the first place?' His hostess for the evening arched one haughty blonde brow over eyes of an exquisite and unusual shade of turquoise blue.

A colour that Darian had previously only associated with the Mediterranean Sea, on a clear summer's day.

Darian had long been aware of this lady's presence in society, of course, first as the Earl of Carlisle's much younger wife and, for these past five years, as that deceased gentleman's very wealthy and scandalous widow.

But this was the first occasion upon which Darian had spent any length of time in her company. Having done so, he now perfectly understood his younger brother's infatuation with the countess; she was, without doubt, a woman of unparalleled beauty.

Her hair was the gold of ripened corn, her complexion as pale and smooth as alabaster; a creamy brow, softly curving cheeks, her neck long, with elegantly plump shoulders shown to advantage by the low *décolletage* of her gown. Those unusual turquoise eyes were surrounded by thick dark lashes, her nose small and pert above generous—and sensual—lips and the ampleness of her breasts revealed above a silk gown of the same deep turquoise colour as her eyes.

No, Darian could not fault his brother's taste in women, for Mariah Beecham was a veritable diamond, in regard to both her beauty and those voluptuous breasts.

Unfortunately, she was also a widow aged four and thirty to Anthony's only four and twenty, and mother to a daughter of seventeen. Indeed her daughter, the Lady Christina Beecham, was newly out this Season, and so also present this evening. She also bore a startling physical resemblance to her mother.

The young Lady Christina Beecham did not, however, as yet have the same scandalous reputation as her mother.

It was that reputation that had prompted Darian's recent concerns in regard to his brother's future happiness and for him to have uncharacteristically decided to interfere in the association.

He would have understood if Anthony had merely wished to discreetly share the lady's bed for a few weeks, or possibly even months. He accepted that all young gentlemen indulged in these sexual diversions—indeed, he had done so himself for many years at that age—for their own enjoyment and in order to gain the physical experience considered necessary for the marriage bed.

Unfortunately, this lady could never be called discreet. And Anthony had made it more than plain, in their conversation two days ago, that he did not regard Mariah Beecham as his mere mistress.

As Anthony's older brother and only relation, Darian could not allow him to entertain such a ruinous marriage. As Anthony's guardian, for at least another few months and so still in control of Anthony's considerable fortune, Darian considered it to be nothing more than an unsuitable infatuation.

His efforts so far to dissuade Anthony from continuing in his pursuit of this woman had been to no avail; his brother could be as stubborn as Darian when he had decided on a course of action.

Consequently, Darian had been left with no choice but to approach and speak to the woman herself, and he had attended the countess's ball this evening for just that purpose. His forays into polite society had been rare these past few years.

He much preferred to spend his evenings at his private club, or gambling establishments, in the company of the four gentlemen who had been his closest friends since their schooldays together. The past ten years had seen the five of them become known collectively in society as The Dangerous Dukes. It was a reputation they had earned for their exploits in the bedchamber, albeit discreetly in recent years, as much as on the battlefield.

Confirmed bachelors all, Darian had recently watched as two of his close friends had succumbed to falling in love—one of them had already married, the second was well on his way to being so.

Much as he might deplore the distance a wife would necessarily put between himself and two of his closest friends, Darian considered the two ladies in question to be more than suitable as his friends' consorts, and had no doubt that both ladies were equally as smitten as his two friends and that the marriages would flourish.

Also, Worthing and Hawksmere were both gentlemen aged two and thirty, the same age as Darian himself, and so both old enough, he considered, to know their own minds, and hearts. His brother, Anthony, was so much younger, and as such Darian did not consider him old enough as yet to know enough of life, let alone the true meaning of love for any woman.

Most especially, he knew Anthony could have no previous experience with a woman of Mariah Beecham's age and reputation. Nor had it helped to quell Darian's disquiet over the association that, when he had arrived here earlier this evening, his first sighting of his younger brother had been as he danced with the countess, a besotted smile upon his youthfully handsome face!

That she now felt just as strongly opposed as Anthony did to Darian's interference in the friendship was in no doubt as he looked down into those cold and challenging turquoise eyes.

It was a long time since Mariah had allowed anyone to anger her to the degree Darian Hunter had just succeeded in doing. Not since her husband, Martin, had been alive, in fact. But Darian Hunter, the arrogantly superior Duke of Wolfingham, had undoubtedly succeeded in annoying her intensely.

How dared this man come into her home and chastise her in this way? As if she were no more than a rebellious and impressionable young girl for him to reprove and reproach for her actions?

Actions of which she was, in this particular instance, completely innocent.

Mariah had, of course, been aware of Anthony Hunter's youthful attentions to her during these past few weeks. Attentions that she had neither encouraged nor discouraged. The former, because Anthony could never be any more to her than an entertaining boy, and the latter, because she had not wanted to hurt those youthful feelings.

All of which she would happily have assured his arrogant duke of a brother, if Wolfingham had not been so determined to be unpleasant to her from the moment they began dancing together.

She should have known that Darian Hunter, a gentleman known for his contempt of all polite social occasions, would have an ulterior motive when he had accepted the invitation to her ball. That he had also claimed a dance with her was unheard of; the duke's usual preference was to stand on the edge of society, looking coldly down his haughty nose at them all.

So much for that particular social feather in her cap! For Mariah now knew that Darian Hunter's only reason for attending her ball, for asking her to dance, had been with the intention of being unpleasant to her.

If only he was not so devilishly handsome, Mariah might have found it in her heart to forgive him. After all, his concern for the welfare of his younger brother and ward was commendable; Mariah also felt that same protectiveness in regard to her daughter, Christina.

And Wolfingham's arrogant handsomeness was

of a kind that no woman could remain completely immune to it. Not even a woman as jaded as herself.

That she knew she was not immune rankled and irritated Mariah more than any of the insulting things Wolfingham had just said to her.

The duke was excessively tall, at least a foot taller than her own five feet, his overlong hair as black as night and inclined to curl slightly on his brow and about his ears. His face—emerald-green eyes fringed by thick dark lashes, a long patrician nose, sharp blades for cheekbones, with sculptured lips that might have graced a Michelangelo statue, along with a strong and determined jaw—possessed a masculine beauty that was undeniably arresting.

The width of his shoulders, and broad and power-fully muscled chest, were all also shown to advantage in his perfectly tailored, black evening clothes. As were his lean and muscled thighs, and the long length of his legs and calves.

Wolfingham was, in fact, everything that Mariah, while acknowledging his male splendour, recoiled from and disliked in a man.

'I was not implying anything, madam.' Those sculptured lips now turned back contemptuously. 'Merely stating a fact.'

Mariah eyed him coldly. 'Indeed?'

Wolfingham nodded tersely. 'I know, for example, that my brother has attended every one of the same excessive amount of entertainments as you have these past three weeks or more. That he then rarely leaves your side for longer than a few minutes. That he calls at your home at least three, sometimes four, times a week and that he stays well beyond the time of any of your other callers. And that, in turn, you—'

'You are having me watched?' Mariah gasped, so disturbed at the thought she had almost stumbled in the dance.

'I am having my brother watched,' Wolfingham corrected grimly, his tightened grip upon her gloved hand having prevented her stumble. 'It is an unfortunate… coincidence that you have always happened to be wherever Anthony is and so your own movements have been afforded that same interest.'

It was truly insupportable that the haughtily contemptuous Duke of Wolfingham dared to so blatantly admit to having monitored those innocent meetings. Totally unacceptable on any level Mariah cared to consider and regardless of Wolfingham's reasons for having done so.

Lord Anthony Hunter was young, yes, but surely old enough to live his own life as he chose, without this excessive interference from his arrogant and disapproving older brother?

As for Mariah, she did not care in the least for having her personal life placed under such close scrutiny.

'Well, madam, what is your answer to be to my request?' Darian prompted impatiently, aware that the dance would soon come to an end and having no desire to waste any more of his evening than was absolutely necessary at the countess's ball. His shoulder, still healing from the recent bullet wound, was currently giving him an excessive amount of pain, following his exertions on the dance floor.

Mariah Beecham pulled her hand from his and stepped back and away from him as the dance came to an end. 'My answer is to make a request of my own, which is that *you* should leave my home forthwith!'

Darian's eyes widened in surprise before he was able to hide it; he had been the Marquis of Durham for all of his life, and the Duke of Wolfingham these past seven years, and as such no one talked to him in such a condescending manner as Mariah Beecham had just done.

He did not know whether to be irritated or amused that she should have done so now. 'And if I should choose not to?'

Her smile was again obviously for the benefit of anyone observing them, rather than genuinely meant, her gaze remaining icily cold as she took the arm he offered to lead her from the dance floor. 'In that case I will have no choice but to ask two of my footmen to forcibly remove you,' she answered with insincere sweetness as she removed her hand and turned to face him.

In contrast, Darian's own smile was perfectly sincere. Indeed, he could not remember being this amused and entertained, by anyone or anything, in a very long time. If ever! 'Are you certain two footmen would be sufficient to the task?' he drawled derisively.

An angry flush coloured those alabaster cheeks at his obvious mockery. 'I do not care how many foot-

men it takes, your Grace, as long as they are successful in removing you, and your insulting presence,
from my home.' Her voluptuous breasts quickly rose
and fell in her agitation.

'I believe I have only been stating the obvious,
madam.' Darian arched a challenging brow.

'Which is that you consider me entirely unsuitable
as a focus for your brother's infatuation?'

'I would go further, madam, and say that I find
you entirely unsuitable to occupy any situation in my
brother's life.' Darian's mouth thinned disapprovingly
at the realisation that *he* now found himself in the position of being attracted to this bewitching woman.
A woman, he had discovered during the course of
the past few minutes, totally unlike any other he had
ever met.

Mariah Beecham was undoubtedly a dazzling
beauty and it was impossible for a man's gaze not
to admire the rise and fall of those voluptuous and
creamy breasts. But he had discovered, as they danced
together, that she was far more than just a beautiful
face and a desirable body.

Her forthright manner, and her obvious contempt
for him, was a refreshing change after the years of
women simpering and flirting in his company, in a
bid to secure his attention and in the hopes they might
one day become his duchess.

Mariah Beecham was obviously a mature and
sophisticated woman. A wealthy and independent
woman more than capable of making her own decisions as well as bringing up her young daughter alone.

Moreover, the countess was a woman who made it perfectly clear that she would do it in exactly the way that *she* pleased.

That sophistication and independence of will was having the strangest effect upon Darian's libido. Indeed, he found himself becoming aroused by her to a degree that he acknowledged his shaft had risen, and was now painfully engorged, in response to the desire he was currently feeling towards her.

Which had not been his intention when he came here this evening. Darian's only *desire* had been to protect Anthony from the woman.

His jaw tightened. 'I will leave willingly, and gladly, madam, if you will first consent to cut my brother loose from your enthralment.'

Mariah's breath caught in her throat at this man's temerity in continuing to insult her after having come to her home for the sole purpose of upbraiding her, in regard to what he considered her encouragement of his brother's attentions to her. 'I believe you must address any such remarks to your brother, rather than to myself, Wolfingham.'

'Anthony is too besotted with you to listen to reason.'

'That would seem to imply that you have tried?' she taunted.

Wolfingham's mouth thinned at her mockery. 'I do not appreciate your humour on the subject, madam.'

Her eyes flashed. 'And I, sir, do not in the least appreciate the insulting manner in which you have chosen to address me this evening.'

'Then it would appear we are at an impasse,' he drawled coldly.

Mariah's eyes narrowed. 'If you will excuse me— Let go of my arm, Wolfingham.' Her warning was dangerously soft as she looked first at those long and elegant fingers currently wrapped about the top of her arm, before raising the coldness of her gaze to stare challengingly into the duke's grimly arrogant face.

Darian had not meant to so much as lay another finger upon Mariah Beecham, not when he was already far too physically aware of her. His action, of reaching out to clasp her arm, had been purely instinctive, a reaction to the fact that she obviously intended to walk away from him.

Something he found he did not like in the slightest.

'I believe we would be better continuing this conversation outside on the terrace,' he bit out grimly as he maintained his hold upon her arm long enough to cross the ballroom and step outside on to the deserted terrace.

He released her arm as abruptly as he had earlier grasped it, before placing both of his hands behind his back and clasping them together as he looked down the length of his nose at her.

'How dare you manhandle me in that way?' Mariah Beecham gasped her outrage at finding herself alone outside on the terrace with him.

'I believe you will find that I dare much in the protection of my impressionable younger brother, madam.' Darian looked down at her coldly. 'Most especially so when I have good reason to believe a woman such as yourself could never have any serious intentions with regard to a man as young and *inexperienced* as Anthony.'

'A woman such as me?' she repeated softly.

Darian nodded tersely. 'We must both be aware of your reputation, madam.'

She eyed him coldly. 'Must we?'

His gaze turned frosty at her tone. 'That reputation apart, you were married to a man at least twenty-five years your senior and now you are dallying with a man at least ten years younger than yourself.' Darian gave a shrug. 'Perhaps it is that you are afraid of entertaining the attentions of a man of your own age?'

Mariah knew that this man could have absolutely no idea of the unhappiness she had suffered during her years of marriage to the much older Martin Beecham; they had both taken great care, for their daughter, Christina's, sake, to ensure that society did not learn of their deep-felt dislike of each other.

As for her dallying with this man's younger brother? It was pure nonsense. The young Lord Anthony had certainly received no encouragement from her, in what Wolfingham now claimed was his brother's infatuation with her.

Truth be told, Mariah did not have a serious interest in any gentleman, her marriage to Martin having soured her towards spending too much time in the company of any man, let alone trusting her emotions, her heart, to one of them. In her opinion, all men were selfish and controlling. And she had no intentions of being controlled by anyone ever again.

Certainly not Wolfingham!

'A man such as yourself, you mean?' she taunted drily.

'I would appear to fit that criteria, yes,' he bit out harshly.

She gave a scornful smile. 'I believe you are still a year or two younger than I, Wolfingham. Nor, after this conversation, would I be foolish enough to ever believe any interest you showed in me, now or in the future, to be in the least sincere.'

Then she would be wrong, Darian acknowledged reluctantly. Because these past few minutes in her company had shown him he was very interested in Mariah Beecham. Intellectually as well as physically.

Not only was it an unwise interest on his part, but it was also a forbidden one, in light of Anthony's feelings for the woman. Darian could not be so disloyal to his brother as to try to win, and bed, the woman Anthony believed himself to be in love with.

'You would be perfectly correct to mistrust any such interest,' he conceded drily.

'Then if we have quite finished this conversation?' She arched haughty brows. 'It is rather chilly out here and I have other guests to attend to.'

'First I wish to know if it is your intention to continue seeing Anthony.'

'As it would appear he attends most, if not all, of the same entertainments as myself, I do not see how I can do otherwise.'

So much for his being a voice of reason, Darian derided himself impatiently. He seemed, in fact, to have only succeeded in making the situation worse, rather than better. By approaching Mariah Beecham and talking to her of his concern for Anthony, he appeared to have angered the lady into doing the opposite of what he asked.

Not only that, but he now seemed to have developed a physical desire for the woman himself!

She looked especially lovely in the moonlight, her hair having turned palest gold, her flawless skin pure ivory against the darker silk of her gown. As for her perfume! It was a mixture of flowers and some heady and exotic scent Darian could not quite place, but that seeped insidiously into his very pores, heightening his senses, so that he was aware only of the woman standing so proudly beautiful before him.

'Must we continue to argue about this, Mariah?' His voice lowered huskily even as he took a step forward.

Her gaze became guarded as she tilted her head further back in order to be able to look up at him. 'I have not given you permission to use my first name,' she bit out frostily. 'Nor am I aware of any argument between the two of us. You have made a request and I have discounted the very idea of there ever being any sort of alliance between your brother and myself. As far as I am concerned, that is an end to the subject.'

Darian drew in a deep breath. 'I do not see how it can be, when Anthony seems so set upon his pursuit of you.'

Mariah was not at all happy at the way Darian Hunter had moved so much closer to her. So close, in fact, that she felt as if her personal space had been invaded. And not in an altogether unpleasant way.

Her years of marriage to Martin had been extremely difficult ones, so much so that in the early years of their marriage she had preferred to remain secluded in the country. Maturity had brought with it a certain confidence, a knowledge, if you will, of her own powers as a woman, if not in regard to her husband, then at least towards the attentions shown to her by other gentlemen. With that confidence had come the art, the safety, of social flirtation, without the promise of there ever being anything more.

It was a veneer of sophistication that had stood her in good stead since Martin's death five years ago, when so many other gentlemen had decided that the now widowed and very wealthy Countess of Carlisle would make them an admirable wife.

As if Mariah would willingly forgo the newfound freedom and wealth that widowhood had given her, in order to become another man's wife and possession!

Oh, she knew well the reputation she had in society, of a woman who took as her lover any man she chose. Knew of it, because it was a reputation she had deliberately fostered; if Mariah Beecham was known only to take lovers, rather than having any intention of ever contemplating remarrying, then the fortune hunters, at least, were kept at bay.

Occasionally—as now!—a gentlemen would attempt to breach those walls she had placed about herself and her private life, but to date she had managed to thwart that interest without offence being taken on either side.

Even on such brief closer acquaintance, she knew that Darian Hunter, the powerful Duke of Wolfingham, was not a man to be gainsaid by flirtatious cajolery or, failing that, the cut direct.

And he was currently standing far too close to Mariah for her comfort.

'I have already told you that you must speak with your brother further on that subject, Wolfingham.' Mariah tilted her chin challengingly. 'Now if you would kindly step aside? As I have said, it is now my wish to return to my other guests.'

Instead of stepping away Darian took another step forward, at once assailed by the warmth of Mariah Beecham's closer proximity and the aroma of that exotic and unique perfume. 'And do you always get what you wish for, Mariah?' he prompted huskily.

The nerve fluttered, pulsed, in the slender length of her neck, as the only outward sign of her disquiet at his persistence. 'Rarely what I wish for,' she bit out tersely, 'but invariably what I want!'

'And what is it that you want now, I wonder?' Darian mused as he continued to breathe in, and be affected by, her heady perfume. 'Can it be that your air of uninterest and detachment is but a ruse? And that secretly, inwardly, you long for a man who will take the initiative, take control of the situation? To take control of you?'

'No!' the countess gasped, her face having paled in the moonlight.

His brow rose. 'Perhaps you protest too much?'

'I protest because it is how I genuinely feel,' she assured vehemently. 'I am no gentleman's plaything, to be controlled.'

'No?' One of Darian's hands moved up of its own volition, with the intention of cupping the smooth curve of her cheek.

'Do not touch me!' She flinched back, her eyes huge turquoise pools now in the pallor of her face.

Darian frowned at her vehemence. 'But I should very much like to touch you, Mariah.'

'I *said*, do not touch me!' Her expression was one of grim determination as she reached up and attempted to physically push Darian away from her.

It was now Darian's turn to gasp, to lose his breath completely, as one of her tiny hands connected with his recently injured and painfully aching shoulder, causing pain such as he had never known before to burst, to course hotly, piercingly, through the whole length and breadth of his body.

He clasped his shoulder as he staggered back, his knees in danger of buckling beneath him at the depth of that pain, black spots appearing in front of his eyes even as his vision began to blur and darken.

'Wolfingham? Tell me what is wrong.'

Mariah Beecham's voice seemed to come from a long distance away as the darkness about Darian first thickened, then became absolute.

Chapter Two

Darian felt totally disorientated as the waves of
darkness began to lift and he slowly awakened.

Quite *where* it was he had awakened to, he had no
idea, as he turned from where he lay on the bed to
look about the unfamiliar bedchamber.

It was most certainly a feminine room, decorated
in pale lavenders and creams, with delicate white
furnishings and lavender brocade curtains at the
windows and about the four-poster bed on which he
currently reclined, the pillows and bedclothes beneath
him of pale lilac satin and lace.

It was Darian's idea of a feminine hell!

Certainly he felt ridiculous lying amongst such
frills and fancies. Nor did he remember how he came
to be here in the first place.

He recalled attending the Countess of Carlisle's
ball, dancing with her, and then that heated conversation with her on the terrace. Followed by the excruciating pain, and then—nothing. He remembered
absolutely nothing of what had happened beyond that.

Either he was still at Mariah Beecham's home, which, considering their argument, he doubted very much, or he had gone on to a club or gaming hell, where he had drunk too much, before spending the night with some woman. Both would be uncharacteristic; Darian never drank too much when he was out and about in the evening, nor did he bed random women.

As such, neither of those explanations seemed likely for his current disorientation.

He struggled to sit up, with the intention of removing himself from his hellish surroundings. All to no avail, as he found it impossible to move his left arm.

Glancing down at the source of the problem, Darian realised that he was wearing only his pantaloons. His jacket, waistcoat, his shirt *and* his boots had all been removed and his left shoulder was now tightly strapped up in a white bandage, his arm immobilised in a sling across the bareness of his chest.

'And just what do you think you are doing?'

Darian, having finally managed to manoeuvre himself into a sitting position on the side of the bed, now turned sharply at the sound of that imperious voice, his eyes widening and then narrowing as Mariah Beecham stepped into the bedchamber and closed the door quietly behind her.

She was no longer dressed in the turquoise silk gown, but now wore a day-dress of sky blue, the style simpler, with just a touch of lace at the cap sleeves. Her hair was also less elaborately styled than at the ball, the blonde curls merely gathered up and secured at her crown and completely unadorned.

The reason for those changes in her appearance became apparent as she lightly crossed the room on slippered feet in order to pull back the lavender brocade curtains from across the windows, allowing the full light of day to shine into the bedchamber.

She turned to look across at him critically. 'You are looking a little better this morning, Wolfingham. The doctor advised last night that you are *not* to attempt to get out of bed for several days,' she continued firmly as Darian would have stood up. 'You had burst several of the stitches on the wound on your shoulder and it was also in need of cleansing before new stitches and a bandage could be applied,' she added reprovingly.

Darian knew his wounded shoulder had been paining him for several days now, but at this moment it throbbed and ached like the very devil!

'Something, the doctor assured me yesterday evening as he reapplied those stitches, that you must have been aware of for some time before last night?' the countess added sternly.

Of course Darian had been aware of it, but his brother's future, and this unsuitable alliance, had been of more importance to him than his own painful shoulder. Nor was it the state of his own health that was now his main concern.

The reason for *that* was the how and why he came to still be in Mariah Beecham's home on the morning following her ball, for he had no choice but to accept that was where he was.

Darian frowned as he recalled their unsatisfactory conversation on the terrace of Carlisle House the evening before. How he had been unable to resist moving closer to Mariah, drawn by her unique perfume and the temptation of the perfection of her skin in the moonlight.

He also had a vague memory of Mariah reaching up to physically push him away after he had ignored her instructions to step back from her. The pain that had followed that push had been excruciating. So intense that it had caused Darian's breath to cease and his knees to buckle as the waves of blackness engulfed him. After that he remembered nothing.

Did that mean he had remained unconscious for the whole of the previous night?

That he had spent that night in Mariah Beecham's home? Possibly in her own bedchamber?

If that was indeed the case, then Darian certainly had no memory of any of those events.

But neither did he recall having departed Carlisle House. Or having been attended by a doctor.

'You are currently in one of my guest bedchambers,' the countess supplied drily, as his horrified expression must have given away at least some of his thoughts. 'My daughter's choice rather than my own,' she continued with a rueful glance at their feminine surroundings.

Darian licked the dryness of his lips before speaking for the first time since he had awoken. 'Lady Christina knows I spent the night here?'

'Why, yes,' Mariah drawled, Wolfingham's obvious discomfort in his surroundings succeeding in dissipating some of her own irritation in having to accommodate him here for the night, following his faint the previous evening. 'There was nothing else to be done once you had fainted dead away on my terrace. What else would you have me call it, Wolfingham?' she added mockingly as he gave a grunt of protest.

He scowled his displeasure. 'I was obviously overcome with pain—to call it a faint makes me sound like a complete ninny.'

'It does rather.' She arched mocking brows. 'Very well, Wolfingham, when you were overcome with pain,' she conceded drily as he continued to glower. 'Whatever the cause, it left me with no choice but to have two of my footmen carry you up the servants' stairs, before placing you in one of the bedchambers and sending for the doctor—much as the temptation was for me to just leave you unconscious upon my terrace, apparently inebriated, for one of my other guests to find!' she added.

Green eyes narrowed. 'I suppose I should thank you for having resisted that particular temptation,' Wolfingham growled.

'I suppose you should, yes,' Mariah drawled dismissively. 'But I doubt you intend doing so?'

'Not at this moment, no,' Wolfingham bit out from between gritted teeth.

She gave a mocking shake of her head. 'Bad show,

Wolfingham, when at considerable inconvenience to myself, I have undoubtedly helped you to maintain your reputation as being the stern and soberly respectable Duke of Wolfingham.'

His brow lowered darkly. 'You have also put me in the position of now having to remove myself from your home, without detection by a third party, on the morning following your ball.'

'And so tarnishing that sterling reputation anyway,' she derided. 'Poor Wolfingham!'

He remained disgruntled. 'My reputation in society is one of sternness and sober respectability?'

'Oh, yes.' Mariah strolled across to where Wolfingham still sat on the side of the bed, the darkness of his hair, tousled and unkempt, succeeding in lessening his usual air of austerity and also taking years off his age of two, or possibly three, and thirty.

Nevertheless, it was far safer for Mariah to take in the tousled appearance of Wolfingham's hair than to allow her gaze to move any lower. To where the removal of his top clothes had rendered Darian Hunter naked from the waist up, apart from the bandage and sling the doctor had placed about his left shoulder and arm the night before.

And a very masculine and muscled chest it was, too, with a light dusting of dark hair, which deepened to a vee down the firm and muscled length of his stomach, before disappearing into the loosened waistband of his black evening trousers.

None of which Mariah was at all happy to realise she had taken note of! 'The doctor remarked that the original injury to your shoulder has all the appearance of being a bullet wound,' she said challengingly. 'And was possibly inflicted a week or so ago?'

'Six days ago, to be precise,' he conceded gruffly. 'I would now have your word that you will not discuss this with anyone else,' he added harshly.

Her eyebrows rose. 'And will you trust my word if it is given?'

'I will.' Darian had little choice in the matter but to trust to Mariah Beecham's discretion. Besides which, there might be plenty of gossip in society in regard to the countess, but he had never heard of her having discussed with anyone the gentlemen with whom she was known to have been intimately involved.

'Then you have it.' She nodded now. 'Nevertheless, I should be interested to learn how you came to receive such a wound. Unless England is already once again at war and I am unaware of it?' She arched mocking blonde brows.

Darian knew that for most women, this would have been her first question upon entering the bedchamber and finding her uninvited guest had finally awoken from his stupor!

But, as he had learnt yesterday evening, Mariah Beecham was not like most women. Indeed, he truly had no idea what manner of woman she was. Which only added to her mystique.

And attraction?

Yesterday evening Mariah Beecham had given the appearance of being the sophisticated and confident woman of society that she undoubtedly was.

Today, free of adornment or artifice, Mariah Beecham looked no older than her seventeen-year-old daughter.

Her figure was that of a mature woman, of course, but her face was smooth and unlined in the sunlight, her eyes a clear Mediterranean turquoise, despite her having hosted a ball the previous evening and no doubt having retired very late to her own bedchamber.

Darian felt that stirring of his arousal, which was rapidly becoming a familiar reaction to being in this woman's company, as he gazed upon her natural loveliness through narrowed lids. 'I fear that peace will not last for too much longer, now that Napoleon has returned to France and is currently reported to be on his way to Paris,' he rasped in an attempt to dampen his physical response to this woman.

'I do not interest myself in such boring things as politics and intrigue,' she drawled dismissively. 'Nor does any of that explain how you came to receive such a wound.' She continued to look at him pointedly, before a derisive smile slowly curved the fullness of her lips at his continued silence. 'Can it be that the cold and haughty Duke of Wolfingham has recently fought a duel? Over a woman? Surely not?' Mocking humour now gleamed in her eyes.

Darian had not cared for the disparaging way in which Mariah Beecham had earlier said his reputation was one of sober respectability. Or that she now referred to him as the cold and haughty Duke of Wolfingham. Nor did Darian like the implication that she doubted he had ever felt so emotional about any woman that he would have fought a duel over her.

Admittedly, he was, by nature, a private man. One who had long preferred his own company or that of his few close friends. But he'd had no idea, until now, that this privacy of nature had resulted in society, in Mariah Beecham, believing him to be sober—boring?—as well as cold and haughty—arrogant?

As the elder son of the sixth Duke of Wolfingham, and Marquis of Durham from birth, Darian had been brought up to know he would one day inherit the title of Duke from his father, along with the management of all the estates entailed with the title. An onerous and unenviable responsibility, which had become his at the age of only five and twenty; much earlier than might have been expected, but his father had been but sixty years of age when he died.

With the title of Duke and its other onerous responsibilities had also come the guardianship of his younger brother, Anthony.

All of these things had made it impossible for Darian to continue with the hedonistic pursuits he had previously enjoyed with his close friends and that, along with his soldiering, had hitherto occupied much of his time.

He had not realised until now that it had also rendered him as being thought stern and sober, as well as haughty. By society as a whole, it would appear, and by this woman in particular.

Nor did he care to be thought so now, for it made him sound as old as Methuselah and just as uninteresting! A circumstance Darian did not enjoy, when he considered his own undoubted physical response to Mariah Beecham.

His mouth tightened. 'I am sure you are as aware as I that the fighting of duels is forbidden.'

She arched blonde brows. 'And do you always follow the rules, Wolfingham?'

Darian gave a humourless smile. 'Your opinion of my reputation would seem to imply as much.'

'But we are all so much more than our reputations, are we not?' Mariah Beecham replied enigmatically.

'Do you include yourself in that statement?' Darian studied her through narrowed lids, taking note of that curling golden hair, the smoothness of her brow, those clear and untroubled blue eyes and the light blush that now coloured her alabaster cheeks, her lips both full and succulent.

A face that appeared utterly without guilt or guile.

Misleadingly so? Or could that air of innocence, so unusual in a woman of four and thirty, possibly be the real Mariah Beecham?

In view of this woman's reputation, Darian found that impossible to believe; the countess could no doubt add 'accomplished actress' to her list of other questionable attributes!

Mariah did not at all care for the way in which Wolfingham was now studying her so intently.

Having Wolfingham point out, the previous evening, that his younger brother had shown a marked interest in her these past weeks was irritating enough.

But to have the far too astute, and equally as intelligent, Darian Hunter, the Duke of Wolfingham, show an interest in her, for whatever reason, was not only disturbing, but could also be dangerous.

For Mariah was most certainly not all that her reputation implied. Indeed, she did not believe, after Wolfingham's revelations the night before regarding that reputation, that she was much of any of what society, or this man, believed her to be.

Deliberately so. For who would suspect that the scandalous Mariah Beecham, the widowed Countess of Carlisle, was also an agent for the Crown, and that she had been so these past seven years and more?

She had not set out for it to be so. She had become embroiled in the intrigues of the English court quite by accident, after discovering that her own husband was a traitor to both his country and his king.

Having no idea what to do with that knowledge, it had taken Mariah some weeks to find a member of the government to whom she might pass along that information.

Only to discover that once she had done so the first time, there was no going back. That her position in society could, and did, open many doors, as it invited confidences from both ladies and gentlemen of the *ton.*

And so, from that time on Mariah had made a point of forming her friendships only with those ladies and gentlemen who might have knowledge that would be of benefit to, or was opposed to, the English monarchy or government.

She had been brought up in the knowledge that her parents' only expectation of her was that she become the wife of a titled gentleman, even if she did not love that gentleman. Her father was himself extremely wealthy, but not completely acceptable to all of society. Indeed, greater acquaintance with society had shown her that love was not a requirement of any of the *ton*'s marriages.

Her husband's only expectation of her had been that she bring a considerable portion of her father's fortune to their marriage, his own fortune having become depleted almost to extinction.

Mariah loved her daughter dearly and, because of that, had willingly sacrificed the years she had suffered of being thought of as just an adjunct of her husband, Lord Martin Beecham, the Earl of Carlisle.

Finding herself suddenly of use, her opinions of importance, had caused Mariah to relish the new role in her life.

As a consequence, the past seven years were the first ones where Mariah had felt useful and valued for herself alone.

She would be unable to continue along that path if anyone in society were to ever discover that she used her title and wealth only as a way in which she might work, and spy, for the Crown.

If the shrewd Darian Hunter, Duke of Wolfingham, were to ever discover her work as a spy for the Crown…

She forced a teasing smile to now curve her lips.

'Surely that is for me to know and for others to find out?'

Darian drew in a sharp breath at Mariah Beecham's huskily flirtatious tone, a quiver of awareness tingling down the length of his spine as his body responded.

At the same time, he sensed that Mariah's flirtation was somehow not genuine, but forced, although he had no idea why that should be.

Indeed, nothing about this woman, or her actions, was in the least clear to him. And until such time as it was, if it ever was, he would be well advised to remain wary in her company.

'Considering that you have refused my request to discourage my brother's interest in you,' he answered her briskly as he stood up, 'and the amount of times our paths have chanced to cross these past seven years or more, I very much doubt there will be any opportunity in future for me to know you any better than I do at this moment.'

'Do I detect a note of regret in your tone?' she taunted.

'Not in the least,' Darian dismissed harshly. 'I am more than ready to leave and so end our acquaintance.'

'Then you had best do so,' she drawled unconcernedly.

His eyes narrowed. 'Did you dismiss my carriage last night?'

The countess laughed huskily. 'Tempted as I was to do otherwise!' She nodded in confirmation. 'It might have been amusing to see how you would have explained that occurrence to any who cared to ask. But, of course, you are Wolfingham, one of The Dangerous Dukes,' she continued drily. 'And like your four friends, Wolfingham does not care to explain himself, to any man or woman!'

Darian's eyes narrowed. 'You do not have a very good opinion of me, do you?'

'Until yesterday evening I do not believe I held any opinion of you whatsoever,' she assured uninterestedly.

His breath caught in his throat at that dismissal; if he did not care to explain himself to man or woman then it was equally as true that same man or woman would never dare to question him, either! 'And now?'

'Now I know without a doubt that you are both arrogant and insulting.'

Darian winced at her dismissive tone, knowing that he had been both of those things in his dealings with this woman. 'If you would kindly send word to Wolfingham House, via one of your obviously capable footmen, and inform my butler that I have need of my carriage, I will then be able to remove my intrusive self from both your household and your presence!'

Mariah felt a sense of disquiet at the abruptness of Wolfingham's departure. 'I had not expected you to capitulate quite so easily, Wolfingham, in regard to my continuing friendship with your brother?' she mocked.

'I am not capitulating, merely withdrawing in order to rethink my strategy,' he assured drily.

'Ah.' Mariah nodded knowingly. 'I remind you that the doctor instructed that you were to remain abed for the next three days at least.'

Having now crossed to where his clothes lay draped over the bedroom chair, Wolfingham turned to look at her with those narrowed green eyes.

Green eyes surrounded by the longest, thickest, darkest lashes Mariah had seen on any man.

Indeed, Darian Hunter was a man of startling and masculine good looks; the nakedness of his back was exceedingly broad and muscled for a man who supposedly ran his estates from the comfort of his home here in London. As were his arms and the flatness of his abdomen, his legs also appearing long and muscled in those black evening trousers. Even his feet, *sans* his boots, bore a long and elegant appearance.

And Mariah could not remember the last time she had noticed the masculine beauty of any man, fully clothed or otherwise!

Perhaps when she had been Christina's age, and on the brink of womanhood, she might have allowed her head to be turned a time or two by a handsome gentleman, but certainly not at any time since. The very nature of her marriage to Martin Beecham had meant there had never been any further inclination on her part to indulge in those girlish infatuations.

But Mariah could not deny, to herself at least, that she had noticed, and been aware of, every muscle and sinew of Darian Hunter's muscular torso these past few minutes. And also been affected by it, as the slight fluttering of her pulse, the warmth in her cheeks and the aching fullness of her breasts all testified.

And she did not want to feel any of those things for any man!

Warning her that Darian Hunter more than lived up to his dangerous reputation, not only to her continued work for the Crown, but also to Mariah's own peace of mind.

'Nor shall I once I am returned to it,' Darian now answered the countess huskily, aware of the sudden, sexual, tension in the heavy stillness of the bedchamber. 'As for my brother, if all else fails, then I fear Anthony must learn of the vagaries of women in the way that all men do—the hard way!' he added derisively.

'Now you are being deliberately insulting again, Wolfingham, not just to me, but all women.' An angry flush now coloured Mariah Beecham's cheeks.

A blush that only succeeded in enhancing her beauty; her eyes glittered that deep turquoise, her cheeks glowing, her lips having become a deep and rosy red.

A very kissable deep and rosy red…

'That was not my intention,' Darian dismissed softly.

'No?'

'I believe my remark was more specific than that,' he assured huskily, holding Mariah's gaze as he slowly crossed to where she stood so stiff and challenging in the middle of the bedchamber. 'Might I ask for your assistance in dressing? I realise it is usual for a man to ask a woman for help to *un*dress,' he added drily as Mariah's brows rose in obvious surprise at his request, 'but I am unable to pull my shirt on over my head on my own.'

Mariah accepted that Wolfingham's request for assistance was perfectly logical, given his injury, and yet she still baulked at the thought of performing such a task of intimacy for him.

She very much doubted that Wolfingham—or any in society!—would believe it if told, but Mariah had seen no man, other than her husband, even half-naked as Wolfingham now was. And Martin, twenty-five years her senior, had certainly never possessed the same muscular and disturbing physique Wolfingham now displayed so splendidly.

Her mouth firmed. 'I will send for one of my footmen to assist you.'

'There is no need for that, surely, when you are standing right here before me?' Darian murmured throatily, his good sense having once again deserted him as he was again assaulted by Mariah Beecham's unique and arousing perfume. An arousal he was finding it more and more difficult to control when in this woman's presence.

In view of Anthony's infatuation with Mariah Beecham, it would be unwise for Darian to allow his own attraction to her to develop into anything deeper than the physical discomfort it already was. Even if Mariah Beecham was herself agreeable to taking it any further, which he already knew that she was not.

On a logical level, Darian knew and accepted all of those things.

Unfortunately, his aroused and hardened body had a completely different opinion on the matter!

'If you please?' His gaze was intent upon her face now as he held out his shirt to her, allowing him to note the deepening of the blush that coloured her cheeks and the pulse throbbing at the base of her slender throat.

A surprising physical reaction, surely, coming from an experienced woman reputed to have indulged in many affairs, both during her marriage and since?

Darian's gaze narrowed searchingly as she stubbornly lifted her chin to meet his challenging gaze. She still made no effort to relieve him of his shirt. 'Unless, of course, you find the idea, and me, too repulsive…?'

It took every effort of Mariah's will to hold back the choked, slightly hysterical, laugh that threatened to burst from her throat, at the mere suggestion that any woman, that *she*, might find anything about Wolfingham in the least repulsive.

For the first time, in more years than she cared to remember, Mariah found herself wholly and completely physically aware of a man.

Of Darian Hunter, the arrogant and contemptuous Duke of Wolfingham, of all men.

Nevertheless, Mariah was aware. Of his reassuring height. His rakishly handsome good looks. And the lean and muscled strength of his body.

And she did not welcome the sensation.

She placed a disdainful curl on her lips. 'It is certainly true that I have always been...particular...as to which men I choose to be intimate with.'

'All evidence to the contrary, madam!'

Mariah drew her breath in sharply at the unexpected and contemptuously delivered insult, before just as quickly masking that response; the sophisticated and experienced Mariah Beecham—a public persona she had deliberately nurtured these past seven years—would laugh derisively in the face of such an insult.

Which was exactly what Mariah did now. 'I am flattered that you should have even taken the time to notice such things in regard to myself, Wolfingham.'

His nostrils flared. 'You take delight in your reputation?'

Did she?

Oh, yes!

It was Mariah's own personal joke on society, that they should all perceive her as being one thing and she knew herself to be something else entirely. Only her darling Christina, now seventeen, and currently enjoying her very first Season, had necessarily been informed of the true reason for Mariah's flirtatious behaviour in public. It was a risk to share that confidence with anyone, of course, but Mariah simply could not have borne for her darling daughter, the person she loved most in all the world, to ever believe the nonsense society gossiped about her.

'No doubt as much as you do your own,' Mariah now dismissed enigmatically.

Darian scowled as he recalled what this woman had described as being his reputation. 'Then that would be not at all.'

She smiled. 'Unfortunately, even you cannot dictate what society thinks of you.'

'Even I?'

'Why, yes, for you are the omnipotent Duke of Wolfingham, are you not?' she dismissed airily. 'Your shirt, if you please,' she instructed briskly, reaching out to take the item of clothing from him. Wolfingham continued to hold on to it, standing far too close to her while he did so.

Darian looked down at her intently, wishing he knew at least some of the thoughts going on inside that surprisingly intelligent head of hers. Before speaking with Mariah Beecham yesterday evening, Darian would have described her, had considered her, as nothing more than an empty-headed flirt, with little in her beautiful head but the pursuit of her own pleasure.

He still had no idea of what or who Mariah Beecham truly was, but an empty-headed flirt she certainly was not.

Rendering her flirtation with Anthony, a man fully ten years her junior, all the more puzzling.

'Mariah—' Darian broke off his husky query as there was the briefest of knocks on the door to the bedchamber before it was opened.

'Mama, I—' Lady Christina Beecham stopped what she had been about to say as she stood in the open doorway, eyes wide as she took in the apparent cameo of intimacy between her mother and their half-dressed guest.

Darian had certainly never been discovered in quite such a scene of apparent intimacy by the daughter of any woman, and he now found himself momentarily nonplussed as he searched his mind for something appropriate to say or do. He frowned down at Mariah Beecham as she looked up at him. She began to chuckle huskily, before that chuckle became a full-throated laugh of pure enjoyment.

At Darian's obvious expense…

Chapter Three

❦

'I trust, Lady Christina, that you do not think too badly of me for the circumstances under which we last met?' Darian murmured politely as the two of them danced together at Lady Stockton's ball, fully a week after their first momentous meeting in a guest bedchamber at Carlisle House.

A week in which Darian had necessarily to spend most of his time in his own bed, recovering from the setback from his bullet wound. For much of that time he'd found his thoughts returning to that morning in Mariah Beecham's guest bedchamber.

Not that there had been a great deal for him to remember and think about once Christina Beecham had appeared in the bedchamber so unexpectedly.

Mariah's amusement at the interruption had been short-lived, her movements having then become brisk and businesslike as she had helped Darian on with his shirt before excusing herself to go downstairs and see to the ordering of his carriage. The two ladies had left the bedchamber arm in arm together.

Darian had felt surprisingly weak after having completed dressing himself as best he could, sitting on the side of the bed to recover as he awaited the arrival of his carriage. Once arrived, his groom had then helped him down the stairs and into that carriage, necessitating that Darian's words of gratitude for the countess's assistance be brief.

Once returned to Wolfingham House, he had sent for his own physician, who'd agreed with his colleague's diagnosis, as he confined Darian to bed for the next three days at least, and rest thereafter for several more days, unless Darian wished to shuffle off his mortal coil completely.

Darian despised any form of weakness, in himself more than others, and that enforced time abed had not sat easily upon his shoulders, despite receiving several visits from his closest friends to help relieve the boredom. Anthony had also called upon him several times and been told that Darian was indisposed and not receiving visitors, which allowed Darian to at least avoid that particular confrontation until he was feeling more himself.

He had to trust that the countess would keep her promise in regard to discussing with others the bullet wound to his shoulder and the night he had necessarily spent in her home. But he had no doubt Mariah would have taken great delight in regaling Anthony with the details of Darian's efforts to persuade her to end their friendship.

Once he felt well enough, Darian had dictated a letter of gratitude to his secretary, to be delivered to the countess, carefully worded so as not to reveal the full extent of his indebtedness to her. He had received no acknowledgement or reply to that missive. As if Mariah Beecham, like himself, would prefer to continue as if that night had not taken place at all.

Consequently, this was the first occasion upon which Darian had been able to offer his apologies in person, to the younger of the two Beecham ladies at least, for the manner of his indisposition the week before.

Mariah Beecham had proved somewhat more elusive this evening than her daughter, always flirting or dancing away on the arm of some other gentleman whenever Darian had attempted to approach her. Christina Beecham had proved far less averse to his request that she dance a set with him. No doubt, unlike her mother before her, Christina Beecham was fully aware of the compliment being paid to her, as the Duke of Wolfingham did not, as a rule, dance at any of these occasions.

She looked up at him shyly now from between thick blonde lashes, her eyes the same beautiful turquoise colour as her mother's, her blonde-haired beauty also similar to that of the countess. 'Mama has already explained the situation to me, your Grace,' she now dismissed huskily.

Darian would be very interested to hear how Mariah had managed to do that, when he was not altogether sure how to explain the situation himself. *To* himself, as well as to others.

'Indeed,' he murmured noncommittally. 'She seems

to be fully occupied this evening.' Another glance about the ballroom had shown him that Mariah Beecham was no longer in the room.

Christina gave a smile of affection. 'Mama's time, and dance card, are always fully occupied at such entertainments as these, your Grace.'

Darian looked down searchingly at the younger of the Beecham ladies. 'And are you not bothered by having to witness the spectacle of seeing so many gentlemen flirting and leering at your mother's— Forgive me,' he bit out stiffly. 'That was unforgivably rude of me.' And, he realised, far too close to his feelings on the matter for his own comfort.

Mariah was wearing a red silk gown this evening, with a very low *décolletage* that revealed the full, ivory swell of the tops of her breasts. A fact Darian had noted several gentlemen taking advantage of as they talked or danced with her.

'Yes, it was,' Christina Beecham answered him with the same bluntness as her mother. 'But then, Mama had already warned me you are very forthright, in both your manner and speech,' she added pertly.

Darian found he did not care for being dismissed so scathingly. Nor did he believe Mariah had used a word so innocent as 'forthright' to describe his previous manner and conversations with her. 'I meant no disrespect to you,' he bit out tersely.

'Only to Mama,' she acknowledged drily. 'Mama has taught me that it is better not to pass comment on what one does not know.'

'Obviously my own mother was neglectful in that particular duty.'

'Obviously.'

Yes, this lady, for all she was very young, was proving to be just as capable of delivering a set-down as her mother!

Darian was also aware that his own reaction to those flirting and leering gentlemen was not one of impartiality, but rather one of complete partiality. Indeed, he had disliked intensely to have to stand by and witness those other gentlemen showing Mariah such marked attentions.

In truth, he had thought of Mariah Beecham far more than was wise this past week. Of her beauty. Her unique perfume. Of his own physical and un-controllable response to the lush curves of her body.

And, quite frankly, he found the whole situation annoying. Distracting. *Unbearable.*

'My dance, I believe, Darian?'

Darian roused himself from those troubling thoughts to look about him almost dazedly; the music had stopped playing and the other couples had left the dance floor, as they now gave curious glances their way. All without Darian having been aware of any of it. His brother, Anthony, was also now standing beside him with eyebrows raised expectantly, as he waited for Darian to release Christina Beecham.

'Of course.' He straightened abruptly as his arms fell back to his sides and he stepped away from Lady Christina. 'I— Thank you,' he added with a belated bow towards the young lady.

Anthony continued to look at him frowningly, eyes narrowed speculatively as he took his brother's place at Christina Beecham's side. 'Are you quite well again now, Darian?'

'Quite, thank you.' Darian nodded abruptly.

'In that case I will call upon you tomorrow,' Anthony stated firmly, his expression challenging, telling Darian that the conversation between the two of them might have been delayed for this past week, whilst he was feeling unwell, but it was not to be avoided altogether!

'Very well.' Darian gave another distracted nod as he once again glanced about the ballroom to see that the three of them were still the focus of more than one group of gossiping people.

'Your Grace?'

'Lady Christina?' Darian turned, one brow raised enquiringly.

A sparkle of humour now brightened those eyes, so like her mother's. 'I believe Mama to have accepted Lord Maystone's invitation to accompany him into the next room to partake of refreshment.'

Had he made his interest in Mariah's whereabouts so obvious that even her daughter was aware of it?

And what the deuce was Mariah doing in Maystone's company, a gentleman Darian had reason to know rather better than might be socially apparent?

Aged in his late fifties, and a widower for more than twenty years, Aubrey Maystone was nevertheless still a handsome man, with his head of silver hair and chiselled features. Nor had his trimness gone to obesity, as had happened to so many of his peers.

He was also Darian's contact at the Foreign Office in regard to his work for the Crown.

Whatever the reason for Aubrey Maystone's interest in Mariah, Darian had no intentions of wasting any more of his own time this evening in an effort to secure the opportunity in which to converse with her again.

He took care to avoid his brother's no-doubt accusing gaze as he gave Lady Christina a rueful smile. 'Thank you.' He gave another bow before turning to cross the ballroom in long and determined strides as he went in search of the refreshment room.

And Mariah Beecham.

'I believe you have accepted an invitation to attend Lord and Lady Nicholses' house party in Kent this weekend?' Lord Maystone nodded his acquaintance to Mrs Moore, as she stood across the room, even as he continued his softly spoken conversation with Mariah.

'I have, yes.' Mariah eyed him curiously. 'Will you also be attending?'

'Good heavens, no!' Maystone turned to give her his full attention, a look of distaste upon his lined but handsome face. 'Subjecting myself to a single tedious evening of socialising in a week is quite enough for me. I assure you, I have no intentions of suffering through a weekend of it.'

'Poor Aubrey.' Mariah chuckled sympathetically,

placing a conciliatory hand briefly on his arm as she sobered. 'Do you have a special reason for asking whether or not I am to attend this particular weekend party?' Aubrey Maystone had long been her contact for the work she did for the Crown.

'I have reason to believe— Ah, Wolfingham.' Aubrey turned to greet the younger man warmly. 'Just the man! The countess is as polite as she is beautiful, but nevertheless I believe her to be in need of far younger company than my own.'

Mariah was relieved she had her back turned towards Darian Hunter, so he would not mistake the colour in her cheeks for anything other than what it was: annoyance at the way in which he had seemed to dog her every step this evening.

Lady Stockton had obviously been as surprised as her guests when the Duke of Wolfingham, a man who rarely attended any of the entertainments of the *ton*, but who had now attended two in as many weeks, had arrived at her home earlier this evening. A surprise that had lasted for only a few seconds, as that lady hastily crossed the room to welcome her illustrious guest.

Mariah's reaction to seeing Wolfingham again had been less enthusiastic. She wondered what he was doing here.

Indeed, she had gone out of her way not to show any reaction at all, but rather to ignore him completely.

Not an easy task, when it seemed that every time she had turned round this evening Wolfingham had been standing there behind her, looking very dark and handsome in his impeccable evening clothes, the darkness of his hair rakishly dishevelled.

Nor did Mariah believe his appearance now, in the refreshment room, to be coincidental, either.

No doubt, whilst forced to convalesce, in order to recover completely from his injury, the duke had also had time to rethink his decision not to leave his younger brother's fate to chance—or Mariah's caprice or whimsy.

Whatever the reasoning behind Wolfingham's dogged persistence this evening, Mariah was more than a little weary of reassuring him that she had absolutely no romantic interest, nor would she ever have, in his brother, Anthony.

'Not at all, Aubrey.' She gave Maystone a warm smile as she now linked her arm with his. 'Indeed, you are so handsome and distinguished that you put all younger men to shame,' she added before turning to look up at Wolfingham now that she felt reassured her cheeks were no longer flushed.

Darian's lips twitched and he held back a smile as he met Mariah Beecham's challenging gaze, recognising her remark for exactly what it was: an insult to him rather than just a compliment to Aubrey Maystone.

Although the warmth of familiarity between the two of them did seem to imply a deeper acquaintance than just a socially polite one.

To the degree that Maystone might be Mariah's current lover? If that was so, then it made a nonsense of Darian's request that she cease her friendship with the far more youthful and inexperienced Anthony.

The possibility of that being true also brought a scowl to Darian's brow. 'Lady Beecham.' He bowed formally as it was the first occasion upon which the two of them had actually spoken this evening; Mariah's avoidance of him had been absolute. 'Maystone.' Darian's nod to the older man was terse.

'Wolfingham.' There was a mischievous twinkle in the older man's eyes, as if he had guessed Darian's thoughts and was amused by them. 'Have you come to steal Mariah away from me for a dance, or are you going to join us in some refreshment?'

'Well, I am certainly not here for refreshment.' Darian made no effort to hide his distaste as he eyed the glasses in their hands. 'I have heard it said that Lady Stockton is parsimonious with the brandy in her punch.'

'Surely it is not necessary to become inebriated in order to enjoy oneself?' Mariah drawled mockingly.

'Not at all.' Darian observed her between narrowed lids. 'But if I wished to drink something as innocuous as fruit juice then I should request fruit juice.' Standing so close to Mariah, he was once again aware of her unique perfume, the lightness of spring flowers and that deeper, more exotic perfume, which he now recognised as being jasmine. It was a heady and arousing combination.

'How true.' Maystone's dismissive laugh broke the tension that had been steadily rising between Darian and Mariah. 'It seems I must forgo your delightful company for now, my dear.' He placed his glass down on the table and raised Mariah's gloved hand to his lips before releasing it. 'And allow a younger man to steal you away from me for a dance.'

Mariah frowned as she answered coolly, 'To my knowledge, his Grace has not had the foresight to request a dance with me this evening. As such, I am afraid my dance card is completely full.'

'Well, there you have it, Wolfingham.' Maystone turned towards him with a grin. 'You will have to be much quicker off the mark in future, if you are to secure a dance with our delightful Mariah,' he teased jovially.

Darian's frustration with his own increasing arousal, as well as Mariah's avoidance of him, was now such that he could barely keep the impatience from his tone and he knew the frown had deepened on his brow. 'A pity, of course, Lady Beecham,' he drawled coldly. 'But as consolation I have just enjoyed the pleasure of dancing with your lovely daughter, Lady Christina. A delightful young woman and a credit to both you and her father.'

Mariah looked up sharply at Wolfingham, easily noting the mocking challenge in his deep green eyes as he returned her gaze unblinkingly. No doubt because he was fully aware of the fact that she would prefer that he stay well away from her young and impressionable daughter.

Oh, Christina had accepted readily enough Mariah's explanations as to Wolfingham's indisposition the previous week having been the reason for his having to remain at Carlisle House overnight. But beneath that acceptance there had been an underlying girlish excitement, a curiosity, about the arrogantly handsome and illustrious Duke of Wolfingham. The last thing Mariah wished was for Christina to develop a crush on the man.

Not that she thought Wolfingham was in the least serious in his attentions to Christina; rather Mariah believed his intention had merely been to annoy her. If so, he had succeeded!

The less she, and Christina, had to do with Darian Hunter, the dangerous Duke of Wolfingham, the better Mariah would like it. Her lifestyle was such, most especially her work for the Crown, that she did not wish to have such an astutely disturbing gentleman as Wolfingham taking an interest in it, or her.

'I believe the music and dancing have now stopped for supper, your Grace.' Mariah had noted the influx of people into the room and strolling towards the supper tables. 'It appears to be raining outside, so perhaps you might care to accompany me for a stroll in the West Gallery?' At which time she intended to warn him to stay away from her daughter!

Darian was not particularly proud of himself for having used Lady Christina Beecham as a means of securing Mariah's company, but neither was he about to apologise for it. Not when it had succeeded in accomplishing his aim, which was to talk with Mariah again. In private.

Although he wasn't sure that being alone with Mariah was an entirely good idea, given his painful state of arousal.

'You will stay away from my daughter!' Mariah barely waited until the two of them had entered the long and deserted picture gallery, lit by a dozen candles or more, before removing her hand from Wolfingham's arm and glaring up at him, her cheeks hot with temper in the candlelight.

'Will I?' he came back with infuriating calm, dark brows raised in equally as mild query.

'Yes—when it is not a serious interest, but merely a means of punishing me.'

'That is not very flattering to Lady Christina.'

'But true.'

'Is it?' he returned mildly.

'What do you want from me, Wolfingham?' Mariah looked up at him in exasperation. 'A public declaration of my uninterest in your brother? Would that appease you? Reassure you?'

He gave a humourless smile. 'It would most certainly not appease or reassure Anthony.' His mouth tightened. 'Nor would it do anything for my own future relationship with him, if you were to tell him that I had been instrumental in bringing about the sudden end to your friendship.'

Mariah drew in a deep breath through her nose. 'Perhaps you should have thought of that before you chose to so arrogantly interfere in his life a week ago?'

'What is your relationship with Maystone?'

Mariah was momentarily disconcerted by this sudden change of topic. As she was meant to be?

She and Aubrey Maystone preferred to keep the true nature of their relationship private and as such it was rare for them to pass any time together in public. Indeed, they would not have done so this evening if Aubrey had not expressed a wish to speak with her urgently. A conversation that had been cut short by the arrival of Darian Hunter.

But the manner of the public acquaintance between Mariah and Lord Maystone was such that Wolfingham could not possibly have guessed that there was a deeper, more private, connection between the two of them. Could he?

Mariah was quickly learning that it would not be wise on her part, or anyone else's, to underestimate the intelligence or astuteness of Darian Hunter.

'My acquaintance with Lord Maystone is a long-standing one,' she answered frostily. 'Come about because he was once a friend of my late husband.'

'And is that all he is to you?'

'What are you accusing me of now, Wolfingham?' Her tone was impatiently exasperated, deliberately so. 'Do you imagine that I am currently enjoying a relationship with Lord Maystone, as well as your brother? Would that not make my bed very overcrowded?' she added scathingly. 'And what business would it be of yours, even if that were the case? I am a widow and they are both unattached gentlemen, so there is no prior claim to hinder the existence of either relationship.' She gave a dismissive shrug.

A nerve pulsed in the duke's tightly clenched jaw. 'Except a moral one.'

'You are a fine one to preach to me of morals, Wolfingham, when you are currently sporting the bullet wound you received whilst fighting a duel over some woman!' Her eyes flashed in the candlelight.

Darian glowered his frustration down at her, wanting to deny the accusation, but knowing that to do so would then bring the real cause of that wound back into question. A question he would not, could not, answer.

Having no answer, he decided to act instead.

Although that was possibly an exaggeration on his part, when his arms seemed to have moved of their own volition as they encircled Mariah's waist and he pulled her in close against the hardness of his body.

Her exotic perfume immediately filled all of his senses as his head swooped down to capture her lips with his own. Soft and delectable lips that had parted with surprise, so allowing for further intimacy as Darian's tongue swept lightly across her lips before plunging into the heated warmth beneath.

She felt so slender in his arms, the fullness of her breasts crushed against his chest, her lips and mouth tasting of honey. A silky-soft sweetness and heat that drew Darian in even closer, as he attempted to claim, to possess, that heat as his own. To claim, to possess, Mariah as his own.

Mariah had been totally unprepared for Wolfingham taking her into his arms, let alone having him kiss her. So unprepared, that for several stunned seconds she found herself responding to that kiss as her hands moved up to cling to the lapels of the duke's evening coat, her body crushed, aligned with Wolfingham's, as his mouth continued to plunder and claim her own. Making her fully aware not only of the hardness of his chest, but also the long length of his arousal pressing against the warmth of her abdomen.

She allowed herself to feel a brief moment of triumph, at the knowledge, this physical evidence, that Darian Hunter, the coldly arrogant Duke of Wolfingham, was aroused by her. From holding her in his arms. From kissing her.

Those brief moments of triumph were quickly followed by ones of panic and a desperate need to free herself. A move she attempted to instigate as she now pushed against that hard and muscled chest even as she wrenched her mouth out from beneath that sensually punishing kiss. 'Release me immediately, Wolfingham!'

Her eyes now gleamed up at him in the candlelight, her chest quickly rising and falling as she breathed heavily, having managed to put several inches between the hardness of his body and her own, but failing to release herself completely.

'You are taking your protection of your brother too far, sir,' she added fiercely as her hands against his chest kept him at a distance but he still made no effort to remove the steel band of his arms from about her waist.

A nerve pulsed in the tightness of his jaw. 'This has nothing to do with my brother.'

'It has everything to do with him.'

Darian was breathing heavily, unable to reason clearly as he looked down at Mariah, his mind and senses too full of her to form a coherent thought, other than the taste of her on his own lips and tongue. The feel of her soft curves against his much harder ones. The smell of her causing his body to throb and pound with need.

A need that the pallor of Mariah's face in the candlelight, and over-bright turquoise eyes, said she did not reciprocate.

He gave a pained frown. 'What did you think would happen when you invited me to join you alone here in the gallery, Mariah?'

'Not this!' Her breasts quickly rose and fell in rhythm with her agitated breathing as she continued to hold him at arm's length. 'Never this!'

Darian's frown deepened to one of concern as he heard the underlying sob in her voice. 'Mariah—'

'I believe the lady has expressed a wish to be set free, Darian!'

Darian's head whipped round at the sound of his brother's harshly reproving voice, a scowl darkening his brow as he saw Anthony watching them from the shadowed doorway into the gallery, the expression on his brother's face one of disgust as well as fury.

A disgust and fury Darian fully deserved, given the circumstances, of Mariah's obvious distress and the feelings Anthony had previously expressed for the woman Darian now held in his arms.

Feelings that Darian had totally forgotten about in his need to claim Mariah's lips for his own.

His arms fell heavily back to his sides as he stepped back and away from her, only to then reach out a hand to steady Mariah as she appeared to stumble.

'Do not touch me!' she lashed out verbally even as she pulled free of his grasp, twin spots of fevered colour now high in her cheeks as she turned away. 'Accompany me back to Lady Stockton's ballroom, if you please, Lord Anthony,' she requested stiffly as she left Darian's side to walk quickly down the gallery to take the arm his brother so gallantly offered her.

Anthony paused to give Darian a warning glance over the top of Mariah's averted head. 'I have changed my mind, Darian, and we will now talk again later tonight, rather than tomorrow morning.'

Darian recognised those words for exactly what they were: a threat, not a promise.

Chapter Four

D arian found himself seated beside the fire at his club the following afternoon, after partaking of luncheon with two of his closest friends; Christian Seaton, the Duke of Sutherland, and Griffin Stone, the Duke of Rotherham.

'You are saying the countess refused to see you when you called at Carlisle House this morning?' Sutherland prompted lightly.

Darian scowled into the depths of his brandy glass. 'Her butler claimed she was indisposed and not receiving visitors.'

'Women do tend to suffer these indelicacies, you know.' Rotherham nodded dismissively.

The scowl remained on Darian's brow as he looked across the fireplace at his friend slumped in the chair opposite. 'So you think the indisposition might be genuine, rather than an excuse not to see me in particular?'

'Well, I would not go quite so far as to say that,' Rotherham drawled. 'From what you told us over lun-

cheon, you did make rather a cake of yourself, you
know, throwing out accusations and insults in that
overbearing manner of yours!'

Darian gave a wince. 'Thank you so much for your
reassurances, Griff.' After Anthony's promised late
visit to Wolfingham House the night before, Darian had every reason to know he had indeed made
a cake of himself where Mariah Beecham was concerned and certainly did not need Rotherham to tell
him as much.

The need to apologise to Mariah was the very reason Darian had attempted to call upon her this morning. Only to be sent away by her butler without so
much as a glimpse of the lady, let alone be allowed
to give the apology owed to her.

'Think nothing of it, old boy.' Rotherham grinned
across at him unabashedly.

'Beautiful woman, the countess,' Sutherland murmured appreciatively as he relaxed in a third chair.

'Oh, yes!' Rotherham nodded.

Darian eyed the two men sharply. 'Have either
of you...?' He could not quite bring himself to say
the words; the thought that Sutherland or Rotherham might have been Mariah's lover was enough to
blacken his mood even more than it already was.

'Never had the pleasure.' Sutherland sighed his
obvious disappointment.

'Unfortunately not.' Rotherham looked equally as
wistful.

Darian found himself breathing a little easier at
knowing that two of his friends, at least, had never

been one of Mariah Beecham's lovers. Even if rumour suggested that plenty of other gentlemen had!

'I suppose there is always the possibility the countess was not actually *at* home when you called this morning?' Sutherland quirked a brow. 'You did say she was rather pally with Maystone yesterday evening, so perhaps she went home with him? Just a thought.' He shrugged dismissively as Darian's scowl deepened.

'The idea did occur to me.' Of course it had occurred to him that Mariah might have spent the night elsewhere than her London home.

Until he had remembered that Mariah had accompanied her young daughter to the Stockton ball and so was hardly likely to have abandoned that young lady in favour of going home with a lover.

Of course Mariah could have gone out again once she had returned Lady Christina to Carlisle House.

He shifted restlessly, aware that he was taking far too much of an interest in front of his two friends, who along with himself were the last of the bachelor Dangerous Dukes, in what Mariah Beecham did or did not do.

'Do you have hopes in that direction yourself?' Sutherland now arched a curious brow.

Did he?

Darian had been unable to sleep last night for thinking of Mariah, of holding her in his arms and kissing her.

Of his desire for her!

A desire he had neither sought nor wanted.

Because every objection he had given Anthony for his brother to bring an end to his involvement with Mariah Beecham—apart from the difference in their ages—also applied to Darian himself. An association, any association on his part with the notorious Mariah Beecham, was unacceptable.

A realisation that seemed not to make a bit of difference to the desire Darian felt for her and that had so disturbed his sleep the night before.

Oh, it was perfectly acceptable for Darian to take a mistress if he so chose, even if he had never chosen to do so before now. But Mariah Beecham, a woman whose private life was gossiped and speculated about constantly, was not suitable even for that role in the public *or* private life of the Duke of Wolfingham.

His continuing work for the Crown had caused Darian to long ago make a conscious decision not to bring any unnecessary attention to his private life. And any liaison with Mariah Beecham would necessarily become public and ultimately throw him front and centre of the same gossip that always surrounded her. Gossip Darian wished to avoid, even if Mariah had been willing to enter into such a relationship with him.

Which Darian had every reason to believe, to *know*—more so than ever, after his clarifying conversation with Anthony the night before—she was not!

So Darian had told himself again and again, as he lay in his bed unable to sleep the previous night.

Today, with the disappointment of not being able to see and speak with Mariah this morning, as he had fully intended that he would, he was not so sure on the matter.

'Of course not,' he answered Sutherland sharply. 'I am merely aware that I owe the woman an apology and I am anxious to get it over and done with.'

'Protesting a little too strongly, do you think, Sutherland?' Griffin Stone turned to prompt the other man drily.

'More than a little, I would say,' Sutherland drawled as they both turned to look at Darian, brows raised over mocking eyes.

Darian withstood that look with a censorious one of his own, having every intention of making his apologies to Mariah Beecham before returning to their previous relationship—that of complete indifference to each other.

Something Darian very much doubted was going to happen, on his part at least, when he was shown into the gold salon of Mariah's home late the following morning and his rebellious body responded immediately.

He had wisely sent her a note late yesterday afternoon, requesting she supply a suitable time for him to call upon her today, rather than run the risk of calling and being turned away for a second time.

Mariah looked ethereally beautiful this morning, in a fashionable gown of the palest lemon, her blonde curls a golden halo about the pale delicacy of her face and throat.

A pallor that implied that perhaps Mariah's claim, of being indisposed yesterday, had indeed been genuine?

'Are you feeling any better today?' Darian prompted gruffly as he crossed the room to where she now stood, taking the gloved hand she raised to him in formal greeting.

'Such politeness, Wolfingham. Indeed, I should hardly recognise you,' Mariah taunted drily as she deftly removed her hand from his before resuming her seat, the gold brocade sofa a perfect foil for her golden loveliness. Deliberately so?

His mouth thinned. 'Could we perhaps at least attempt a modicum of politeness between the two of us, rather than begin to argue immediately after we see each other again?'

'I do not believe it is a question of us arguing, Wolfingham. We simply do not like each other!'

He drew in a sharp breath, knowing that for his part that claim was untrue, that he liked—indeed, he *desired*—Mariah Beecham far more than was comfortable.

Mariah studied Wolfingham from beneath lowered lashes as he made no reply to her taunt.

It had been her dearest wish never to find herself alone with this gentleman again. She had only agreed to this morning's meeting because she knew he was not a man she could continue to avoid indefinitely, if he had decided it should be otherwise. Her claim of being indisposed yesterday, as a way of avoiding Wolfingham when he called, had not been all fabrication; Mariah had stayed in her bed late yesterday morning, her head aching after suffering a restless and sleepless night.

Because she had not been able to stop thinking of Darian Hunter. Or his having kissed her.

Or remembering that she had responded.

A response that was so unprecedented, and had troubled Mariah so deeply, that she had found it impossible to sleep these past two nights for thinking of it.

A response she had since assured herself would not happen again.

Could not happen again!

So it was entirely frustrating for her to acknowledge her awareness of how arrogantly handsome Wolfingham looked this morning, dressed in a dark green superfine and buff-and-green-striped waistcoat, his linen snowy white, buff-coloured pantaloons moulded to the muscular length of his long thighs above his brown-topped black Hessians. His hair was in its usual fashionable disarray about his sharply etched features.

As she also noted the pallor to those sharply etched features and the dark shadows beneath his deep green eyes. As evidence, perhaps, that Wolfingham had not rested any better than she had herself these past two nights?

Although she doubted it was for the same reasons.

Against all the odds—her dislike of Wolfingham and the years of her unhappy marriage to Martin— for the first time in her life Mariah had found herself actually enjoying being held in a man's arms two nights ago.

Even more surprising was the realisation of how she had *responded* to that depth of passion Wolfingham had ignited in her.

Her marriage to Martin had been completely without love and affection from the onset, on either side, and equally as without passion. Indeed, for the first ten years of their marriage, the two of them had spent very little time even living in the same house, Mariah languishing in the country with their daughter, while Martin preferred to spend most of the year living in London. At best they had been polite strangers to each other on the rare occasions they did meet, for the sake of their daughter, and more often than not they had ignored each other completely.

That had changed slightly seven years ago, when Mariah began to spend the Season in London, Martin necessarily having to accompany her to at least some of those social engagements. But even so, those occasions had only been for appearances' sake, and they had continued to retain their separate bedchambers, and for the most part live their separate lives, on the occasions they were forced to reside in the same house together.

So, it had been all the more surprising to Mariah that she had not only responded to, but enjoyed being held in Darian Hunter's arms and being kissed by him, the night of Lady Stockton's ball. Not only an unprecedented response, but an unwanted one as well, and ensuring that Mariah was all the more determined it would not occur for a second time.

'Did you have something in particular you wished to discuss with me when you called upon me yesterday morning, then sent a note requesting a convenient time you might call again today? Or is it as I suspected and you merely wish to add to the insults you invariably make when we meet?'

Darian's breath left him in a hiss at this deliberate challenge; at least when he was breathing out his senses were not being invaded by Mariah Beecham's heady and arousing perfume.

Darian had once again been aware of that perfume the moment he stepped into the salon. Indeed, he believed he now knew that unique aroma so well he would be able to pick Mariah Beecham out of a roomful of veiled and heavily robed women, just by the smell of that heady perfume alone.

Seeing Mariah again this morning, being with her again, his senses once again invaded by her beauty and aroused by that heady perfume, made a complete nonsense of his denials of yesterday to Rotherham and Sutherland, in regard to his not having the slightest interest in pursuing a relationship with Mariah Beecham.

He might not *want* to feel this desire for her, but he did feel it nonetheless.

'Oh, do stop scowling, Wolfingham, for it is giving me a headache,' Mariah snapped at his continued silence. 'I am sure there are many women who might find all this brooding intensity attractive, but I am not one of them.' She wrinkled her nose in disgust. 'Personally, such behaviour has always filled me with a burning desire to administer a weighty smack to the cheek of the gentleman in question.'

The situation in which Darian currently found himself did not at all call for any sign of levity on his part. Consequently he did try very hard not to give in to the laughter that threatened to burst forth.

To no avail, unfortunately; his amusement was such that it refused to be denied and he found himself chuckling with husky appreciation for Mariah's obviously heartfelt sentiments.

'You are incorrigible, madam,' he admonished once he had regained his breath enough to speak.

'I, sir, merely remain unimpressed by any gentleman's angst,' Mariah returned disparagingly.

'But more so when that gentleman is me,' Wolfingham acknowledged drily.

'Yes.' She did not even attempt to deny it as she gave an impatient shake of her head. 'It was *you* who asked if you might call upon me today, Wolfingham, so I ask once again that you state your business and then leave. I find maintaining even this level of politeness between the two of us to be taxing in the extreme.'

Darian knew he fully deserved Mariah's lack of enjoyment of his company. He had made so many mistakes in their short acquaintance, it seemed. Too many for her to forgive him? Easily, if at all.

He drew in a deep breath. 'I needed to speak

with you again because it appears that I owe you an apology, Mariah.'

Her eyes widened in obvious surprise. 'Indeed?'

His jaw grated he held it so tightly clenched. 'Yes.'

'For what, pray? You have made far too many insults, to me and about me, for me to ever be able to pick out a specific one for which you might apologise.'

Darian bristled. 'Such as?'

'The disgusting thoughts you so obviously held two evenings ago, with regard to my friendship with Aubrey Maystone, for one.'

Ah. Yes. Well, there was that, of course…

He shifted uncomfortably. 'It was a natural conclusion to have come to, surely, given the circumstances of the ease of the friendship between the two of you?'

'Only if your mind was already in the gutter, as yours so often appears to be where I am concerned!' Her eyes flashed.

Darian could not deny that he had thought the worst of Mariah before he had even met her, hence his initial alarm regarding Anthony's involvement with her. But in his defence Mariah Beecham's reputation in society was such that surely, at the time, he could have formed no other opinion, in regard to Anthony's obvious and public attentions to her.

At the time.

Darian knew differently now, of course. Which was the very reason he had been so determined to speak with Mariah these past two days. So that he might apologise and, hopefully, discuss the matter with her further.

'It was doubly insulting, when you had already accused me of being involved in an affair with your younger brother,' she now accused coldly.

And now, Darian recognised heavily, was the perfect opportunity in which to make that apology and inform her of his mistake.

He grimaced. 'I have had the opportunity to speak with Anthony again, since the two of us parted so badly at the Stockton ball.' He ignored her scathing snort; she knew as well as he did that it had been Anthony's parting remark—promise—that had caused the two brothers to talk again later that very same night. 'And it would seem—it would seem—'

Darian was not accustomed to apologising for his actions, to anyone, and yet in this particular instance he knew he had no choice; he had seriously wronged Mariah and now he must apologise for it.

He sighed. 'My brother has now made it more than clear to me that his affections lie elsewhere than yourself.'

'Hah!' Those turquoise-blue eyes gleamed across at him with triumphant satisfaction. 'Did I not tell you that you were mistaken in your accusations?'

'It is very unbecoming in a woman to say "I told you so" in that gleeful manner, Mariah.' Darian scowled, still more than a little irritated with himself for having initially jumped to the wrong conclusion where his brother's affections were concerned, and even more so for having then acted upon those conclusions by insulting Mariah to such a degree he now owed her an apology.

He was equally as irritated that by doing so he had now placed himself in the position of being the one to tell Mariah the truth of that situation.

'Not when that woman has been proved right and you have been proved wrong.' she came back tartly.

Darian chose his words carefully. 'I was only half-wrong—'

'How can a person, even the illustrious and arrogant Duke of Wolfingham, be half-wrong?' she scorned. 'Admit it, Wolfingham. In this matter you were completely and utterly in the wrong.'

'No, I was not.' Darian sighed deeply, choosing to ignore the scathing comment in regard to himself; no doubt Mariah would have more, far stronger insults to hurl at him before this conversation was over. 'I was merely mistaken as to which of the Beecham ladies held Anthony's affections and consequently, the reason for his polite and public attentions to you.'

He also had absolutely no idea how Mariah was going to react upon learning that Anthony was paying court to her young daughter, Christina, rather than to herself. Even if he only took into consideration Mariah's feelings towards *him*, Anthony's despicable and insulting older brother, then Darian was sure that it could not be in a favourable way.

Any more than were his own feelings on the matter. Admittedly, he could not help but feel a certain amount of relief at having learnt that Anthony was not besotted with Mariah Beecham, after all. For the reasons he had previously stated.

But also on a personal level.

Unwanted as his own desire for Mariah might be, Darian nevertheless felt a certain relief at knowing he was not harbouring a desire for the same woman for whom he had believed his brother had serious intentions.

As for the real object of his brother's affections…

Admittedly the seventeen-year-old Lady Christina Beecham was more acceptable as a wife for Anthony than her mother could ever have been. But, in Darian's opinion, only marginally so. Christina Beecham could not escape the fact that she was the daughter of a woman with a notorious and scandalous reputation.

A woman with a notorious and scandalous reputation who, he realised belatedly, for the moment seemed to have been struck uncharacteristically dumb. At having learnt that his brother, Anthony's, romantic inclinations were directed towards her young daughter rather than herself?

Mariah drew a harsh breath into her starved lungs as she realised she had forgotten to do so these past few seconds. 'Forgive me, but I— Am I to understand that your brother, Lord Anthony Hunter, a gentleman aged almost five and twenty, believes himself to be in love with—that he has serious intentions towards my seventeen-year-old daughter?'

Wolfingham gave a terse nod of his head. 'That is exactly what I am saying, yes. I have no reason to be-

lieve that your daughter returns Anthony's feelings.'
His eyes narrowed. 'But perhaps you do?'

'Not as such, no.'

'You seem unduly concerned?'

'She is seventeen years of age, Wolfingham. At the
very least Christina will have been flattered by the
attentions of an eligible and sophisticated gentleman
such as your brother,' Mariah answered distractedly
as she now recalled all those occasions these past
few weeks when Lord Anthony Hunter had been included in the group of admirers surrounding herself
and Christina.

As she also remembered the polite attentions the
young Lord Anthony had paid to her and the visits he
had made to Carlisle House—and that Wolfingham
had mistaken for a romantic interest in Mariah—in
an effort, no doubt, to ingratiate himself into Mariah's
good opinion.

And Christina's youthful heart?

The more Mariah considered the matter, the more
she believed that her daughter could not help but be
aware of Anthony Hunter's romantic interest in her.

Having spent much of Christina's early years clos-
eted alone together in the country, Mariah believed
she and Christina were closer than most mothers and
daughters of the *ton*. But Christina was fully grown
now—or believed that she was!—and Mariah now realised that those childhood confidences had become
fewer and fewer during these past few weeks spent
together in London.

Perhaps because Christina harboured a secret passion for her handsome admirer?

A secret passion that, because of her age, she knew Mariah could not, and would not, approve of?

Oh, she had been unable to deny Christina her first Season; her daughter was seventeen, after all. But Mariah had not launched Christina into society with any intentions of seeing her young daughter engaged to be married within weeks of her having made that appearance.

As she herself had been.

Mariah gave a determined shake of her head. 'Whether she does or does not, it will not do, Wolfingham.'

He arched dark brows. 'You would refuse Anthony's suit?'

'Her uncle, the earl, is her male guardian, but I will strongly advise against it, yes.'

'Why would you?' Having been so set against the match himself, Darian now felt contrarily defensive on his brother's behalf. Anthony might be young, and occasionally irresponsible, but none could doubt his eligibility in the marriage mart. 'Lady Christina is seventeen years of age—'

'And so far too young to fall in love, or consider taking on the duties of marriage!' Mariah scorned.

'Surely she is the same age as you must have been when you married?'

'We were not discussing me!' Those turquoise-coloured eyes now glittered fiercely across the room at him.

Wolfingham's gaze became quizzical at her vehemence. 'I thought an advantageous marriage was the whole purpose of a young lady making her debut in society?'

'That is a typically male assessment of the situation.'

He arched a dark brow. 'Then perhaps it is that you consider that having a daughter married to be ageing to yourself?'

'Do not be any more ridiculous than you have already been, Wolfingham!' Mariah stood up agitatedly. 'My reservations have absolutely nothing to do with myself and everything to do with Christina. She is far too young to know her own mind in such matters.'

'She seemed a prepossessing young lady when I danced with her the other evening.'

'So she is.' Mariah nodded her impatience. 'And no doubt I will one day, in the distant future, be happy to dance at her wedding. But not now, when Christina has only been out for a matter of weeks, rather than years. Nor do I have any reason to believe that you would approve of an alliance between your brother and my daughter?' She looked up at him challengingly.

No, of course Darian did not approve of it and he had voiced his reservations regarding the match to his brother when the two of them had spoken so frankly together two evenings ago. A disapproval that Darian knew had once again fallen on deaf ears; Anthony was bound and determined in his pursuit of Christina Beecham.

A determination that was obviously to now be thwarted by that young lady's mother.

Again, Darian found himself playing devil's advocate. 'I still fail to see, apart from your daughter's youth, what your own objections can be to the match. Anthony will come into his own fortune on the occasion of his twenty-fifth birthday in just a few months' time. He is the grandson, the son and now the brother of a duke—'

'I am fully aware of who Lord Anthony is and of his family connections,' Mariah assured him dismissively.

'And the fact that the severe and sober Duke of Wolfingham is his brother is no doubt part of the reason for your own objections to the match?' Darian surmised drily.

'Do not even pretend to be insulted, Wolfingham, when you know full well your feelings on this matter entirely match my own.' Mariah sighed her impatience.

'I repeat, why are they?'

Mariah drew in a deep and controlling breath, knowing she was overreacting to this situation, allowing her own unhappy marriage at the age of seventeen, the same age as her daughter was now, to colour her judgement. And in front of the astute and intelligent Darian Hunter, of all people. 'Of course I wish for Christina's future happiness. Just not yet. She is so young and has not yet had chance to enjoy even her first Season.'

'Is it only because he is my younger brother?' he guessed shrewdly.

Mariah gave a determined shake of her head. 'I also have no doubt that, if Christina were ever to become your brother's wife, you would make her life, as your sister-in-law, nothing but a misery.'

He stiffened. 'You are insulting, madam, to believe I would ever treat any woman so shabbily.'

'You would treat any daughter of *mine* more than shabbily,' she insisted. 'And I do not want that for Christina. She deserves so much more than that.' So much more than Mariah had suffered herself as Martin's wife, unloved by her husband and disapproved of and ignored by his family for her more humble beginnings. 'No.' She shuddered at the thought of Christina suffering the same fate. 'If Lord Anthony should ask, I will not ever give my blessing to such a match.'

Darian frowned darkly. 'And what of your daughter's feelings on the matter? Have you considered that perhaps she might return Anthony's affections? If not now, then at some future date?'

'It is perhaps a possibility that she may one day *believe* she returns those feelings,' Mariah allowed grudgingly. 'But at seventeen she is too young to know her own heart and mind.'

'As you yourself were at the same age?'

She stiffened. 'Again, we were not talking about me.'

'Then perhaps we should be.'

'No, we will not,' Mariah informed Wolfingham coldly. 'Not now, nor at any time in the future.'

Darian studied Mariah intently, knowing by the stubborn set of her mouth, and those flashing turquoise eyes, that she would not be moved on the subject of her own marriage.

And so adding to the mystery that Mariah Beecham had become to him.

A mystery that had already occupied far too much of his time and thoughts these past ten days.

He gave a grimace. 'Have you considered how your husband might have felt regarding an alliance between his daughter and the Hunter family?'

Her chin rose. 'I had no interest in my husband's opinions whilst he was alive and I certainly have none now that he is dead.'

Because, as he had begun to suspect, like so many marriages of the *ton*, the Beecham marriage had been one of convenience rather than a love match? A question of marrying wealth to a title? The wealth of Mariah's father matched to Beecham's title as the Earl of Carlisle?

Darian's own parents had married under similar circumstances, but they had been two of the lucky ones, in that they had come to feel a deep love and respect for each other, ensuring that their two sons had grown up in a family filled with that same love and respect.

The fact that Mariah had only been seventeen to Beecham's two and forty when their marriage took place, and the rumours of her numerous affairs since, would seem to imply she might not have been so fortunate.

'That is a very enlightening comment,' he said slowly.

'Is it?' Mariah returned scathingly. 'I doubt I am the first woman to admit to having felt a lack of love for the man who was her husband.'

'Your words implied a lack of respect, too.'

Those eyes flashed again. 'Respect has to be earned. It is not just given.'

'And Carlisle did not earn yours?'

'The feeling was mutual, I assure you.'

'And yet the two of you had a daughter together.'

A cold shiver ran down the length of Mariah's spine as she remembered the night of Christina's conception. A painful and frightening experience for Mariah and a triumphant one for Martin.

Her gaze now avoided Wolfingham's probing green one. 'I believe it is time you left.'

'Mariah—'

'*Now*, Wolfingham!' Before Mariah broke down completely. Something she dared not do, in front of the one man who had already somehow managed to get through the barrier Mariah had long ago placed about both her emotions and the memories of the past. For fear they might destroy her utterly.

Darian had no idea what would have happened next. Whether he would have acceded to Mariah's request for him to leave, or whether he would have followed his own instincts and instead taken Mariah in his arms and comforted her. This talk of her marriage to Carlisle seemed to have shaken her cool self-confidence in a way nothing else had.

Instead, their privacy was interrupted as the butler entered the room bearing a card upon a silver tray, which he proceeded to present to Mariah.

She picked up the card and quickly read it, before tucking it into the pocket of her gown as she spoke to her butler. 'Please show his Lordship into my private parlour, Fuller,' she instructed briskly. 'And then return here and show his Grace out.' Her gaze was challenging as she turned and waited for the butler to leave before looking across the room at Darian.

Darian breathed out his frustration, both with what was obviously Mariah's dismissal of him and a burning curiosity to know the identity of the man the dismissed butler was even now escorting to Mariah's private parlour.

Which was utterly ridiculous of him.

He had lived for two and thirty years without having the slightest interest in Mariah Beecham, or any of her friendships, and for him to now feel disgruntled, even jealous, of this other man was ludicrous on his part.

And yet Darian could not deny that was exactly how he now felt.

Just as he knew Mariah was equally as determined that her two male visitors would not meet each other.

'I believe I am perfectly capable of showing myself out, Mariah,' Darian informed her harshly.

She blinked. 'Fuller will return in just a moment.'

'And I am ready to depart now.'

'But—'

'Good day to you, Mariah.' Darian bowed to her stiffly before crossing the room and stepping out into the cavernous hallway, only to come to an abrupt halt as he saw the identity of Mariah's caller.

'Wolfingham!' Lord Aubrey Maystone turned at the bottom of the staircase to greet him enthusiastically; eyes alight with pleasure as he strode forward to shake Darian warmly by the hand. 'How fortuitous this is, for you are just the man I wanted to see.'

Darian failed to see how that was possible, when Maystone could not have had any idea that Darian would be at Mariah Beecham's home this morning.

Or could he?

As Darian knew only too well, from working so closely with the older man for so many years, Maystone was deceptively wily. A man capable of weaving webs within webs and all without losing sight of a single thread of those intricate weavings.

Although Darian seriously doubted that the other man's role as spymaster was his reason for calling upon Mariah this morning.

Indeed, Mariah's instruction, for Maystone to be taken to her private parlour, left only one conclusion in regard to Maystone's presence here this morning: that the older man was indeed the man Mariah was currently intimately involved with and his joviality was now merely a politeness in front of Mariah's butler.

Chapter Five

Mariah had hurriedly followed Wolfingham out into the entrance hall and had arrived just in time to witness Aubrey Maystone warmly greeting and shaking the younger man by the hand. Much, she noted ruefully, to Darian Hunter's stony-faced displeasure.

No doubt because Wolfingham had now deduced, despite her denials to the contrary, that she was indeed involved in an affair with Aubrey Maystone.

Just as she was sure that Aubrey Mayston's real reason for calling upon her so unexpectedly this morning was sure to be a matter of some delicacy and no doubt related to her work for the Crown.

In which case, the arrogantly disapproving Darian Hunter would just have to continue to think what he would regarding her relationship with the older man. As, it seemed, he always chose to think the worst of her.

'Aubrey!' She greeted the older man with a warm smile as she crossed the hallway to link her arm with his and allowed him to kiss her lightly on the cheek. 'His Grace was just leaving.' She turned to look at Wolfingham with coldly challenging eyes.

'I would prefer him to remain, my dear.'

To Mariah's surprise it was Aubrey Maystone who answered her softly, rather than the harsh response she had fully expected from Wolfingham regarding her obvious dismissal of him. A frown marred her brow as she turned to give the older man a puzzled glance.

Maystone raised his brows pointedly towards her hovering butler before answering her. 'Might I suggest you consider ordering us all some refreshment?'

'Er—of course.' Mariah was more than a little disconcerted. 'Bring tea and brandy, if you please, Fuller,' she instructed distractedly before the three of them turned to enter the gold salon. Mariah was still totally at a loss to understand why Aubrey Maystone should have deliberately delayed Wolfingham's departure.

'What is this all about, Maystone?' Darian Hunter felt no hesitation in expressing his own impatience with the older man's request, as he restlessly paced the length of the room once the three of them were alone together with the door closed behind them. A disdainful smile curled his top lip. 'I trust we are not about to engage in a proprietary claim of ownership on your part, in response to your having discovered my having paid the countess a visit this morning?'

'Wolfingham!' the older man snapped reprovingly.

Mariah also gasped at Wolfingham's deliberate

insult. 'I am not a hunting dog, nor a piece of horse-flesh, Wolfingham, to be *owned* by any man!'

In truth, it had not been Darian's intention to insult Mariah. He had merely meant to challenge the older man for what he perceived must be Maystone's displeasure at finding Darian in the home of his mistress.

Darian had not *meant* to insult Mariah, but he could see by the stiff way that she now held herself, the fierce glitter in her eyes and the two spots of angry colour that had appeared in her otherwise pale cheeks, that was exactly what he had done. 'I meant you no disrespect—'

'Did you not?' she scorned.

Had he?

Darian frowned as he realised that *he* was the one who felt displeased and unsettled, both at the other man's arrival and the unmistakable familiarity that he knew existed between Maystone and Mariah.

It was obvious, from the warmth of Mariah's tone and manner whenever she spoke to the older man, that she liked and approved of Aubrey Maystone. Just as it was equally as obvious, from the coldness of her tone and manner whenever she addressed Darian, that she disliked and disapproved of *him* intensely.

And he, Darian acknowledged heavily, had done little in their acquaintance so far to dispel or temper those feelings of dislike. The opposite, in fact. 'I sincerely apologise if I spoke out of turn.' He bowed stiffly to Mariah before turning to the older man. 'Perhaps, if you have something you wish to say to me, Maystone, it might be better if we arrange another time and place in which to have that conversation?'

'I trust you are not considering engaging in *another* duel, Wolfingham?' Mariah Beecham scorned.

'Another duel?' Lord Maystone looked confused.

'A misunderstanding on Lady Beecham's part,' Darian dismissed coolly; Aubrey Maystone was one of the few people who knew in exactly what manner Darian had received the bullet wound to his shoulder. 'If you will send word when it is convenient for me to call upon you, Maystone?'

'I was perfectly serious when I said it was fortuitous that you happened to be here this morning.' The older man eyed him impatiently.

Darian studied the older man through narrowed lids, noting the hard glitter to Maystone's eyes and the lines of strain etched beside his nose and mouth. Evidence that the other man's mood was not as cheerfully relaxed as it had appeared to be when he had arrived? 'What could you possibly have to discuss with me if not my visit this morning to Mar—Lady Beecham?'

Mariah was wondering the same thing, as she also wondered why Aubrey Maystone had called at her home at all; as a precaution, the two of them had never met at Aubrey's offices in the Foreign Office or here in her home, but chose instead to pass information on to each other whenever Aubrey arranged for them to meet socially. The fact that Aubrey had chosen to call on her here this morning must mean that he had something of a serious nature to import.

Although that still did not explain why it was he wished Wolfingham to remain.

'That will be all, thank you, Fuller.' Mariah smiled at the butler once he had straightened from placing the tray bearing the tea and brandy on the low coffee table. 'I am not at home to any more callers this morning,' she added, waiting until her butler had left the room and closed the door behind him before turning back to Aubrey Maystone. 'What—'

'I shall begin this conversation,' Maystone spoke firmly, 'by first stating that it is necessary that I now inform both of you of the other's involvement in certain matters of secrecy and delicacy to the Crown.'

Mariah was so stunned by Aubrey's announcement that she instantly sank down weakly into one of the armchairs, before she even dared to look up and see that Wolfingham's expression was one of equal shock—proof that he was just as stunned as she was at being so bluntly outed as an agent for the Crown, by the very man who acted as her—no, their?—spymaster?

Mariah was more than shocked; she was having great difficulty believing Aubrey Maystone's announcement in regard to the haughtily disapproving and condescending Duke of Wolfingham.

The man Mariah knew society believed to be both sober and stern.

A man she personally knew to be arrogant and unpleasant, as well as insulting.

That same gentleman worked secretly, as she did, for the Crown?

It seemed barely possible it could be true, yet it must be so if Aubrey Maystone said that it was.

The puzzle was why Aubrey Maystone had now revealed something that had, in Mariah's case, remained a secret to all but her daughter for seven years.

A sentiment, a confidence, that Wolfingham echoed, if the glittering green of his eyes was any indication. 'What do you mean by talking so frankly, Maystone?'

'Recent developments have made it necessary, Darian,' the older man excused heavily as he gave a dismissive wave of his hand. 'And I also suggest that the two of you get over your shock as quickly as possible, so that we might then proceed.'

Darian *was* shocked by Maystone's unexpected announcement, too much so to be able to hide the emotion.

And it was a knowledge, in regard to Mariah Beecham, that instantly posed a dozen other questions in Darian's mind.

Such as how long had Mariah been engaged in such dangerous and secret work for the Crown?

And why had she?

When did she?

Where?

And how?

It was perhaps the answer to that last question that interested Darian the most.

For surely there was only one way in which a woman in society might go about gaining secret information?

'It would seem, Aubrey, that Wolfingham is too

busy drawing his own conclusions as to the methods I might utilise—flirtation, teasing, *seduction*—in order to be able to garner that information, to be able to proceed at the moment,' Mariah drawled coldly, for once Wolfingham's thoughts having been crystal clear to her. Unpleasantly so!

He scowled. 'I was merely—'

'I am well aware of what you were *merely thinking*, Wolfingham,' she snapped disgustedly.

His jaw tightened. 'Do not presume to know the thoughts in my head, madam—'

'Enough,' the older man interrupted wearily. 'We do not have time for petty arguments this morning.'

Those green eyes turned as hard as the emeralds they resembled as Wolfingham turned his attention back to the other man. 'Then perhaps you might state what it is we do need to talk about so urgently that you have deliberately chosen to put both myself and Lady Beecham in a position of personal vulnerability?'

'Only to each other.'

'Exactly!' Wolfingham scowled darkly.

Maystone grimaced. 'It was necessary, Darian.'

'As I said, I would be interested to know why.'

'Plots and treason, Wolfingham,' Maystone stated emphatically.

'There is always talk of plots and treason,' Wolfingham dismissed scathingly.

'This time it is different.' The older man frowned darkly. 'Perhaps you will better understand the situation if I tell you that in the past week plots to assassinate the tsar and the Austrian emperor have been discovered and the assassins dealt with. That such a plot, despite all our efforts to make it otherwise, still exists in regard to our own Prince Regent.'

'Good lord!' Wolfingham slowly lowered his body down into one of the armchairs, his face pale.

Maystone nodded. 'Five days ago two people, a tutor and a footman, attached to and working in the households of two prominent politicians, were taken in for questioning on the matter. My own private secretary was taken into custody late last night,' Maystone continued grimly. 'And he is even now being questioned as to the part he has played in the plot to assassinate the Regent himself.'

'How is such a thing possible?' Mariah breathed faintly, her hand shaking as she lifted it to her mouth.

Maystone gave Darian a telling glance. 'I am sure *you*, at least, will better understand the seriousness of this threat if I say that your old friend Rousseau was involved?'

Both men were well aware that the Frenchman was no friend of Darian's. Indeed, Rousseau was responsible for the bullet wound in Darian's shoulder. As Darian was responsible for having brought the other man's life to a swift and sudden end.

He gave a shake of his head. 'He left England and returned to France almost a year ago.'

'But not before he had set up a network of his own spies and assassins amongst the households of some of the leading members of the English government,' Maystone rasped disgustedly. 'All set in place and ready to act when or if Napoleon departed Elba and attempted to return to France as emperor, which, as we all know, he is currently doing. At which time the heads of the allied countries were to be eliminated, an act designed to throw the governments of the alliance into chaos.'

Darian lay his head back against the chair and closed his eyes, better understanding the reason for Maystone's agitation now. Such a plot as the other man was outlining could have had, might still have, a devastating effect on the shaky alliance formed against Napoleon.

Especially so, as Napoleon was even now marching triumphantly towards Paris, an army of hundreds of thousands at his back. And all without, as Napoleon had claimed it would be, a shot being fired.

'How was it even possible for a Frenchman to do such a thing?' Mariah frowned.

Maystone gave a humourless grimace. 'Because he worked and lived in England for a year under the guise of tutor to a son of a member of the aristocracy. Jeffrey Lancaster, the future heir and now the Earl of Malvern, to be exact.'

'You are referring to the French tutor the Lancaster chit eloped with last year?' Mariah gasped. 'Does it surprise you, knowing what you do now, that I have made a point of knowing these things?' she added dismissively as Wolfingham gave her a frowning glance.

'That "Lancaster chit" is now the Duchess of Hawksmere and the wife of a close friend of mine!' he reminded stiffly.

'She was also the lover of this man, André Rousseau, for several months, if I am to understand this situation correctly,' Mariah maintained stubbornly.

'Situations are not always as they appear.'

'As I once reminded you,' Mariah said pointedly 'You—'

'Could we please concentrate on the subject at hand?' Maystone interrupted irritably, before sighing heavily. 'Yes, my dear Mariah, for the sake of clarity, I can confirm that you are quite correct in believing that André Rousseau was tutor to young Jeffrey Lancaster for a year and also the same man who persuaded Lancaster's sister Georgianna into eloping with him. I would like to add in her defence,' he continued firmly, 'that she was also responsible for bringing us information vital to our government just weeks ago. Information that also resulted in Rousseau's death in Paris just fifteen days ago.'

'Fifteen days ago?' Mariah did a quick calculation in her head as she recalled that it had been nine days ago that Wolfingham had told her he had been shot 'six days ago, to be precise'.

It did not take a genius to add nine and six together and come up with the correct answer.

She slowly turned to look at Wolfingham, knowing by the challenging glitter in those emerald-green eyes as he returned her gaze, that her calculations were correct.

Wolfingham had killed André Rousseau in Paris fifteen days ago.

And in doing so he had received a bullet wound to his shoulder.

She had no doubt now that Darian Hunter, the haughty Duke of Wolfingham, was not only a spy for the Crown, as she was, but that he had also travelled to France in the past three weeks, in the midst of the turmoil of the Corsican's escape and return to France, and succeeded in killing the man who was a known spy for Napoleon.

As Wolfingham had killed others, in the past, who had threatened the security of the Crown?

It was both shocking and a little daunting to realise there was so much more to the Duke of Wolfingham than the disdain he chose to show outwardly and those flashes of passion he had so ably demonstrated to Mariah privately.

So much so that Mariah now viewed him with new and wary eyes. She had already considered her unwanted physical response to Darian Hunter to be a risk to her peace of mind, but this new information, on exactly what sort of a man the Duke of Wolfingham really was, now caused Mariah to consider him as being completely dangerous.

Indeed, he reminded her of a stalking predator, a wolf, hiding behind a mask of stern urbanity.

Proof indeed that he had more than earned his place as being thought of as one of the five Dangerous Dukes.

'If we could return to the more immediate problem of this plot to assassinate the Regent?' Lord Maystone prompted drily as he obviously saw this silent battle of wills between Mariah and Wolfingham.

Mariah found it hard to breathe, let alone break

away from that glittering green gaze, feeling as if she were a butterfly stuck on the end of a pin and with no way of escape.

She began to breathe again only when Darian Hunter, after giving her a hard and mocking smile, turned his attention back to Aubrey Maystone.

'I am presuming that your own private secretary's involvement with Rousseau will also have exposed the names of the network of people who work for you?' Wolfingham prompted astutely.

Mariah's eyes widened in alarm as she saw the truth of that statement in the heavy mantle of responsibility that instantly settled on Aubrey Maystone's slumped and aged shoulders.

'Almost all.' The older man nodded. 'We had our first inkling of that exposure, of course, when Rousseau revealed to Georgianna Lancaster that he knew of Hawksmere's work for the Crown.'

Darian nodded grimly, that information having meant that Hawksmere could no longer play an active role in Maystone's network of spies. Perhaps it was as well, now that Hawksmere was a married man, but even so...

'I am also presuming, as you wished to speak with both of us this morning, that perhaps Lady Beecham and myself have so far not been exposed?'

'That is so, yes,' Maystone confirmed tightly. 'I do not keep written records of my agents, as you know, but of the twelve in my network, only the two of you have never had reason to call at the Foreign Office or my home.'

'And would not the fact that you have chosen to call at the countess's home this morning have succeeded in alerting any now watching you to the possibility that she—'

'I am not completely without the resource of stealth myself, Wolfingham,' the older man snapped impatiently. 'I left my home by the servants' entrance, hired a hackney cab to bring me to within two streets of this house and walked the rest of the way. All whilst keeping watch for any who might be taking any undue interest in my movements.'

'I apologise.' Darian gave a rueful inclination of his head.

'Apology accepted.' Maystone nodded briskly. 'Could we now return to the subject of these assassins and their infernal plots?'

Darian sank back into his armchair. 'I presume you are now about to tell us what part you expect the two of us to play in foiling this plot?'

Mariah had been aware of the sharpness and acuity of Wolfingham's intelligence, but she had also learnt a wary respect for his astuteness these past few minutes as the two gentlemen talked and knew, by the irritation in Aubrey Maystone's face, that the Duke's words had once again hit their mark.

'What could the two of us possibly do that you have not already done yourself?' she prompted guardedly; positively the last thing she wished for was to spend any more time in Darian Hunter's company than she needed to.

Aubrey Maystone seemed completely unaware of

her reservations as his next words instantly trampled that wish. 'Mariah has already told me that she has accepted her invitation to go to Lord and Lady Nicholses' house party in Kent this weekend. I now wish for you to accompany her, Wolfingham.'

'But—'

'I am aware it is not your usual choice of entertainment, Wolfingham,' the older man acknowledged drily. 'But in this instance it is too dangerous for Mariah to attend alone.'

'Then why attend at all?' she questioned sharply, her heart having leapt in alarm just at the thought of spending a weekend in the company of the judgemental Darian Hunter. He despised her utterly already, enjoyed thinking the worst of her, without the added humiliation of knowing he was watching her with those cold green eyes as she moved about flirtatiously at one of Clara Nichols's licentious weekend house parties. 'It will be no hardship to me to send my apologies to Clara Nichols.'

'That is the last thing I wish you to do, my dear,' Aubrey Maystone assured gently, before launching into an explanation of exactly why the two of them must attend the Nicholses' house party together.

'And to think that you once told me that such things as politics and intrigue bored you,' Wolfingham drawled mockingly.

Lord Maystone, having stated his business, had now departed as abruptly as he had arrived, after stating that he would now leave the two of them alone together, so that they might discuss and consider his request, before giving him their answer later on today.

A request, as far as Mariah was concerned, that was so outrageous as to be unthinkable.

And yet...

She had never said no to anything that Aubrey Maystone had asked of her in the past and she could not bear to think of doing so now, either.

Except for the fact that this time it involved Wolfingham, a man she had serious reason to be wary of.

Her gaze flickered across to where Wolfingham now lounged in the armchair opposite her own, both the pot of tea and the decanter of brandy now empty, after almost an hour of intense discussion. 'I believe you also allowed me to continue to think that you came by your bullet wound by engaging in a duel rather than disposing of André Rousseau?'

'How delicately you put it, my dear Mariah!' Wolfingham drawled. 'But I also have reason to believe that you have greatly enjoyed tormenting *me* with the possibility of it coming about because of some tragic love affair?' He arched a mocking brow.

Yes, Mariah had indeed enjoyed taunting the haughtily disapproving Duke of Wolfingham with the possibility of his having fought a duel over a woman.

Only to now know that he had come by his bullet wound after days of secretly scouting the French countryside for information to bring back to the English government. Followed by a hand-to-hand fight in which the other man—the Frenchman André Rousseau, a spy for Napoleon, both here in England and in France—had died and Darian Hunter had been shot.

'It would seem that we have both had something to hide,' Wolfingham bit out abruptly. 'The question is, what do we do now in regard to Maystone's audacious request of the two of us?'

It *was* outrageous, Mariah acknowledged with a pained wince. Worse than outrageous, as it involved herself and Darian Hunter giving every appearance, in public at least, of being intimately involved with each other. An affair they were to use as their cover when, if, the two of them agreed to attend the house party at Lord and Lady Nicholses' house in Kent this following weekend.

Because the Nicholses had, apparently, been named in the plot against the Prince.

The Nicholses were notorious for giving licentious house parties once or twice a Season. Parties at which the Prince Regent, usually resident in a house nearby, always made an appearance on the Saturday evening of the masked ball, although Aubrey Maystone and other members of the government had succeeded in persuading the Regent into not attending this one.

The Prince Regent particularly enjoyed making an appearance at such parties as these, occasions not designed for the attendance of the young debutantes and their marriage-minded mamas, but for the older, more sophisticated members of the *ton*, where their *risqué* behaviour would not be frowned upon.

Mariah would never dream of allowing Christina to attend, for example. Having accepted her own in-

vitation, Mariah had instantly made arrangements
for her young daughter to spend the weekend at the
home of her friend Diana Gilbert. Diana's mother,
Lady Gilbert, intended to chaperon her own daughter and Christina to a musical soirée on Friday evening and then a ball on Saturday evening, followed
by church on Sunday morning, and Mariah would
return in the evening.

Mariah had always made a point of attending the
Nicholses' weekend parties, when inhibitions became
relaxed and information was more freely given.

A lowering of inhibitions that Mariah now accepted could—and according to Aubrey Maystone's
information, had—equally have been used to Lord
or Lady Nicholses' advantage.

Aubrey Maystone's suggestion was that, the danger being high, Wolfingham would now accompany
Mariah into Kent, posing as her lover. Explaining that
it would not be unexpected, when the two of them
had been seen talking and dancing together several
times this past week or so, and apparently giving rise
to a certain amount of gossip and speculation concerning whether or not there might be a relationship
between the two of them.

Mariah could not claim to have heard any of that
unwelcome gossip herself, but then she could not expect to have done, when that gossip was about her.

It would be an easy step, Maystone had assured,
for the two of them to attend the house party together
and so confirm the gossip and speculation.

But it was a pretence that Mariah, despite those two occasions in which Wolfingham had held her in his arms or kissed her, would not have believed the austere and disdainful Duke of Wolfingham to be capable of.

Before today...

Mariah had no doubts now that Wolfingham had indeed chosen to hide his real self behind the guise of that cold and disdainful duke, because she now suspected—*knew*—that behind that haughty exterior was a man of deep passions.

Deep and unrelenting passions that terrified her at the same time as they caused a wild fluttering inside her.

She straightened determinedly. 'You do understand that, if I should agree to do this in order to flush out the traitors, the public liaison between the two of us would be for appearances' sake only? That there would be no actual intimacy?'

Her eyes widened as Wolfingham gave a rueful chuckle, the signs of that humour, in the warmth of his green eyes and the soft curve of chiselled lips, instantly lessening his veneer of austerity and making him appear years younger than his age.

'You do have a certain way with words, Mariah.' Darian gave a wry shake of his head. 'And I assure you, I never doubted for a moment that our liaison,' he drily echoed her own words, 'would be for appearances' sake only.' He sobered. '*If* we should agree to go forward with Maystone's proposal,' he added harshly, 'which neither of us has yet done.'

Mariah did not see how either of them had any real choice in the matter, if the perpetrators of this plot to assassinate the Prince Regent were to be arrested.

Chapter Six

'What have you done with Lady Christina this weekend?' Darian prompted as he and Mariah travelled into Kent on Friday evening in the warmth of his lamplit coach. His valet and Mariah's maid, along with their luggage, had already travelled into Kent in a second coach sent on ahead earlier today.

Cool turquoise eyes turned to look at him across the width of the coach. Mariah looked cosily warm in a travelling cloak, bonnet and muff for her hands of that same vibrant turquoise colour. 'She is staying with friends.'

'And do you trust that my younger brother will not take advantage of your absence?' Darian had sent a note informing his brother that he would be away in the country this weekend, but not with whom; he fully expected to hear of his brother's displeasure if or when Anthony learnt that Darian had spent the weekend in the company of the mother of the young lady about whom he had serious intentions.

'I trust my daughter not to allow any gentleman to take advantage of my absence.' Mariah had chosen not to speak to Christina regarding Anthony Hunter in particular, believing that to do so would only cause her independent-minded young daughter's attention to fixate on the gentleman. But a casual conversation between mother and daughter had confirmed that Christina did not have serious feelings for any of the young gentlemen who flocked to her side on every social occasion.

Wolfingham nodded. 'And Lady Nichols was receptive to my accompanying you?'

Mariah gave a dismissive snort. 'What society hostess would not be receptive to counting the elusive Duke of Wolfingham amongst her guests?'

'The Countess of Carlisle?' Darian arched a mocking brow.

'True,' that countess drawled dismissively before turning away to look out of the window into the dark of the night.

This was the first time that Darian had seen Mariah since they had informed Maystone of their decision to attend the Nicholses' weekend house party together, their arrangements having then been made through an exchange of terse notes.

A terseness that obviously still existed between the two of them now that they were together again.

Darian straightened on his side of the coach. 'And how successful do you think we shall be at this ruse of an affair between the two of us, when you cannot even bring yourself to look at me for longer than a few seconds?'

Mariah closed her eyes briefly behind the brim of her bonnet before gathering herself to once again look coolly across the carriage at Wolfingham. 'We have not arrived at Eton Park yet, your Grace.'

Darian Hunter gave a mocking shake of his head. 'It is then that I am to expect that the woman who now calls me your Grace so condescendingly will suddenly turn into my adoring lover?'

Mariah firmly repressed the shiver that ran the length of her spine—she did not care to search too deeply as to whether it was a shudder of revulsion or a quiver of anticipation!—at the mere suggestion of herself and this forcefully powerful man ever really becoming lovers.

Wolfingham was just so *immediate*. So overpoweringly male. Just so—so *Wolfingham* that he would totally possess any woman brave enough to attempt to match herself against the passions that Mariah now knew, without a doubt, burned so fiercely behind that mask of stern disapproval.

Even seated in the confines of this coach with him Mariah was aware of that fire smouldering, burning, beneath his outwardly relaxed, even bored, countenance.

'I will never be any man's adoring lover, Wolfingham,' she scorned—or any man's lover at all! 'And I will only be your *pretend* lover for this one weekend,' she assured firmly. 'I believe that you will also find my acting skills are more than sufficient as to be convincing once we are in the company of others.' How could they not be, when for years she had managed, in public at least, to look as if she found pleasure in being at her husband's side?

'And might I enquire as to where and how you might have attained and honed these acting skills?' Wolfingham arched a sceptical brow.

'Perhaps you should turn your attention to your own performance rather than worrying about mine?' she challenged sharply rather than answer his question.

Darian noted that the asperity, which usually edged Mariah's tone whenever she spoke to him, had now returned. It was an improvement on her earlier cool uninterest, but only barely!

He settled more comfortably against the plush cushions of the seat. 'I do not recall ever having received any complaints in the past regarding my performance,' he drawled mockingly.

A flush now coloured Mariah's cheeks, of either embarrassment or anger—though Darian would guess at it being the latter; there was no reason for Mariah to feel embarrassment discussing such a subject when she had been a married lady for many years and so familiar with her husband's performance. And that of the other gentlemen who had shared her bed during and after her marriage!

A thought that did not give Darian any pleasure whatsoever.

He eyed her with frustration from behind lowered lids. Indeed, it had been long days—and nights—of frustrations since the morning he had called at her home and they had been joined by Aubrey Maystone.

Not least because Mariah had proved so elusive on the occasions Darian had asked for the two of them to meet in person since that time, so that they might discuss how they were to proceed this weekend. Requests Mariah had consistently refused, on the excuse of having far too many other engagements, and the arrangements to be made for their weekend away in Kent, to be able to fit a visit from him into that busy schedule.

Darian's suggestion that, as her lover, he was *supposed* to be visiting her had been met with a wall of silence on Mariah's part. A silence that had not been broken until he had called at her home to collect her earlier this evening.

Another frustration had been Maystone's inability to persuade any of the three men, now being held and questioned, into giving them more information regarding one or both of the Nicholses' involvement in this plot against the Prince.

Thankfully, Maystone and other members of the government had succeeded in continuing to convince the Prince Regent that it was for the best that he not attend even the Nicholses' masked ball on Saturday evening.

Instead, Aubrey Maystone and several of his agents would take up residence at Winterton Manor for the weekend, just five miles away from Eton Park, and await word from Darian and Mariah as to the Nicholses' reaction to the note the Prince Regent would have delivered to them at Eton Park at precisely five o'clock on Saturday afternoon, explaining his absence. Five o'clock had been chosen deliberately, when all would be gathered for tea, so that Mariah and Darian might observe Lord and Lady Nicholses' reaction to the news, and also what followed. If anything.

It was the thought of being thrust into the midst of this weekend of licentiousness that had become yet another thorn in Darian's side, when he would normally avoid such events like the plague. Not because, as Mariah was so fond of telling him, he was too proper and austere to attend, but simply because he preferred to perform acts of intimacy without an audience. *All* acts of intimacy.

Such as the numerous acts of intimacy he had imagined engaging in with Mariah, the moment he had retired to his bed these past three nights.

Resulting in him rising early each morning following a restless night's sleep, in order to take a cold bath, before joining one or other of his friends at the boxing saloon and so allowing him to dispel some of his frustration in the boxing ring.

All of which Darian doubted would be a possible outlet for all of his restless energy during this weekend spent in Kent at Mariah's side.

No, he fully expected to be put through even worse torture whilst in the Nicholses' home. Especially since, as was usual at these types of unrestrained weekends of entertainment, his bedchamber would no doubt tactfully adjoin Mariah's own.

Having already spent several hours in the coach

with Mariah, that exotic and erotic perfume once again invading his senses, Darian was unsure whether or not he would be able to withstand the nightly temptation of opening the door that connected his bedchamber to hers.

'Do you always wear the same perfume?'

Mariah looked sharply across at Wolfingham, surprised by the sudden, and harshly spoken, change of subject, but also searching for some sign of criticism. As usual his expression proved too enigmatic for her to decipher.

Her chin rose. 'You do not like it?'

'It is unusual,' he answered noncommittally.

Mariah laughed softly. 'That does not answer my question, Wolfingham.'

'Darian.'

She blinked. 'I beg your pardon?'

'So far we have progressed from having you address me as your Grace to the more familiar Wolfingham. I thought now might be as good a time as any for you to begin calling me Darian.'

'Did you?' Mariah returned with the coolness that had become her only defence against the fire of emotions she now knew burned behind those cold green eyes. Emotions that surprisingly sparked something similar within her own fast-beating heart.

Wolfingham now shrugged those exceptionally wide shoulders, shown to such advantage in the black fitted superfine, as was the flatness of his stomach beneath a grey waistcoat and snowy white linen, his pantaloons also black, his legs long and sprawling as he relaxed back against his side of the carriage. 'I believe most couples, in a situation such as ours is supposed to be, address each other by their given names rather than their titles.'

'You believe?' Mariah gave a taunting smile. 'Do you not know for certain?'

Darian's mouth thinned at what he knew to be her deliberate mockery. 'The ladies I have bedded in the past have not usually had the privilege of a title,' he drawled dismissively and had the satisfaction of seeing that blush once again colour Mariah's cheeks. 'But I have no particular aversion to addressing you at all times as Countess, if that is the game you like to play?' His brief moment of satisfaction quickly faded as he saw the smile instantly waver and then disappear from those beautiful red lips, her gaze equally as uncertain. He rose abruptly to his feet. 'Mariah—'

'Stay on your own side of the carriage, Wolfingham.' She held up a hand to ward him off from his obvious intention of crossing the carriage to sit on the seat beside her.

Darian froze even as he studied her face intently, noting the shadows beneath those beautiful eyes and the way the colour had now deserted her cheeks, leaving her pale and delicate. At thoughts of his moving closer to her? 'Are you sure you wish to go ahead with this charade, Mariah?' he finally prompted gently.

She smiled tightly. 'Who else will do it if we do not?'

He had no answer to that argument, knowing as he did, as Mariah did, that time was not their friend.

That Napoleon, having been joined by the defector Marshal Ney, and his army ever increasing, was now fast approaching Paris. There were already riots in the capitol in support of their emperor's return and King Louis was preparing to flee. If something were to now happen to England's Prince Regent, it was guaranteed to throw the allies into total disarray, so allowing Napoleon's return to the capitol to be a double-edged triumph.

Darian sank back down on to his seat, but remained sitting forward so that he might reach out and take both Mariah's hands from inside her muff, frowning as he felt the way that her fingers trembled as he held them in his own. 'There is nothing for you to be frightened of, Mariah,' he assured gruffly. 'I promise I will do my utmost to ensure that no harm shall come to you this weekend.'

Mariah held back the hysterical laugh that threatened to burst forth at the obvious sincerity of Darian's promise of allowing no harm to come to her—when the person she now feared the most was *him*.

Oh, not him exactly, but her responses to him certainly. Responses, of heat and desire, that did not seem to have dissipated or lessened in these past three days of not seeing him, as she had hoped that they might.

Responses that she had believed herself to be incapable of feeling towards any man.

Until Wolfingham.

Just a few minutes of being back in his company and Mariah had known that she was still aware of everything about him. The dark and glossy thickness of his hair. Those beautiful emerald-green eyes. The stark and chiselled handsomeness of his features. The strength of his muscled body.

The gentleness of the long and sensitive hands that now held her hands so lightly, but securely, within his own.

Hands that Mariah could only too easily imagine moving, exploring her body, lighting a fire wherever they touched, giving pleasure wherever they caressed. And what did she know of the pleasure of her body at any man's hands?

Nothing, came the blunt and unequivocal answer.

If she really were a normal widow, the woman of experience Wolfingham believed her to be, then she would know. Just as she would take every advantage of their weekend together to explore this attraction she felt for him.

Except Mariah was not normal, as a widow or a woman.

Christina had been conceived on the one and only occasion Martin had— No, Mariah could never think of what he had done to her that night as making love! It had been force and pain, and humiliation for her, nothing more and nothing less.

Their marriage had been nothing but a sham from the beginning, Martin spending most of his nights in the bed of his mistress, the same woman who acted as housekeeper in their London home, and had done so for twenty years or more before Mariah and Martin were married.

Many wives might have resented having her husband's mistress actually living in one of their homes, but Mariah had felt only gratitude; whilst Martin's nights were occupied with Mrs Smith then he would not think of coming to her bed. She had dismissed Mrs Smith after Martin's death, of course, for Christina's sake as well as her own, but Mariah's gratitude to that lady had been such that she had provided the other woman with a large enough pension for her to live comfortably for the rest of her life.

What would Wolfingham—a man who believed her to have been an adulteress in her marriage and to have had a multitude of lovers during her five years of widowhood—what would such a man think if he were to learn that Mariah had had but a single night of carnal knowledge in her life and that one occasion had been the most horrible, degrading, painful—

'Where have you gone, Mariah?' Darian had not liked the way in which her expression had grown distant, turned inwards, her thoughts giving a shadow to the depths of those beautiful eyes. He liked it even less when she had given an obvious shudder just now of what seemed like revulsion...

Because she did genuinely fear the coming events at the Nicholses' home?

Or because she felt revulsion for the idea of even that *pretence* of an intimate relationship with him?

Unfortunately, Darian had no answer to that question.

She roused herself with effort, purposefully pulling her hands from his as she straightened, a bright and meaningless smile now curving those ruby-red lips, a smile that did nothing to take away the shadows in her eyes. 'Why, I am right here in the carriage with you, Wolfingham,' she assured him with unmistakable brittleness. 'And I do believe we are now on the driveway approaching Eton Park,' she added with obvious relief.

Darian leant back abruptly against the cushions, knowing that their brief moment of tenderness was over. If it had ever really begun on Mariah's part.

His expression was grim as he turned to look out of the window to view the brightly lit house in the distance. He inwardly cursed himself for being a fool. He might have spent the past days and nights thinking of, desiring, Mariah, might even have anticipated being with her again, but she had shown him time and time again that she did not feel that same desire towards him.

He gave a shake of his head as he once again turned his own thoughts to the business of the weekend ahead. 'What sort of entertainments might I expect to endure this evening?'

Mariah shrugged. 'The full entertainments will not begin until tomorrow, obviously, but after dinner this evening I expect there will be cards and dancing.'

Darian grimaced. 'Sounds boringly normal to me.'

She chuckled huskily. 'I assure you there is nothing "normal" about cards and dancing in the Nicholses' home!'

Darian eyed her speculatively. 'Meaning?'

A small, secretive smile hovered at the corners of her mouth. 'You will see soon enough!'

Darian disliked the sound of that. As he disliked feeling as if he were at a disadvantage, as he surely was where such weekends as this were concerned.

And meaning that he would have to look to Mariah for guidance as to the correct way for him to behave.

But first, it seemed, he had to endure the simpering and coquettish Lady Clara Nichols as she gushingly welcomed him to her home, whilst her husband showed Mariah similar attentions. Attentions, he noted with satisfaction, that she laughed off quite easily.

Darian was not so successful where Lady Clara was concerned, as she proudly introduced them to the rest of the company still assembled in the drawing room after tea: several lords, an earl, half a dozen Members of Parliament, some with their wives, but most not. There were also a dozen or so other female members of the *ton*, a titled lady or two, several Honourables, three well-known actresses and an opera singer, and all without the escort of their husbands.

Lady Clara then insisted, her arm firmly linked with Darian's, on personally accompanying them up the stairs to show them to their bedchambers.

Darian felt quite sickened by her attentions by the time that lady finally took herself off to rejoin her other guests and no doubt indulge in gossip about the duke and the countess.

His top lip curled with distaste the moment the door of the bedchamber had closed behind his simpering hostess. 'There is something particularly sickening about a lady of possibly forty years giggling like a schoolgirl.'

Mariah chuckled, no doubt at the look of disgust on his face, as she untied her bonnet and threw it down on to her bed. 'How very ungrateful of you, Darian, when I do believe, from their situation of being at the front of the house and the opulence of these bedchambers, that Clara and Richard must have moved out of their own bedchambers in order to accommodate the two of us.'

As expected, the two of them had been given adjoining bedchambers, the door between those rooms having been left pointedly open, and no doubt the reason Darian had been subjected to Clara Nichols's girlishly suggestive giggles when she reminded them that dinner would be served in a little over two hours. No doubt she expected the two of them to indulge in some love play before that time.

Darian's room was acceptable, but Mariah's— Clara Nichols's own bedchamber?—was a ghastly nightmare of pink and cream lace and flounces. 'How will you ever be able to sleep in such an explosion of pink?' He grimaced as he stood in the doorway between their two rooms.

Mariah gave a dismissive shrug. 'I shall simply blow out the candles and then I shall not be able to see it.'

Darian admired the picture of grace and beauty Mariah made in the candle and firelight as she stood in the middle of that ghastly pink room. A veritable vision in turquoise and cream, her hair appearing like spun gold, colour now warming her cheeks.

His blood stirred and he felt that tingling at the base of his spine and between his thighs, the rising and thickening of his erection, as he imagined how much more lovely Mariah would look without any clothes on at all.

Would the curls between her thighs be that same gold or possibly a shade darker?

Would her nipples be the same ruby red as her lips?

And would the folds between her thighs—

'If you would not mind, Darian?' Mariah's voice softly interrupted his erotic musings. 'My maid will be here shortly to help me bathe and dress for dinner, as no doubt will your own valet. Oh, and, Darian…?' she added as he gave a terse bow of acceptance before turning to leave, waiting until he had slowly turned back to her before speaking again. 'Close the door on your way out, please.'

His jaw tightened at the dismissal as he stepped through the doorway and closed the door behind him, knowing he needed the privacy in order to take care of the need throbbing through his body, before he dared to rejoin Mariah!

'You are not intending to appear in that gown in public!'

Mariah turned from where she had been gazing at her reflection in the mirror as she put the last of the pearl clips into her hair, to now look at Wolfing-ham as he once again stood in the open doorway between their two bedchambers. His appearance was as resplendent as usual in black evening clothes and snowy white linen, an ebony sheen to his hair, his features once again as hard as granite.

It was the look of horror on those hard features, as he gazed back at her unblinkingly, that now brought a wry smile to her lips. 'You do not like it?'

Like it? Darian had never seen a gown like it before! Well, not outside the walls of a brothel, at least.

The gown left Mariah's shoulders bare except for two tiny ribbon straps and was made of some diaphanous cream material, lined with the sheerest of lace. It clearly revealed the bare outline of the curvaceous body beneath and darkening at the apex between Mariah's thighs—revealing the nakedness of the darker curls covering her mound.

As for the bodice of the gown! It was almost non-existent, just that cream diaphanous material covering the fullness of Mariah's breasts, the nipples plump berries and clearly showing through as being as ruby red as her lips—that ruby colour aided by rouge, if he was not mistaken.

His traitorous body had surged back into full attention the moment he looked at the reflection of those plump nipples in the mirror, and imagined Mariah applying that rouge to those succulent berries. 'I see that a certain part of you does, at least.' Mariah looked pointedly at the unmistakable evidence of his arousal.

Darian did not in the least enjoy feeling like a callow youth taking his first look at a naked woman.

Except Mariah was not naked.

Perhaps he would not have reacted so strongly if she had been!

Of course he would, Darian instantly chastised himself. It was only that there was something so provocative about the tantalising glimpses of those slender and obviously naked curves as Mariah moved across the room to collect her gloves from the bed, giving just the hint of those golden curls nestling between her thighs. And her breasts were magnificent; creamy, full and plump, with those red and succulent rouged nipples just begging to be tasted and suckled.

Darian wanted nothing more at that moment than to lay Mariah down upon the bed before taking those berries into his mouth and sucking and tasting their plumpness until he was sated.

If he ever was!

As for the shadow of those darker golden curls and the promise of what lay hidden between her thighs—

Darian imagined lowering her gently down on to the bed and pushing her gown up her thighs so that he might explore every silken inch of that hidden treasure. To caress the plumpness of her folds. Taste and suck the tiny nubbin above—

Beads of perspiration broke out on Darian's forehead as he fought an inward battle not to give in to the urge to cross the room and take Mariah in his arms, to fulfil every single one of the fantasies that had been slowly driving him insane and that he now found impossible to stop.

'I am ready to go downstairs and join the other guests, if you are?'

It took every effort of his indomitable will to pull Darian back from the brink of giving in to his desires, his voice harsh as he answered her. 'Do you have a shawl or something you can wear about your shoulders?' The thought of other men ogling Mariah's almost naked breasts, and that tantalising outline of her naked curves beneath her gown, was enough to make him clench his fists violently.

Mariah gave a bell-like laugh as she collected up a fan from her dressing table rather than a shawl. 'You will see, Darian, my gown is quite modest in comparison with the gowns some of the other ladies will be wearing this evening.'

He had no interest in what the other ladies were wearing this evening; they could all walk around stark naked for all Darian cared. But if he caught one single gentleman in the act of ogling Mariah— He was behaving more than ridiculously, Darian recognised self-disgustedly, when he had no more right to approve or disapprove of other gentlemen ogling Mariah, tonight or any other night, than—than the Prince Regent did!

Although he had no doubt that the Prince Regent, if he had been one of the guests this evening, would have taken great delight in enjoying Mariah's appearance. The man might be plumper and more dissipated than he had been in his youth, but he still had charm enough to seduce the ladies.

Whereas Darian's charm, what little he did possess—and no doubt Mariah would say he possessed none!—seemed to have completely deserted him for the moment.

'Darian?' Mariah prompted again lightly.

He gathered himself to straighten determinedly before crossing the room to hold out his arm to her, feeling much as he had when he had necessarily to prepare himself before a battle.

And unsure whether that battle this evening would be with his own wayward emotions, or with the other gentlemen present.

Chapter Seven

Mariah was enjoying herself.

Actually enjoying herself, when normally she would simply have gone through the motions of doing so at this sort of entertainment, flirting and laughing with the gentlemen whilst at the same time keeping them in line—and their groping hands firmly at bay—with a delicately aimed flick of her fan.

And the reason she was enjoying herself was standing broodingly at her side now that all the guests had retired to the drawing room following dinner, giving every appearance of a dark and avenging angel, ready to swoop down on any who might even think of crossing over the invisible line he had drawn about the two of them since they had sat down to dinner earlier.

The dark and avenging angel Darian Hunter, the Duke of Wolfingham.

As she had warned Wolfingham before coming down the stairs earlier, most of the other ladies were dressed much more daringly than she was this evening. Indeed, there was a plethora of completely bared breasts visible about the drawing room as the gentlemen, and many of the ladies, completely against the normal rules of polite society, enjoyed an after-dinner brandy together. Most of the gowns were without the benefit of that layer of lace that covered Mariah's breasts and several of the gowns were made of a totally transparent and gauzy material that left absolutely nothing to the imagination.

And for all the notice Wolfingham had taken— was still taking!—of any of those erotically displayed ladies, they might as well have been wearing sackcloth.

It was a refreshing change for Mariah to be in the presence of a gentleman whose gaze was not constantly wandering to the half-naked bodies of other women.

Just as Wolfingham's glowering and tight-lipped disapproval of the approach of both the ladies and the gentlemen present this evening had kept everyone but their hostess from attempting to interrupt their privacy. Wolfingham had wasted no time in dispatching that lady, too, with a few choice and tersely spoken words.

Instead, he had centred all of his attention on Mariah as they ate the sumptuously prepared dinner served to them earlier, his conversation exclusive, and occasionally feeding her the odd delicacy of food from his own plate, as a way, no doubt, of giving further illusion to their intimacy.

Mariah had blushed like a schoolgirl the first time

Darian behaved so unexpectedly, that blush having deepened as he centred his hawklike gaze upon her lips when she finally leant forward to take the food from his fork. She had been better prepared the second time it had happened, but still felt unaccountably hot at the way his green gaze stared so intently at her lips.

And throughout all of it Darian had seemed completely unaware of the sexual play going on about them.

The assembled company had been slightly restrained to begin with, all obviously aware of having the imposing Duke of Wolfingham within their midst, but several glasses of wine later, along with Wolfingham's apparent distraction with Mariah, and those inhibitions had quickly fallen away.

Several of the gentlemen had openly caressed and tweaked bared breasts, and one gentleman had even crawled beneath the table for several minutes, the expression of rapture on the flushed face of the actress seated next to him, followed by her breathy and noisy gasps of pleasure as she climaxed, clearly showing where that gentleman was lavishing his attentions.

Mariah had glanced away as if bored as the gentleman crawled back up into his seat, his mouth moist and lips swollen, the expression on his flushed face becoming one of equal rapture as that lady returned the favour, by unbuttoning his pantaloons and openly stroking him until he, too, reached a completion.

It was a disgusting and embarrassing display, and one that Mariah had been forced to witness at least a dozen times during these past seven years of spying for the Crown.

And one that tonight had caused a flush of heat to course through Mariah's own veins and an unaccustomed tingling and warmth to spread between her thighs.

A heat and tingling that she had preferred not to question too deeply.

'Say no, Darian,' she warned Wolfingham softly now as she shook her own head at Clara Nichols as the other woman moved about the room gathering up the people who wished to play cards.

Darian gave a terse shake of his own head to their poutingly disappointed hostess before moving to stand slightly in front of Mariah, the broadness of his back and shoulders blocking her from the view of the majority of the other guests in the room. 'Why?' he returned as softly.

Mariah looked up at him beneath lowered lashes. 'Because I doubt you will like the forfeit if you lose. Do you ever lose?'

Darian raised one dark brow. 'At cards?'

'At anything!'

Well, he was certainly losing his battle tonight in regard to the desire he felt for Mariah.

Dinner with the Nicholses' guests had been a disgusting display of body parts and licentious behaviour, which he had found distinctly untitillating and which had actually turned his stomach on several occasions. Several sexual acts had actually occurred at the dinner table, made all the more incongruous by the fact that they were all seated about a formal dining table in an equally formal dining room and were being waited upon by the Nicholses' placid-faced butler and footmen.

He had noticed several gentlemen eyeing Mariah covetously when they first sat down at the dinner table. Glances he had frowned darkly upon. Those glances had then turned towards Darian, envious in some cases and actually belligerent in one or two others.

Because none of those gentlemen had been numbered amongst Mariah's lovers? Darian hoped it was so.

He had soon forgotten all but Mariah, as he shut out the presence and behaviour of the people around them and concentrated all of his attentions on her.

He had enjoyed talking with her, their conversations intelligent and witty. He had also fed her sweetmeats on occasion, initially as a way of publically demonstrating the intimacy of their relationship, but continuing to do so time and time again as his shaft hardened as he watched her lips encircle his fork and imagined how those soft and full lips would feel encircling him in the same sensuous way. He had almost come undone completely when she had once run her tongue along her bottom lip as she licked away an excess of cream from a bonbon he had just fed her.

'Very rarely,' he answered her drily now. 'What exactly is it that you forfeit here for losing at cards?'

'Watch.' She turned to where two tables had now been set up with four card players on each, two gentleman and two ladies on one and three gentlemen and one lady on the other.

'Good gracious.' Darian gave a shudder just seconds later as Clara Nichols, obviously the loser of the first hand of cards, instantly stood up to remove her gown, resuming her seat dressed only in silk drawers and pale stockings held up by two pink—what other colour would the woman choose!—garters, her breasts hanging down like two giant udders. 'There should be a law against such an unpleasant display.' Darian's mouth twisted with distaste.

'No doubt there is outside of the privacy of one's home.' Mariah smiled up at him impishly. 'And some gentlemen find such full breasts...erotic.'

'I cannot see how they could!'

'Watch,' she encouraged again, just in time for Darian to glance across the room and see a prominent member of the government—prominent in more ways than one at this precise moment!—lying back upon Lady Clara's bare thighs and placing his head beneath one of her pendulous breasts before sucking the nipple heartily into his mouth.

'He looks like a giant baby taking suck from its mother!' Darian muttered with disgust.

'I believe that is Lord Edgewood's little fetish, yes.' Mariah nodded. 'And many women's breasts become less pert as we age, especially when we have borne children,' she added with a playful tap of her fan on his shoulder.

Whether intended or not—and Darian suspected not, in his particular case—the movement drew attention to her own perfectly formed and jiggling breasts, beautifully pert rouge-tipped breasts that peeped out at him temptingly from beneath that thin barrier of lace. 'I am pleased to note your own have not suffered from a similar malaise,' he murmured gruffly.

Mariah's breath caught in her throat, her eyes widening in alarm, as she realised she had actually been *flirting* with Darian Hunter, the imposing and disapproving Duke of Wolfingham, these past few minutes. Openly, coquettishly, *flirting*.

'I believe I have seen quite enough for one evening,' Wolfingham now muttered harshly as he turned away as one of the gentlemen on the second card table, a short and overly plump member of the aristocracy, stood up to remove his trousers, revealing his small and glistening manhood sticking out from the opening of his smallclothes. 'Shall we retire?' He held out his arm to Mariah, a nerve pulsing in the hardness of his cheek.

She raised teasing brows as she rested her gloved hand lightly upon his arm and allowed him to accompany her from the room, aware of several pairs of eyes following their abrupt departure. 'You do realise that everyone will assume we are going upstairs for the sole purpose of making love together?' she teased drily as Wolfingham took a lighted candle from the butler before they ascended the staircase together.

'Let them think it!' Darian doubted he had ever actually made love to any woman. Had sex with, yes, but never made love with or to.

But this evening—*that* had been nothing more than

several hours of a sickening display of unrestrained debauchery and was beyond enduring for even another moment.

He gave a shudder as they came to a halt as they reached the top of the staircase. 'I do believe that just the memory of that image of Clara Nichols's pendulous breasts will make it difficult for me ever to be able to become aroused again, let alone have sexual relations with a woman. I dread to think what outrageous entertainments they will think of for the masked ball tomorrow evening!'

Mariah cursed the blush that had warmed her cheeks as Wolfingham talked so frankly of his arousal. She was a widow aged four and thirty, had been a married woman for twelve of those years. And Wolfingham, along with many others, believed her to have first been an adulteress, then a mistress several times over these past five years. Women as sophisticated and experienced as Mariah Beecham was reputed to be did not blush like a schoolgirl when a man talked of his arousal.

'This is just a small house party—the majority of the guests will arrive tomorrow evening just for the ball,' she dismissed lightly. 'This evening's guests will no doubt sleep most of the day away after tonight's excesses.'

'One blessing, I suppose,' he muttered.

Mariah nodded. 'I am afraid the wearing of masks tomorrow evening allows for even more licentious behaviour than you have witnessed this evening. Also, the Nicholses' smaller and private ballroom is...well, perhaps I should leave that as a surprise for you for tomorrow evening.'

He gave another shudder. 'I would rather you did not!'

Mariah was about to answer him when there came the sound of loud shouts and whistles of approval from down the stairs. 'I do believe another lady or gentleman has just been divested of another article of clothing.'

Wolfingham looked frostily down the long length of his nose. 'In that case I see little reason to celebrate.' He drew in a deep breath. 'Please tell me that you have never— Assure me that none of those *gentlemen* have ever—'

'No,' Mariah assured him hastily, the warmth deepening in her cheeks.

Those green eyes narrowed. 'None of them?'

Mariah's jaw tightened. 'No.'

'There is a God, after all!' he rasped with feeling as he took hold of her arm, the candle in his other hand lighting their way as they began walking down the hallway to their bedchambers.

Mariah eyed him quizzically. 'I fail to see why it should matter to you one way or the other.'

'It matters!' he ground out between clenched teeth.

'As I said, I do not see why. This, what is supposed to be between the two of us, is merely play—' The breath was knocked from Mariah's lungs as she suddenly found herself thrust up against the wall, the candle placed on a small side table as an ominous-looking Wolfingham towered over her. He had placed his hands on the wall either side of her head, making her a prisoner of both his encircling arms and the lean and muscled strength of his body. 'Darian…?' She looked up at him uncertainly between long, thick lashes.

Darian was breathing deeply, in an effort to retain his control. He had already been enraged, just at the thought of Mariah having ever been intimate with any of the other men present this weekend—he refused to think of any of those men again as ever being *gentlemen*! But being dismissed by Mariah, as if he were of no more importance to her, that he was no better than any of them, was beyond endurance.

His nostrils flared as he looked down at her between hooded lids, his senses aflame, flooded, *filled*, with both the sight of her and the increasing smell of that insidious and arousing perfume.

Her eyes were a deep and drowning turquoise, her skin creamy smooth, with that becoming blush to her cheeks. Her parted lips were so plump and tempting! The bareness of her shoulders made him ache to touch them, the hollows of her throat begging further investigation, with his lips and tongue. And her breasts moved, swelled enticingly beneath that thin lace barrier, as she breathed shallowly.

And all the time Darian gazed down at her hungrily, the very air about them seeming to have stilled, the intensity of that erotic perfume having deepened and swelled, engulfing him, *enslaving* him and threatening to destroy his last shreds of resistance.

Why had her perfume deepened now? How was it possible?

'Mariah, do you stroke your perfume across and between your breasts and between your thighs?' he prompted gruffly.

'Darian!' she gasped breathlessly.

'Do you?' he pressed raggedly.

'I— Yes. Yes!' she confirmed achingly.

And telling Darian that, for the perfume to have become stronger, Mariah's body heat must have deepened, and so increasing the perfume escaping from those secret, hot places.

He closed his eyes briefly, hoping it might aid him in holding on to his fast-slipping control. But closing his eyes only intensified his sensitivity to her perfume. He slowly opened half-raised lids, his heated gaze immediately homing in on the soft pout of Mariah's parted lips. Lips he had been longing to taste again since she climbed into his carriage earlier today.

An ache he found he could no longer resist as he held her gaze with his own, his arms on the wall beside her keeping his body from touching hers, as he slowly lowered his head to run his lips lightly across her slightly parted ones.

They were soft and hesitant beneath his own, tasting of sweetmeats and brandy as he ran his tongue gently along and between them, running lightly across the ridge of her teeth, stroking along the moist length of her own tongue, before retreating to start the caress all over again, their ragged breathing becoming hot and humid between them.

Mariah had never been kissed so gently before, so slowly and so *erotically*, her pulse leaping, and her heart beating loudly beneath breasts that had become swollen and sensitised, just the gentle brush of that lace across them causing her nipples to harden and ache as they became engorged and swollen almost to the point of pain. Just as she was aware of a similar swelling, heat, between her thighs.

Her neck arched as Darian's lips now travelled across her cheek, teeth nibbling her earlobe before moving lower still. Her hands moved out to grasp Darian's shoulders as she felt his lips against her throat, gently sucking on that flesh, tongue lathing moistly to ease the pain before moving lower still, the brush of that hot and moist tongue now dipping into the deep and sensitive hollows at the base of her arched throat.

'Darian!' Mariah was so beset with new and unfamiliar emotions that she had no idea whether her gasp was one of protest for him to stop, or a plea for him to continue.

The response and heat of her body felt so strange to her. Not an unpleasant strange—far from it! She had never felt such pleasure before, or this deep and yearning ache she had to press closer against Darian's body, to rub herself against him, in an effort— a plea—to find relief for this hot and burning need, both in her breasts and between her thighs.

She groaned low in her throat, her knees threatening to buckle beneath her as Darian's lips and stroking tongue now explored the tops of her creamy breasts.

Sighing her pleasure as she at last felt the heavy weight of Darian's thighs against her own as he leant inwards to prevent her fall, allowing her to feel his own long and engorged arousal pressed against her softness—and giving instant lie to his earlier claim!

Mariah should have felt trapped, should have felt awash with the usual panic she suffered whenever a man attempted to touch or kiss her. That need she always felt to escape. To free herself.

And yet she felt none of that with Darian, wanted only to press herself closer still, to rub herself over and against him, anything to be able to somehow alleviate the burning ache in her breasts and between her thighs.

'Darian!' Mariah gave a helpless gasp as she felt the moist stroke of his tongue across her bared nipple, the first indication she had that he had pulled down that delicate lace barrier and bared her breasts.

That stroke of his tongue was quickly followed by the hot and deliberate brush of his breath over the sensitised tip. The stroking of his tongue again, followed by that soft breath, her nipple standing erect and begging for more as he moved to lavish that same attention to its twin.

It was pleasure like nothing Mariah had ever known before, had never guessed existed.

'After you for a taste, if you don't mind, Wolfingham?'

Mariah had frozen at the first sound of that intrusive voice. She now turned her head quickly, her gaze stricken as she saw Lord Richard Nichols standing just feet away down the hallway, his face flushed with arousal, eyes fevered as he gazed unabashedly at Mariah's completely bared breasts.

That fevered gaze remained fixed lasciviously on her bared breasts as he took a step forward. 'I've long wanted a taste of this particular beauty.'

Mariah was barely aware of Wolfingham moving, aware only of the loss of his heat pressed against her as he strode ominously down the hallway towards the other man, allowing her time to pull the lace quickly back in place before looking up again as she heard Richard Nichols's squeak of protest and seeing that Darian now had the older man pressed up against the wall of the hallway, Nichols's feet dangling as he was held several inches above the floor by Wolfingham's hand about his throat. Darian's expression was one of cold fury as he looked at the other man.

'I do mind, as it happens, Nichols!' he grated harshly. 'In fact, I would mind very much if I were ever to learn that you had come within six feet of touching Mariah.'

'But—'

'Do I make myself clear?'

'Very—very clear.' The other man appeared to be having trouble breathing, let alone speaking. 'L-leave off, do, Wolfingham!' Nichols choked out, his hand about the younger man's wrist as he struggled to free himself.

Darian gazed contemptuously at Richard Nichols for several long seconds more, his gaze glacial as he conveyed a stronger, more silent threat to the older man. One of violence and retribution such as Nichols had never seen before.

'Darian?'

He was so angry, so filled with a need to shake the older man like a rag doll, like the insufferable cur that he was, that for several long moments Darian could think of nothing but the desire he felt to beat this man to within an inch of his life. He was so angry that he could not respond to Mariah's pleading.

'Darian, please!'

He heard the sob in Mariah's voice this time, causing him to break his murderous gaze away from Nichols in order to turn and look at her. She looked so pale, so tiny and vulnerable, in the softness of the candlelight, her shadowed gaze holding his with that same pleading he had detected in her voice.

His expression softened slightly as he continued to look at her. 'Do not worry, Mariah, I do not intend to kill Nichols. Not this time,' he added harshly as he turned back to look challengingly at the other man.

His reassurance did nothing to alleviate Nichols's obvious panic, the other man's face having become an unpleasant puce colour—much like the unpleasant colour of his wife's bedchamber!—his pale eyes bulging.

Perhaps because Darian still had his hand about his throat!

Darian gave a disgusted snort as he removed his hand before taking a step back, uncaring as the other man lost his balance and almost fell to his knees as he dropped those several inches back down to the floor.

'I advise that you stay away from Mariah in future, if you know what is good for you.'

Richard Nichols had his hand raised to his bruised throat, his expression one of belligerent irritation. 'You only had to say no, old chap. There's no need for—for such violence. There is plenty to go round—' He broke off as he obviously saw the savagery of Darian's expression. 'I— Well— Yes. I think I will go and rejoin my other guests down the stairs.'

At any other time Mariah might have found amusement in seeing the indignity of the obnoxious Richard Nichols scuttling hastily down the hallway before quickly turning the corner and disappearing in the direction of the staircase.

Here and now, the older man having stood witness to the heated lovemaking between Mariah and Darian—and who knew how long he had stood observing the two of them before he spoke up!—Mariah was too upset to be able to find any amusement in the situation.

Instead, she felt humiliated and sickened, the pleasure of that lovemaking becoming as degrading as the rest of this evening's events had been. She shuddered just thinking of Richard Nichols having lasciviously watched as Darian suckled and pleasured her breasts. Having heard her gasps and moans as the heat coursed through her body. It was— Her gaze sharpened on Wolfingham as she realised he had made no move since he had stepped back after releasing Nichols, those icy green eyes now narrowed in concentrated thought. 'What is it, Darian?' she prompted abruptly.

He drew in a deep breath before answering her distractedly. 'What was Nichols doing wandering about up here in the first place when the entertainment is downstairs?'

She gave a dismissive shrug. 'Perhaps he came to collect something?'

'Or perhaps he came up here for another reason entirely!' Darian rasped as he turned and strode determinedly down the hallway towards her, collecting up the candle and taking a firm grasp of her arm before continuing on his way to their bedchambers.

'Darian?' Mariah was totally at a loss to know what was bothering him as he stepped aside and waited for her to enter her bedchamber ahead of him, before following her inside and closing the door firmly behind him. Because something most assuredly was.

For herself, she could imagine nothing more humiliating than the two of them, their lovemaking, now being the amusing topic of conversation down the stairs, when no doubt Richard Nichols would skip over his cowardly response to Wolfingham's violent reaction, but enlarge and embellish what he had observed, for the lascivious pleasure of his listeners. It was—

'What are you doing?' She frowned as she watched Darian now moving about her bedchamber, lighting several more candles before he commenced prowling about the room. His expression was grim as he moved several paintings aside before moving on to examine the four-poster bed, stepping up on to the pink bed-spread to examine the top and back of it. 'Darian?'

Angry colour stood out in the hardness of his cheeks when he finally stepped down from the bed, a nerve pulsing in his tightly clenched jaw. 'There are peepholes, through several of the paintings and the frame at the back of the bed, all neatly disguised so that none would know if not aware of them, but there nonetheless.'

'Peepholes?' Mariah repeated uncomprehendingly.

'You had no idea they were there?'

'I—' She gave a dazed shake of her head. 'I do not even know what they are.'

He grimaced. 'No doubt Nichols came up the stairs just now to check on which bedchamber we had gone into, yours or my own. His intention then being to go back down the stairs and invite his guests to come up here and observe the two of us together through those peepholes, no doubt accessed through a shallow passage between the walls.'

Mariah dropped weakly down on to the side of the bed and felt all the colour leach from her cheeks as she took in the full import of what Darian was saying to her.

A peep show. They were to have been nothing more than a—

'It did not happen, Mariah,' Darian soothed as he moved to sit on the bed beside her before taking her into his arms as she collapsed weakly against his chest; one look at the blank shock on Mariah's deathly white face had been enough to tell him that this was the first she had known of those strategically placed peepholes in the walls of Lady Nichols's bedchamber.

He felt ashamed now for having harboured even the briefest of doubts that Mariah might have been a willing participant in the entertainment the Nichols had now intended providing for their guests.

An understandable doubt, perhaps, in view of Mariah's reputation, but Darian now felt a heady relief at realising, from her collapse against him, that if they had made love together she would have been as innocently unaware of the people watching as he was.

A reputation Darian had already started to question earlier this evening and about which he now had serious doubts.

She had been at deep pains in his carriage earlier to ensure that he understood that any show of intimacy between the two of them was for show only.

The gown she wore this evening was positively virginal in comparison with the other ladies' attire.

Mariah had seemed relieved rather than disappointed when his glowering presence beside her had kept all other gentlemen at bay this evening.

She had been as disgusted as he by the sexual play they had witnessed during dinner and since.

Lastly, he would swear that her responses just now, to his kisses and the caress of his hands, lips and tongue, had been completely without guile or pretence.

As had her dismay when she realised that Richard Nichols had been watching them.

'It could have,' she choked now. 'It could have!'

Mariah pulled out of Wolfingham's arms before standing up abruptly, knowing, that if Richard Nichols had not played his hand too early, that she had been on the brink—the very brink!—of allowing her emotions to rule her head.

She had *wanted* Darian Hunter to make love to her.

She had *hungered* for it.

Had been so lost to the pleasure of his hands and mouth, of wanting that pleasure to continue, that she had almost been on the point of *begging* him to make love to her!

It was incomprehensible.

Unbelievable.

Unacceptable!

She did not find pleasure in a man's arms, in his closeness, in his lovemaking. She never had. She never would. How could she when the single memory of that act was of the violation of her body rather than pleasure?

When Martin Beecham, the man who had later become her husband, had forced himself upon her shortly before her seventeenth birthday.

A rape of her body and her soul of which Christina was the result, thus forcing Mariah into becoming Martin's wife.

Chapter Eight

'What is it, Mariah?' Darian questioned sharply as he stood up.

He made no move to touch her again; Mariah now looked so fragile, in her emotions as well as her body, that he feared she might crumple and fall at his feet if he attempted to place so much as a finger upon her.

'You can ask me that?' she choked out incredulously, those turquoise eyes glittering brightly in the pallor of her face. 'After learning that the two of us were to be nothing more than exhibits in the Nicholses' peep show?'

He grimaced. 'Only if we had proceeded to make love together. Which we have not.'

Mariah could no longer meet his gaze. 'That does nothing to change the fact— Oh! Do you think anyone could have been behind those walls earlier this evening?' she gasped, eyes wide as she twisted her gloved fingers together.

Darian shrugged. 'I doubt, with the responsibility

of his other guests, that Nichols would have found the time to come up the stairs and observe you dressing.'

'I was referring to our conversation, Darian! Did we say anything in this room earlier that might have— Do you seriously think that weasel Nichols might have *watched* me bathing and dressing earlier this evening?' Mariah's face had taken on a sickly green hue at the thought of it.

'As I recall, our conversation was perfectly innocuous earlier,' he reassured. 'I also think it more likely that Lady Nichols, after escorting us to our bedchambers, would have lingered upstairs to observe *me*!' Darian's mouth twisted with distaste for the very idea of having that pale blue gaze moving lasciviously over his naked body whilst he'd bathed and dressed earlier.

Mariah stilled. 'You believe there to be similar peepholes in your own bedchamber? In *all* the bedchambers?' she added aghast.

'After tonight I believe the master and mistress of this house to be capable of anything! After all, this is not the Nicholses' main country residence.' He shrugged. 'They do not bring their children here, for example, but leave them at their Norfolk estate with their nurse. Thank heavens for small mercies!'

Mariah thought of the other occasions when she had stayed in this house, totally unaware of the eyes that might have been secretly watching her. As she bathed. As she went about her *toilette*. As she stood completely naked before dressing.

She felt ill.

Unclean.

Violated!

As violated as she had been that night eighteen years ago when Martin had lured her into one of the private rooms at a ball they were both attending, locked the door behind them and then coldly and calculatedly assaulted her. Warning her after the event that no one would believe the word of the daughter of a minor landowner and merchant against an earl's, if she were to accuse him of the deed.

Mariah had been but sixteen years old and was too frightened, too devastated, felt too unclean, to dare take the risk of telling anyone what Martin Beecham, the Earl of Carlisle, had done to her.

Most especially so as he had also warned her that he would repeat the violation, again, and then again, until such time as she was with child. Not because he particularly wished for an heir, but so that she was forced into marrying him, thus bringing a good portion of her father's fortune into the marriage.

And it had all worked out perfectly for Martin, of course, because Mariah had become pregnant with that very first attempt. She had tried to tell her parents the truth then, but as promised, Martin had denied her accusation of his having forced her, claiming that she had been as eager as he for the coupling. He also insisted that she was merely frightened of the repercussions after the event, now that she found herself with child. Repercussions that would cease to exist when she accepted his offer of marriage.

Whether or not her parents had believed Mariah's

version of events had not mattered at this point, although she liked to think that they had; she was an only child and their relationship had always been a close one.

But whether they believed her or not, her mother and father had been left with no more choice in the matter than Mariah. She would have to accept the earl's offer of marriage. A babe born seven months after the wedding could be overlooked by society and very often was! But if Mariah refused to marry the father of her child—the more-than-willing father!—then she would be ruined and both she and her parents ostracised from society.

Faced with those choices there had been only one decision that Mariah could make.

Marriage to the very man who had raped her.

Her body might not have been violated tonight, but her privacy, her very person, had.

She was no longer a girl of sixteen, of course, too frightened to accuse the person responsible for that violation. But the reputation she had nurtured in society, as the sophisticated and flirtatious Countess of Carlisle, would most certainly be in danger if she were to now voice her complaints to her host and hostess.

As her obvious shock now had already placed that reputation in danger in regard to Darian Hunter, the astute and intelligent Duke of Wolfingham.

Mariah drew in a deep breath before straightening her shoulders and unclasping her fingers, her chin high as she turned to give Wolfingham a derisive smile. 'How unfortunate, for the Nichols, that you grew wise to their little scheme!'

Darian was relieved to see that some of the colour had now returned to Mariah's cheeks. Although he did not believe for a moment that she was as composed as she now wished to appear; her obvious shock a few minutes ago had most certainly been genuine.

A shock he might not have expected from one as promiscuous as Mariah Beecham was reputed to be.

He also wondered what thoughts had been going through her head just a few minutes ago. Whatever they were, they had brought a grey tinge to her already pale cheeks and haunted shadows to those beautiful eyes.

'Very unfortunate,' he echoed drily, prepared, for the moment, to accept that Mariah was determined to place those walls back about her emotions. This was not the time, and certainly not the place, to question her further on the subject.

But the very fact that she had not as yet upbraided him for their lovemaking earlier was surely evidence of her inner unease?

A lovemaking, and Mariah's response, that Darian knew was going to haunt and disturb his own rest tonight—again!

'Do you have any shawls or handkerchiefs with you? I could place them over the pictures and the head of the bed to ensure your privacy,' he explained at her questioning frown.

'Oh. Oh, yes, of course,' she breathed in obvious relief as she moved to open the wardrobe and look through the things on the shelves in there. 'Here.' She handed Darian several handkerchiefs and two shawls. 'Will they be enough to prevent anyone from at least seeing into this room?'

'Oh, yes.' Darian tied the two shawls securely to the paintings before moving on to do the same to the bed with the handkerchiefs. 'There.' He nodded his satisfaction as he stepped back.

'What of your own bedchamber?'

'I have some handkerchiefs of my own,' he dismissed.

'I— Then I will wish you a good night.'

He frowned. 'Mariah—'

'I believe we have provided enough of a display for our audience for one night, Wolfingham. Besides which, it is late and I am very tired.' She arched one pointed brow.

Darian knew himself well and truly dismissed, without either of them having made direct reference to their heated lovemaking earlier.

If Nichols had not interrupted them then Darian might not have left this bedchamber at all tonight.

But equally, if Nichols had not interrupted the two of them, allowing Darian the time to think of what the other man was doing there at all, then they might even now be providing entertainment for the other guests.

Not that Darian was the prude Mariah had once thought him. Far from it. He had spent his share of time in gaming hells and the houses of the *demi-monde*, and knew full well the games played in such establishments. But that play was at the consent of both parties, not the intrusion, the violation, tonight's game would have been to the privacy of their love-making. He did not perform for the entertainment of strangers.

'Very well, Mariah.' He nodded as he strode across the room to bend down and kiss her lightly upon her brow. 'I wish you a good night,' he added huskily as he looked down at her intently.

Mariah felt flustered by Darian's close proximity, coming so soon after this shocking discovery of the peepholes in her bedchamber.

So soon after she had felt those strange and wonderful sensations as he made love to her earlier out in the hallway.

Sensations Mariah could still feel, in the tingling fullness of her breasts and the swollen dampness between her thighs.

And so reminiscent of those sensations she had felt when he'd kissed her at Lady Stockton's ball.

Was it possible, after all these years of feeling nothing, that her body was actually awakening to sexual arousal?

A sexual arousal caused solely and completely by Darian Hunter, the Duke of Wolfingham?

And felt only for him?

Mariah stepped back abruptly, too alarmed by even the possibility of that being true to be able to suffer his close proximity a moment longer. 'Goodnight, Wolfingham,' she stated firmly.

Darian studied her from between narrowed lids for several seconds longer, knowing from the determined set of Mariah's mouth and chin that she considered this conversation over.

He gave a terse nod. 'If you should need me, you know where I am.'

Her brows rose. 'You are suggesting that I might possibly be overcome with lust for you in the middle of the night?'

Darian grimaced at her scathingly derisive tone. 'I am suggesting that I noticed there is no key in the lock to this bedchamber. We could place a chair beneath the door handle,' he suggested as he saw the alarmed look Mariah gave in the direction of the door.

'Yes! Yes, please do,' she confirmed more coolly. 'Thank you,' she added softly, eyes downcast, as Darian saw to the placing of that chair.

Darian sighed his frustration as he looked at her bent head for several seconds more. Not sexual frustration—that seemed to be with him constantly whenever he was with Mariah. And when he was not!

No, his frustration now was due to another reason entirely.

With Mariah he so often felt as if he took one step forward and then was forced, by circumstances, into taking two steps back. As now. Their lovemaking had been beyond enjoyable. Darian could not remember ever having been aroused quite so quickly, or so strongly, by any other woman. And he knew, from the obvious responses of her body, her breathless sighs of pleasure, that Mariah had been just as aroused. And yet now she was dismissing him as if that closeness had never happened.

It was beyond frustrating; it was infuriating.

Mariah was a woman of four and thirty, had been a married woman for twelve of those years, and as such she could not be unaware of how much he had wanted to make love to and with her a short time ago. Or that she returned that desire for him to make love to and with her. And yet she behaved now as if that desire had never happened.

Was that only because of the unpleasantness of the circumstances here at Eton Park?

Or because, beneath that desire, she disliked him still?

Darian breathed out his frustration with the situation. 'Goodnight, Mariah,' he repeated harshly before turning on his heel and leaving the room abruptly, firmly closing the door adjoining their two bedchambers behind him.

Mariah sank back down on to the side of the bed the moment Darian closed the door between their rooms, her thoughts in turmoil. Not because, unpleasant as it was, of the knowledge of those intrusive peepholes in the walls of her bedchamber. Nor was she overly concerned as to what might or might not transpire tomorrow, after the Regent's note of apology had been delivered.

No, the reason for the present disquiet of her emotions was all due to Darian Hunter and the desire she could no longer deny, to herself at least, that she felt for him.

And him alone.

* * *

'Would you care to go for a ride, or perhaps a walk, in the fresh air this morning, Mariah?' Darian suggested as he looked across the breakfast table at her.

A breakfast table at which only the two of them sat, the other guests, as Mariah had suggested might be the case, either still asleep after their late night, or choosing to break their fast in the privacy of their bedchambers.

Darian had been awake shortly after seven o'clock, earlier than was usual for him, but as he had expected, he had passed another restless night and, once fully awake, could not bear to stay abed any longer. He had known, from the sounds and soft conversation he could hear in the adjoining room, that Mariah was also awake and talking to her maid.

He had found several peepholes in his own bedchamber the night before and used his handkerchiefs accordingly, but they had both agreed the coverings should come down during the day, if only so that the Nicholses did not realise they both knew of the peepholes.

If the Nicholses' butler—he had introduced himself as Benson, when Mariah had enquired—was surprised to see any of the guests appearing in the breakfast room a little after eight o'clock in the morning, then the blandness of his expression did not show it. He remained as stoically impassive as he had yesterday evening, as he served the Nicholses' guests dinner.

It did not help Darian's peace of mind that Mariah

looked beautiful and untroubled this morning, in a russet-coloured silk morning gown, her golden hair swept up and secured at her crown, with clusters of curls at her temple and nape.

She had also been coolly polite to him so far this morning, to the point of irritation.

As if their closeness last night had never happened.

As if Darian had not feasted upon her bared breasts.

As if she had not thoroughly enjoyed having him feast upon her bared breasts.

As if she was annoyed with him for having taken such liberties?

The temper that seemed to burn just below the surface of Darian's emotions whenever it came to Mariah once again raised its ugly head at her lack of response to his suggestion. 'Unless you would rather wait for some of the other guests to come down and perhaps join them?'

Mariah looked at Wolfingham beneath lowered lashes, having sensed that he was angry with her from the moment he knocked briskly on the door adjoining their two bedchambers earlier, then waited for her permission before entering. It had been her experience that Wolfingham did not wait for permission to do anything he pleased.

He looked very severe in his anger. Very much Wolfingham.

The darkness of his hair was brushed back severely from the harshness of his face. His eyes were a flinty, uncompromising green. And there were brackets of displeasure beside his nose and mouth. His movements were also brisk and impatient.

She raised cool brows. 'I shall be quite happy to seek my own entertainment this morning if you are too busy to accompany me on a walk.'

He speared her with that impatient green gaze across the width of the table. 'And what else could there possibly be here to keep me busy this morning?'

Mariah turned to smile at the butler as he lingered by the array of breakfast trays, in readiness for serving them more food. 'Could we possibly have some more coffee, Benson? Thank you.' She waited until the butler had left the room before turning back to Darian. 'If you wish to argue with me, might I suggest that you wait until after we have gone outside,' she hissed in warning.

His brows rose autocratically. 'Why should you imagine I might wish to argue with you?'

Mariah could think of only one reason for Darian's bad humour this morning: the same sexual frustration she had suffered last night!

She was not completely innocent in the ways of men, knew that a man's passion, once aroused, was apt to make him irritable if it was not assuaged; the housekeeper, Mrs Smith, had once taken a week's leave to visit her sick sister and Martin had been unbearable for the whole time she had been gone. To the point that Mariah had feared he might turn his attentions towards her in the other woman's absence. As a precaution against that possibility, Mariah had wisely taken herself off to the country for the rest of that week.

She could not avoid Darian Hunter's company by doing the same. Not for this weekend, at least.

Nor was she altogether sure she wished to.

She had lain awake in bed for hours after they had parted the night before, her body uncomfortably achy and needy. Her breasts had felt swollen, the tips seeming to tingle and burn, occasionally sending shards of pleasure coursing through her as they rubbed against the material of her night-rail. Between her thighs had felt uncomfortably hot and damp, despite her having used a washcloth before going to bed. And there had been an ache amongst the curls down there that had throbbed even harder when she pressed her thighs together, in an effort to dispel that unaccustomed heat.

For the first time in her life Mariah had suffered what she was sure must be sexual frustration.

And it was both frightening and exhilarating, to realise how attracted she had become to Darian Hunter in such a short space of time. How much she desired him. How much she desired to have him make love to and with her.

That realisation frightened her more than anything else!

She lowered her lashes in case that desire should now be reflected in her eyes. 'I know that you do, Darian,' she answered him quietly. 'And I am sorry for it—' She broke off as he stood up abruptly, his chair scraping back noisily on the polished wooden floor. 'Darian?'

His eyes glittered dangerously as he stood beside the table glowering down at her. 'Exactly what are you apologising for, Mariah?' he demanded exasperatedly.

She swallowed. 'I realise that last night—that it did not proceed, as you might have wished it to have done—'

'As *I* might have wished?' he repeated softly, dangerously so. 'Are you denying that your own wishes were exactly the same as my own?'

'I—'

'I advise caution with your answer, Mariah,' he warned softly, those green eyes glittering dangerously, a nerve pulsing in his clenched jaw. 'I am not some callow youth who does not *know* when a woman feels desire.'

Colour warmed Mariah's cheeks and she was unsure whether it was from embarrassment at the intimacy of their conversation, or jealousy, because Darian must have intimate knowledge of *other* women's desire to be so well informed. 'This is neither the time nor the place for—'

'Will it ever be, Mariah?' he bit out scathingly. 'Will you ever be willing to give yourself to me?'

Mariah drew her breath in sharply even as a bite of longing twisted almost painfully between her thighs. What would it be like to give herself to this man? Not just any man, but to Darian Hunter, the Duke of Wolfingham?

Nothing like that horrendous single experience with Martin, she was sure. Even in her limited experience, she knew Darian had already demonstrated that he was a generous and attentive lover, with more of an interest in ensuring his partner's pleasure than taking his own.

Could she give herself to this man? Could she let down her guard, her inhibitions, and open herself up to such intimacy? Such *vulnerability*?

She was starting to believe, that with Darian Hunter, she just might be able to do so...

She straightened her shoulders as she made her decision. 'Perhaps,' she allowed gruffly.

Darian's eyes widened as he barely heard Mariah's softly spoken reply. He had feared the worst minutes ago, as Mariah's eyes once again took on that look of distance, as if she were no longer quite here with him in this room, but somewhere else entirely. Lost in memories, perhaps? Some of them unpleasant ones, if he had read her expression correctly.

Of her husband? Or some other man she had been involved with during her marriage or since?

Darian's ire rose just at the thought of a man, any man, ever having hurt her, in any way.

'Mariah?' He sat down in the chair beside her before taking one of her hands in both of his. Instantly becoming aware of the trembling of her fingers beneath delicate lace gloves—evidence that those thoughts had indeed been unhappy ones? Whatever the reason, he felt heartened by the fact that she did not instantly pull her hand away from his.

'Do you think we could please get out of this oppressive house, if only for a few hours?'

She blinked long lashes. 'I ordered fresh coffee.'

'I am sure that Benson is an understanding fellow. He would have to be to suffer working for the Nicholses!' Darian grimaced.

'Ah, Benson.' The butler appeared in the room almost as if he had been cued to do so. 'The countess and I have decided to go for a walk in the grounds this morning—do you recommend any direction in particular?'

The butler poured fresh coffee into their cups as he answered, his face as expressionless as ever. 'I believe most of her ladyship's guests find Aphrodite's Temple of interest, your Grace.'

'Aphrodite's Temple?' Darian repeated doubtfully; if he remembered his Greek mythology correctly, from his years spent at Eton, Aphrodite had been the goddess of love, beauty and sexuality, but better known as being a goddess who indulged her own selfish sexual desires and lust.

Totally suited to the Nicholses' lifestyle, of course, but not necessarily Darian's own.

'It is Lady Nichols's name for it, your Grace.' Benson seemed to guess some of his thoughts, his expression still stoic and unrevealing. 'It is situated amongst the trees to the left of the lake at the back of the house.'

'Mariah?' Darian turned to prompt, aware that she had not taken part in the conversation as yet. But still Darian felt heartened by the fact that she had allowed her hand to remain in both of his.

She looked up at the butler. 'It sounds…intriguing, Benson.'

She dutifully picked up her cup with her other hand and drank some of the coffee.

The butler nodded. 'And it is always deserted during the day.'

Darian narrowed his eyes. 'But not in the evenings?'

'Not this evening, certainly, your Grace.'

To say Darian was intrigued would be putting it mildly. Although, bearing in mind the sexual games the Nicholses liked to play, he could well imagine that Aphrodite's Temple might prove a little too much for what he now believed to be Mariah's sensibilities. She was much more easily shocked than he might ever have imagined, or hoped for, before spending so much time in her company.

She had become, in fact, the most intriguing woman he had ever met. And was becoming more so rather than less, the more time he spent in her company. It was a certainty he had never been in the least bored when with her.

'Thank you, Benson.' Mariah smiled up at the butler warmly. 'Perhaps you might ask my maid to bring down my pelisse and bonnet from my bedchamber?'

'Of course, my lady.' He bowed.

The silence in the breakfast room seemed charged once the butler had left the two of them alone there. Almost as if the very air itself was waiting expectantly.

For what, Darian was unsure. He only knew that

he wanted to get out of this unpleasant and cloyingly decadent household, if only for a few hours. And that he wanted more than anything for Mariah to accompany him.

He stood up, retaining his hold upon her hand as he pulled her up beside him, so close he could almost feel the brush of her hair against his jaw, her perfume once again invading and capturing his senses. 'Ready?'

Mariah's heart leapt in her chest, as she knew instinctively that Darian was asking for more than if she was ready to go for their walk. That he was continuing their previous conversation rather than starting a new one.

Was she ready?

Was she prepared to take their relationship a step further?

To give in to the desires of her own body and engage in intimacy with Darian?

Could she do that?

Or would the memories of the past intrude once again and bring with them the fear and aversion that was all she had known as Martin's wife?

Mariah looked up at him searchingly, not at his handsomeness; that was all too apparent. No, she looked into his eyes, those clear, deep and unwavering green eyes. Eyes that spoke of a man of both honour and truth. A man capable of killing his enemy, if necessary, but totally incapable of physically hurting a woman, most especially one he desired. And Wolfingham did desire her, was making no effort to hide that fact as he steadily met and returned her searching gaze.

Was she ready?

Was it time for her to release her memories of the past, along with her inhibitions, and give in to these new, and at times uncomfortable, yearnings of her own body?

Was she ready to do that?

Chapter Nine

'Good gracious!' Darian winced up at the pale pink marble structure of what could only be described as a miniature copy of the Greek Parthenon he had visited whilst taking the Grand Tour ten years ago or more.

Nestled amongst the woodland to the left of the lake at Eton Park, exactly as Benson had said it would be, it had six small Doric-style marble columns fronting the building, with ten more along each side, and a domed cupola on the roof. And standing in pride of place before the huge wooden doors at its entrance was a nude statue, of what Darian could only assume was Aphrodite, cupping and stroking her own breast.

A nude statue that should not have been there, considering that, if Darian remembered his Greek mythology correctly, the Parthenon in Greece was dedicated to Athena, the virginal goddess of wisdom and philosophy.

'I can only assume that Lord and Lady Nicholses' knowledge of the Greek gods must be as lacking as their good taste,' Mariah drawled beside him, revealing that her own knowledge on the subject was not lacking at all.

Darian chuckled huskily. 'One does not need to make assumptions once they have seen this.'

Mariah's eyes danced merrily as she glanced up at him. 'It does err rather on the side of ostentatious.'

'That is one word for it!' Darian gave a disgusted shake of his head. 'I sincerely hope that Benson is not of the opinion that the two of us share his employers' bad taste!'

Mariah peered around the statue at the huge oak doors. 'What do you think is inside?'

'Even more lewd statues?'

'Perhaps,' she murmured distractedly as she moved forward to rest one gloved hand on the handle of the door. 'Shall we go inside and see?' she invited huskily.

Darian had to admit to feeling as if a heavy weight had been lifted from his shoulders since leaving the oppression of the Nicholses' household, having enjoyed being out in the fresh air with Mariah walking companionably beside him and wearing a pelisse and bonnet the same russet colour as her gown.

He was in no hurry to forgo that feeling of companionship by entering what he could only assume, in the knowledge of the Nicholses' tastes, and Benson's warning that it would not be empty this evening, was more than likely to be a place where the Nicholses continued their debauchery. 'I doubt it will be any more tasteful inside than out.' He grimaced.

Mariah turned the handle and pushed open the

door. 'We will not know— Oh!' She gave a gasp as she stepped inside. 'Oh, do come and look, Darian,' she encouraged breathlessly. 'It is— You will never believe what is in here!'

Darian found himself moving forward to join Mariah inside the temple, partially lured there at having her address him by his first name, something she rarely did voluntarily, but also out of the need to discover exactly what sort of debauchery had awaited her inside and rendered her so breathless.

Darian felt the difference in temperature as soon as he stepped inside—the cavernous marble building was filled with an inexplicable heat. Or perhaps not so inexplicable, as he breathed in the slightly sulphurous smell only thinly disguised by the scent of lavender and realised that the mixture of smells was emanating from the deep sunken bathing pool of water in the centre of the rose marble building.

Mariah's eyes were glowing with pleasure as she turned to look at him. 'I believe it is a natural hot spring!'

That was exactly what it appeared to be. Darian knew that there were a dozen or more of these natural hot springs in England and that society made a point of flocking to them, usually during the summer months, in order to drink or bathe in what they considered to be the health-giving waters.

But he had never before seen or even heard of there being a private hot spring such as this one obviously was...

He shrugged. 'We are close to Tunbridge Wells, so perhaps this is an offshoot of the one there?'

'It is wonderful!' Mariah drew off one of her gloves before stepping forward to crouch down and dip her fingers into the scented water. 'And it is lovely and warm!' she announced excitedly.

Darian was more than a little grateful for Mariah's distraction with the sunken bathing pool, once his gaze had skimmed over the rest of the interior of the marble building.

There were half a dozen tall candleholders about the cavernous room, fresh candles in them, no doubt in preparation for this evening's entertainments. And a dozen or more slightly raised platforms, each littered with sumptuous and brightly coloured silk cushions.

Darian gave a grimace, his gaze moving swiftly on, as he easily guessed the purpose for *those*.

The two-foot-high frieze on the walls was a plethora of painted scenes of the mythical gods engaged in acts of debauchery with man, woman and beast, as was the domed ceiling above them. But it was the five statues placed about the side of the pool that now caused him to draw his breath in sharply.

Each and every one of them was of Aphrodite, in all her naked glory, engaged in a variety of sexual acts so explicit that no imagination was necessary and causing Darian's mouth to set grimly.

It was so typical of the Nicholses that they had taken a thing of beauty and turned it into yet another scene for their own very questionable sexual tastes.

'Have you ever seen anything like it before, Darian?' Mariah was totally enthralled by the pool, her expression enrapt, as she moved her bare fingers backwards and forwards in the warmth of the water.

With its dozen or so steps down into the water it reminded Mariah of a painting she had once seen, of Queen Cleopatra bathing in such a pool filled with the ass's milk reputed to have preserved her wondrous beauty.

'No, I cannot say I have ever seen anything quite like this before,' Darian answered coolly.

She turned to look at him quizzically, noting the emerald glitter of his eyes and the slight flush to his cheeks, caused by the warmth of the temple. His mouth was pressed into a thin, uncompromising line. She straightened slowly. 'What is it?'

A nerve pulsed in his tightly clenched jaw. 'We should leave! And continue with our walk,' he added tersely as she looked confused by his vehemence.

Mariah blinked at the harshness of his tone. 'But it is so cosy and warm in here, and surely the perfect place for us to escape the company of the other guests until luncheon.' She had thought Darian had desired to be alone with *her* just a short time ago.

His shoulders were tensed beneath his perfectly tailored dark green superfine. 'I agree that the bathing pool is of interest.'

'But?'

He sighed his impatience. 'But the rest of the temple is far less so.'

Mariah had been so enthralled, so enchanted, at

the discovery of the beautiful sunken pool that she had not bothered to look at anything else in the room.

She did so now. And instantly felt the colour heat her own cheeks as she saw the erotic scenes painted on the walls and the ceiling above them. 'I am afraid this has ruined the surprise of the Nicholses' smaller ballroom—' Mariah drew in a sharp breath as she now saw the statues posed about the edge of the pool.

The naked goddess Aphrodite was cradling the head of an equally naked man, whose proportions were worthy of the name Adonis, as he suckled one of her breasts whilst the other hand cupped beneath its twin, thumb and finger in the act of pinching the turgid nipple.

The next was of Aphrodite sprawled upon a couch, the Adonis still at her breasts, her legs parted, a look of ecstasy upon her face as another man feasted on the bounty between her thighs.

Aphrodite reclining upon the same couch, one of the men now lying between her thighs, the hardness of his arousal poised at her entrance— Mariah's gaze moved quickly to the next statue, only to move quickly on again as she saw that Aphrodite was now posed on her hands and knees, her tongue licking her lips as a man stood behind her holding her hips in place, ready for him to enter her like a stallion covering a mare, whilst another man knelt in front of her, his hard arousal jutting forward—

Mariah ceased breathing altogether, her cheeks burning as her gaze hurriedly shifted to the last statue. She saw that the man behind Aphrodite had now buried himself to the hilt between her thighs, a smile now curving the fullness of her lips as she arched her throat, the huge erection of the second man in her mouth.

'You have never been in here before?' Wolfingham enquired harshly.

'I— No.' Mariah was too stunned still to be able to think straight. Or even attempt the sophisticated response that might have been expected of her! 'No, thank goodness,' she repeated irritably. 'I usually retire earlier than the other guests at these affairs and have never— I have never seen any of this before now.' She waved a dismissive hand, eyes downcast so that she did not have to actually look at those statues again.

Statues that should not have shocked the notorious Lady Mariah Beecham and would surely have amused the sophisticated Countess of Carlisle. And yet Mariah *was* shocked and far from amused.

She was also aware that her thoughts had taken flight as she imagined herself and Darian engaged in those intimacies.

His mouth on her breast.

His mouth feasting between her thighs.

His shaft buried to the hilt between those same thighs.

His entering her from behind with the fierceness of a stallion coupling with a mare.

Mariah's fingers encircling his hardness as she parted her own lips and took that swollen length into her mouth. She turned sharply on her heel, *knowing* her response should have been one of sophistication, and perhaps even boredom, at such an erotic display, but for the moment she was unable to even attempt to be either. 'You are right. We should leave.'

'Mariah?' Darian reached out and grasped her wrist as she would have brushed past him as she hurried to the door.

His gaze was searching on her flushed cheeks, and he drew in a sharp breath as she raised her lashes and he saw the fevered glitter in her eyes. An *aroused* and fevered glitter?

Mariah had presented him with one puzzle after another since the moment they'd first met, it seemed. One moment behaving every inch the sophisticated and notorious woman of society she was reputed to be. The next, as she appeared now, seeming to be as shocked as a girl barely out of the schoolroom, by this evidence of the excesses of the less reputable members of the *ton*.

The more time Darian spent in Mariah's company, the more of a mystery she became to him. And it was a mystery that Darian was fast becoming addicted to solving.

He had no wish for it to be that way. Had no wish to ever become so enthralled by one particular woman that he could think of nothing and no one else.

So enthralled that his every waking thought was of making love to and with her. As the pulsing and throbbing of his erection now testified he wished to do. With Mariah.

Perhaps if he made love with her, witnessed her

in the throes of sexual pleasure, saw that she was a flesh-and-blood woman with carnal needs that matched, or even exceeded, his own, then this hunger would go away?

His fingers tightened about her wrist. 'There is no reason for us to leave here just yet if you wish to remain.'

Mariah's heart leapt in her chest, the heat increasing in her cheeks, as she looked up and saw the burning intensity of Darian's gaze fixed so intently upon her lips. Lips that instantly tingled with the memory of his kisses from the evening before.

Lips that parted instinctively as Darian's gaze held hers captive as his head lowered towards her own.

It was as if the hours between their time together the previous evening and this morning had never happened; the desire was instant. Tongues duelled, hands caressed, their breathing sounding ragged in the silence of the temple as they kissed hungrily.

It was as if they could not get enough of each other. Could not get close enough.

Mariah could *feel* the evidence of Darian's desire pressing hot and heavy against her softness as the kiss continued, tongues tasting, teeth gently biting. She felt the pulse, the thrill, of that arousal, all the way from the top of her head to the tips of her toes. Her breasts swelled, ached painfully, against the bodice of her gown. She felt a gush of wetness between her thighs in response to that desire and she was aware of Darian groaning low in his throat as he now arched, ground that arousal, against and into her.

She felt her folds swell, become wet and slick, as Darian moved one of his hands down and in between them in order to cup her mound through her gown. His palm pressed against her, unerringly finding and putting rhythmic pressure upon the sensitive nubbin nestled amongst her curls, as his fingers curled to trace the delicate folds beneath. Teasing. Caressing.

Mariah wanted more, needed more, as she instinctively thrust up and into those caressing fingers, the pleasure building, growing unbearable as she arched her throat, head back, eyes widening— And instantly found herself looking up at those scenes of debauchery painted upon the ceiling!

It was as if a bucket of cold water had been thrown over her, dousing every measure of arousal and desire as Mariah wrenched her mouth from Darian's to draw in a deep and shaky breath at the same time as she pushed against Darian's chest and put herself at arm's length. 'I do not—' She gave a shake of her head. 'This place makes me feel...uncomfortable.'

Darian's eyes glittered down at her heatedly. 'Uncomfortable or aroused?'

Mariah's breath hitched in her throat and the trembling increased in her limbs. A trembling that Darian could not help but be aware of when his hands were still on her waist. 'A little of both,' she acknowledged gruffly.

She heard Darian draw in his own breath sharply before he answered her huskily, 'I feel the same way.'

Mariah glanced about them at the erotica depicted so graphically on the frieze on the walls and ceiling, and those explicitly erotic statues. And knowing that she could not—

'Not here, Darian. I could not bear to do this here—' She broke off with a shudder. 'I can only imagine the scenes of excess this room has witnessed during the Nicholses' weekend parties! And will no doubt witness again this very night.' She was so tense now that she flinched as one of Darian's hands moved up to cup her cheek before he gently lifted her face up towards his own.

Darian looked down at Mariah searchingly, once again struck by her beauty, at the same time as he recognised those familiar shadows in her eyes and the slight trembling of her lips.

As he also knew that the flush in her cheeks was partly due to the arousal the eroticism in this temple could not help but evoke.

Not completely because of him, or for him.

And it might be a matter of false pride on Darian's part, but when—*if*—he ever made love to Mariah completely, then *he* wished to be the only reason for her arousal.

He drew in a steadying breath before nodding abruptly and releasing her before stepping back. 'Then again I suggest we continue with our walk.'

Mariah was more than a little unsettled by the abruptness of Darian's acceptance of her withdrawal as she led the way out of the marble temple. Could it be that he had actually *wanted* to remain in the temple and indulge in those sexual fantasies depicted by the paintings and statues?

Sexual fantasies that still made the blood boil in her veins and her body ache for—for *Darian*.

Only for Darian.

She had never felt this attraction to any other man. Never felt this ache for a man's touch. Never wanted, hungered for, a physical closeness with any man. Never burned for the promise of pleasure his lips and hands had evoked.

Until Darian.

She looked up at him from beneath lowered lashes once they were outside again in the crisp March air. 'I apologise if my words of earlier led you to expect otherwise, Darian. But I simply could not bear the thought of us being together in such a place.' She gave a shudder of revulsion. 'It was—'

'Unpleasant at best and thoroughly disgusting at worst?' He nodded grimly. 'I thought so, too.'

'You did?'

'I did,' he rasped harshly. 'You may rest assured, I shall be having words with Benson on the subject once we have returned to the house,' he added grimly.

'You are not disappointed?'

A frown appeared between his eyes. 'Why should I be disappointed?'

'I gave the impression earlier—I all but implied— that we, the two of us, might—' She straightened her shoulders. 'I am aware that a man does not take sexual disappointment well.'

'From your husband?'

'No!' Mariah gasped in protest, only to quickly seek composure as she realised how telling her answer might have been. She strived to adopt a derisively dismissive smile. 'No man needs suffer sexual disappointment in regard to his own wife, when the law allows him to do with her whatever, and as often as he wills it.'

Wolfingham's eyes narrowed. 'Were you happy in your marriage, Mariah?'

She eyed him coolly. 'I believe I have already intimated to you, in a previous conversation, that I was not.'

'Ever?'

Her mouth tightened. 'No.'

Darian could read nothing from the stiffness of Mariah's expression. Or perhaps that stiffness was telling in itself.

'Was Carlisle cruel to you?' He found himself tensing as he waited for her answer.

Her chin rose proudly. 'Only if indifference can be called cruelty. And in the case of my husband, I did not consider it to be so.'

'His indifference? He did not love you?' Darian's gaze sharpened on the paleness of her face.

'No more than I loved him, no.'

'Then why marry him at all?' Darian frowned. 'Your daughter's age now intimates you yourself were barely out of the schoolroom when you married. That it was in all probability your first Season. Surely, as you informed me regarding your daughter, there was no hurry for you to accept the first offer of marriage made to you?' His mouth twisted harshly. 'Or perhaps you fancied yourself as being a countess?'

'No!' Her denial came out sharply this time, her eyes glittering as she looked up at him coldly. 'Sometimes—sometimes we cannot do as we wish but as we must,' she added tautly as Darian continued to look down at her beneath hooded lids.

'And you *must* needs marry Carlisle?'

'Yes!' she hissed vehemently.

Darian's gaze narrowed as he studied her intently, looking, searching for the answers he knew Mariah had not yet given him. That the closed expression on her face said she might never give him...

Part of Mariah's mystery was her unwillingness to discuss the past with him. Her past. A past that he was now sure had made her the coolly detached woman she so often was today.

A past that had also led to her being here with him now, acting as an agent for the Crown?

'Talk to me, Mariah. Help me to understand,' he invited gently. 'Explain why you felt you had to marry Carlisle when, as you have said, you did not love him, or he you, and you did not fancy yourself as becoming his countess. Was your family in financial difficulty? Did your father have debts owing to Carlisle directly? Help me to understand, Mariah,' he repeated gruffly.

'Why?'

'Because I *need* to!' he ground out harshly.

'Again, why?'

Darian forced all trace of anger from his voice and expression, already knowing that Mariah did not react well to either. 'Perhaps you might humour me by doing so?'

Her eyes flashed darkly. 'There was nothing in the least humorous about my marriage.'

He sighed. 'Perhaps I chose the wrong word. It would *please* me if you would do me the honour of confiding in me, Mariah,' he amended softly.

She looked at him searchingly for several long seconds, no doubt looking for sarcasm or mockery in his expression, but surely she would find only sincerity.

'Please, Mariah,' Darian encouraged again gently.

She breathed heavily. 'I married Carlisle for none of the reasons you have mentioned.' Her tone was still cold, uncompromising. 'My father was—still is, a very wealthy man. But Carlisle's coffers were bare and he required some of that wealth.' She shrugged. 'Enough to marry a woman he did not love and who did not love him. As might well be expected from such an ill-matched alliance, it was not a happy marriage. For either of us. And that is an end to it.'

Darian doubted that very much. 'And is that the reason you had affairs with other men? Why you now attend licentious weekend parties such as this one?'

'You are being deliberately insulting!' Her cheeks were flushed.

'I am trying to understand.' Darian drew in a deep and controlling breath as he saw the way in which Mariah drew back at his forcefulness. 'Can you not see, I am trying to understand *you*, Mariah,' he spoke more calmly, evenly, knowing his impatience would not endear him to Mariah, or encourage her in the confidences he wanted, needed, to hear from her.

'Why?' She eyed him challengingly. 'What should

it matter one way or another whether or not you understand me?'

Darian ground his teeth together. 'It matters to me.'

She smiled without humour. 'That is no answer at all.'

He sighed. 'Can you not see I am puzzled as to why any young and beautiful woman would marry a man she admits she did not love, who did not love her and who was so much older than herself? I could better understand it if Carlisle had been rich and you or your family had been in need. Or even if you fancied yourself as being Carlisle's countess. But you have denied any and all of those as being the reason for entering into a marriage that you admit to knowing would bring you no happiness. I can think of no other reason why—' Darian broke off abruptly, eyes widening as a third alternative began to take form and root in his mind.

A third alternative that would most certainly have required that Mariah *must* marry Carlisle.

Could that possibly be the answer to this puzzle?

Mariah admitted to being four and thirty, and her daughter, Christina, was now aged seventeen, which meant that Mariah could only have been sixteen when that daughter was conceived.

'You were with child when you married Carlisle,' he breathed softly, knowing he had guessed correctly as he saw every last vestige of colour leach from Mariah's already pale cheeks.

Mariah drew her breath sharply, wishing she could

deny it, yet at the same time she knew there was no point in her doing so.

Wolfingham had been intelligent enough, determined enough, to accurately guess as to the reason for her marriage to Martin. If she denied it now he would only need to ask any who had been part of society seventeen years ago to discover—to confirm— that the Earl and Countess of Carlisle's daughter had been born not quite seven months after their wedding had taken place.

Her chin rose challengingly. 'Yes, I was with child when Martin and I married.'

Those intelligent green eyes continued to look down at her, searching, probing, as if Wolfingham might pluck the answers to the rest of this mystery from inside her head.

Outwardly Mariah withstood the probe of that astute green gaze, her chin raised in challenge as her turquoise gaze returned his unflinchingly.

But inwardly she was far less secure in her emotions. In being able to withstand these probing questions, coming so soon after they had visited Aphrodite's Temple together. Not just because of those erotic and disturbing paintings and statues, but also because her body was still deeply aroused from Darian's kisses coming so soon after, and the manner in which he had touched her, aroused her, between her thighs.

An arousal, a desire for *more*, that she knew had already battered her shaky defences.

'How was such a thing possible?' Darian breathed softly.

Mariah gave a humourless laugh at the incongruity of the question. 'I believe Christina to have been conceived in the same manner in which all children are!'

Darian reached out to grasp the tops of her arms, relaxing his hold slightly as he instantly became aware of the way in which Mariah was trembling. 'You are avoiding answering the question directly, Mariah.'

Her gaze also avoided meeting his. 'No—'

'Yes,' he insisted gently. 'You did not love Carlisle. Your manner when you speak of him implies that you did not even like him. You have stated that he was indifferent to you and did not love you any more than you loved him. There have been no other children in your marriage. If those were the true circumstances—'

'I do not tell lies, Darian,' Mariah bit out tautly, her chin defensively high, while inside, much as she fought against it, she felt those walls about her emotions slowly but surely crumbling at her feet. 'I abhor it in others and will not allow it in or to myself.'

'Then why, young as you were, would you have given yourself to a man such as Carlisle—' Wolfingham broke off with a gasp, his cheeks taking on a shocking pallor. 'Carlisle took you against your will.' It was a statement, not a question.

It was too much. *Darian* was too much. And Mariah could no longer bear it. She could not look at him any longer!

'No.' Darian's hands tightened on Mariah's arms

as she would have pulled away from him, with the obvious intention of escaping. Of possibly returning to the house without him. 'No, Mariah,' he repeated softly, even as he released his grip to instead gather her into his arms as he cradled her close against him. 'We have come so far in this conversation, now we must finish it.'

'Why must we?' She held herself stiffly in his arms.

'Perhaps for your own sake?'

She gave a choked laugh. 'I already know the events of the past, Darian, I certainly do not need to talk of them in order to remember them with sickening clarity.'

'Please, Mariah,' Darian encouraged gruffly, holding back his need to know the truth as he sensed the emotions now raging within her.

He could sense her anger, certainly. Her pain. And perhaps still a little of the desire they had felt for each other earlier? Which, he realised ruefully, was perhaps the only reason that she had not already issued him one of her icy set-downs before marching back to the house. Alone.

Darian's arms tightened about Mariah. 'Was I right when I said that Carlisle took you against your will?'

She drew in a ragged breath. 'Yes.'

'Oh, Mariah,' he breathed out raggedly.

'Carlisle was— I told you, he was in need of funds,' she continued forcefully, as if to ward off any show of compassion from Darian. 'He knew, all of society knew, that my father was extremely wealthy.'

'And?' Darian encouraged gently.

She drew in a ragged breath. 'Can you not leave this alone?'

'No more than I can leave *you* alone,' he assured tautly.

Mariah sighed softly before answering him. 'The Season was only weeks old and Carlisle had danced with me several times at various balls. He could not have failed to know I did not—that I had no particular liking for him. Nor would I ever willingly accept a marriage proposal from him. No matter what his title,' she added ruefully.

Darian was now ashamed of himself for ever having suggested that might have been her motive for marrying a man so much older than herself. 'It was a natural, if insulting, assumption to have made.'

'Perhaps,' she allowed flatly before continuing. 'Carlisle was not a man to accept a refusal, most especially not from the daughter of a man he, and his family, considered as being so inferior to himself.'

'His family were cruel to you?' If that was so, then it explained Mariah's overprotectiveness towards her daughter's future husband and family.

'They considered me beneath them and treated me accordingly,' Mariah confirmed huskily, licking the dryness of her lips before speaking again. 'Knowing of my aversion, Carlisle lay in wait for me at one of those balls, trapped me alone in a room and—and then he— I will leave you to draw your own conclusion as to what happened next!' She shivered in Darian's arms.

'Mariah?' A black haze had passed in front of Darian's eyes at all that Mariah had not said. That she could not say. 'Why did your father not deal with him? Call him out? Expose him in society for the beast he was?'

'I did not— I dared not tell either of my parents what had happened.'

'Why not?' Darian scowled darkly.

Mariah shook her head. 'My father was very wealthy, but even so he was only a minor landowner, had made his money in trade and was only accepted into the fringes of society, as was I. Carlisle, on the other hand, might not have been rich, but his title made him extremely powerful in society. And if my father had challenged him, or Carlisle had called him out for making his accusations against him, I have absolutely no doubt as to which of them would have walked away.' She gave a shudder.

Nor did Darian; Martin Beecham had been known as an excellent shot and swordsman.

'Besides,' Mariah continued in that same flat voice, 'Carlisle had made it clear to me after—afterwards...' a little colour flared briefly in her cheeks before as quickly fading again '...that if I told my father what had happened, then he would deny my accusations, claim that it was just my own guilty conscience regarding our having acted on our desire for each other. And that the only outcome to my confession would be the one that he wanted anyway, our immediate betrothal and marriage. He also threatened—' She breathed shakily. 'He said he would do *that* again, and again, until I carried his child, so leaving me with no choice but to marry him.'

'The utter and complete bastard!' If Carlisle had been alive today then Darian knew that he would happily have thrust a sword or knife blade through the other man's cruel black heart, for what he had done to Mariah. Or put a bullet in that same warped and twisted heart.

Mariah pressed her face against Darian's chest, causing him to bend lower in order to hear her next words. 'When I discovered just weeks later that I was indeed expecting his child, I wanted to die, to run away. I even thought of ending my own life. And yet I could not do that either, not with the babe inside me. It would have been nothing less than murder. And my father, as Carlisle had predicted, once told of my condition could not refuse the earl's offer of marriage. Not without causing scandal and ruin for all of us. I was well and truly trapped. Into marrying a man I not only hated, but also had every reason to fear—' She broke off as a sob caught at the back of her throat.

Darian inwardly cursed himself for having forced the subject to the point that he had put Mariah through the pain of reliving those unhappy memories of her past.

The memory of the taking of what Darian was sure would have to have been her young and inexperienced body.

A body that now trembled almost uncontrollably against his own as Mariah battled to stop the tears from falling.

Darian had no doubt they were tears Mariah should have shed eighteen years ago. For the manner in which she had lost her innocence. For the babe, conceived in fear on Mariah's part and greed on Carlisle's.

For the twelve years of unhappiness she had spent as wife to the very man who had raped her.

Chapter Ten

Darian shifted slightly so that his arms were beneath Mariah's thighs and shoulders as he lifted her up and against his chest before striding across to sit down on one of the ledges along the outside of the temple. He settled Mariah comfortably on his thighs, her head, for the moment, resting against his shoulder.

Darian held on to her tightly. 'I believe it would be better if you now tell me all, Mariah, when you have already come so far.'

She gave a shake of her head. 'And I do not care to talk, or think, any more about those horrible memories.'

'The memories of when Carlisle raped you. What he did was the rape of an innocent, Mariah, nothing more, nothing less,' Darian insisted grimly as she stiffened in his arms.

'I am well aware of what it was.'

'After which, he then forced you into years of suffering an unhappy marriage with him, because of your daughter.' Darian could barely contain the violence he felt at learning of Carlisle's brutish behaviour. An impotent violence, in view of the fact that Carlisle was no longer alive to feel the lash of his tongue or the flash of his blade. Carlisle might have been an excellent swordsman, but Darian knew he was better.

'I may not have wanted the marriage, or Carlisle, but I have loved Christina since the day she was born,' Mariah instantly defended. 'She has always been the one shining light in my life.'

Darian nodded, only too well aware of the protectiveness she felt towards her daughter.

As he was also now aware of her reason for objecting so vehemently to the idea of Lady Christina marrying anyone at the age of only seventeen years. The same age as Mariah had been when she was forced to marry Carlisle.

'But there was no heir?' Darian prompted slowly.

'Carlisle did not— He had no interest in my producing his heir. He had a younger cousin he was perfectly happy should inherit the title. His only reason for marrying me was to attain a portion of my father's considerable fortune.'

'I have noted that marriage has a way of producing children, whether they are wanted or not,' Darian drawled ruefully.

'And I have already told you that Carlisle was completely indifferent to me as his wife.'

Darian looked down at Mariah with incredulous eyes. 'Are you saying— You cannot possibly mean—'

'What, Darian?' Mariah lifted her head to look up at him, her eyes dark and shadowed in the pallor of her face. 'I cannot possibly mean that my husband's uninterest in me was such that he did not share my bed, even once, after we were married?' Her smile was completely lacking in humour as she gave a shake of her head. 'Why can I not mean that, Darian, when it is the truth?'

A truth that Darian could not even begin to comprehend, when his own desire for Mariah was such that he found it difficult to sleep at night, to stop thinking about her day and night, of the ways in which he wished to make love with her. She had been Carlisle's *wife* for twelve years. Surely the other man could not have—

Mariah took advantage of his distraction to pull herself abruptly out of his arms before standing up and turning the paleness of her face away in profile, a shutter seeming to have come down over her emotions—no doubt because she deeply regretted having revealed them in the first place.

'Why should Carlisle have need of the attentions of his very young and very inexperienced wife,' she continued drily, 'when his mistress of over twenty years was the housekeeper of our London home?'

'Carlisle kept his mistress in your home after you were married?' Darian stood up slowly.

It was well known that many gentlemen of the *ton* kept a mistress after they were married. But never, ever, in the same house as their wife. It was not done.

It simply was not done. And yet, it appeared that that was exactly what Carlisle had done.

'In truth, I was grateful for Mrs Smith's existence.' Mariah shrugged dismissively as she briskly pulled her glove back on to the hand she had earlier dipped into the heated pool. 'And I was not made uncomfortable by the arrangement, visiting London rarely during the first ten years of our marriage. I much preferred to remain in the country with Christina.'

Darian breathed deeply. 'But something happened to change that? Did you and Carlisle perhaps reconcile?'

'There was nothing *to* reconcile.' She turned to frown at him. 'How could there be, when we had never been husband and wife in the true sense of the word?'

'But something did change.'

Mariah knew she had said too much already, revealed too much—more than she had ever told anyone else about the past and the reason for her marriage to Martin. The only thing she had not shared with Darian was Martin's treasonous behaviour. And the lie that was the rumour of her numerous affairs...

She had never confided as much to anyone about the past as she now had to Darian Hunter. Knew she had only been lulled into doing so this time because her emotions had already been disturbed by what she had seen and done in the temple. From her imaginings as to what it would be like to engage in those acts with Darian. Imaginings that had deepened, flourished, during the kiss that had followed.

And that momentary weakness had now cost her dearly.

Damn it, she had told him of Carlisle's brutality. Her forced marriage. She had *cried* in Wolfingham's arms. She, who never cried, preferring never to show any sign of weakness. To anyone.

And she did not intend to continue to do so now where Wolfingham was concerned, either. Had made a vow to herself long ago not to allow *anyone*, apart from Christina, to come so close to her, to know her so well, they were capable of hurting her. 'Do you still wish to continue with our walk, or has all this ridiculous emotion dampened not only your shirt but your enthusiasm for walking?' she prompted coolly.

That astute green gaze remained narrowed on her as Wolfingham stepped closer. 'There was nothing in the least ridiculous about your upset just now, Mariah.'

'And I believe it to have been an utterly ridiculous waste of time,' she insisted coldly, 'when the past, talking about it, changes nothing.'

'And what of the future, Mariah?' He stepped so close to her now that she could feel the warmth of his breath against her brow. 'What of *your* future?'

She gave a dismissive shrug. 'Once this weekend is over, I do not believe that to be any of your business.' Mariah clasped her hands together so that Darian could not see they were trembling still, evidence that her emotions were not as back under her control as she would have wished them to be. Her complete lack of control, just minutes ago, now made her feel vulnerable, in a way she found most disturbing.

Wolfingham raised his hands to cup both her cheeks before he tilted her face up so that he might look directly into her eyes. 'And what if I wish to make it my business?'

Wolfingham's gentleness was unbearable, before and again now, when Mariah knew her emotions, despite her denials to the contrary, remained ragged and torn. When her *defence* against Darian's gentleness remained ragged and torn.

'I am sure I am not the first woman to have been trapped into an unhappy marriage,' she said drily. 'Nor will I be the last. And as you say, I did become a countess because of it.'

'Do not attempt to make light of it, Mariah!' Wolfingham rasped harshly.

'How do you wish me to behave, Darian?' Her eyes flashed darkly as she looked up at him defiantly. 'I have wailed and railed, and now I wish to forget it. As I have forgotten it these past seventeen years.'

'Did you forget, Mariah?' He looked down at her searchingly. 'Did you ever really forget what that man did to you?'

Of course Mariah had never forgotten. She had not wanted to forget, was the woman she was today because of it.

Her chin rose. 'Enough so that I do not require, or need, your own or anyone's pity because of it.'

'Does this feel like pity to you?' Wolfingham had grasped one of her hands and placed it over the noticeable bulge in his pantaloons. 'Does it?' He pushed for an answer, his eyes glittering down at her darkly.

'And how long will that desire last, Wolfingham?' Mariah fell back on derision as her defence as she deliberately removed her hand at the same time as she returned his gaze mockingly. 'Until you have sated your lust between my thighs and then wish to move on to some other conquest? Possibly to a woman who is younger and less complicated!'

He gave a slow shake of his head. 'I find your complications intriguing and your age of four and thirty is unimportant to me.' A nerve pulsed in the tightness of his jaw. 'And I resent your assumption that my desire for you is a fleeting thing.'

'Perhaps I presume as much because it has been my experience that a man will say anything, promise anything, when he wishes to bed a certain woman.' She eyed him scornfully.

Darian frowned his frustration. He did not give a damn what Mariah's previous lovers had told her, or promised her, when *he* was the man now standing before her, telling her, physically *showing* her, how much he desired her. How much he desired to *be* with her.

A desire of such intensity that Darian had no doubt it would not abate for some time. If ever.

More than anything he wished to take Mariah to his bed. To gently kiss her, caress her, to *taste* her, to worship every satiny inch of her, and show her the depth of his desire for her. And then he wished to start all over again. And again. And then again. Again, and again, and again, until Mariah was left in absolutely no doubt as to the depth of his desire for her.

At the same time as he knew that this place, Eton Park, with its peepholes into the bedchambers and a temple worthy of the debauchery of the Roman Empire at the height of its power, and the guests to match, plus the Nicholses' intrigues, was not where he wished to lie with Mariah the first time. Not where he wished to make love with her, to worship her and her body, as she so deserved to be worshipped.

His hands fell back to his sides as he stepped back. 'Very well, we will continue with our walk for now. But we will talk on this subject again once we are back in London,' he added softly.

She arched a taunting brow. 'Not if I do not wish to do so.'

Darian's mouth quirked into an equally mocking smile. 'A word of advice, Mariah. I am not like any of your previous lovers. When you know me better, which you most assuredly will, I believe you will find that I am a man who *always* means what he says as well as *always* keeps his promises!'

Mariah masked her uneasiness as she fell into step beside him as he began to walk back in the direction of the lake, very much afraid that Darian Hunter was indeed a man who always meant what he said as well as kept all of his promises.

Afraid?

Oh, yes, Mariah was very much afraid, in spite of everything that had happened between them since they first met, that she desired Darian Hunter as much as he now claimed to desire her.

That she desired to know Darian in a way she had never desired any other man.

'Do try to smile, Darian, rather than scowl and glower in that dark and disapproving way,' Mariah advised lightly later that afternoon, viewing his reflection in the mirror after he had entered her bedchamber through the door adjoining their two rooms, after only the briefest of knocks. His appearance was elegantly foreboding in a black superfine, grey waistcoat and pantaloons. 'Else, once we arrive downstairs for tea, the other guests will think that the two of us have argued.' She looked at her own reflection in the mirror to give her already perfectly styled hair another pat, rather than continue to look at Darian's more disturbing reflection.

Everything about this man disturbed her.

The way he looked.

Her undeniable response to his touch.

The desire she was finding it more and more difficult to deny or control.

And the fact that she had confided so much of her past to him earlier today.

That breach in the barrier she had kept so firmly about her emotions for so many years disturbed Mariah most of all, so much so that she had spent the past four hours, since they parted downstairs after returning from their walk, attempting to shore up or replace that barrier.

Only to have taken but a single glance at Darian's reflection in the mirror as he strode forcefully into her bedchamber just now to know that those efforts, determined as they might have been, had been a complete waste of her time.

What was it about this man in particular that affected her so? Oh, he was handsome enough. Forceful enough. But he was far from the first handsome or forceful man to have expressed a desire to bed her. Desire she had found absolutely no difficulty in rejecting in the past.

No doubt because she had not felt a return of that desire for any of those other men.

The same desire that had so shaken and disturbed her earlier, to a degree that she had confided more of her past to this man than she had ever wished anyone to know.

The very same desire that made her feel so vulnerable whenever she was in his presence.

'I have absolutely no interest in what they do or do not think,' Darian answered her impatiently now, the scowl still dark upon his brow as he stepped further into the room.

Mariah turned slowly, a slight frown creasing her own brow now. 'Has something happened?'

Darian stared at her incredulously.

Had something happened?

As far as Darian's life was concerned, Mariah Beecham had happened.

So much so that just one look at her, when he entered her bedchamber just seconds ago and saw how beautiful she looked in an afternoon gown of the palest turquoise, her breasts a creamy and tempting swell, the very low and curved neckline of that gown revealing the tops of her nipples as being a deep rose, and he was forced to endure a hard and painful throb inside his pantaloons yet again.

At the same time he felt a ridiculous desire to cover up those beautiful breasts, so that no other man could look at or see any part of them. Or become aroused and tempted by looking at them, as he undoubtedly was.

A ridiculous reaction, when Mariah's coolness towards him this morning, once they had left the temple, and then completed their walk about the lake together in complete silence, had spoken only too clearly not only of her need to put a physical distance between them, but also of a return of that emotional one.

Darian had lingered in the hallway to have that promised word with Benson while Mariah went up the stairs alone. By the time he arrived up the stairs, the door to Mariah's bedchamber, and the door adjoining their two rooms, had both been firmly closed. He had known instinctively that Mariah meant them as a barrier between the two of them. One he crossed at his peril.

Because she had revealed too much about herself to him this morning? Because he now knew things about her life, her marriage to Carlisle, that perhaps no one else did?

Darian did not believe that Mariah was the type

of woman who would confide her deepest, darkest secrets easily. To anyone. And he knew from personal experience that Mariah's role as an agent for the Crown would also make it difficult for her to have close friends, male or female, for fear they might discover her secret.

The murderous rage Darian had felt earlier today, towards Martin Beecham, had not abated in the slightest in the hours that had passed since Darian and Mariah had parted so stiffly. Her husband had been an out-and-out bastard who had raped and terrified a young and inexperienced girl for the sole purpose of forcing his child and marriage on her, trampling all of the young girl's romantic dreams into the dust beneath his own greedy need for the bride's portion of her father's money.

Not only that, but Carlisle had doubly insulted Mariah by having his mistress in residence as housekeeper in one of the homes Mariah herself had necessarily to visit on occasion.

How did any woman survive that? But especially one as young and innocent as Mariah had been then?

Darian knew it would be difficult for a woman of any age to have survived such base and selfish cruelty.

Yet here Mariah stood before him, a lady in every sense of the word. So graciously beautiful, as well as being the most desirable woman he had ever known.

Nor was it any wonder, after all that she had suffered at Beecham's hands, that Mariah had turned to the comforting arms and desire of other men, both during and after her marriage.

Had any of those other men *made love* to her? Darian wondered as he continued to admire her beauty and poise. Truly made love to her? Showering Mariah with the gentleness, the care and consideration that was her due?

Or had they all without fail, as she had so scathingly scorned earlier, treated her as just another conquest in their bed? So that they might afterwards claim, to their male friends and associates, to have bedded the beautiful Countess of Carlisle?

'Darian?' Mariah prompted again, her expression having become wary at his continued silence.

Darian had spent most of the past four hours pacing his bedchamber and thinking of Mariah. Of all that she had told him of her past, at the same time as he now knew it was that past that had made her the woman she was today: cool, poised and determined to remain totally removed from emotional entanglements with any man.

It had brought Darian to the question that concerned him the most: how the two of them were to now proceed—or *if* Mariah would allow them to proceed at all.

For he had promised himself he would not use any type of force upon Mariah. That he might perhaps allow himself to cajole, tease and seduce her, but he would not, could not, ever use coercion or force of any kind.

'Nothing has happened.' He drew in a ragged

breath. 'I want— I need— No, I *ask*—' He broke off abruptly, only now appreciating how difficult it was going to be to keep the promise he had made to himself earlier, when just to look at Mariah again made his blood burn in his veins and his erection throb.

Mariah was now truly alarmed by Darian's behaviour. Of what might possibly have happened to put the arrogantly assured Duke of Wolfingham in such an obvious state of uncertainty. 'Yes?' she prompted tensely.

He straightened his shoulders, emerald gaze fixed intently upon her as he spoke abruptly. 'I would ask if you will allow me to kiss you before we go downstairs?'

Darian Hunter was a man Mariah had every reason to know was always and completely assured as to the rightness of his own actions.

As he had believed he was in the right two weeks ago, when he had warned her not to encourage his younger brother in his attentions to her.

As he had believed her friendship with Aubrey Maystone must be one based on intimacy.

As he believed her to be a woman who had indulged in many affairs, both during and after her marriage.

Wolfingham had believed he was in the right in all of those things.

Admittedly, he had already been proven wrong in two of those things, but the latter? Darian still believed in that legion of lovers Mariah was reputed to have had these past seven years, no doubt believed them to have been her comfort for the coldness of her marriage.

And yet he now asked if he might kiss her?

To say Mariah was flustered by Darian's request would be putting it mildly. Especially when she had every reason to know that the arrogantly self-assured Duke of Wolfingham never 'asked' permission to do anything, let alone asked permission to kiss *her*. The notorious and scandalous Mariah Beecham, Countess of Carlisle...

She attempted a sophisticated and dismissive laugh, hoping Wolfingham did not recognise it, as she certainly did, as sounding more nervous than assured. 'I thought we had agreed not to continue with that conversation until after we have returned to London.' She gave a pointed glance to where her shawls and handkerchiefs were once again draped over those peepholes into her bedchamber, in order to preserve her privacy, both while she'd bathed and changed her clothes earlier.

A nerve pulsed in his tightly clenched jaw. 'I find that my desire to at least touch you again cannot wait that long.'

His desire to touch her again!

It was Wolfingham's touch that had been her undoing from the beginning. Not just once, but so many times. On the terrace of her own home. In the guest bedchamber of her home, where he had necessarily to stay in order to recover after his collapse. In the gallery of Lady Stockton's home. And here. Here at

Eton Park she had allowed Darian to touch her more intimately than any other man had ever done before.

Mariah now feared her response to his touch.

Not because she thought Darian would ever physically hurt her—she was already sure he would never use force upon any woman. She had come to know him these past two weeks, knew he was not a man who showed his strength or power through physical dominance over others, but by the sheer force of his indomitable will.

No, she did not fear Darian would physically hurt her, as Carlisle had hurt and humiliated her, to such an extent she had never cared to repeat the experience.

Darian Hunter was capable of hurting her in a much different way.

She was not only aroused by him, felt desire for him, she also liked and admired him. His strength. His honesty. His family loyalty. His devotion to his country. He was, as she had learnt these past weeks, in all things an honourable man.

A man she might love.

And Mariah did not wish to love any man, even one as handsome and honourable as she now knew Darian Hunter, the Duke of Wolfingham, to be.

The independence of nature she so enjoyed now had been hard won, after years of living only half a life, hidden away in the country, and for the most part ignored by the husband she hated and despised. For the past seven years, since revealing Martin's treasonous behaviour to Aubrey Maystone, she had no longer had reason to fear Martin, or anything he might try to do to her. Aubrey Maystone had taken care of that.

For the first time in her life Mariah had done exactly as she pleased, her worthwhile work for the Crown enabling her to become a woman she could not only respect, but also like.

For her to fall in love, with any man, would, she believed, be to put all of that at risk.

To fall in love with Darian Hunter, the much respected and admired Duke of Wolfingham, would most certainly lead to heartbreak on the day he cast her aside and left her for another female who had caught his fancy.

Wolfingham might have a reputation in society as being severe and very proper, nor had there ever been any gossip as to his ever having taken a permanent mistress. But that did not mean there had not been other rumours, of his liaisons with several ladies of the *ton*, and the gaming hells and the houses of the *demi-monde* he had visited on the evenings he spent with the other Dangerous Dukes.

Dangerous.

Yes, where Mariah was concerned Darian Hunter more than lived up to his reputation as being dangerous. To her independence. To her untutored body. To her untouched heart.

And that she could not, dare not, allow.

'Goodness, Wolfingham, where on earth has all this politeness and solicitude come from?' she taunted him mockingly. 'If it is because of our conversation earlier today, then let me assure you that it is of no consequence.'

'No consequence?'

'Absolutely none,' she dismissed coolly in the face of his vehemence. 'It was too many years ago to be of any significance to the here and now. Nor, as I assured you earlier, do I have need of anyone's pity. Least of all your own,' she added with deliberate scorn.

'Least of all mine?' Wolfingham's eyes were steely now as he looked at her through narrowed lids.

'But of course.' Mariah returned that hard gaze with a challenging one of her own. 'You really are arrogance personified if you believed otherwise. In the circumstances I described to you earlier, a woman can either grow stronger from the experience or allow herself to be beaten down by it. I am certain that by now you know me well enough to have realised which one of those women I have become?' She arched haughty brows.

Oh, yes, Darian knew full well which one of those women best described Mariah. Her fortitude was only one of the reasons he admired and liked her so much. Desired her so much. A desire she was now at pains to inform him she wanted no part of.

To a degree she would not even give permission for him to so much as kiss or touch her again.

Was that avoidance not telling in itself?

Or was he simply grasping at straws, because he so much wished for Mariah to return his desire?

It was a question Darian intended to explore with

all thoroughness once they were well away from Eton Park.

He nodded. 'As it is almost five o'clock, might I suggest that we join the other guests downstairs for tea?'

A surprised blink of Mariah's long dark lashes was her only outward sign that she was surprised at his ease in accepting her refusal. 'But of course.' She nodded graciously as she collected up her fan before sweeping past him and preceding him out of the bedchamber.

Darian smiled grimly as he followed her out into the hallway before offering her his arm to escort her down the stairs.

Mariah might believe him to have been routed by her set-down, but if she had come to know him half as well as he now knew her, then she would very soon realise that his patience, in achieving his goals, was infinite.

And his most pressing goal, desire, was to make love with Mariah.

Chapter Eleven

'If one knows where to look, it is almost possible to see the bruises in the shape of fingerprints upon Lord Nichols's neck,' Mariah remarked conversationally a short time later before taking a sip of tea from her cup, as she and Wolfingham sat together on a *chaise* in the Nicholses' salon. Its placement by one of the windows allowed them to observe the other guests.

'He's lucky he still has a neck to bruise,' Wolfingham muttered, the ice in his gaze the only sign of his displeasure, as he gave every outward appearance of relaxation, lounging on the *chaise* beside her.

Mariah chuckled softly. 'I am not sure I ever thanked you properly for your gallantry last night.'

He turned to face her. 'No, I do not believe you did,' he drawled drily.

'Well, I do thank you.' Mariah was unnerved to once again find herself the focus of those piercing green eyes. 'These people really are an unpleasant lot, aren't they?' Her gaze now swept contemptuously over the other guests.

The men were drinking brandy instead of tea, with most of them already well on their way to being inebriated yet again. Including their host, as he occasionally cast a furtively nervous glance in Wolfingham's direction.

The women were once again wearing an assortment of gowns that would be more suited to a bordello or brothel. Not that Mariah had ever been in either establishment, but she could well imagine the state of *déshabillé* of the women who did.

Normally Mariah would have had no difficulty in maintaining a certain distance, from both the gentlemen's drinking and the ladies' state of undress, when attending one of these weekend parties. She had no doubt it was the challenge her coolness represented to the gentlemen that caused the *ton*'s hostesses to continue to include her in these weekend invitations. The gentlemen made no secret that they began each of these weekends with a wager on which one of them might succeed in bedding the Countess of Carlisle.

Yes, normally Mariah would not have the slightest difficulty maintaining that distance.

Wolfingham's presence, and Mariah's complete awareness of the lean and muscled length of his body as he lounged on the *chaise* beside her, had heightened her senses to such a degree, she now seemed to feel and view everything as if through a magnifying glass.

The way in which even the statuary and decor in this house seemed to be attuned to the debauchery that went on under its roof.

The gentlemen's red and bloated faces, and their avidly glittering eyes as they ogled the ladies' state of undress.

Those same ladies vying with each other, with more and more outrageous behaviour, in order to attract and hold the attention of the gentleman, or gentlemen, they had decided to bed.

The way in which Wolfingham's austere handsomeness, in the formal black of his clothing and snowy white linen, succeeded in putting him above any and all of the other gentlemen present.

Knowing that, *aware* of that, this weekend, and Mariah's forced association with Wolfingham, could not come to an end soon enough for her.

'Very,' Wolfingham now drawled disdainfully. 'I feel soiled just by being in the same room with them.'

Mariah arched a mocking brow. 'And yet you and the other Dangerous Dukes are rumoured to frequent brothels and the houses of the *demi-monde.*'

His eyes narrowed. 'I draw the line at brothels. And the ladies of the *demi-monde* do not pretend to be upstanding members of society.'

Mariah's curiosity was piqued by the fact that he had not denied frequenting *those* houses. 'Do you—'

'And what are you two whispering about together so secretly?'

Without either of them having been aware of it— Darian was sure that Mariah's attention had been as focused on him as his was on her—their hostess had crossed the room to join them and now stood looking down at them with coquettish curiosity. A lapse in concentration on their part, which Darian knew could have been very costly indeed, if they had chanced to be talking of their real reason for being here this weekend.

He stood up politely and instantly regretted doing so as his superior height gave him a clear view down the front of Clara Nichols's loose gown, as far as her navel—decidedly *not* an arousing sight. 'We were discussing the...merits of the temple in your garden, madam.'

Lady Nichols's rouged lips gave a knowing smile. 'So *that's* where the two of you have been all day.'

'This morning, at least.' Darian gave an acknowledging nod. 'Your butler was most helpful, this morning, in telling us of its existence.'

'Benson *has* turned out to be a treasure.' His hostess smiled fondly at the butler as he circulated amongst the guests, calmly refilling the gentlemen's brandy glasses with the same aplomb as he did the ladies' teacups, before withdrawing from the room with that same calm after one of the footmen had entered and drawn him aside to speak to him quietly. 'One is never quite sure, when one takes on new household staff, whether or not they are going to suit, but Benson did come personally recommended and he has more than lived up to it these past few months.' Lady Nichols turned to eye them speculatively. 'I trust you both enjoyed our little temple?'

'Most diverting,' Darian answered noncommittally, a glance at the clock on the mantelpiece revealing that it was just a few minutes after five o'clock, time for the Prince Regent's note to be delivered, for which he and Mariah had been patiently waiting these past twenty-four hours. And, hopefully, the reason Benson had been summoned from the room?

Well, the waiting had perhaps not been quite so patient, on Darian's part! Indeed, it had been unimaginable torture, having to suffer the company of such people and made all the worse by his increasing desire for Mariah. His only wish now was to have this charade over as soon as was possible, so that they might return to town and he could concentrate his considerable attention on seducing Mariah.

'You will have the opportunity to return there later on tonight, of course,' Lady Nichols continued to chatter. 'It is *so* romantic in the evenings.'

Darian almost choked on the sip of brandy he had been about to take, at the very idea of the erotica displayed in that temple ever being thought of as romantic. Certainly it appeared that Lady Nichols's idea of romance, and his own, differed greatly!

How long did it take Benson to collect the Prince's note of apology from the rider and return with it?

'We are both so looking forward to the masked ball this evening, Clara.' Mariah claimed their hostess's attention as Darian made no reply.

'And I trust that you will not remain quite so… exclusive…this evening, sir?' Lady Nichols gave Darian's arm a playful tap with her fan. 'There are many more ladies present who would welcome your attentions.'

Darian narrowed his gaze on her. 'Indeed.'

Where the hell was Benson with the Prince's note?

'Oh, yes.' Their hostess gave another of those tittering giggles, so incongruous in a woman who was aged in her forties, at the least. 'Indeed, the ladies have talked and speculated of nothing else since your arrival yesterday.'

'Indeed?' Darian repeated stiltedly, his hands clenching tensely into fists at his sides.

'Oh, my goodness, yes!' Lady Nichols looked up at him with what she no doubt thought was a winning smile, obviously having absolutely no idea how close Darian was to telling her to go to the devil and take her simpering flirtation with her! 'I myself would dearly love to—'

'I do believe Benson is trying to attract your attention, Clara,' Mariah put in hastily, having thankfully spotted the butler approaching them, a silver tray held aloft on one hand; the increasing coldness of Darian's expression, and those hands clenched at his sides, warned Mariah he was seriously in danger of telling Clara Nichols exactly how repugnant he found both her and her guests. Their reason for being here be damned!

'What *is* it, Benson?' Their hostess could barely contain her irritation at the interruption as she frowned at her butler.

'This was just delivered for you, madam.' Benson offered the silver tray. 'I took the liberty of asking the rider to wait, in case there is a reply,' he added helpfully.

Mariah could feel Darian's tension as the two of

them watched their hostess break the seal on the letter before quickly scanning its contents. Mariah actually held her breath as she waited for Clara Nichols's response, which for the moment appeared to be only a displeased frown.

'What is it, my dear?' Richard Nichols called out across the room.

A pout appeared on Clara Nichols's too-red lips. 'The Prince Regent is unable to attend the ball this evening, after all. Some urgent business requiring he return to town earlier than expected.'

There were several murmurs of 'too bad' and 'bad show' from the other guests, but it was Richard and Clara Nichols whom Mariah continued to study intently, as she knew that Darian did also.

'That is a pity.' Richard Nichols strolled over to join his wife before reading the note for himself. 'Oh well, can't be helped, old girl.' He patted his wife awkwardly on the shoulder. 'The country's needs must come first and all that.'

Lady Nichols continued to pout her disappointment. 'It really is too bad of him,' she snapped waspishly. 'I only invited Lady Henley on his instructions I should do so.'

'I am sure that there are plenty of other gentlemen present to keep that lady entertained. Hey, Wolfingham?' Richard Nichols attempted a conspiratorial and conciliatory smile at the haughty duke.

'You are welcome to do so, by all means, Nichols.' That smile was not returned as Darian looked coldly down the length of his nose at the older man. 'As I am sure I have made perfectly clear, I am happy in the company of Lady Beecham.'

'A man can have too much of a good thing, though, don't you think?' Nichols suggested slyly.

Wolfingham's jaw was tight. 'No, I most certainly do not think,' he bit out tautly, eyes glacial as he continued to look contemptuously at the other man.

A contempt, a danger, that Mariah knew the older man would be foolish to ignore. Most especially so when he still bore the bruises on his neck from the last time he had managed to infuriate Wolfingham.

She stood up to tuck her gloved hand into the crook of Darian's arm, administering a gentle squeeze of caution even as she turned to smile at Richard Nichols. 'I am afraid our…friendship…is relatively new, Lord Nichols, and Wolfingham is quite besotted still.' She felt the tension in Darian's arm beneath her fingertips as his response to such a ridiculous claim.

As it was indeed ridiculous to think of the haughty Duke of Wolfingham as ever being besotted with any woman, least of all the scandalous Countess of Carlisle!

'Well, can't blame a man for that.' Richard Nichols wisely backed down. 'Oh, do cheer up, Clara,' he turned to instruct his sulking wife impatiently. 'I am sure we shall manage quite well this evening without the Prince's presence. After all, we do have the elusive Duke of Wolfingham as one of our guests!'

'So he is.' Clara Nichols brightened before turning to the waiting butler. 'There is no reply, Benson.' She placed the note back on the tray. 'Could you see that this is put in my private parlour?' she added dismissively.

'Of course, milady.' The butler bowed politely before withdrawing.

Mariah frowned her puzzlement as she continued to study Richard and Clara Nichols; there did not seem to be any undue reaction to the Prince's note of apology, apart from Clara's obvious disappointment.

Clara Nichols now directed another of those coquettish smiles at Wolfingham. 'Where were we?'

'I believe that Mariah and I were about to return upstairs,' he bit out tautly.

'Again? So soon?' Clara Nichols gave Mariah an envious smile. 'My, he is a lusty one, isn't he, my dear?'

Mariah felt the warmth of colour enter her cheeks and dearly hoped that the other woman would see it as the burn of anticipation at being the recipient of Wolfingham's passion, rather than the embarrassment it really was. 'I am sure we are both very grateful to you for allowing us the privacy, in which to fully indulge ourselves, this weekend.' She curled her nails painfully, and quite deliberately, into Darian's tensed arm.

He moved his other hand to cover hers, squeezing with just enough pressure not to cause pain, but to administer a warning of his own. 'Very grateful,' he drawled drily.

'We appear to be completely superfluous here, my dear. Shall we return to the entertainment of our other guests?' Richard Nichols extended an arm politely to his wife. 'If you will both excuse us?' He bowed politely to Mariah and Wolfingham as the other couple moved away, Clara Nichols still twittering her disappointment over the Prince Regent as they did so.

Mariah waited only long enough for the Nicholses to be out of earshot before turning to Darian. 'Should we not wait here awhile longer before returning upstairs?'

'No.'

'But—'

'I believe we have seen all that we needed to see, Mariah,' he assured grimly.

'We have?'

He nodded tersely. 'Besides which, if I do not leave this company very soon, then I am afraid I might lose my temper completely.'

Mariah could see the truth of that claim in the dangerous glitter of his eyes and the nerve pulsing erratically in his tightly clenched jaw.

She held her head high as she accompanied him across the room, knowing they were being observed with interest as she heard the outbreak of whispering and laughter in the room behind them as they stepped out into the hallway. 'Must you always be so—so *obvious* as to our supposed intention of disappearing to make love together?' she hissed the moment they were out in the deserted entrance hall.

Darian was feeling murderous rather than obvious. How much longer must he endure this torture, of watching men like Nichols lusting after the woman he—the woman he—the woman he what? Exactly what was it that he felt towards Mariah?

Protective, certainly.

Proprietary.

Possessive.

To the extent he could quite cheerfully have taken on every man in that room who had so much as looked at Mariah sideways—which was all of them, damn it!

'You are missing the point, Mariah.'

'And it *appears* to me that you are enjoying yourself altogether too much at my expense!' she came back heatedly.

'Could we talk of this further once we reach your bedchamber?' he prompted softly as Benson appeared at the top of the stairs, no doubt after having delivered Lady Nichols's letter to her private parlour.

'May I get you anything, your Grace?' he offered politely as he reached the bottom of the staircase.

'No, thank you, Benson,' Darian answered distractedly, his hand firmly beneath Mariah's elbow as he pulled her up the stairs beside him.

'Darian?'

'You are missing the point, Mariah,' he repeated through gritted teeth as they reached the top of the staircase before turning into the hallway leading to their adjoining bedchambers.

'Which is?' she prompted as she opened the door to her room.

'The letter,' he reminded impatiently as he followed Mariah into her bedchamber. 'The response to the Prince's letter.' He closed the door firmly behind him.

All of Mariah's indignation fled as she realised

she had indeed allowed her embarrassment to distract her, that she was the one now guilty—however briefly!—of forgetting their reason for being at Eton Park at all this weekend. 'Apart from Clara's obvious disappointment as hostess that the Prince would not be gracing her ball tonight after all, there did not appear to be any response at all to his note,' she stated belatedly. 'No pointed looks, or conversation, with anyone else in the room. No one hastily leaving the room. There was no response whatsoever.'

'Exactly.' Wolfingham paced the room restlessly.

Mariah continued to frown. 'Does that mean Aubrey Maystone's information was wrong?'

'Maystone is never wrong,' he assured grimly.

'Then what happened just now?'

'Nothing. That is the problem.' Wolfingham looked grim.

Mariah chewed briefly on her bottom lip. 'Do you think that might be because someone suspects that we—'

'Came back upstairs to make love?' Wolfingham interrupted huskily. 'Oh, I think that was more than obvious, my love.'

Mariah blinked, momentarily confused at the sudden change in his tone. 'What—'

'I am sure that we have been more than obvious in our obsession to bed each other,' Wolfingham acknowledged indulgently. 'Indeed, I find I cannot wait another minute to undress you and make love with you,' he added gruffly, at the same time as the fierceness of his gaze now moved pointedly to the shawls and handkerchiefs Mariah had left in place over the peepholes about the bedchamber. 'Come over here, love,' he invited huskily.

A warning to Mariah that someone was standing behind one of the walls at this very minute, listening to their conversation?

And necessitating in their continuing with the act of lovers once again eager to be alone together, so that they could make love?

Oh, heavens!

She gave an abrupt nod of her head, in silent acknowledgement of their eavesdropper, as she crossed the room to Wolfingham's side. Her heart was pounding loudly in her chest, her pulse racing, as she wondered for how long, and how far, they would need to continue with their act of eager lovers.

At the same time she felt an inner yearning to satisfy, just a little, the desire she had discovered she felt for Darian.

All thoughts of anything else fled Darian's head as Mariah now stood in front of him, so close he could feel her breath brushing warmly against his throat as she moved up on tiptoe. 'Oh, yes, Mariah,' he groaned in approval—both of her quickness of mind, in realising they were not completely alone, *and* most certainly of the fact that her teeth were now nibbling in earnest on the sensitivity of his earlobe; surely an unnecessary embellishment to their act when they could be overheard, but not observed?

He turned his head slightly so that he could look into Mariah's eyes, the fullness of her parted lips now just inches beneath his own as their gazes clashed and held, both of them breathing softly, expectantly.

Darian took full advantage of Mariah's closeness as his arms moved about her waist to pull her in tightly against him, his gaze continuing to hold hers as his head lowered and he took fierce possession of those parted lips with his own.

Something Darian had wanted—*hungered for*—since they had parted so coolly after their walk earlier today.

So much so that there was no way to stop the avalanche of desire that now swept over and through him as he felt Mariah's lips part beneath his own, her arms about his waist.

Darian deepened the kiss, his tongue sweeping, tasting her parted lips, before plunging, thrusting into the moist heat beyond.

Mariah tasted of the honey cake she had eaten with her tea; sweet and utterly delicious. Combined with her exotic perfume, it was addictive.

Darian continued the depth of those kisses as, for the second time that day, he swept her up into his arms. Carrying Mariah across the room before placing her on top of the bedcovers and following her down. Settling his thighs between her parted ones, he took his weight on his elbows before cupping either side of her face with his hands and continuing to kiss her hungrily. Tasting, sipping, possessing!

Mariah gave a throaty groan as Darian's lips and tongue continued to claim her own. Even as his hands deftly removed the pins from her hair before loosening it on to the pillows beneath her, she moved her arms up over his shoulders as her fingers became entangled in the dark silkiness of his own hair.

She was filled with a yearning ache as the heat of Darian's arousal throbbed between her parted thighs. Pressing, shifting slowly against and into her, pleasure surging through her as that friction stroked against the throbbing nubbin between her now slick and swollen folds.

Darian broke the kiss, breathing heavily as moist lips now travelled the length of her throat. 'God, how I want you!' he groaned achingly. 'You are so beautiful, Mariah. So very beautiful.' One of his hands now moved caressingly, restlessly, beneath the curve of her breast, before pulling down that silken barrier to bare their fullness, his hand now cupping her breast in sacrifice to his questing lips and tongue.

'Darian!' Mariah's back arched off the bed as he claimed one aroused and sensitive nipple into the heat of his mouth, pleasure surging, filling her, as his tongue flicked against that hardened nub, teeth gently biting before he suckled deeply, drawing the whole of her nipple into the heat of his mouth.

Darian's mouth was heat and fire, pleasure beyond description. A pleasure that surged and intensified unbearably between Mariah's parted thighs, causing her to arch up against his hardness, in need of a greater friction as she searched, ached for the full promise of that pleasure.

'Yes!' she cried out as Darian shifted slightly to her side, his lips and tongue still drawing fiercely on her breast as his hand moved to push her gown up her thighs. Caressing, seeking, *finding* the opening in her drawers that allowed his fingers access to caress the slick moisture of her swollen folds, at the same time as the soft pad of his thumb stroked the throbbing nubbin above. 'Please, Darian! Yes!' Mariah was mindless with pleasure as she arched up into those caresses, wanting, needing, something *more*.

'Come for me, Mariah,' Darian encouraged throatily at the same time as first one finger, then two, entered the slickness of her core. 'Please come for me, Mariah!' He suckled hard on her nipple at the same time as those fingers now moved rhythmically, his thumb stroking, pressing down on that swollen nubbin above.

Pleasure, unlike anything Mariah had ever known, or imagined, now exploded between her thighs, her head thrashing from side to side on the pillows as that release coursed hotly, claiming the rest of her body in wave after wave of seemingly endless pleasure.

She was still lost to the wonder, the euphoria of that pleasure, as Darian gazed down at her darkly before sliding down the length of her body until he knelt between her parted thighs. Mariah offered no resistance as he slowly pushed her gown up to her waist before moving aside to allow for the removal of her drawers and bared her to his heated gaze as he parted her legs so that he might once again kneel between them.

'So pretty. Like a rose in bloom,' he murmured appreciatively as his fingers moved to part her swollen folds, allowing him to gaze his fill of her before he lay down between her thighs, his tongue a hot and pleasurable rasp against her highly sensitised and aroused flesh.

'Darian?' Mariah felt she should protest at such intimacy, but in truth she felt so satiated still, so lost in wonder as she felt the stirring of her arousal for a second time in as many minutes, that she could barely speak, let alone offer words of protest.

'Let me.' The coolness of his breath was sweet torture against her hot and aching flesh. 'You are so beautiful here, Mariah,' he groaned as he touched her gently. 'So beautiful!'

His lips and tongue caressed her at the same time as his hands moved up to cup her breasts. Mariah gazed down in wonder as those long fingers and thumbs tweaked and pinched her swollen nipples, at the same time as Darian's head was buried between her thighs, the sight of such intimacy enough to cause her to gasp anew.

'Again, Mariah,' he encouraged roughly. 'I want you to come for me again.'

Mariah felt captured, swept along in a relentless tide as a second wave of pleasure built higher deep inside her and then higher still. Higher and higher—

'Darian!' Her back arched to push her breasts into Darian's hands, encouraging, welcoming the pleasure-pain as he now squeezed and pinched her nipples to the same rhythm as her thighs moved into the stroking of his lips and tongue.

She gave a gasp, eyes wide with shock as pleasure even more intense than the first suddenly ripped through her.

This was what all the poets wrote about so ardently. What singers crooned about so achingly. What lovers so hungered for they were willing to throw away all caution and reputation in order to achieve it.

Mariah had never known, never guessed, that lovemaking, this wonderful feeling of completion, would be so all-consuming. So much so that nothing else mattered, the outside world, and everyone in it, ceasing to exist. Only Darian and Mariah remained at that moment.

'Oh, goodness.' She groaned weakly as she remembered that the two of them were not *all* that existed in the world, that they had a listening audience.

Darian raised his head to look at her, his face flushed, lips moist and slightly swollen from ministering to Mariah's pleasure. 'He or she left some time ago,' he assured gruffly, pulling her gown slightly down over her legs before he moved up the bed to lie down beside her.

Mariah looked at him anxiously. 'How do you know?'

'I heard the click of the door shutting as they left. I did not spend all my afternoon in my bedchamber, but explored those peepholes and passages' he explained as her eyes widened. 'I would never allow anyone to see or hear your pleasure but me, Mariah,' he assured softly as he lifted a hand to smooth back the hair at her temple.

Mariah felt grateful for Darian's reassurances,

even as she trembled at the full realisation of what had just happened between the two of them. What she had all but begged to happen, as she arched and thrust against the caress of Darian's mouth and hands.

She should feel mortification just thinking of those intimacies. Should feel embarrassment, if not horror, at her own wanton response and encouragement of those intimacies. Her complete lack of inhibition.

Mariah could feel none of those things.

Instead, for the first time in her life, Mariah felt totally fulfilled as a desirable woman. A desired and now totally satiated woman.

It was exhilarating.

Liberating, in a way Mariah had never imagined.

So much so that there was no room inside her for embarrassment or self-consciousness.

Darian Hunter, the austere and exacting Duke of Wolfingham, had just made thorough love to her. Had touched and caressed her more intimately than any other man had ever done. Than any other man had ever wanted to do. And he had not found her wanting.

Wolfingham had not found her wanting.

For so many years Mariah had wondered if it was because she was so undesirable that Martin had never wanted a normal marriage with her. Not that she had ever wanted a normal marriage with the man she had considered as being her rapist, but Martin's complete lack of interest in her physically, and for so many years, had certainly caused her to question her own desirability.

Oh, she had played her part well these past seven

years, had flirted and teased whichever gentlemen had needed to be flirted with and teased, in order for her to extract the information from them that she needed. But she had never felt like this with any of those other men, never *wanted* as she had wanted with Darian. Never felt even tempted with those other men, had known that she would just be another conquest to them.

In contrast, Darian had made love to her like a thirsty man in a desert, praising her all the while, telling her time and time again how beautiful she was to him. How much he desired her. How much he wanted and appreciated her body.

Gifting Mariah with that freedom, that liberation in her own sexuality that she had long believed dead inside her.

And in doing so Darian had given her pleasure unlike anything Mariah had ever known before.

A pleasure she now fully intended to gift back to him.

A seductive smile curved her lips as she recalled that look of bliss on the male statue's face as Aphrodite took his full and burgeoning length into her mouth.

Chapter Twelve

Darian did not believe he had ever seen anything as beautiful as Mariah looked at this moment; her loosened hair was a golden halo about her flushed face, her eyes soft and languid, her cheeks creamy smooth, her lips slightly swollen from their earlier kisses, her breasts still bared to the heat of his gaze. Perfectly rounded and pert breasts, tipped with ruby berries still puckered and reddened from his ministrations.

And beneath all that visual beauty was the smell of her pleasure and that tantalising and erotic perfume that Darian associated only with her.

The hardness of his shaft shifted, surged, as he continued to breathe in that perfume and gaze down at those perfect and desirable globes, as a painful reminder that his own arousal still needed to be dealt with. And sooner rather than later.

'You are very sure our eavesdropper has left?' Mariah murmured as she obviously felt that impatient movement of his arousal against her thigh. She sat up beside him to gaze down at that telling bulge in his pantaloons, her breasts still fully exposed to Darian's heated gaze, resulting in another fierce pulsing of his aching arousal.

Darian had been fully aware of Mariah's initial resistance to give in to the pleasure he offered, when she believed they had a listening audience. 'Very sure,' he confirmed gruffly.

'Then I believe it is now my turn to pleasure you.' Her fingers moved to unfasten the buttons of his pantaloons, the bared fullness of her breasts jiggling tantalisingly at the movement. 'I would not wish for anyone but me to see or hear your own pleasure, either...' she added softly.

'Mariah?' Darian placed one of his hands over both of hers as he looked up at her searchingly, wondering if she really meant what he thought she did.

He had bedded his first woman at the age of sixteen and there had been too many more women since then for him to remember all their faces, let alone their names. Several ladies of the *demi-monde* had also chosen to take him into their mouth and give him pleasure that way. Could Mariah really be suggesting she might do the same?

Just the idea of having Mariah placing those delectable and pouting lips about his shaft, of having her suck him into her mouth and all the way to the back of her throat, excited Darian to such a pitch he could barely contain it.

Mariah could see that she had momentarily surprised Darian with her intentions. Because, despite the licentiousness she had witnessed during this, and other weekend parties, most of the ladies of the *ton* were believed to be too delicate, too prim and proper, to be exposed to such acts as she had witnessed earlier today between those statues in Aphrodite's Temple?

Mariah's newly found pleasure and sexual liberation, her curiosity, was now such that she *must* know all. Whether or not she would be any good at this was another matter, but she fully intended to make up with enthusiasm what she lacked in experience.

Mariah looked down searchingly into Darian's face, noting the glitter to those dark green eyes as he looked back at her, the flush to his cheeks.

And knowing that her own eyes were probably just as fevered, her cheeks as flushed. In anticipation of freeing, of seeing, that enormous bulge inside Darian's pantaloons…

She had never seen that part of a man in the flesh, so to speak.

She had not seen Darian naked as yet, but even so a glance down at that telling bulge in his pantaloons told her he was so much bigger than Martin had been.

'Do not think of it, Mariah,' Darian rasped abruptly, his hand gentle on her cheek as he turned her averted face back towards him. 'The past has no place here between the two of us, Mariah,' he assured softly.

Mariah continued to look at him blankly for several long seconds, held captive by those memories, those awful, painful, disturbing memories.

'You shall be in charge here and now between the two of us, Mariah,' Darian assured her huskily. 'Or not. It is your choice to make. I assure you no one shall make you do anything you do not wish to do,' he promised gruffly as his hands dropped down to his sides. 'I am yours to do with exactly as you wish, Mariah. Or not,' he repeated gruffly.

'But—you have not found your own pleasure yet.' She frowned. 'Once aroused, I believed men to need that release more than a woman?'

Darian had to once again fight down his murderous feelings towards Martin Beecham. Because Mariah required his gentleness now, rather than a show of the anger he felt towards her dead husband. For having inflicted, over so many years of his indifference, such an uncertainty of her own sexuality, her desirability. A cruelty indeed to such a beautiful and courageous lady as he now knew Mariah to be.

Darian sat up slightly to run the soft pad of his thumb over the fullness of her bottom lip to take any sting from his next words. 'You do not have to do anything else, Mariah. I can return to my bedchamber and deal with my arousal myself,' he assured gently.

Her eyes widened. 'You are talking of— You would—'

'Yes.' He smiled at her reassuringly.

'You have done that before?'

'Many times. All young boys do it,' he dismissed without embarrassment as her eyes widened. 'Indeed, I believe it becomes their favourite pastime during adolescence.'

'But it has been many years since you were that age.'

Darian shrugged. 'A man's member tends to wake

up before him each morning. And without a wife to ease that arousal, it often becomes necessary for a man to take himself in hand.'

'I see,' she said slowly. 'And which would you prefer now, to feel your own hand or mine?'

Darian drew his breath in sharply at the candour of her question. 'Neither. I would prefer to have your mouth on me, Mariah,' he explained as she looked at him questioningly.

Delicate colour bloomed in her cheeks. 'As would I.'

Darian groaned low in his throat as he watched Mariah moisten her lips, as if in anticipation of the act. 'May I watch? It would enhance my own pleasure to do so, Mariah,' he explained as she gave him another of those curious glances.

Curious and slightly shy glances, which to Darian's mind did not sit well with the reputation of her being the scandalous and adulterous Countess of Carlisle.

The gossip of Mariah's adultery Darian could now understand, when her husband had been such an out-and-out and indifferent bastard to the needs of his own wife. That curiosity and shyness needed explaining—

All thoughts fled Darian's mind as Mariah moved up on her knees beside him so that she might place several pillows behind his head, her bared breasts jutting forward pertly as she moved, allowing her nipples to dangle, so swollen and tempting, just inches away from his rapidly moistening mouth.

'Give me just a taste of you first, Mariah!' he groaned achingly.

Mariah tilted her head as she looked down at Darian, easily noting that his fevered gaze was now transfixed on her bared breasts. She leant forward slightly in order to allow one of her nipples to touch his moist and parted lips, gasping slightly as he instantly suckled that fullness into his mouth, eyes closing, lashes resting darkly against his flushed cheeks, as his hand cupped beneath that breast as he drew hungrily on the nipple.

And allowing Mariah to learn another sexual revelation...

That a man could be just as vulnerable during lovemaking as a woman.

Perhaps more so, she realised, as she turned her head so that she might guide one of her hands to untie the ribbon on Darian's drawers, before turning back the folds of those drawers and finally exposing that impressive bulge.

Darian's shaft was incredibly long and thick as it jutted up from its nest of dark curls.

Mariah licked her lips. What would he taste like? Salty or sweet? And would—

'Darian!' She gave a sudden gasp as she felt a now familiar burn of pleasure growing, swelling, between her own thighs, Darian's mouth almost painful on her nipple as he suckled deeply, hungrily, teeth biting as his other hand alternately stroked and then squeezed its twin. 'Darian, I believe I am going to—'

'Come for me, Mariah!' he urged fiercely, both hands cupping her breasts now, squeezing and pinching her nipples as he gazed up into her flushed face.

'I—' She cried out her pleasure as another climax suddenly ripped through her body, the longest and strongest yet, as her empty sheath contracted and pulsed hungrily, again and again, the swollen nubbin above throbbing. 'I had no idea I could— That it could happen so—so spontaneously.' She rested her head weakly on Darian's shoulder.

It had never happened for Darian with any other woman before now. But as he now knew only too well, Mariah was indeed a woman unlike any other. And the fact that he had been able to give her such pleasure, just by touching her breasts, gave him more satisfaction than he could describe.

Not that he had time to dwell too long on those feelings of wonderment as Mariah now moved sinuously down the length of his body, her bared breasts briefly resting either side of his fiercely jutting erection before she moved to lie between his parted thighs and take him in hand.

'You are so wondrously big,' she murmured admiringly as she stroked the length of him. 'Your skin so velvety soft,' she added huskily before wrapping the fingers of both hands about the thickness of his engorged and throbbing length. 'And so wet.' The soft pad of her thumbs stroked over the tip of his shaft.

Darian felt his groin tighten as her fingers continued to caress him sensually. 'Mariah!' he groaned harshly, tensing, as he watched her little pink tongue flick out to taste the tip.

'Would you like me to stop?' Her glance up at him, from beneath her long lashes, was wickedly teasing.

'No!' Darian protested, groaning as he saw her smile widen, his head falling back on the pillows as he watched her continue to lick him, her tongue a sensuous rasp across his highly sensitised skin, her long golden hair cascading forward to drape sensuously across his thighs.

'You taste delicious,' she murmured appreciatively, her breath hot against his dampness.

'As do you,' he assured gruffly.

'Really? Let me see!' She moved quickly up the bed to lick her own juices from his parted lips. 'Mmm.' She nodded, her smile sensuous as she moved back down the bed to kneel between his thighs, before once again taking him in hand and holding him up as she parted her lips and took him into her mouth, her lips tight just beneath the tip and stretched tautly about his thickness.

Darian groaned, hips bucking, the second he was engulfed by the heat of Mariah's mouth, totally unable to stop himself from thrusting up rhythmically into that wet heat. His hands clenched into the bedclothes at his sides as he fought to hold off, to prolong the moment of his release.

An almost impossible task as he watched Mariah's head bob up and then down. Up and then down. Each time taking him deeper and then deeper still, her tongue swirling, dipping, as she rose up, before plunging him deeper on the downward stroke. Little by tortuous little, until he finally hit the back of her throat and she began to suck in earnest.

Finally, when Darian thought he might go insane

from the pleasure, she released him on the next upward stroke, eyes dark as she looked up at him at the same time as she moved one of her hands lower, caressing him tenderly. 'Come for me now, Darian,' she invited as her gaze held his at the same time as she parted her lips and slowly took him to the back of her throat.

Darian felt the tingling at the base of his spine, the painful tightening through his groin, and knew his climax was imminent. 'You must release me now, Mariah—'

Her own second and throaty 'Now!' vibrated down the length of him, sending Darian spiralling over the edge, totally unable to stop from coming as he became lost in the fiercest, most prolonged orgasm he had ever experienced in his life.

Mariah continued to suck on him greedily, cheeks hollowed, and she refused to release him until she had swallowed down all of Darian's salty-sweet release. Even then she could not resist licking the last few drops from the tip before sitting back on her heels to look up at him.

His dark hair was dishevelled, the dark curls lying damply tousled on his brow. Eyes glittered the colour of emeralds between sleepy half-closed lids, his cheeks were flushed, his lips parted. His body was completely relaxed and exposed to her as his erection lay half-hard still against the tautness of his stomach.

He was beautiful.

Completely satiated, wickedly decadent and utterly beautiful.

And she had done this. She, Mariah Elizabeth Beecham, Countess of Carlisle, had given Darian Hunter, the severe and oh-so-proper Duke of Wolfingham, that look of satiation.

A thrill of satisfaction rose up beneath Mariah's breasts, filling her chest to bursting, in the knowledge that she had succeeded in giving Darian the same pleasure he had given her.

'Come up here and lie beside me, Mariah, and let us both catch our breath,' he invited gruffly now as he opened his arms to her.

Mariah moved up the bed gladly before lying down at his side, her head resting on one broad shoulder, one of her arms draped across the muscled hardness of his stomach as he stroked the long tendrils of her hair. She had never felt so relaxed, never known such peace as this existed, as she glowed in the aftermath of their lovemaking.

This, this closeness, was what it should be like between a man and a woman. What she had been denied for so many years.

What she had denied *herself* for so many years, too afraid to risk this vulnerability with any man. A vulnerability that Mariah now knew applied to both the man and the woman; a man could not be any more vulnerable than when he allowed a woman to take that precious part of himself into her mouth and pleasure him. As she had been just as vulnerable when she'd allowed Darian to pleasure her in the same way.

Such intimacies required complete trust, from both the man and the woman.

As Mariah had learnt to trust Darian.

Not just with her body, but with the secrets of her past, as well as her work for the Crown. She had not told him all of her secrets, of course. Had not, for instance, confided that Martin had been a traitor to his country. Or revealed that that awful time with Martin had been her only physical experience with any man before today. But she had trusted Darian with so much more than that.

Had told him what had happened to her the night of Christina's conception.

Trusted him with the knowledge Aubrey Maystone had imparted, of the work she had carried out secretly for the Crown these past seven years.

Mariah believed she could trust Darian never to reveal those secrets to another living soul.

As she now trusted him with her life.

With her love?

Mariah tensed, barely breathing, as she considered what her feelings were for the man beside her. For Darian Hunter, the severe and sober Duke of Wolfingham.

She did trust him, yes. She also admired him. Truly believed he was a man she could trust with her life.

But with her love?

No!

Mariah dared not allow herself to fall in love with any man. It was too much of a vulnerability. Too much power—

'Mariah?' Darian could feel her sudden tension as

she lay so still beside him. 'What are you thinking about?' he prompted gently.

She made no answer for several long seconds before replying huskily, 'Do you think the person listening to us behind the wall might have been the assassin?'

'In all probability, yes,' he bit out grimly. 'Damn it, I shall have to send a note to Winterton Manor informing Aubrey Maystone of these most recent events.'

They both knew that the reason he had not already done so was because they had been too engrossed in each other, in the desire between them.

'I shall do so as soon as I have regained the strength to get out of bed and go down to the stables in search of my groom,' Darian added.

'Is it possible, as we were followed up the stairs, that perhaps we have not been as clever in our deception of being lovers as we had hoped to be?'

Darian did not believe for a moment any of this conversation had been the reason behind Mariah's sudden tension a few minutes ago; she had paused too long, considered her words for too long, before answering him. Nor was he insensitive to the fact that she seemed to be distancing herself from him once again, despite still being held in his arms, her half-naked body draped alongside his own, her hand resting warmly—trustingly?—on his chest.

At the same time he was aware of how tenuous still was the closeness between the two of them, despite the depths of the intimacies they had just shared.

That unless he wished to call Mariah a liar and risk alienating her even further, he had no choice but to accept this as her explanation for her sudden quiet.

For now...

'From the speed with which they left, once the two of us began to make love, I believe they can have no further doubt regarding the latter— Mariah?' he questioned again sharply as he felt her increase in tension. He turned on his side to look at her searchingly, easily noting the pallor of her cheeks, the shadows in those beautiful turquoise eyes, before she lowered her long, dark silky lashes and hid those shadows from his view. 'Do you regret what just happened between the two of us?'

She moistened her lips with the tip of her tongue— tasting him there, as Darian could still taste her on his own lips? The colour that suddenly warmed her cheeks, as she became aware of her movements, would seem to imply that she did.

'I accept it was necessary,' she answered him evenly now. 'If we were to successfully keep up this pretence that we are lovers.'

'It is no longer a pretence, Mariah!' Darian felt stung into snapping his frustration with her coolness. With the fact that they both knew there had been no need for the continuation of that pretence, once he had assured Mariah their eavesdropper had departed.

She swallowed, those long lashes still hiding the expression in her eyes. 'We have shared...certain intimacies. That does not make us lovers.'

'Then what does?' Darian scowled down at her

darkly. 'I will admit that this was far from the ideal place, or situation, for the two of us to have become lovers,' he continued impatiently, very aware that he had previously decided he could not allow such a thing to happen at Eton Park. But he could no more have resisted, denied himself the pleasure of making love to and with Mariah just now, than King Canute had been able to turn back the tide! 'But that does not change the fact that it is now exactly what the two of us are,' he added huskily.

Mariah drew in a ragged breath even as she gave a definitive shake of her head. 'I believe we have allowed the licentiousness and erotica at this place to colour our judgement. That once we return to town we shall both see how...ridiculous such a relationship would be between us.'

'Ridiculous?' Darian knew the frown had deepened on his brow.

'Of course.' She gave a dismissive laugh as she finally looked up at him, those eyes reflecting her derision. 'We have absolutely nothing in common outside of this current situation. No common interests, or friends. Indeed, in London you are every inch the austere and sober Duke of Wolfingham as I am the scandalous Countess of Carlisle.'

Having come to know Mariah better, Darian was now extremely sceptical about the latter.

'And this?' He reached out to grasp the tops of her arms. 'What was it that just happened between the two of us?'

'A very enjoyable but unrepeatable interlude,' she

dismissed drily. 'As I have said, I believe we have both allowed our forced alliance, along with the licentiousness of our surroundings, and the people here, to arouse and cloud our better judgement. Left to our own devices in town, the two of us would never have so much as spared each other an approving glance.'

Darian could not deny that his opinion of Mariah, before meeting her, had been far from favourable. Nor had that opinion changed once he *had* met and spoken to her, despite the unwanted and begrudging desire he had felt for her.

But sometime during these past few weeks his opinion of Mariah *had* changed. Dramatically. He now knew her to be a woman of great courage and fortitude. A woman who risked her own life and reputation, on a daily basis, in order to work secretly for the Crown. For that alone Darian might have admired and respected her.

But there was so much more to Mariah than that.

Darian now knew that she had also fought her own personal demons of the past and not just survived them, but had become a gracious lady of great dignity and personal independence.

Much like a soldier after a success in battle.

Truly, Darian believed Mariah to have as much courage, to be as heroic, as he or any of his four closest friends had been in their fight against tyranny, openly and secretly.

None of which changed the fact that Mariah was now rejecting, out of hand, the very idea of the two of them continuing any sort of relationship once they had returned to town.

A rejection, the challenge of her expression, as she met his gaze so fearlessly, he would do well to heed.

Darian had never been one to back down from any sort of fight. Least of all one that mattered to him as much as this one did. As much as continuing to see Mariah, to be with Mariah, now did.

But she was absolutely correct in one regard. This was not the time, or the place, for them to have this conversation. There was too much else at stake: a would-be assassin in this house they still had to identify and bring to justice.

As such, Darian would agree to delay the conversation between himself and Mariah.

For now.

Once they had left Eton Park and returned to town, he had every intention of pursuing a satisfactory conclusion to this conversation.

Of pursuing Mariah.

Chapter Thirteen

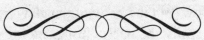

'Does our hostess seem less than composed to you this evening?' Darian murmured softly to Mariah, eyes narrowed as he observed a rather red-faced Clara Nichols across the crowded ballroom, as she issued low-voiced instructions to a somewhat panicked-looking young footman.

A small ballroom that, along with the hundred or so masked and indecently clothed guests laughing and talking too loudly, was every bit as outrageously decadent as Mariah had earlier warned him it would be.

The walls were all mirrors, reflecting back the dozens of candles illuminating the room, as well as the lurid and explicit frescoes painted on the ceiling above. Although to Darian's way of thinking, it was hard to decide which was worse, those erotic frescoes above, or the half-clothed guests milling about below.

He had certainly breathed a sigh of relief once he had realised that Mariah's gown, a delicate gold confection of some gossamer material to match the gold of her mask, was actually not as revealing as it at first appeared.

Her beautiful and creamy shoulders were completely bare, admittedly, but there was at least a bodice to the gown, albeit a sheer and delicate lace that did little to hide the fullness of her breasts and rouged nipples below. But the body of the gown was at least lined, with only the barest hint—literally!—of the silky limbs and blonde curls hidden beneath.

With things so unsettled between the two of them still, Darian did not believe he would have been able to hold on to his temper if he also had to cope with other gentlemen ogling Mariah's near nakedness!

'She does,' Mariah now answered him equally as softly. 'Perhaps I should stroll over and see what is amiss?'

Darian's first instinct was to say no, to keep Mariah safely beside him, rather than risk her moving through the crowded room, and the possible groping hands of the other gentlemen present, to where their hostess stood beside the doorway.

There was also a would-be assassin still somewhere in their midst.

Darian quickly repressed his overprotectiveness, knowing that Mariah would no more accept that than she had wished to listen to his conversation earlier, in regard to the continuation of their relationship once they were back in town. He had no doubt that she would especially baulk at any sign of possessiveness towards her on his part. Even if that was exactly how he felt!

Just the thought of any other man but himself so much as looking at Mariah with more than admiration was enough to cause his jaw to tighten and his back teeth to grind together.

'We shall both go,' he compromised as he held out his arm to her.

Mariah eyed Darian from behind her mask as she placed her gloved hand on his arm before allowing him to escort her across the crowded ballroom, knowing that the avidly covetous eyes of at least a dozen other women followed his progress.

He was, without a doubt, the most handsome and striking-looking gentleman in the room, formidably so.

Once again dressed all in black, accompanied by snowy white linen, the mask that covered the top half of Wolfingham's face was also a plain and unrelenting black, green eyes glinting warningly through the two eye-slits to ward off the approach of any of the other guests.

Mariah repressed a shiver at just how devilish Darian looked this evening. Dark and watchful. Cold and unrelenting.

Nothing at all like the warm and satiated man who had made love to her, and to whom she had made love, earlier this evening.

'Cold?' Darian turned to her solicitously as he obviously felt her shiver.

Mariah straightened determinedly; after all, she

was the one who had insisted there was nothing be-tween them but the intimacy of the circumstances under which they now found themselves. She was a little disappointed, hurt, at how easily Darian had ac-cepted her dismissal after making only a token pro-test, but that was for her to deal with, not him. Darian had promised nothing and she had asked for noth-ing, which was how it should be. How it *must* be, if she was to continue to maintain her emotional inde-pendence.

'Not at all.' She now gave him an over-bright smile. 'Did you manage to send your groom with a note to Winterton Manor?' she prompted softly.

'Yes,' Wolfingham confirmed. 'Although he has not returned as yet with Maystone's reply,' he added grimly.

'Do you think that something might have hap-pened to him along the way?' Mariah frowned; Au-brey had told them that Winterton Manor, where the older man had waited these past twenty-four hours or so, along with several other of his agents, until he heard word from them, was only situated five miles or so from Eton Park.

Darian frowned. 'We shall go out to the stables and check for news of his return, once we have talked to Clara Nichols.'

Mariah's brows rose. 'Surely there is no reason for both of us to go?'

Perhaps not, but Darian still felt that reluctance to leave Mariah's side. 'We shall both go, Mariah,' he repeated uncompromisingly, returning the searching glance Mariah gave him with one of cool determination.

Darian sensed an underlying air of tension in the Nicholses' ballroom this evening, one that smacked almost of desperation. As if someone in this room knew they were being hunted. And if anything amiss was about to happen, then Darian intended being at Mariah's side when and wherever it did.

'Very well.' Mariah finally nodded acquiescence, her eyes narrowing as they approached their flustered hostess and her obviously nervously trembling footman.

'Something definitely has Clara on the verge of a fit of the vapours,' she murmured softly to Darian, her voice rising as they reached Clara Nichols's side. 'Clara, darling, whatever is the matter?' She left Darian's side to link her arm companionably through the older woman's.

Lady Nichols dismissed the footman before answering. 'Oh, Mariah,' she wailed. 'Nothing this evening is going as it should, and— Oh! Good evening, your Grace,' she greeted hastily as she saw Darian was standing just behind Mariah.

'Can the countess and I be of any help?' he queried lightly, senses now on full alert, knowing it was most unusual for ladies of the *ton* to become so discomposed in front of their guests, no matter what the situation.

'Oh, no!' Clara Nichols looked horrified at the suggestion. 'No, thank you, Wolfingham,' she added with more calm. 'It was just a— There were several domestic matters in need of my attention. It is all settled now.'

Mariah somehow doubted that, from the hunted look still in Clara Nichols's pale and constantly shifting blue eyes. 'Could the capable Benson not have dealt with them?'

The older woman's mouth thinned, those angry spots returning to her cheeks. 'Benson is the main cause of the problem! Indeed, personal recommendation or not, I am seriously thinking of dismissing him the moment he returns.' Her eyes now glittered with her anger. 'The servants are all in disarray without his guidance.' She had obviously forgotten her earlier reassurances to the contrary, in her agitation. 'And I am sure that there are far more guests here this evening than were actually invited.' She looked askance at the very overcrowded ballroom.

'Indeed?' Wolfingham was narrow-eyed as he also glanced at the overabundance of masked guests.

'No doubt they had heard of the entertainments here and wished to be a part of it, whether invited or not,' Clara twittered coyly.

'No doubt,' Wolfingham drawled drily. 'When Benson returns from where?' he added softly.

Clara gave an impatient shake of her head. 'He has gone to be at the bedside of his sick father. Against my instructions, I might add,' she added agitatedly. 'When he asked earlier I refused him leave to go until tomorrow, but I learnt just minutes ago that he has gone this evening anyway!'

Mariah's breath caught in her throat as she turned to give Darian a wincing glance.

Stupid!

How could they both have been so utterly, utterly stupid?

Or, perhaps more accurately, how could she and Darian have allowed themselves to become so distracted, by their ever-deepening attraction to each other, as to totally miss what had been right in front of their noses this whole time?

Of course neither Richard nor Clara Nichols had reacted as had been expected to the news that the Prince would not be attending their masked ball this evening, after all. Why should they, when neither of them was the assassin or one of the conspirators, whom Mariah and Darian had been sent here to find, in the discovered attempt to assassinate the Prince Regent.

To date, all of the known network of arrested spies, set up by André Rousseau during the year he had spent working as a tutor in England, had been employees in the households of rich or politically powerful people. Servants of one kind or another who could move about at will without attracting attention. A private secretary. A tutor. A footman.

A *butler…*

Benson!

Benson had been Rousseau's spy in the Nicholses' household.

Benson, who had only been employed in the Nicholses' household for a matter of months.

Benson, who had proved to be such 'a treasure' since coming to work in the Nicholses' household.

Benson, who *had* been the only person to leave the Nicholses' sitting room after the Prince's note had been delivered and read.

Benson, who had carried that note up the stairs to Clara Nichols's private sitting room, before no doubt proceeding to read its contents!

Benson, his suspicions perhaps aroused, who had then followed Mariah and Darian back up the stairs, before entering that passageway behind the wall in Mariah's bedchamber, for the sole purpose of listening to their conversation?

Mariah knew by Darian's slight nod of acknowledgement, and the grimness of his expression, that he had already drawn those same conclusions.

As they both must now also be aware that Benson had already departed Eton Park, before either of them had been able to make that connection.

To go where, though, and for what purpose? Did Benson intend to go to London and somehow attempt to assassinate the Prince Regent still?

'You said that Benson came to you through personal recommendation?' Wolfingham, obviously one step ahead in his thinking than Mariah, now prompted their hostess shrewdly.

'Why, yes.' Clara Nichols looked slightly surprised by his interest, before then giving an affectionate smile. 'But, of course, I could not possibly be cross with dear Wedgy. I can only assume that Benson must have fooled him as to his reliability, in the same way that he has fooled all of us.'

'"Wedgy"?' Darian had little or no patience left for the woman's prattling, especially so when she obviously had absolutely no knowledge of just how *much*, and in what way, Benson had fooled them all.

His hostess continued to smile. 'Darling Wedgy. Lord William Edgewood,' she supplied irritably as Darian continued to glower down his aristocratic nose at her. 'But I have always called him Wedgy. William and Edgewood—Wedgy, do you see?'

Darian did indeed see. He saw exactly how the slightly rotund and jolly, and apparently innocuous, Lord Edgewood, a man he now recalled was also attached to the Foreign Office and so privy to certain information—such as the Prince Regent's social engagements!—might have conspired with others in an attempt to assassinate the Prince Regent.

'We have been friends since childhood, you see,' Clara continued to confide. 'More than friends in recent years, of course,' she added coyly, obviously in reference to the debauched display of that affection they had been forced to witness the evening before. 'But I have always considered that friends make the best lovers.'

'What colour mask is Wedgewood wearing this evening?' Darian could not even pretend to listen politely to this dreadful woman another moment longer.

Clara blinked at his obvious aggression. 'He is wearing the red mask of the devil.'

How appropriate! 'And have you seen him yet this evening?'

His hostess frowned as she nodded. 'Just before this latest crisis, as it happens.'

'Where?'

Clara frowned her irritation. 'Really, Wolfingham, you are being less than polite.'

'Where did you last see him, madam?' he demanded tautly.

She blinked pale lashes. 'He was talking to one of the musicians as they prepared their instruments before they commenced playing. Why, Mariah, what on earth is wrong with Wolfingham this evening?' She looked totally bewildered as the duke turned sharply on his highly polished heels to disappear into the melee of the crowded ballroom, without so much as a word of apology or explanation.

Mariah knew exactly what was wrong with Darian, and the reason for his having left so abruptly, and her heart began to beat a wild tattoo in her chest at the realisation that Darian had every intention of confronting Lord Edgewood. 'I will explain later.' She threw the words distractedly at Clara before herself hurrying off in Darian's wake.

Very aware that the assassin's plans for this weekend had been thwarted on two levels. First, by the arrival of the Prince Regent's note of apology. And second, by Benson's hurried departure.

Whether or not Lord Edgewood knew of the disappearance of his co-conspirator, *Mariah* certainly knew that a cornered animal was more likely to come out fighting, rather than cowering in the corner. And William Edgewood, once he became aware of Benson's defection, was obviously intelligent enough to realise he no longer had anything else to lose.

A single glance at the grimness of Darian's expression, before he left to go in search of the older man, had told her that the dangerous Duke of Wolfingham fully intended to confront the older man as being the traitor he so obviously was.

As Mariah was also aware that Darian had barely survived André Rousseau's bullet just weeks ago.

'A little caution, if you please, Wolfingham!'

Darian came to an abrupt halt to turn sharply in the middle of the ballroom, having easily recognised the softly spoken warning as coming from one of his closest friends, Christian Seaton, the Duke of Sutherland. And obviously also one of those uninvited guests Clara Nichols had referred to just minutes ago!

'These masks hide a multitude of sins.' Sutherland confirmed drily, dressed similarly to Darian, in dark clothing and a black mask, his eyes glinting violet through the eye-slits. 'Your groom arrived at Winterton Manor with your note and we arrived here just in time to stop and question the Nicholses' butler as he was attempting to leave,' he supplied economically. 'Rotherham and Maystone are here somewhere, too.'

'You know of Edgewood's involvement?'

'Oh, yes. Benson squeaked like a stuck pig once he knew the game was up. No doubt hoping to shift some of the blame!' The other man gave a grim smile.

'Griff and Maystone are watching him even as we speak.'

Darian nodded abruptly. 'Do we have a plan of extraction?'

'Maystone suggests— Good heavens, what is she doing?' Sutherland growled with a sudden start of surprise.

Darian tensed, very much afraid he knew exactly which 'she' his friend was referring to. 'Where?'

'The little fool!' Sutherland had now turned fully in order to look across the heads of the other guests in the direction of the musicians. 'Can you not keep your woman under control, Darian?' he demanded disgustedly as the two of them began to push their way towards where Mariah now stood in conversation with Lord William Edgewood.

'She is not my woman—' Darian broke off with a start as he realised that, yes, that was *exactly* what Mariah now was.

His woman.

The woman he wished to protect, with his own life if necessary.

The woman he admired and respected more than any other.

The woman he now realised meant more to him than any other woman ever had. Or ever would?

And at this moment *his woman* was deliberately endangering herself by engaging in conversation with the very man they both knew to have been one of the conspirators in the intended assassination of their beloved Regent.

His mouth thinned as he prompted again, 'Do we have a plan, Christian?'

'We did, yes,' the other man confirmed just as grimly. 'That may be a little more difficult now that— Where is she going now?' Sutherland demanded incredulously, both men coming to a halt and watching helplessly as Mariah, her hand companionably in the crook of Lord Edgewood's arm, now crossed to the French doors and strolled outside on to the terrace with him.

'Damn it to hell!' Darian had never felt so helpless in his life before as he did at that moment. Or so much like putting Mariah across his knee and administering a sound thrashing, for having endangered herself so deliberately. A thrashing, because of his earlier promise to himself never to cause Mariah any physical harm, that would have to take a verbal form. A verbal tongue-lashing he fully intended to carry out the moment the two of them were alone together again.

If they were ever alone together again.

'There is such an uncomfortable crush in there already,' Mariah remarked lightly as she stepped outside into the briskness of the March evening air beside William Edgewood.

He released his arm from her hold. 'You may drop the pretence now, Countess,' he dismissed scornfully.

'Pretence?' She gazed up at him guilelessly.

Edgewood gave a scathing snort. 'I am sure that we both know, with Wolfingham so obviously your lover, that you have absolutely no real interest in stepping outside into the moonlight with an old man like me.'

In truth, Mariah had not thought any further beyond the need she felt to prevent Darian from challenging the older man, as she had known he fully intended doing when he left her side so precipitously.

Outside, and alone on the terrace with William Edgewood—who appeared to have dropped all pretence of being that amiable fool everyone believed him to be and now looked at her with shrewdly calculating eyes—she now had time and opportunity to realise her mistake.

To realise that cornered animal had now turned its rabid attentions on to her.

She faced Edgewood unflinchingly as she decided to do exactly as he had suggested and cease all pretence. 'Your cohort has already fled.'

'So Clara unwittingly informed me a few minutes ago.' He nodded tersely.

Mariah nodded briskly. 'There is no way of escaping, nowhere you might go now where you will not be caught and held for trial as a traitor and attempted assassin.'

'Would not France be the practical choice?' he derided.

Mariah gave a pained frown. 'Why? Why would you turn traitor on your own country? On your Regent?' She had once asked Martin the same question.

'You can ask me that here, in the midst of this debauchery that has become England?' Edgewood scoffed. 'And with a Regent more licentious than the rest?'

And Martin's answer had been just the same.

'You are just as guilty of that licentiousness—'

'Necessarily so...' he nodded '...if I was to fool others into not suspecting my real feelings on the matter. My mother was French, you know. I am half-French, and my loyalties lie there rather than— Ah, Wolfingham, I wondered how long it would take for you to follow your mistress!' Edgewood murmured derisively as he glanced over Mariah's shoulder. 'And I see you have brought several of your friends with you, too!'

Mariah turned sharply to look at where Darian— and several of his friends?—had now joined them outside on the terrace.

At least, she had fully intended to turn and look at them.

Instead, she found herself suddenly held as Lord Edgewood's prisoner, as he pulled her roughly in front of him and anchored her there, by placing an arm about her throat and pressing a pistol painfully against her temple.

A single glance at Darian showed his eyes to be glittering intently behind his mask in the moonlight, his displeasure, at the vulnerable position in which Mariah now found herself, clear for all to see as he glared at her furiously.

She quickly moved her gaze to the three masked gentlemen standing behind him, believing she rec-ognised one of them as being the grey-haired Aubrey

Maystone, but the identity of the other two were hidden behind their masks. 'It would seem you are outnumbered, Lord Edgewood,' she remarked slightly huskily, the tightness of his arm about her throat preventing her from breathing properly.

'But I have the pistol,' he pointed out conversationally.

'We all have pistols, Edgewood,' Aubrey Maystone assured drily as those pistols now appeared in all the other gentlemen's hands.

Including Darian's, Mariah realised, wondering where on his person he could have kept it hidden until now.

Was she becoming slightly hysterical, in questioning something so trivial, when Lord Edgewood had a pistol pressed so painfully against her temple? Lord, she hoped not!

'But I also have the Countess of Carlisle,' Edgewood came back confidently. 'Eh, Wolfingham?' he added challengingly.

Darian was well aware of the fact that Edgewood now held a pistol against Mariah's temple. Could see all too clearly how the end of the barrel of that pistol was digging into her tender flesh. Hurting her.

'You are only making your situation worse, Edgewood.' Aubrey Maystone drew the other man's attention back to him.

'Could it possibly be any worse, when I am obviously already known as a conspirator and traitor against the Crown?' The other man eyed Maystone coldly.

Darian took advantage of Edgewood's distraction to inch his way slowly to the side and then forward, aided in his stealth of movement by Sutherland and Rotherham, as they both moved to flank Aubrey Maystone.

If Darian could just move a little further forward he might be able to—

'Stay exactly where you are, Wolfingham,' Edgewood warned harshly as he now pointed the pistol in Darian's direction.

It needed only that brief moment of Edgewood's distraction from Mariah for there to be a blur of movement at Darian's side as Sutherland dived downwards towards Edgewood's legs, at the same time as Rotherham leapt forward, with the obvious intention of wrestling the raised pistol from Edgewood's hand.

Leaving Darian to stand and watch as the scene played out before him.

Mariah was deafened as Lord Edgewood's pistol suddenly went off beside her ear, quickly followed by the report of another shot being fired, before she then felt herself toppling over as Lord Edgewood's legs were knocked from beneath him, pulling her down heavily on top of him. Her last vision was of a horrified Darian before she hit her head hard on the floor of the terrace and she knew no more.

Chapter Fourteen

'I trust you know that I am still very angry with you for behaving so recklessly, madam?'

Mariah was nestled comfortably against Darian's shoulder, held securely in his arms as they travelled back to London in his ducal coach several hours later. Despite the lateness of the hour neither one of them had wished to remain at Eton Park a moment longer than they had to, once the worst of the furore had died down.

Clara Nichols had been hysterical, of course, as had many of her female guests, at learning that her friend and lover Wedgy now lay dead upon the terrace at Eton Park, a bullet through his heart.

The gentlemen present had been more prosaic regarding the situation, readily accepting Aubrey Maystone's explanation of Lord Wedgewood having been caught in the act, by the Duke of Wolfingham, of forcing his attentions upon the Countess of Carlisle, before then being accidentally killed by his own pistol in the tussle that had followed. An act witnessed and confirmed by the Dukes of Sutherland and Rother-ham.

It was far from an accurate account of the truth, of course, the fatal bullet having been fired by Aubrey Maystone himself. But none present had wished to challenge the word of men as powerful as Lord May-stone, and the Dukes of Wolfingham, Rotherham and Sutherland. And Clara Nichols had been too hysteri-cal to question the fact that Lord Maystone, and the Dukes of Rotherham and Sutherland, had not even been invited to her masked ball.

No doubt the other woman would remember that fact once she had calmed down, but she had been far too busy enjoying being at the centre of the scandal, and the scandalous success of her masked ball, when Darian and Mariah had quietly taken their leave ear-lier.

The two of them had gone up the stairs to their rooms so that Mariah might change her bloodied clothes before departing, leaving Mariah's maid and Darian's valet to pack up their things before follow-ing tomorrow.

'Mariah, you are not to fall asleep until you have listened to what I have to say!' Darian gave her shoul-ders a shake to prevent that from happening. 'Do you have any idea how I felt when I looked down and saw you unconscious upon the floor and cov-ered in blood?' he demanded harshly, his impatience barely contained. 'Do you even realise that my own heart stopped beating, when I thought Maystone had missed Edgewood and had shot you instead?'

Mariah was too tired, felt too safe in Darian's arms, to care about much of anything else at the moment. 'As you see, by my presence here, he did not and I was not.'

'Mariah!'

'Darian.' She moved slightly in his arms so that she might look up at him in the lamplight, noting the dark shadows in his magnificent green eyes, the grey tinge to his tightly etched face and clenched jaw. She reached up now to gently touch that clenched jaw. 'I am safe. We are both safe.' *Darian* was safe. Which, after all, had been Mariah's only intent earlier, when she hurried across the ballroom in order to reach William Edgewood's side ahead of Darian.

Her only *interest* had been to prevent Darian from challenging the other man and perhaps being hurt or killed in the process.

Because, she had realised, she was in love with him.

She loved, and was in love with, Darian Hunter, the Duke of Wolfingham.

And strangely that realisation no longer terrified her. The emotion was no longer something for her to fear. Nor did it make her less, as she had believed loving someone would, but somehow more.

Darian now repressed a shudder. 'He might have killed you.'

She smiled. 'But he did not.'

Darian looked down at Mariah searchingly, noting

the calmness of her expression and the tranquillity in those beautiful turquoise-coloured eyes.

While he was still a churning mass of emotions. Fear, for Mariah's life. Devastation, when he had believed her dead. Relief, when he had realised the blood on her gown was from Edgewood rather than her own. Elation, when she had opened her eyes minutes later and smiled at him.

Unfortunately, *all* those emotions had been followed by anger. That Mariah could have been so reckless as to have put herself in danger in the first place.

'What possessed you?' he demanded now. 'What on earth went through your mind when you deliberately placed yourself in a position of vulnerability by going outside alone on to the terrace with Edgewood?'

Her smile became rueful. 'I do not believe I was thinking much of anything at the time. It just seemed— It was the right thing for me to do, Darian.'

'It was the worst thing you could have done!' he contradicted explosively.

Her fingers rested lightly against the tautness of his cheek. 'Let us not discuss this any further just now, Darian. It is over. The Prince Regent is safe. The would-be assassins are all dead or in custody. Napoleon himself has been thwarted in his plan to devastate the alliance. It is all finally over, Darian.'

He tensed beneath those caressing fingers. '*We* are not over, Mariah!' His arms tightened about her. '*We* will never be over!'

She looked up at him quizzically. 'What do you mean?'

'Exactly as I say.' A nerve pulsed strongly in his clenched jaw. 'We have begun something this weekend, Mariah. Something good. Something wonderful. And I will not allow you to just calmly walk away from that. To walk away from *me*!'

Leaving Darian was the last thing that Mariah wanted to do. Indeed, she never wished to be apart from him ever again. Wished to spend her every waking moment with him, and her sleeping ones, too, for the rest of her life.

That was how much she had realised she loved Darian. More than life itself. More than any of the fears of love and intimacy that had plagued her for over half of her lifetime.

She looked up at him shyly beneath the sweep of her lashes. 'Did I say that I wished to walk away from you?'

'Well. No. But—' He looked nonplussed. 'It will not do, Mariah. I will not have you running all over London and putting yourself in danger as you have been doing these past few years. I will not countenance—' He broke off as she began to chuckle softly at his bluster, a dark scowl on his brow. 'I fail to see what is so funny, Mariah.'

'We are. The two of us.' She sobered as she saw that Darian was still bursting with anger. 'We are both so afraid to admit that we might care for or need anyone. In any way. Darian, I will not walk away from you once we are returned to London,' she assured him seriously. 'I will be yours for as long as you wish me to be,' she assured him huskily.

'You will?'

'I will,' she confirmed huskily. 'Of course there are still many things that need to be discussed between the two of us.' Her supposed affairs with other men being one of them. Her lack of experience in physical matters being another. 'But I am sure, once we have done so, that we will be able to come to some sort of arrangement, whereby the two of us—'

'Arrangement?' Darian repeated softly, dangerously. 'I am talking of the two of us marrying, Mariah, not forming an arrangement!'

The shock on Mariah's face at his pronouncement might have been amusing, if Darian were not so much in earnest. If he did not love this woman more than life itself. If he did not love, admire and respect Mariah more than he had realised it was possible to love, admire and respect any woman.

Except he did. Knew that he felt all of those things for Mariah. So much so that he really had thought his heart had stopped when he looked down at her earlier, covered in blood, and had thought her dead. His own life had ended, too, in those few brief moments. He had ceased to exist. Darian had ceased to live or breathe, in the belief that Mariah Beecham, Countess of Carlisle, and the woman he loved, no longer lived or breathed. All that had remained was a shell, a body, without emotions or feeling.

Until Mariah's eyes had fluttered open and she had looked up at him and smiled.

It was at that moment that Darian had decided that he was never going to let Mariah out of his sight ever again. Whatever he had to do, however long it took, he intended that Mariah would be his wife, his duchess, and at his side for the rest of their lives.

'I love you, Mariah,' he told her now, fiercely, his arms tightening about her. 'I love you and want to marry you. To spend the rest of my days and nights with you. I love you, Mariah,' he repeated determinedly. 'And however long it takes to convince you, I intend having you for my—'

'Yes.'

'—wife,' he concluded purposefully before his gaze sharpened as he realised what Mariah had said, if not why. 'Yes what?' he questioned guardedly.

'Yes, I will marry you, Darian!' She smiled up at him glowingly, tears now glistening in her eyes. 'I love you, too, my darling Darian. I love you!'

Darian continued to look down at her searchingly. Hardly daring to believe—to hope that—

'You love me? How can you possibly love me?' He frowned darkly. 'When I have been nothing but judgemental of you from the first. So disapproving. Scornful. Critical—'

'And kind, caring, protective and passionate,' Mariah spoke huskily. 'Would you prefer it if I did not love you, Darian?' she added teasingly as he still looked down at her in disbelief. 'I suppose I might try,' she continued conversationally. 'But it is so very difficult, when I believe you to be so much all of those things *I* mentioned in regard to how you are with me.

I could *try* not to love you but— Darian!' She gave a strangled cry as his mouth finally claimed hers, his arms gathering her in so close against him it felt as if he was trying to make her a part of himself.

And perhaps he was, because for the next several minutes there was nothing else between them but those passionate kisses interspersed with words of love and adoration.

'I intend that we shall be married as soon as is possible,' Darian finally warned as he continued to hold Mariah tightly in his arms, as if afraid, if he let her go, she might disappear in a puff of smoke. 'I believe the least we are owed, for helping to foil this plot against the Prince Regent, is the granting of a Special Licence. Unless, of course, you would prefer to have a big grand wedding, with all of the *ton* in attendance?' he added uncertainly as the idea occurred to him that Mariah had never really had a happy wedding day. 'I suppose I might be persuaded into waiting for a few weeks longer, as long as you will allow me to spend all of my days and nights before the wedding by your side.'

'A Special Licence sounds perfect,' Mariah assured him happily. 'I have already had the big white wedding attended by the *ton*,' she dismissed huskily. 'Neither it, nor that marriage, brought me any happiness.'

'Apart from Christina.'

She gave a shake of her head. 'I have always seen Christina as somehow being apart from that marriage.

As if she were only ever mine, to love and to cherish. Does that sound ridiculous, in the circumstances?'

Darian's arms tightened about her. 'Nothing you say ever sounds ridiculous to me. But I hope— I sincerely hope, would deem it an honour, if you would allow me to become another father to Christina once the two of us are married?'

Mariah's heart was already full to bursting with the love she felt for Darian, but in that moment she believed it truly overflowed with the emotion. 'I should like that very much,' she accepted emotionally. 'As, I am sure, would Christina. Martin was never a proper father to her anyway.' She frowned. 'He took as little interest in her as he did in me.'

'Carlisle was a fool.' Darian scowled. 'But his loss is my gain,' he dismissed firmly. 'I assure you that I intend telling and showing both of you, each and every day, how much you are both loved and cherished.'

'I know you will.' Mariah smiled up at him gratefully, before biting her bottom lip worriedly. 'There are still some things we need to discuss, before we make any more of these wonderful plans. Things you need to know about me—'

'No,' Darian bit out harshly.

'But—'

'I do not need to know anything more about you, Mariah, than that I love you and you love me. Nothing else matters but that,' he stated firmly.

'You have no idea how happy that makes me, Darian.' Mariah smiled tremulously. 'But these are things you really do need to know, if you are to become my husband.'

'I most assuredly am!'

'Then you *must* listen to me, Darian,' she insisted as he seemed about to deny her once again.

His jaw was tightly clenched. 'Not if you are about to tell me about the other men who have been in your life. I do not want to know, Mariah. They are unimportant, irrelevant—'

'Non-existent,' Mariah put in softly, although it inwardly thrilled her to hear Darian dismiss the existence of those lovers as being irrelevant to the two of them.

Darian's voice trailed off as he seemed to hear what she had just said, a frown between his eyes now as he looked down at her searchingly.

A searching look that Mariah returned with a steady gaze as she began to talk again. 'Seven years ago I discovered, quite by chance, that my husband was a traitor to the Crown. Let me tell all, before I lose my nerve, and then you may speak, Darian,' she pleaded as he would have interrupted once again.

'Very well.' Darian nodded slowly; in truth he was still completely stunned at Mariah's claim that she had taken no other lovers.

And so he listened. As Mariah told him of her husband's treachery to his country. Of how she had gone to London, and Aubrey Maystone, with the information. And how Aubrey Maystone had used that knowledge, and Mariah, to garner even more information from Carlisle during the last two years of that man's life. Of how she had continued her own work for the Crown for these seven years, and the sense of self and self-worth it had given her. The first she had known in her life, apart from being mother to Christina.

Darian was finally left speechless when Mariah confided in him that there had been no lovers in her life. That she had flirted, cajoled, teased information from certain gentlemen, but that she had never bedded a single one of them. That the rumour and speculation of scandal about her had grown over the years, because pride had dictated that none of those gentleman had ever wished to own to the fact that they had not been, nor ever would be, a lover to the Countess of Carlisle.

The conclusion this final revelation gave Darian was simply mind-numbing. 'Then that single, awful occasion with Carlisle, the evening Christina was conceived, was the only occasion—'

'Yes,' Mariah confirmed flatly.

'My darling!' Darian gave a pained groan. 'Then our own lovemaking—the things we did together—'

'Were utterly beautiful,' Mariah assured him firmly. 'You could not have been a more gentle, more caring, a more passionate lover, even if you had known the truth, Darian.'

Darian begged to differ. If he had known, if he had once guessed at Mariah's innocence in regard to physical love, then he would have taken things more slowly, more gently, been less physically demanding.

That Mariah had been able to respond so passionately as she had earlier today to his caresses, that she had attained her peak not once but three times, was a miracle!

Although Mariah's revelations did help to explain those puzzling moments of innocence he had sensed in her, those blushes that had seemed so out of character with the experienced siren she was reputed to be.

'I trust you are not having regrets about our love-making earlier today, Darian,' Mariah now teased him reprovingly. 'Because I am dearly hoping that we shall be continuing with my education, in that regard, as soon as we reach London. Christina is away until tomorrow evening,' she reminded huskily. 'And we shall have the house all to ourselves till then...'

Darian would like nothing more than to spend the night with Mariah, to make love to and with her for hours and hours without end. But he would also settle for just being in the same bed with her, of just holding her, as difficult as that might be, if she would rather wait until they were married for them to make love again.

'I would not be at all happy to wait,' Mariah answered decisively, Darian's first indication that he had spoken his reservations out loud. 'Darian, I am simply *dying* for us to make love again. I have so many years to make up for. So much I have missed. That I want to learn about and enjoy.' She curved her body seductively against his. 'You are not going to continue to deny me, are you, Darian?'

How could Darian ever deny this woman anything?

This woman whom he loved, and would always love, with every fibre of his being.

'Do you know what I thought after we had made love at Eton Park earlier today—yesterday now?' Mariah realised after a glance at the bedside clock revealed it was well after midnight, her fingers swirling in the darkness of the hair on Darian's naked chest as she leant up on her elbow beside him in the comfort of her dishevelled bed.

'Earlier today?' He arched his brows as he glanced down at their satiated and well-loved nakedness.

'Earlier today,' she insisted firmly. 'I thought, so this is what poets all write about, singers croon over and lovers will risk anything to possess. But I was wrong, Darian, because *this*, the absolute joy we have just found in each other's arms, is what poets write about, singers croon over and lovers will risk everything to possess!' Their lovemaking had been a revelation to Mariah.

She had never dreamed such pleasure existed, had never realised how wonderful it was to literally become a part of another person. To be joined to them, body, soul and heart.

To be joined to *Darian*, body, soul and heart.

'I love you, Darian,' she told him achingly, emotionally. 'I love you so very much, my darling.'

'As I love you.' His arms tightened about her once again. 'And I will love you for the rest of our lives together.'

'Promise?'

'Without a doubt. You?'

'Oh, yes!'

Mariah had absolutely no doubt it was a promise they would both cherish in their hearts and happily keep.

Epilogue

Two weeks later—Wolfingham House, London

'Was that a very despondent-looking Anthony I saw leaving just now?' Mariah prompted as she entered Darian's study.

'It was, yes.' Darian smiled as she walked across the room and straight into his welcoming arms.

She looked up at him quizzically. 'What on earth did you say to him to make him look so down-hearted?'

His smile widened into a grin. 'As we had already discussed, I told him that my duchess and I had decided to give him permission to pay court to our daughter, Christina.'

After only a week of marriage, Mariah still felt a thrill in her chest at hearing herself referred to as Darian's duchess. For that was who she was now, Mariah Hunter, the Duchess of Wolfingham. How grand it sounded. And yet she knew she loved Darian so much, wanted to be with him so much, that she would have married him even if he had not been the top-lofty and wealthy Duke of Wolfingham.

Although she did not altogether trust that wicked grin upon her husband's face right now.

'If you told him that, why was Anthony looking less than happy?'

That wicked grin widened, green eyes glowing with laughter. 'Because I told him that not only does he have to win Christina's heart, but that as her stepfather, I will also expect him to prove himself as being sober and responsible, before we would agree to the match. And that even then we will not countenance there being a wedding until after Christina's eighteenth birthday.'

'What a wicked stepfather and brother you are, when you know full well that Christina has already admitted to us that she is smitten.' Mariah chuckled reprovingly.

'A little uncertainty will do my little brother good,' Darian dismissed unrepentantly, his arms now tightening about her waist as a different sort of wickedness now gleamed in his eyes. 'Have I told you yet this morning how beautiful you look?'

'About an hour ago, I believe.' She blushed as she remembered the *way* in which he had told her.

'Have I *shown* you yet this morning how beautiful you are to me?'

'Also about an hour ago,' Mariah answered shyly.

'And would my duchess be interested in my demonstrating the depths of those feelings for her again right this minute?'

Mariah felt the thrill in her chest at just how willing she was to allow Darian to do exactly that. A thrill of excitement that now coursed hotly through the whole of her body. 'I should like to demonstrate the depth of my feelings for you first,' she suggested huskily.

Darian chuckled softly. 'Then shall we retire to the ducal bedchamber?'

The ducal bedchamber that the two of them had shared every night before their wedding and again every night since, the two of them having decided there would be no separate bedchambers for them. Ever. That they would spend all of their nights, as well as all of their days, together.

Mariah had no idea what the future would bring. Another war to quell Napoleon was most certainly imminent. A wedding for her daughter and Anthony next year, she hoped. Perhaps a child or two of their own, for Darian and herself. A handsome boy who looked exactly like his father and a little girl, also with her father's dark hair and green eyes, so that their parents might spoil and pet them both. Mariah certainly hoped it would be so.

But she had no doubt whatsoever, that whatever the future might hold for the two of them, that they would face it together.

Always, and for ever, together…

* * * * *

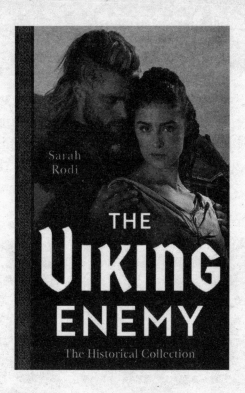